GILDED CAGE

A RUSSIAN MAFIA ROMANCE

NICOLE FOX

Copyright © 2021 by Nicole Fox

All rights reserved.

No part of this book may be reproduced in any form or by any electronic or mechanical means, including information storage and retrieval systems, without written permission from the author, except for the use of brief quotations in a book review.

❀ Created with Vellum

MAILING LIST

Sign up to my mailing list!
New subscribers receive a FREE steamy bad boy romance novel.

Click the link below to join.
https://sendfox.com/nicolefox

ALSO BY NICOLE FOX

Kovalyov Bratva Duet

Gilded Cage (Book 1)

Gilded Tears (Book 2)

Princes of Ravenlake Academy (Bully Romance)

Can be read as standalones!

Cruel Prep

Cruel Academy

Cruel Elite

Bratva Crime Syndicate

Can be read in any order!

Lies He Told Me

Scars He Gave Me

Sins He Taught Me

Belluci Mafia Trilogy

Corrupted Angel (Book 1)

Corrupted Queen (Book 2)

Corrupted Empire (Book 3)

De Maggio Mafia Duet

Devil in a Suit (Book 1)

Devil at the Altar (Book 2)

Kornilov Bratva Duet

Married to the Don (Book 1)

Til Death Do Us Part (Book 2)

Heirs to the Bratva Empire

Can be read in any order!

Kostya

Maksim

Andrei

Tsezar Bratva

Nightfall (Book 1)

Daybreak (Book 2)

Russian Crime Brotherhood

Can be read in any order!

Owned by the Mob Boss

Unprotected with the Mob Boss

Knocked Up by the Mob Boss

Sold to the Mob Boss

Stolen by the Mob Boss

Trapped with the Mob Boss

Volkov Bratva

Broken Vows (Book 1)

Broken Hope (Book 2)

Broken Sins *(standalone)*

Other Standalones

Vin: A Mafia Romance

Box Sets

Bratva Mob Bosses (Russian Crime Brotherhood Books 1-6)

Tsezar Bratva (Tsezar Bratva Duet Books 1-2)

Heirs to the Bratva Empire

The Mafia Dons Collection

The Don's Corruption

GILDED CAGE
BOOK ONE OF THE KOVALYOV BRATVA DUET

I'LL LOCK HER IN A GILDED CAGE AND THROW AWAY THE KEY.

The night we met, she thought she was tasting freedom.

I devoured her once and left before I even knew her name.

Four months later, Bratva business leads me to the house of my enemy with one objective:

Burn it down and kill everyone inside.

That's exactly what I plan to do…

Until I find her cowering before me.

The innocent girl from the club.

My beautiful caged bird.

I'm not here to save her—I'm here to ruin her.

But something stops me in my tracks.

Something I never expected.

Did she say that's *my* baby in her womb?

1

ESME

A SECRET LOCATION ON THE PACIFIC COAST OF MEXICO

I look around at my bedroom and fight the urge to scream.

It's beautiful by any measure. The finest furniture. The most expensive art.

But I see it for what it really is: a gilded fucking cage.

My eyes settle on the picture board I set up when I was fifteen years old. I still remember the first thing I stuck up there—a glossy postcard of Florence, Italy.

Seven years have passed since I first pinned it up. The postcard is no longer glossy. It stares back at me, old and faded, a constant reminder of the invisible steel bars that surround my life.

The board shows all the places I've always wanted to go. The Coliseum in Rome. The Great Wall of China. The pyramids in Egypt.

But they're all just fantasies. I've only left my father's home once.

The picture of that lone trip is up there, too. I reach up and take it down.

In the photograph, my older brother, Cesar, stands beside me, his arm wrapped protectively around my shoulders. The Eiffel Tower pierces the low clouds behind us.

We're both smiling.

Oblivious to the future.

Oblivious to how little time he and I had left together.

It's been years since Cesar's death and yet it still hurts to think about him.

You should be here with me, I think. *Maybe then things would be different.*

My fingers caress Cesar's face for a moment. But when tears start to prick at the corners of my eyes, I pin the picture back up on the bulletin board—facedown, so I don't have to look at it and remember everything I've lost.

A knock on my door interrupts my thoughts.

I turn to face the door. "Yes?"

"Señorita Esme, your father requests your presence downstairs in the formal sitting room."

The muffled voice belongs to Sofia, one of the maids who works here at my father's compound. I close my eyes for a moment and breathe deeply.

The only reason Papa would "request" my presence in the formal sitting room is so I can be his show pony.

My father likes to flaunt his possessions.

And unfortunately for me, I'm his crown jewel.

I open the door and come face to face with the woman. She's small, Mexican, shy, beautiful.

"I guess I shouldn't 'request' that he go fuck himself, should I?" I drawl.

Sofia flinches like I slapped her.

It's just a joke, of course. But she's seen what my father is capable of.

We both know that saying that to his face would earn me a month in the cellar.

I sigh. "Never mind. Gracias, Sofia. Tell Papa I'll be down soon."

I expect her to nod in her usual respectful manner and walk away, but she continues to stand there in her black and white maid's uniform, wringing her hands together nervously.

Not a good sign.

"Is there something else, Sofia?"

"Señorita..." Her tone is apologetic already.

I frown. "What else does he want?"

Sofia raises her brown eyes up to meet mine. She is a little paler than usual, which is pretty standard when my father is in the house. We all walk on eggshells whenever he is around.

"He also said would like you to wear a dress," she finishes, lowering her eyes again. "'*Something a man would like*,' he said."

So he wants to impress some unspecified male guest or guests.

That's not a good sign at all.

I offer Sofia a forced smile. "As Papa wishes, he shall receive. Gracias, Sofia."

With her task completed, relief washes over her face. She hurries down the long hall towards the kitchen.

I close the door with another sigh and head to my walk-in closet.

It's large enough to be a room in its own right. A large center island holds my basics, jewelry, and underwear. Opposite the island is an elaborate dressing table, over which hangs a back-lit mirror.

The racks hidden behind mahogany panels are loaded with tons of designer clothing. Probably half a million dollars' worth of the finest fashion the world has to offer.

I've hardly worn any of it.

Why bother? I never leave the grounds.

But tonight is different. Something is happening. I don't like it at all.

I pick a sleeveless vintage Prada dress with a high neckline and slip on a pair of Jimmy Choos with a one-inch wedge.

Before I go downstairs, I step in front of the full-length mirror to make sure I'm dressed for the part. Papa would be furious if I'm anything less than dazzling.

The jade of the dress brings out the tiny flecks of green in my hazel eyes. My dark brown hair cascades in messy waves down my back and my cheeks still retain a little color from my morning run. I add a pair of diamond studded earrings and smear a little nude gloss onto my lips.

And then the transformation is complete.

Abracadabra, presto change-o: the don's daughter.

His beautiful, caged bird.

It makes me sick to my fucking stomach.

When I'm done, I leave my bedroom and begin the trek to the formal sitting room.

The Moreno household—more like a fortress, really—is a sprawling labyrinth, so it takes me almost five full minutes to get there. I pass tennis courts, swimming pools, several lush gardens, and both kitchens. All filled with the nicest things money can buy.

Drug money, to be specific.

I hear the voices of laughing men when I reach the brass-studded door to the sitting room. I rest my hand on the doorknob, but before I open it, I take a moment to breathe and gather myself.

Cesar's face from that Paris photograph is still floating behind my eyelids. Laughing, care-free.

I swallow my bitterness down.

Put your "good daughter" mask on, I remind myself, *or there will be hell to pay later.*

Just like that, I feel my mask settle into place.

Perfect smile, perfect daughter—that's the motto that keeps me alive.

Papa won't accept anything less.

I remind myself of who I am—or at least, who I'm expected to be: Esmeralda Moreno, princess of the Moreno cartel, the most eligible bachelorette in the entire Mexican drug world.

Then I push open the heavy door and slip inside.

Immediately, the chatter softens. Eyes turn to me.

Papa's voice cuts across the room, booming and resonant.

"Ah, Esme! There you are."

He gets up from his leather armchair and strides towards me, laying his hand on the small of my back and pushing me forward towards his guests as though he's trying to feed me to the sharks.

To the suited men seated in the other chairs, he says, "Caballeros, meet my daughter, my pride and joy, Esmeralda Moreno."

Pride and joy. That's a lie. So misleading it makes me sick.

I can't even begin to explain how fucked up our relationship is. How fucked up my father himself is.

But you'd never know it by looking at him. That broad smile, that fatherly hand on my back—it's so fake, so staged that I want to puke.

If only these men knew what it was really like to be Joaquin Moreno's daughter.

If only *anyone* knew what he truly is like.

Papa's guests stare up at me, each darker and slipperier-looking than the last. I trust none of them. Their honeyed smiles are normal enough, but their sharp eyes travel over my body without an ounce of shame.

They introduce themselves to me one by one, offering hands to shake and names I don't bother trying to remember.

I study their accents with detachment. Colombian, I think. Probably the higher-ups from one of my father's cocaine suppliers down there.

In other words, it's business as usual in the Moreno household.

"Esme is a pianist," Papa announces. He pushes me towards the grand piano over by the curtained windows. "Play something for us, cariña."

I nod, smile still riveted to my face, and move towards the piano gratefully. Anything to avoid looking at their faces.

It's easier to breathe when I'm playing. I'm more relaxed in those moments. I can close my eyes and be transported to another place. Somewhere I'm free.

I settle on the piano bench and poise my hands over the keys. I usually play Chopin, but today, I decide instead to perform Mozart. It's more dramatic, more mournful.

Suits my mood.

My fingers meet the keys. One high, sweet note rises up, blissful and simple. Then the next. And the next. And the next.

I can hear the men's murmurs but I ignore them. I don't care if they pay attention or not. If they like it or not.

Because I'm not playing for them.

I'm playing for myself.

For several minutes, my fingers dance across the piano.

For several minutes, I'm free of this ugly cage I'm trapped in.

It ends far too soon.

Don't forget the mask, I remind myself when I finish. I plaster my good-daughter smile back on my face as I rise and turn to face my father and his colleagues. They applaud. I offer a small curtsy.

"Didn't I tell you, gentlemen? Isn't she a marvel?" Papa boasts, turning away from me. "Esme, you may be excused."

I nod and escape into the hallway. My fingers twitch again as I close the door on the sitting room.

Retreating to my room, I pull off the Prada dress and leave it crumpled on the floor of my closet. I crawl under the silk sheets and try to fall asleep, praying that at least my dreams will transport me somewhere different.

But sleep never comes. I end up staring at the ceiling above my bed for an hour. Maybe I'm just too depressed to dream.

After a while, I give up. I pull back the sheets and get out of bed to trade my pajamas for a pair of leggings and a sports bra.

Then I sneak downstairs, through the French doors, and out into the moonlit garden.

Fresh air fills my lungs. It makes me feel better—just barely.

A voice in the darkness calls my name. "Señorita Esme?"

I turn to find Miguel, one of our home's security guards, standing a few feet away from me.

His features are hidden by shadow but I can sense from his tone that he's concerned for me. Then again, he's always concerned about me. He's sweet like that.

"Is everything okay?" he asks.

He steps into the light and grins. Miguel is a rough-featured man, all blunt nose and bushy eyebrows, but there's a tenderness to him that I always appreciate. It stands in stark contrast to my father's cruelty.

I give him a kiss on the cheek. "Hi, Miguel. How's your wife?"

A smile transforms his face. It strikes me that, despite the black suit and the massive rifle slung across his chest, he's not much older than I am. Like a big brother looking out for his kid sister.

He knows he's not supposed to be casually chatting with me—that's strictly against my father's orders—so he glances around to make sure no one else is in sight before stepping closer and pulling out his cell phone.

"She gave birth last week," Miguel tells me excitedly. "Look, look—I have a daughter now!"

My heart thrills for him. The warm glow in his eyes, the happiness radiating off of him—*this* is how a father is supposed to talk about his baby girl. Not like an item to be sold to the highest bidder.

"Here!" he says as he pulls up the picture on the phone and hands it over to me with reverence. "Her name is Selena. We named her after my abuela."

I look down at the round-faced baby girl, wrapped up tight in a yellow blanket with pink flowers embroidered around the edges.

My chest squeezes tight. "She's beautiful, Miguel."

He nods and winks. "She looks like her mother, thankfully."

"I'm so happy for you. For both of you," I say, handing the picture back to him.

"What are you doing up so late?" Miguel asks hesitantly.

I gnaw my lip anxiously. "I was planning on going for a run."

His dark eyes turn nervous. "I can accompany you around the grounds if you'd like," he offers.

I put a hand on his forearm. "Please, Miguel," I beg. "I need to get off the compound, just for an hour or two. I want to run by the ocean."

"I'm not authorized to let you go unaccompanied…"

"I know that. You don't need to come with me. I'll be fast. Safe. No one will see me."

He's tugging nervously at his mustache. "Señorita, you know I can't allow that. I'm under strict instructions from your father. You are not supposed to leave the compound without his permission."

"Papa will never know, Miguel," I plead. "Please? Just this once?"

I feel bad about putting him in this position, but I'm desperate to feel the salt air on my face.

Just for a little while… let me pretend I'm free.

"No one will know," I promise him again.

He sighs, looks down between his feet, then back up to me. I see his eyes softening and I know I've won.

"Only an hour?" he asks solemnly.

"Not a minute more," I tell him. "I swear."

He nods once, gruffly. I could hug him I'm so happy, but the clock is already ticking. Instead, I give him my most grateful smile and take off in a hurry towards the back of the compound, to a little side door in the garden wall that leads me out to the ocean.

I can smell the salt air as I reach the sand and break into a run. It feels good to move, to sweat, to taste the ocean breeze. It tastes like freedom.

I didn't know it then, but it was the last freedom I'd have for a long, long time.

2

ESME

I promised Miguel I'd only be gone for an hour. True to my word, I make it back with two minutes to spare.

It's near midnight and the night is quiet. Once I'm back within the walls however, I notice that the house is still lit up. Artificial light filters in from the first floor onto the lawn, turning the grass purple.

I circle around the house in search of Miguel. I arrive at his post but he's nowhere to be found.

My heart starts thudding in my chest. Silently, I head into the house and towards to my room as fast as I can. Towards safety.

I'm passing the third-floor drawing room when I hear Papa call my name.

"Esme."

I freeze. Dread settles over me like a blanket of thorns. I think about ignoring him, but years of experience tells me that'll only make things worse.

The door to the drawing room is ajar. I push it open a little further and walk in.

The room's balcony doors are open to the ocean breeze. Papa sits outside, his back to me, his face angled up towards the moon. How had he even heard me passing by?

"Yes, Papa?"

"Esme, my darling," he repeats. "Come and sit with me for a moment."

I gnaw my lip. I don't really have a choice, though. I just have to hope for the best.

I walk out onto the large balcony and sit down in the chair next to his. There's a disturbing tension in the air.

Something is most definitely not right.

"What is it, Papa?"

He offers me his hand. I have no choice but to take it. He squeezes my fingers for a moment. It's an old gesture, one that he hasn't done in many years, not since I was a little girl.

"Did you have a nice run?" he asks casually.

I hesitate for a second before admitting the truth "I, uh... yes, I did."

Papa nods. "Cesar liked late night runs as well."

My face pales. He hasn't spoken Cesar's name in so long. It sounds so wrong coming from his lips.

Ever since the funeral, Papa has refused to speak my brother's name. It's like he blames Cesar for his own death. Despises him for it. All the pictures of him were taken down and his name became a dirty word.

As if he wanted his only son—my only brother—permanently erased from existence.

I fidget uncomfortably in my seat. I try to withdraw my hand from my father's, but he doesn't let go.

"You played well tonight, you know," he murmurs. "The men from Colombia were impressed." He's smiling, but the warmth of it doesn't reach his eyes.

"Gracias, Papa," I mumble, only because I know how irritated he gets when I don't respond to him.

He tsks in annoyance anyway. "Look at me when I'm talking to you."

He's still smiling, but I know that look of his—it's a deliberate smile. He called me out here for a reason.

"Yes, Papa," I say respectfully.

"My beautiful daughter," he continues. "What a prize you are."

I look down, say nothing.

"I've seen all the women in the world," he tells me. "There are plenty of beauties out there. You are pretty enough, yes, but there are many women who are prettier."

He reaches out with his other hand, grabs my chin, and turns my face side to side like he's studying me for flaws.

He releases my chin and brushes back a strand of hair from my face. "I have good news for you, my doll."

My body tenses up. This is it. We're getting to the point of this late-night visit.

His grin broadens, but there's still no warmth in his eyes. There never has been. It's just like a wolf smiling at you before he takes a bite.

"The time has come," he announces, "for you to get married."

His words engulf me with ice-cold dread.

No. Please, God, no.

This can't be happening. Not yet.

I thought I had longer.

The words are out of my mouth before I can stop them: "Please, Papa, don't make me get married."

The smile never wavers off his face.

Not even when his hand rears back in the darkness and then swings through the air, making harsh contact with my cheek and the left side of my jaw.

The sharp crack of knuckle on flesh rings out.

He slapped me.

I collapse backwards, skull rapping against the back of the chair. Pain sears through my face and my eyes start to water.

Don't cry, I hiss inwardly. *Don't you dare cry in front of him.*

"What a shame, Esmeralda," Papa continues calmly, as if nothing had happened. "You sound ungrateful. I did not raise you to be an ungrateful child."

My instinct is to lay my hand across my stinging cheek, but I resist the urge and blink back my unshed tears.

I let my mask slip. I should've known better than that.

"Papa, I didn't mean to be ungrateful," I say, keeping my voice soft. "I know you will only ever do what's best for me."

I hate myself for saying it, but it's what he wants to hear. And as sick as it is, that's the only thing that will make this nightmare stop.

Tell him what he wants to hear.

Wait until he's gone.

Only then can I cry. Only then can I retreat into my room, scream into my pillow, and pretend none of this is happening.

"You are young and beautiful," Papa continues, his eyes glazing over. He wears the same look anytime he is trying to broker a new deal. "You must do your part for the family. You *will* do your part for the family. Won't you, Esme?"

He turns to look at me. The smile is back, the cold sneer that cuts like the sharp edge of a dagger.

I nod, not daring to look up at him. "Yes, Papa. I will do my part."

"That's my little bird. Now, come with me. I want to show you something."

I frown. Surprises from my father are never good. But he's still clinging tight onto my hand, and just like everything else that's happening around me, I don't have a choice in the matter.

Robotically, I follow him out of the drawing room. I expect him to turn right, but he turns left instead and goes downstairs. My heart thuds unevenly as he leads me to a room at the bottom of the staircase.

The thick steel door is flanked by two of Papa's guards. One of them opens the door for us to pass through.

The moment I walk into the room, I scream, my voice cuts through the quiet of night like a siren's wail.

"No!"

Miguel sits limp on a chair. He's bound and gagged and his head hangs low on his chest. His clothes are ripped, bloodied, and his features are marred by the vicious beating his face has taken.

"Miguel," I whisper as hot tears roll down my cheeks.

He doesn't stir. Doesn't look up. I don't even think he hears me at all. He's just groaning softly as blood streams from the many cuts on his swollen cheeks and forehead.

I turn to my father in horror.

He's regarding me with cool detachment. "You see what your actions have caused?"

"Is… is he dead?" The words feel like acid coming out of my mouth but I have to ask.

Oh, God, his wife, his newborn daughter. What have I done?

"No," Papa replies in a bored voice. "But the next time he disobeys one of my orders, he will be. He understands that now. Do you?"

His eyes bore into mine. I nod slowly. "Yes, Papa."

"There will be no more midnight outings for you, my daughter," he continues. "I have turned a blind eye for too long. But you are not a child anymore. It is time you learned to obey. Do I make myself clear?"

"Yes, Papa."

He smiles. I wonder if there was ever a time when I had loved the man standing in front of me.

All I can see now is a monster.

"Good."

I glance towards Miguel but I dare not move any closer to him. I only hope he knows how sorry I am.

I flee the room as fast as I can and run to my bedroom. Then I throw myself down on my bed and cry until sleep takes me.

∼

"Señorita Esme?"

A voice calls me out of my dreams the next morning. I open my eyes, but I can barely see. They're still puffy and red from crying until I fell asleep.

A stocky man with a thick, dark mustache is standing over me, gently shaking my shoulder. Could it be...?

"Miguel?" I say sleepily, hopefully.

Maybe last night was just a horrible nightmare.

Maybe it never happened at all.

Then I blink and my vision clears.

It's not Miguel.

Instead, I'm looking up at a stone-faced man I've never seen before. He has a shaved head and several serrated scars along his jaw. His eyes are cold as marble.

The hope vanishes as quickly as it came.

"Who are you?" I ask in alarm.

"Your new guard, señorita," he replies. "Your father sent me to wake you. You need to get up and pack your things."

I scramble upright in alarm. "Pack my things? Why?"

The man's expression doesn't change. "Your father has a meeting in Los Angeles. You will be accompanying him."

My frown deepens and my heart beats faster. "What's in Los Angeles?"

But the man is turning away from me. He doesn't answer. He already has one of my bags out and opened up on the luggage stand. A Louis Vuitton duffle I've used only once—the time Cesar and I flew to Paris, when we took the picture I was looking at last night. Just the sight of it makes my heart throb painfully.

My brother swore he would protect me from Papa.

But he lied.

He died and left me here alone.

No one can protect me now.

3

ARTEM

A PENTHOUSE IN LOS ANGELES, CALIFORNIA

Grebanyye koshmary.

Fucking nightmares.

I haven't dreamed of her in months. And now, out of nowhere, comes that old fucking nightmare.

Marisha in her white dress.

The silent, black O of her mouth as her screams fade to silence.

And the blood.

So much blood.

Red and thick, staining the white of her dress...

I swing my legs off the bed and drop my head into my hands, trying to shake away the black whirlpool that threatens to pull me apart from the inside.

When that doesn't work, I do what I always do—reach for the whiskey.

I keep a bottle by my bedside for moments like this. I take a swig straight from the bottle and relish the welcome burn that surges down my throat.

"*Sukin syn*," I mutter gratefully under my breath in Russian. "I fucking needed that."

The images fade at once.

I'm good again.

Until I feel a hand graze my bare back.

I whip around, seizing the arm and twisting it back, ready to snap the elbow if need be. It's an automatic reflex from years of training—break first, ask questions later.

I hear the girl's panicked cry before I see her face. Her blue eyes stare back at me, wide with terror and confusion.

She is lying naked and tangled in my sheets. Her short blonde hair no longer holds the glossy sheen that caught my attention last night.

"You're hurting me," she whimpers shakily.

I look down and realize that I'm still pinning her arm.

Sighing, I release her. She lets out a pained little gasp before scurrying away to the opposite corner of the king-sized bed in terror.

I turn from her and rise to my feet. "Get dressed and get out."

I try to remember what we did last night, but I can recall only a few vague grey flashes. I do remember that she screamed so loudly that she had given me a headache. I'd finally shut her up by putting my cock in her mouth.

But even that left me feeling unsatisfied.

Then again, it's been a long time since any woman has come close to making me feel satisfaction.

I expect her to high tail it out of here. But when I hear no movement, I pivot again and catch her staring at me.

"Do I need to pay you or something?"

"Pay me?" she sounds confused. "For what?"

"For last night."

Her blue eyes go wide as she realizes what I'm asking. The fear gets flushed out by indignation.

"I'm not a fucking hooker, asshole!" she spits.

I shrug. "Then what are you waiting for?"

Furious color floods her face as she leaps out of bed and starts stumbling around in search of her clothes, huffing in anger. She has to step over several empty bottles of whiskey to get to the sequined silver dress lying on the ground next to my bar cart.

She bends over to snatch up her dress and wiggle it on. I remember now why I picked her from the crowd last night: those tits are the work of a very talented plastic surgeon.

Once she's grabbed her fuck-me Manolo Blahnik stilettos and neon-red Bottega Veneta clutch, she turns to me.

Her bloodshot eyes are rimmed with smudged mascara and eyeliner. "Do you even remember my name?"

I laugh out loud. "What do *you* think, princess?"

She glowers at me for a moment, too pissed for words, before storming past me and out of my bedroom.

I stand still, head pounding from last night's booze, until I hear the front door of my penthouse slam shut.

Good fucking riddance.

When the apparently-not-a-hooker is gone, I head to the bathroom to survey the toll last night took on me.

I look like shit. I probably shouldn't have gone so hard with the drugs and the drinking. It was a stupid thing to do the day before a big meeting.

My reflection stares back at me. Out of habit, I reach up and touch the scar next to my left eye. My body stiffens, and I force the hand back down to my side.

Not today. I won't go there today.

The dream of Marisha had stirred old memories, ones I've spent several years drowning. But it only takes the smallest of reminders to make them resurface.

I don't have time for distractions today, though. Father will be watching at the meeting. He has been watching me closely for the last few months. Testing me.

Tonight will be the culmination of everything.

I step into the shower and turn it on. The water is so cold that it stings, but that's what I'm after—a little pain to keep my mind sharp, present, aware.

More importantly, it keeps the memories at bay.

When I've had enough, I dry off quickly and pull on a pair of dark pants and a long-sleeved henley shirt. My father prefers that I wear suits to these meetings, but I deliberately avoid them.

Fuck what he wants from me.

No one tells me what to do—not even my father.

Even if he is the don of the Kovalyov Bratva.

I roll up the sleeves, displaying the tattoos that encircle my arms. My Rolex reads eight fifty-six in the evening—I've slept the whole day away—which means my ride will be pulling up in front of the building in exactly four minutes.

Father is never late.

I head downstairs to the lobby in my personal elevator. The elevator doors peel apart in the main foyer to reveal a straight-line path towards the glass entrance of the building.

"Good morning, Mr. Kovalyov," the concierge greets, just as I spot the top-of-the-line Range Rover that my father favors pulling up in front of the building.

There's no denying the luxury SUV is a sleek ride. Even at first glance, it's intimidating as fuck. And that's without knowing about the performance tread tires, the bulletproof ballistic glass windshield, or the high-powered automatic weapons stashed in various compartments around the vehicle.

That's all by design. My father is not one for traveling unprotected.

In his case, it is more than justified. When you've survived as many assassination attempts as he has, investing in proper protection just makes good business sense.

I see only my own reflection in the tinted window before I open the back door and duck into the car.

My father and uncle are waiting for me inside, both dressed in sharp gray suits and open-collared white shirts.

When they were younger men, it was obvious to anyone that Stanislav and Budimir Kovalyov were brothers. They had the same square jawline and hollowed-in cheekbones that I inherited.

The same bushy eyebrows. The same beer bellies. And the same intolerance for disrespect.

But as they've aged, they've begun to look less and less similar. My father, Stanislav, has shrank into himself, developing a slight hunch that has him looking up at the world through narrowed eyes.

Five years ago, his lustrous black hair fell out, a by-product of the cancer treatment. When it grew back, it came in stark white.

None of this has made him less frightening, however. He is still the don of the Kovalyov Bratva. And he still wears that title like a crown of gold.

With his curly hair and easy smile, Uncle Budimir is less imposing. But there's a coldness in him that runs deep. He's ruthless in a way that my father isn't. The kind of man who is cruel just for sport, whereas my father is cruel only out of necessity.

"You look like shit," my uncle remarks with a booming laugh.

I sigh as I slide into my seat. "Good to see you, too, Uncle."

"Budimir is right. And you did not wear a suit," Stanislav observes, his lips pursed up with displeasure. Thirty years in America, but his Russian accent is still thick and well-preserved.

"I don't want to feel like I'm being strangled by a tie all night."

"It's not about what *you* want," Budimir replies coolly. His accent is slight. Only the faintest hint of the motherland still lingers. "Your father prefers you dress the part."

I grit my teeth. "And what part is that, Uncle?"

"You are the heir to the Kovalyov Bratva—"

"You are not a child anymore, Artem," Stanislav interrupts, his tone impatient.

Budimir shuts his mouth immediately. I've seen this happen so many times that it doesn't stand out to me anymore. Stanislav is the older brother. He is the don. It's expected that everyone else takes a back seat whenever he walks into the room.

But I've started to notice little things about my uncle lately. In particular, the way his mouth turns down at the corners every time my father cuts him off or overrules him.

Like it's eating him up inside.

"So nice of you to notice, Father," I answer sarcastically, trying and failing to keep the bitterness from my tone. "Seeing as how I'm thirty as of last month."

Stanislav's eyes narrow on me. "It takes more than age to be a man, my son."

No one else says a word for the rest of the ride. We pull up at the back entrance of The Siren, the Bratva-owned nightclub where tonight's meeting is taking place.

"Who will be at the meeting?" I ask, changing the subject.

Budimir answers first. "Don Maggadino and his sons. Gallo. Brooklier. And Dragna."

"Dragna?" I repeat in surprise, sitting up a little straighter and turning to my father. "You actually invited him?"

"This is a meeting for all the cartels that answer to me," Stanislav says, glancing out the window. "Dragna answers to me. Therefore, he will be at the meeting."

"Yeah? Then why didn't he tell you about the drug shipment from the Antonio cartel he was trying to import without our approval?"

A vein across his forehead pops a little but he keeps looking out the window. "I dealt with that."

Budimir gestures for me to keep quiet. I ignore him. I'm short on patience this morning.

"He was trying to cheat you out of four million dollars!" I snap. "You're going to reward that disloyalty by including him in a meeting?

At the very least, he should be excluded from the inner circle for a while. See if that improves his attitude."

My father sighs. "That would humiliate and offend him."

"That is the fucking *point*," I growl.

At last, Stanislav turns his gaze on me, but his expression is icy. "Being the don is not just about throwing your weight and watching the ants scatter to the wind, Artem. Diplomacy is needed. Intelligence is needed. Brute force is never enough to hold power."

I've heard variations of this speech before.

Just like always, it takes everything I have not to roll my eyes.

"So that's it?" I persist. "You're going to look the other way and let him walk all over you?"

At that, my father's eyes spark with a fiery anger I have not seen in a long time. That fire, that fury—*that* is what has allowed him to reign supreme in the Los Angeles underworld for so long.

"Do you take me for a fool, boy?"

Boy. He called me *boy*. It is a slap in the face—he knows it, I know it, Budimir knows it. Hell, the driver in the front seat and the hot dog guy on the street corner probably know it too.

My anger swells up in my chest, but I bite it back and keep my mouth shut.

His gaze is still rooted on me. "Well?" he asks. "I don't ask questions for the sake of hearing myself speak. Answer. Do you take me for a fool?"

I squeeze my fists at my side as tight as I can. "I take you for the don," I grit icily.

"Good," he nods. "As it should be."

We clamber out of the Range Rover and into the side door of The Siren.

It's packed to the rafters already. Lights arc across the ceiling. Bodies grind together on the dancefloor. Rising above it all is the thunder of the music.

But we don't go out to the main dancefloor. One of the Bratva men on security detail leads us down a dark hall and up to another imposing iron door.

On the other side is where the meeting will take place. No doubt the other Family heads are already here. Father does not tolerate tardiness.

Just before the bodyguard opens the door for us, Father holds up a hand to signal for him to wait.

He turns to me and rests a wrinkled old hand on my wrist.

I frown in confusion. "What?" I ask.

He's got that look on his face, the one I've learned not to like.

"You're not coming in," he says finally.

I blink. "What?"

Budimir lays a reassuring hand on my shoulder. "It's okay, nephew."

I shrug them both off and turn back to my father. "What the fuck is going on?"

"You're not coming in, son," my father repeats. "Not today. You're not ready."

I'm too stunned and furious to speak. He looks into my eyes and nods once.

Then he turns once more and walks through the steel door.

Leaving me alone in the hallway, with rage boiling in my veins.

4

ESME

MONDRIAN HOTEL—LOS ANGELES, CALIFORNIA

"Hey girrrl! The fun has arrived!"

I force a smile as my cousin Tamara bounces into my hotel suite at the Mondrian Hotel in Los Angeles.

Everything about Tamara screams "socialite party girl." She's wearing a black leather mini skirt and an oversized white linen blouse that hangs carelessly off one shoulder. It's very Cali, very fashion-forward.

Classic Tam-Tam.

She pauses suddenly once she registers my glum face.

"Seriously?" she asks, pouting a little. "Is that the welcome you give your favorite cousin?"

"What makes you think you're my favorite cousin?" I tease.

She wrinkles her nose and flicks her long, straightened black hair off her shoulder. "First of all, duh. And secondly, um, yeah, this is most definitely *not* the welcome you give your favorite cousin. I'm gonna go back outside and we can try this a second time, kay? Kay."

I snort a laugh and shake my head at my ditzy cousin. Tamara is definitely a good time and I love when we get to hang out, but I'm just not in a very social mood today.

Not after what happened just before we left Mexico.

I'd planned on spending this whole trip cooped up in the hotel room. Still, a part of me is glad not to be alone.

I stand and give Tamara the hug she's been waiting for. To my surprise, even when I try to pull away, she holds on to me, prolonging the hug a little.

"You okay, chica?" she asks as she releases me.

I frown. It isn't like Tamara to get all serious right off the bat.

"I'm fine," I reply with a shrug, even though I feel anything but fine.

Tamara's voice drops low. "Has he been awful lately?"

She doesn't have to say my father's name for me to know who she's talking about.

But I hesitate anyways. "Why do you ask?"

"Because of this." She traces the bruise along my jaw tenderly with her fingers. Her eyes are wide with sympathy.

"Oh." I'd forgot all about the slap. "It's not a big deal."

I can feel Tamara's eyes on me for a moment before she opens the large, trendy leather bag she's carrying. Her blonde highlights glint under the sunlight as she rummages through her bag.

When she comes up for air, she's got a makeup kit in hand.

"What are you doing?" I ask, confused.

"I'm gonna fix your face."

"My face is fine," I argue. "You can barely see the bruise anymore."

"I beg to differ. Trust me, you don't want that thing exposed when we're hitting the clubs later."

I laugh bitterly. "I hate to burst your bubble, but we won't be hitting anything tonight except for an early bedtime."

Tamara rolls her eyes and starts pulling out a range of different concealers and some blush.

"What he doesn't know won't hurt him."

"Tamara..."

"Hush up, girl, unless you wanna get stabbed in the eye with mascara," she says absent-mindedly.

She forces me to sit down on the white sofa facing the window and gets to work on my face.

I concede defeat and let her do what she wants to. It's easier than arguing.

My thoughts float aimlessly as I stare out at the LA skyline.

I can imagine Papa's voice in my ear. *Sit in your cage and be quiet, little bird. Sit and smile. It doesn't matter if you're happy or not. Just keep smiling.*

"Earth to Esme! Where's your head at, girl?"

I blink and focus on Tamara. "Doesn't matter," I mumble. "How about we head to the spa now? I'd really love to get out of this room."

She doesn't argue. We get our bags and head down to the spa with two of my new guards in tow.

I notice Tamara checking out Ansel. He's the taller of the two guards and he's got a pair of tattoos on his face, which contribute to how dangerous he looks. I'm willing to bet anything that's a large part of why she's attracted to him.

"I wouldn't go there," I mutter to her as we enter the spa, leaving my guards stationed at the entrance. "Matter of fact, I wouldn't get involved with anyone who works for my father."

Tamara snorts. "What makes you think I want to get involved with him?" she asks. "I'm just interested in fucking him."

She says it casually, but it leaves me reeling. Maybe because it's just such a foreign idea.

What must it be like to do something just because you can? Just because you feel like it?

The spa has exactly two tones, pearly greys and muted ivories. I know it's meant to promote calm and healing, but to me, it feels lackluster, completely devoid of personality or life.

We're greeted by a petite blonde woman who is as pale as her surroundings.

She leads us to a private room, which is, surprise surprise, as white and dull as the rest of the spa.

"Please make yourselves comfortable," she says with a smile. "I'll be back with some refreshments for you both."

The moment the door is closed, I turn to Tamara, feeling the immense need to unburden myself. "He's trying to marry me off, you know. My father."

Tamara's eyes grow wide. "You're only twenty-two!"

"Apparently, that doesn't matter," I say. "Nothing I want matters. And I don't think it ever will."

"You need to get out of here."

"Yeah." I nod. "That's exactly what I need to do. But I can't see a way out of this life."

"No," Tamara says, shaking her head, "I mean, out of this spa. What you need is to take control of your life, and it starts with baby steps."

I roll my eyes. "That's an elaborate plan to get yourself to a club tonight."

Tamara puts a manicured hand on my leg. "Okay, forget about me. What do *you* want to do today?"

"Does it matter?"

Tamara squeals in delight and claps her hands together excitedly. "Then it sounds like my plan is the winner!"

I just sigh. "Have you forgotten the two armed guards waiting outside this spa for us?"

She rolls her eyes dismissively. "Please, girl. I've been sneaking out since I was thirteen years old," she says. "Those two don't scare me. If they happen to catch us… well, they'll just have punish us, won't they?" She winks flirtatiously.

I can't help but laugh. "You're insane."

"Come on. Let's go," Tamara says enthusiastically. "Pretty please?"

I realize how much I actually want to go.

A night out with my cousin—who has never even heard of the concept of having something to worry about—sounds like the perfect antidote to all my despair.

But then I think of Miguel.

The image of him beaten and bloodied on that chair has haunted me for days now.

What happened to him was my fault.

"I don't know," I say nervously. "Let's just enjoy our spa appointments, okay? We don't have to do anything reckless right now."

Tamara sighs noisily but I ignore her and swap my clothes out for the soft robes that were left for us.

I settle on the spa table and try to relax, but I realize how tense my body is. No matter how much I try to breathe, I can never get enough air into my lungs.

This is what my life is going to be for the next several decades.

Perfect.

Pampered.

And completely horrible.

Endless spa appointments, private piano performances for Papa's colleagues, eventually a nightmare of a wedding to some pig of a man.

I'll be a living, breathing doll with no voice and no freedom. Forever trapped in my colorless world, counting regrets like other people count money.

I sit up suddenly, get off the table, and reach for my clothes.

Tamara looks at me in alarm. "Chica, what's going on?"

"New plan. Let's get out of here right this second," I say, before I can change my mind.

"What?"

"Let's go," I say.

A dazzling smile lights up Tamara's face. "Now we're fucking talking. Follow my lead."

5

ESME

I follow Tamara back through the spa, towards the entrance. The doors are closed, but I know my guards will still be at their posts just outside.

"How do you plan on doing this without being seen?" I ask.

Tamara throws me a pitying look. "Oh, sweet, innocent Esme," she murmurs. "Do you really think there's only one way in and out of here?"

"You're heading for the entrance," I point out.

"You really don't pay attention, do you?" Tamara asks. "There was a door to the left as we walked in. Staff quarters. There'll be an exit through there."

Tam is a psycho, but she's a fun psycho. Life always works out for people like her.

And, true to form, it works perfectly and smoothly. The staff quarters are empty, with an exit door at the far side of the room like the pot of gold at the end of a rainbow.

We're about three steps away from freedom—when the door opens and one of the spa therapists comes in.

She too is decked out in an all-beige ensemble, but she's not the woman who greeted us when we entered. At least, I don't think she is. Everyone who works here looks the same, though, so I can't say for sure.

"May I help you?" she asks politely.

"Sorry, we got a little turned around," Tamara says, flashing a smile. "We'll head back into the spa now."

Tamara grabs my hand and pulls me towards another door off to the side.

"Um, ma'am, that door will take you back into the hotel," the therapist says in confusion.

"Same difference!" Tamara chirps. She pulls me through the door before the woman can say anything.

The moment we step out of the blinding whiteness of the spa and into the color of the hotel, we both start running. We probably don't even need to, but it feels good.

We rush through the massive lobby to the grand golden doors of the hotel. Then we burst outside into the perfect L.A. sunshine.

As Tamara hails a cab, a laugh bursts from my lips. She looks at me for a moment, a smile settling over her face, but she doesn't say anything.

The cab drops us off outside of Tam's building, a huge, pink building with a lattice of roses up the front. We race upstairs, still cackling like maniacs, and into her chic two-bedroom apartment.

The moment Tamara closes the door behind us, I breathe a sigh of relief and throw my bag down on the glass coffee table.

"I can't believe it," I laugh. "We did it!"

"Well, I did it," Tamara reminds me with a friendly nudge in the ribs. "You just tagged along."

"Fair enough," I smile. "You can have all the credit."

She grins. "Aren't you glad you decided to listen to me?"

"Yeah, yeah, yeah. Don't get a big head about it."

But we both know I'm lying. I would've never done something this reckless on my own. And truth be told, I'm not stupid enough to think I've gotten away with anything just yet.

No doubt there'll be hell to pay if my father finds out.

But that's a problem for future Esme. If there are any consequences, I'll deal with them later.

My life is closing in on me even faster than I've always feared. I want to live a little—while I still can.

"Come on. Let me doll you up. You can borrow something from my wardrobe for tonight," Tamara says, leading me into her bedroom.

I raise my eyebrows as I walk in. Tamara's room is complete and utter chaos. Clothes piled everywhere, makeup littering the top of her vanity, half-eaten snacks lying on the bedside table.

"Oh, don't look at me like that. The maid's coming tomorrow," she sasses as she flings open her wardrobe and starts riffling through it.

I stand in the doorway, scared to go any further for fear of triggering a hidden landmine or something, as she throws clothing items over her shoulder without looking.

"Ah ha!" She re-emerges, holding something up triumphantly. "Here. This little number will suit you perfectly."

I stare in disbelief at the dress she's picked out for me. "You cannot possibly be serious."

Tamara frowns. "What? Too much?"

I laugh. The dress is made of what looks like sheer chainmail. The neckline seems explicitly designed to reveal my boobs to the world and a thigh slit that rises up to show everything else.

"It would have to be invisible to be any more revealing," I drawl.

Tamara laughs. "Don't be a drama queen."

"Can you even wear underwear with it?" I ask. I'm genuinely curious.

"The point is to *show off* your underwear," Tamara tells me with a wink.

I shake my head. "Pass. I think I'll choose something myself for tonight."

Tamara sighs dramatically, but she moves over to make room for me.

We spend the next couple of hours playing dress up and laughing. At some point, Tamara pours us each a huge glass of red wine—full enough that mine sloshes over the rim a bit when she hands it to me—and we start drinking.

In the end, the dress I choose is a simple, black mini, but the cut is really sexy. It has thin straps and a bustier that emphasizes my cleavage while still keeping the look classy. The hemline is short, ending just a couple of inches below my butt, but the structure is figure-hugging and flattering, highlighting my curves and making me look sophisticated and a little more mature.

I slip on a pair of strappy silver stilettos and let Tammy go to work on me with some lipstick, eyeliner, and rouge.

"Nothing too dramatic," she reassures me. "Just enough to make your natural features pop a little more."

So she says. I'm not in an arguing mood. I'm mostly happy to sip on my wine and let Tam take control of the night. She knows better than I do how to live it up.

We go back and forth about what to do with my hair. Ultimately, I just pull it free from its messy top knot and leave it hanging down my shoulders.

Tam laughs. "Like a fierce lioness! Rawr!"

But then she smiles and gives me a mushy kiss on the cheek and I know that it's a good look for me.

I stare at myself in the mirror, almost in disbelief. Papa never allowed me to dress too sexy. Claimed it would make me look like a "whore."

But as I cast a critical eye over my look, I feel strong and confident.

Fuck what Papa thinks.

"Damn, girl!" Tamara exclaims as she turns me around to take one final look. "You look hot as hell."

I smile. "Thanks. So do you."

She really does. She's wearing a red halter with a low neckline and a black leather skirt that's even shorter than mine.

"Please," Tamara snorts dismissively, "no one's gonna be looking at me with you in the room."

The sun set at some point while we were drinking and laughing. The L.A. day has turned into a warm and bustling L.A. night.

I'm feeling really good as we head to one of Tamara's favorite haunts in the city: an upscale club called The Siren.

As we pay for our ride and hop out of the taxi, I can see how popular it is by the huge line extending out of its doors.

"Oh, jeez. How are we gonna get in?" I ask nervously.

"Um, have you seen yourself?" she chuckles. "Have you seen me? It's no problema. Come on, baby cousin, let me show you how it's done."

Tamara ignores the line of people completely as she heads for the bouncer at the entrance to the club.

Some of the women queued up there shoot us angry glances.

The men, on the other hand, yell compliments that oscillate between flattering and creepy.

I ignore them all and follow Tamara. I expect her to take the lead, but the moment we get to the bouncer, Tamara grabs my hand and pushes me forward in front of her.

The bouncer, a tall, handsome guy in a black leather jacket, takes one slow look up and down at each of us, then flashes a dazzling smile.

I shiver. *Is everyone in Los Angeles this good looking?*

"You girls have fun in there." He unhooks the velvet rope and ushers us in through the VIP entrance.

I laugh as we tumble inside, feeling a strange sense of euphoria settle over me.

Tomorrow, I have to go back to my claustrophobic, Papa-controlled world.

But for tonight, I'm in control of the next few hours.

I'm going to make them count.

Tamara is still holding my hand as we emerge from the darkened VIP hallway into the main area of the club.

It's a booming, overwhelming maze of sweaty bodies and bright lights. The music is so loud I can't hear myself think. I'm sweating already, too.

Tamara screams something in my ear, but I can't make out what she said.

"What?" I scream back.

"I said, let's get someone to buy us shots!"

I give her a thumbs up and a hesitant smile. I'm just overwhelmed, that's all.

But if I stop to try and gather my thoughts, the image of Miguel beaten and slumped over in that tiny room flashes in front of my eyes.

I shudder.

Can't be doing that. Look at Tammy—she's dancing already, having fun, arms in the air and not a care in the world.

I try to smile and mimic her.

But I can't help feeling like I'm being watched.

I tap Tam on the shoulder. "Does it feel like someone's staring at us?" I yell.

She makes me repeat it a few times, but eventually she gets it.

When she does, she laughs out loud. "Of course we're being watched!" she yells back. "We're the hottest girls in the club!"

I feign another smile and try to breathe. *Follow Tamara's lead.*

But I still can't shake that feeling of being watched.

And when I turn around, I realize why.

Someone's staring right at me from a small, innocuous doorway along one wall. He's got dark hair raked back carelessly from his forehead. Tattoos trace over his brawny forearms, and more peek out from beneath the open collar of his henley shirt.

But it's his eyes that draw my attention the most.

Even in this chaotic club, they stand out.

They're darker than anything else.

Angrier. More intense.

And they're locked dead on me.

6

ESME

I notice two things right off the bat.

First off, he's deadly handsome. Handsome in a way that feels raw and primal. It doesn't hurt that he's big, muscular—over six feet and built like an athlete.

His features are somewhat exotic but still familiar. Foreign, maybe. His coloring is dark. Dark hair. Dark eyes. Dark everything, really.

His nose is sharp, proud, aristocratic. His cheekbones are defined, his jaw an aggressive square that offsets the fullness of his lips.

I might have called him "beautiful," but the word just isn't appropriate for him. Not with the light stubble coating his jaw, the piercing directness of his eyes, the careless way he rakes his fingers through his hair, as though he hasn't given it a second thought his entire life.

Other people notice him, too. Their eyes keep flitting his direction, just like mine do.

He's a man people want to be close to.

But they're scared of getting *too* close.

I can understand that feeling. I'm a hundred yards away from him with a thousand people between us and even I'm a little scared.

There's just something about the reckless way he surveys the crowd, the arrogant way he leans against the doorjamb...

He looks the kind of man who breaks things and laughs about it.

The second thing I notice about him is the way he's looking at *me*.

I'm used to being looked at, admired, cat-called. Tam and I have been out for less than three hours and you could already fill a stadium with the number of men who've commented on my ass or tits.

Point is, I'm familiar with salacious glances and lust-filled gazes from men.

This is... not that.

Not by a longshot.

The man on the railing isn't undressing me with his eyes like other men are. His gaze feels thoughtful. Almost curious.

But there's an edge of possessiveness in his stance. A sense of ownership that I don't understand.

"Esme? Hello... what are you looking at...? Oh, *whoa*." Tamara trails off when she notices who's got my attention.

I drop my eyes instantly, embarrassed to have been caught.

"Damn... now that's a man," Tamara says. She grins wickedly at me. "You know how to pick 'em, boo."

I laugh scornfully at that. I can count on two fingers the number of guys I've slept with.

There's Mattias, the assistant of the man who cleaned the pool at my family's compound. My father had him beaten senseless when he found out we'd slept together.

Then there was Felipe, the son of a supplier Papa used to do business with. Papa found out about him, too. He had the man's father locked in the basement for a month.

I never saw either of them again.

So it's safe to say that I have no clue "how to pick 'em."

"Come on," I tell her, grabbing her arm and pulling her deeper into the club. "Let's go get another drink."

"Fuck that," Tamara says, her eyes still fixed on him. "Let's head over there and say hi to the Greek god with the Superman chin."

"No," I say, without hesitation.

"Why not?" Tamara asks, whirling me around to face her. "Oh, I see… You *like* him."

I roll my eyes, trying to pretend as though none of this had any effect on me. "Grow up, Tam."

"You do," Tamara laughs. "Admit it. You're attracted to him."

"I… I mean, he's not unattractive—"

"Understatement of the year."

"But it doesn't matter," I tell her. "We need to leave soon anyway."

"What the fuck are you talking about?" Tamara asks. "The night's just getting started!"

"Which means Papa's probably got his men scouring L.A. in search of us right now," I tell her. "We should go."

"I thought we were going to the bar?" Tamara pouts. She's clearly not ready to leave yet.

Just then, she stumbles and turns her ankle in her four-inch stilettos, falling right into my arms with a squeal.

I catch her, thank goodness, but it's a dead giveaway that the night should be over a lot sooner than she wants. She's drank way more than I have and she's starting to get a little sloppy.

"Okay," I concede. "Let's go to the bar." My real plan is to get my cousin a tall drink of water, but she doesn't have to know that just yet.

We fight our way to the bar, going through the dance floor, turning down offers to dance from a bunch of different men who grab us anyways as we pass.

I cringe away from their hands, but Tamara revels in it.

When we get to the bar, Tamara immediately orders two Moscow mules and then proceeds to flirt brazenly with the bartender.

I ignore her and turn to survey the crowd.

"Hey, sexy," someone rumbles way too close to my ear.

I ignore the deep voice for a second. But the tap of a blunt finger on my shoulder is too intrusive to shrug off.

I turn and look at the man who has planted himself behind me. He's huge and shaped like a boulder in a too-tight black t-shirt and overlarge veneers on his teeth.

Something about him makes my skin crawl.

So I just give him a tight, *no thanks* smile and turn my back on him with finality.

He doesn't seem to get the message.

"How about I buy you a drink, doll?" Boulder Man bellows over the thundering music.

I glance at him and shake my head. "No, thank you," I answer curtly. "My friend already bought our drinks."

"Your friend is sloshed off her ass," he says, leaning in a little. "How about we ditch the deadweight and have a little fun?"

"Good idea. If we're ditching deadweight, then why don't you fuck off and bother someone else?"

Safe to say that the onrush of sudden anxiety has made me a little feistier than usual.

This was a fun idea, a good idea… until it very much wasn't anymore.

Now, all I can think about—once again—is Miguel.

It's time to go home.

I don't catch Boulder Man's reaction, because just then, Tamara throws back a shot that I wasn't aware she had ordered.

Then she promptly spits it back out… right on the bar counter.

The bartender she'd been flirting with looks murderous as he turns to me.

"Okay, she's cut off," he tells me. "Time to get her home."

"Good call." I nod in agreement and grab Tamara, pulling her away from the bar. She doesn't resist this time. In fact, she actually moans a little.

I know then that something is really wrong.

"Tamara?"

I've got her arm around my neck, so it's hard for me to see her face. But a quick side glance tells me that her color is not quite right.

"Esm', I don't feel so… *urgh*…"

She stops talking. I watch her turn a nasty shade of yellow right in front of my eyes.

"Oh, God," I gasp. "We need to get you home right now."

Tamara shakes her head violently. "No… *urgh!* Bathroom…"

Shit. Looks like home is out of the question. T-minus sixty seconds or so until projectile vomiting commences.

Nodding, I try and support her as best I can as I half-drag, half-carry her past Boulder Man and off to the bathroom on the other side of the club.

On our way there, several men accost me with offers to "help" carry Tamara.

"Come on, baby. Let me carry her for you. If you're jealous, I'll carry you too."

"What will you give me if I help you with your skank friend?"

"I like my women barely conscious when I fuck 'em."

I act as though I hear none of them. I just keep my head down and power through, ignoring the comments as well as the stares and wolf whistles. Even though the increasingly vulgar comments make my skin shiver.

Men are vile.

Drunk men doubly so.

I'm panting by the time we reach the restrooms.

Tam looks even worse than she did back at the bar. Her face is an unnatural green and the sounds coming out of her are like baby gurgles mixed with a clogged garbage disposal.

Fuck. Fuckity fucking fuck.

I have to kick the door of the bathroom open, but I manage to get us both inside.

For the first time since she threw up on the bar, Tam moves of her own volition. Her drunken, wobbly legs carry her towards one of the open stalls.

She's down on her knees in seconds, spewing her guts out into the open toilet.

Suppressing my own gag reflex, I reach forward and pull back her hair. Tamara grips the toilet as though it's a lifeline. Her bare knees scrape against the silver-grey slate tiles beneath us.

In that moment, I'm grateful that Tamara decided on one of the more upscale clubs in the city. There are worse floors to be kneeling on, that's for sure.

Some time passes. I'm not sure how long. Three or four *yaaakks'* worth, if that's a unit of measurement.

But eventually—mercifully—Tamara's puking slows.

I brush another flyaway back from her sweaty forehead.

"Tammy, hon? You feeling a little better?"

"*Urgh*," is all she can muster up.

At least she's stopped puking. She slumps against one wall of the bathroom stall and sighs deeply, grimacing.

There's still a dribble of vomit running down one side of her mouth. I grab some toilet paper and rush to the marble sink to wet the corner slightly. Then I dart back to Tamara and clean her up a bit.

She just lies there, nearly lifeless, her eyes fluttering closed. It's like cleaning up a corpse.

"Tamara." I pat her cheek. "Hey, babe, let's go back to your apartment okay? You can sleep when we get there."

"No," she whines, closing her eyes on me. "I'm so tired. Lemme rest."

I'm somewhat reassured by the fact that she's talking in full, coherent sentences again, and her color definitely looks better.

But she needs rest, and she's most definitely going to have a killer hangover in the morning.

"We're in a bathroom," I remind her. "We're in a *club* bathroom, Tam-Tam. You'll feel better in your own bed."

"Five more minutes," she tells me like a petulant child. "Please? I just wanna rest…"

She trails off there, leaving me kneeling in front of her, frustrated and exhausted.

Fine. I suppose I can give her a few minutes.

I position Tamara against the wall of the stall so that she doesn't slump over onto the ground, then I go back over to the sink to wash my hands.

I'm still rinsing my hands when I feel eyes on me.

The hair on the back of my neck stands on end as I raise my gaze to the back-lit mirror in front of me.

That's when I see *his* reflection in the mirror.

He's standing right behind me, leaning against the doorframe with a scowl on his face.

It's the man from the bar, the one who offered to buy me a drink just before Tamara threw up.

Boulder Man.

7

ESME

I whirl around to face him. "What are you doing in here?"

He looks perfectly relaxed as he stares at me. There's even a smile on his face.

But it's not a nice smile. It's the kind that makes your legs heavy with fear.

He looks even bigger in this small, fluorescent bathroom than he did out by the bar. His head nearly brushes against the ceiling.

He flexes his hands like he can't wait to tear me limb from limb.

"Our conversation was cut short," he rumbles acidly. "I wanted to finish it."

My heart thunders painfully in my chest as instinct tells me to run. To scream. Get away from this man as fast as I can.

But my eyes slip to the partially closed door of the stall Tamara's in.

I can't leave her.

"Please," I say. "I need to get my cousin home."

"Cousin, huh?" he says conversationally. "You two don't look related."

I haven't moved an inch. But he takes a step toward me and I turn slowly on the spot.

"Yeah, well, she's my cousin, and she got sick, so..."

He nods. It's almost convincingly sympathetic. "Yeah, you should probably get her home quickly."

"Exactly—"

"The sooner you suck my cock, the sooner that's gonna happen."

A gasp catches in my throat. *No fucking way did he just say that.*

But his grin widens a notch, and I know that he very much did.

I can't deal with all this right now. The fear of Papa, of Boulder Man, of every drunk faceless horny moron out preying on the club floor right now—it's all piling up, choking me out, clouding my brain.

I pray for someone to enter the bathroom. Anyone will do—beggars can't be choosers.

The fear is worsening. It's choking me. Making me dizzy. Making me weak.

Do something, Esme! screams the voice of self-preservation in my head.

"That's never going to happen," I snap at him with strength I don't actually feel.

He chuckles. "I'm not really giving you a choice, darlin'."

Then, all at once, he lunges forward.

A scream rises in the back of my throat, but nothing comes out.

I stumble to the side in an attempt to get away from him.

Not fast enough, though.

Boulder Man seizes my hair and pulls me back-to-front against him. His breath is sticky against my neck as he brushes my hair aside and licks from my collarbone up to my jaw.

He stinks of alcohol and sweat and cheap cologne.

The rapist trifecta.

Worst of all, I can feel his nasty erection pressing against the fabric on the back of my dress.

For some reason, that does it—releases the scream in my throat.

The tiny, tiled bathroom echoes with the sound of my fear.

And my instincts switch from *flight* to *fight*.

I jab my elbow as hard as I can back into his stomach. He's got easily a hundred or more pounds on me, so it's not like I do any real damage.

But the move startles him so much he actually loosens his grip on me and I wriggle free.

Released from his grasp, I try to run again. If I can just reach the door, call for help...

But my legs are shaky and he's three times my height and ten times my bodyweight.

With one huge hand, he slams me back against the closed door of a stall. The impact sends stars shooting across my vision.

The man's eyes narrow to ugly slits as he moves towards me.

I've succeeded mostly in pissing him off, apparently.

Well, buddy, there's more where that came from.

When he's close enough, I jam my knee upwards into his groin.

He grunts in pain. Unfortunately, my aim was off, so he doesn't go down like I intended him to.

Instead, I have just enough time to see his palm slice across the air towards me.

In the next second, pain erupts on the side of my face. The shooting stars double and my vision goes black at the edges.

By the time I process that he just slapped me—hell, he might've given me a concussion with how hard he swung—he's got his hands on me.

He yanks up the front of my dress and rips it in the process. All that's left is my panties between him and me.

I continue to fight even though I know I can't win. Writhing, screaming, thrashing with all my might.

At this point, it's a matter of pride.

I will not just lie still.

I will not just *accept* being assaulted.

I will fight him every step of the way. He'll have to knock me unconscious if he wants me to lay back and take it.

He seems to realize exactly that as his hands close in around my neck.

"I will break every bone in your body, you little bitch," he snarls at me. "Fucking cut it out."

"Go ahead!" I scream back at him. "Break every bone in my body. It still won't make you a fucking man."

His eyes go wide with anger and his meaty fingers tighten around my neck. My vision blurs more.

His other hand is scrabbling at his fly, trying to unzip and pull himself out so he can finish what he started.

I feel the sting of incoming tears, but I squeeze my eyes against them.

I refuse to let him see me cry. Maybe I can't stop him from taking my body.

But he doesn't get to take my dignity with it.

I gasp in pain as his nails scratch my thighs. His hand on my throat is so tight I can barely breathe.

Don't you cry, Esme. Don't you dare cry.

"Get the fuck off her."

My eyes fly open. I look towards the door, in the direction of the deep, commanding voice.

And I see him standing there. Like some kind of dark avenging angel.

The man from earlier. The one with the square jaw, the beautiful lips, the midnight-black eyes.

His stare is even more intense up close.

And right now, he looks absolutely murderous.

"Yo, buddy, get the fuck out of here," the monster on top of me says. "Go find another whore to stick your cock into. This one's mine."

My guardian angel doesn't bother responding.

He takes one step forward, grabs Boulder Man by the throat, and hurls him to the ground.

I feel the pressure around my neck disappear and my legs suddenly feel like jelly. It takes all my strength to stay on my feet.

I draw in a deep, shuddering breath.

Then I look up to see what's happening.

The two men are on the ground. My rapist is at least fifty pounds heavier than the dark-eyed man—mostly in the beer gut department—but that doesn't seem to make a difference.

All I can see is a flurry of fists.

All I can hear is a series of muffled groans and sickening crunches.

There's blood on the tiles, I notice suddenly.

Then—one more crunch.

I scream and look away, but not before I see Boulder Man's elbow bent exactly the wrong direction. The image sears itself into my brain.

I'm still covering my eyes as I hear more muffled noises.

When I look up again, I see that my attacker has dragged the rapist out into the hallway.

He delivers one more swift, brutal kick to the man's ribs—*CRUNCH*—spits on him, and then slams the door shut. Locks it with a *click*.

Then he turns to me.

And my heart does a platform dive into the acid of my stomach.

I thought the dark-eyed man was my savior.

What if I was wrong?

I'm shaking like a leaf. Horrified all over again. One bad thought leads to the next.

Is this better? Is it worse? What have I gotten myself into? What is going to happen next?

My dress is ripped, my face is bruised, and I'm sweating all over.

But despite the brutal beatdown this man just administered, he looks perfectly calm.

Perfectly composed.

The very picture of icy control.

"Did he hurt you?" he asks.

His voice resonates with something inside me. I'm still too choked up to answer.

When I don't reply, he takes a step forward.

I flinch instantly. "Don't come any closer," I order.

"And here I was expecting a thank you," he drawls. But to his credit, he stops in his tracks.

His eyes bore into my face. Something rises, hot and desperate, inside me. I've never quite felt anything like it before and it takes me off guard.

"Why?" I ask. "So you can finish what he started?"

His eyes flash dangerously. "Do I look like the kind of man who needs to force himself on a woman?"

"How would I know?" I spit. "I don't know you."

"No, but you've been staring at me like you do."

My mouth pops open in shock. I thought I was being subtle. I try and recover, but I fear he's already seen through me.

"You were the one staring at me."

He smiles, a slow, tilted grin that sends a bolt of electricity shooting up between my legs. *What the fuck is that?*

"Yes, I was," he admits freely.

"Why?" I ask.

"*Why?*" he repeats, raising one dusky eyebrow. "Because men like me live to claim women like you."

My breath catches in my throat.

Without thinking, I take a step towards him. Something magnetic takes ahold of me.

I make a decision in that moment.

For no one else but me.

Because *I* want to.

"He had his hands all over me," I say softly.

Anger flashes across his eyes, bitter and terrible. He says nothing though. Waits for me to go on.

"Make me forget," I whisper. "Make me forget that he ever touched me."

My savior closes the final distance. Raises his hand. Lets his thumb trail along my bottom lip.

It's the only moment made of tenderness.

In the next second, his lips crash down on mine like a storm and my arms wrap around his neck.

I can feel his hands on my back, before they slip down, squeezing my ass and hoisting me up around his waist.

He turns and carries me to the bathroom counter. He sets me down on the marble, right between two sinks.

My body registers how cool the marble is, but it's extinguished almost immediately by the heat of his hands.

They rake across my skin, leaving trails of fire that somehow find their way between my legs. I can feel his cock pressed up against my thigh and it makes me moan.

Desire—that's what I feel with this stranger.

Aching, craving, desperate desire.

The kind I had always assumed was simply an elaborate fiction dreamed up just to sell books and movies.

But this is real. This is happening.

He settles between my legs, pushing my thighs further apart, his sheathed cock rubbing against my pussy.

His lips ravage mine, and I let him. I open for him. Beg for more.

When his tongue meets mine, I try twisting into him as close as I possibly can. I'm aware how clumsy I am as my hand reaches down between us, but I want to feel him.

Before I can reach his cock, however, he grabs both my hands and pulls them back behind me. He holds them there, keeps them bound together with one of his hands, as the other falls on my pussy.

I gasp as he shoves aside my panties and strokes my lips for a few seconds before he slips a finger inside me, then another.

I gasp again, shocked at how my body is reacting to this.

He's not gentle.

And I realize one thing: I don't want him to be.

My wetness coats his fingers. All I can do is writhe around helplessly, unable to move my hands.

Totally and completely at his mercy.

He finger-fucks me until I'm bent into him, my face pressed up against his neck.

He smells of oak and sandalwood. Deep, earthy scents that make me think of icy mountains and dark forests.

My body feels like a raw nerve ending, ready to explode.

And just when I think I might, he stops, he pulls out of me and raises his hand to his lips.

I can see my juices on his fingers just before he slips them into his mouth. When he removes them, his fingers come out clean.

His eyes never leave mine.

They're swirling pools of lust.

Endless.

Possessive.

Only then does he release my hands. I grip the counter and watch as he unzips himself. My eyes fall hungrily to his cock. It's a thing of beauty. Hard, long, and cruelly curved.

His eyes meet mine as he lines himself up with my entrance and pushes into me with one hard thrust that has me crying out.

I have to hold on tight because he rams into me so hard, I nearly come apart at the seams.

His body feels harder and stronger than the marble beneath me. I cling to him with all the desperation of a woman who knows she's about to fall.

Sweat drips down between my breasts as he fucks me, his body slamming into mine so hard that the sound bounces off the walls in echoes.

My back arches as my pussy begins to clench…

Until, all at once, I burst.

I come so fast I'm not prepared for it. Definitely not expecting it, which is why I moan so loudly I'm pretty sure I can be heard above the music in the club.

But the dark stranger doesn't care. He doesn't stop.

He just keeps fucking me, his thrusts getting faster and faster.

Until he explodes, too, hardly a minute after me.

I feel him unleashing inside me. I'm just drunk enough not to care.

When he's fully spent, I collapse into him. I can hardly breathe. The air in this tiny, cramped bathroom is thick and steamy.

He leans against me, the stubble of his jaw grazing my cheek.

We're both panting heavily, but he gets ahold of himself faster than I do.

My legs are still wrapped around his waist when he pulls back, his eyes penetrating into mine.

"My name is—"

"No!" I blurt before he can tell me. "Please, no."

I shake my head. I'm thinking of Miguel. Of Cesar. Of Mattias and Felipe and all the countless people that have come into my life, only to leave again in blood and tears—or, worse, in a coffin.

"Please," I whimper. "No names."

His eyes cloud over for a second before he regains composure.

Then he nods and moves back. I can feel his seed seep out of me and I feel an inextricable sense of loss.

I watch him zip himself back up. The top buttons of his henley shirt are open, revealing more inky tattoos across his collarbone.

I want to trace them with my fingertips. Explore the rest of his body.

The stranger's gaze flickers over me for a few short seconds.

Then, he turns and walks out of the bathroom without so much as a backward glance.

I exhale. My breath comes out in short, shuddering bursts. I'm oscillating between tears and giddy euphoria, overwhelmed and shocked.

I have no idea what that was. No idea what came over me.

I'm not sure about much in life, but I know one thing for sure now: *that* is what sex is supposed to feel like.

Too bad I'll never see him again.

8

ARTEM

FOUR MONTHS LATER

THE PORT OF LONG BEACH—LOS ANGELES, CALIFORNIA—MIDNIGHT

"Why is it that whenever we're on a stakeout, you're fucking sleeping?" I demand.

Cillian O'Sullivan sighs and opens one eye to glance at me scornfully.

My best friend has feathery blonde hair that he keeps a few inches too long and baby blue eyes.

It's ironic, really. He has an all-American, boy-next-door vibe going for him despite the fact that he's Irish through and through.

"Because this isn't a fucking movie," he replies. "It takes a while for the action to get started and I need—"

"Your beauty sleep," I finish, rolling my eyes. "If the point was to improve your appearance, I would start by shaving the pubes off your face."

At that, Cillian sits up and looks at me with mock hurt. "Are you knocking my beard?" he asks pridefully.

"If you can even call it that."

Cillian runs his hand through the scant blonde hair of his chin and checks his reflection in the car mirror.

"I just have to give it more time to fill out. It's only been four months."

I snort. "If four months isn't enough to turn that dead rat on your lip into a real man's beard, then you're shit out of luck, amigo."

"Blow me," he retorts. Not his most eloquent comeback.

Four months. Has it really been that long?

An image of the girl's face flashes across my eyes. I see her swollen lips, her matted hair, the rise and fall of her chest as she watched me zip myself up.

I'd walked out of that club bathroom without looking back.

That was four months ago.

"Is it really that bad?" Cillian asks, turning to me.

"You want my honest opinion?"

"I wasn't aware that you had anything else to offer."

"It looks like you covered your chin in honey and rolled around the floor of a barbershop."

"For fuck's sake, you're an asshole."

I chuckle. "You asked. I delivered."

"I'm going to deliver a fist to your face if you keep it up."

"That won't end well for you, Irish boy."

He scowls and goes back to examining his sparse blond whispers in the mirror. "Girls haven't said anything," he comments after a while.

I raise my eyebrows at him. "You don't pay them for that."

"Fuck you again. I don't pay for sex."

"You're paying for my drinks tonight, though," I remind him.

"Goddammit, you're really holding me to that?"

I chuckle. "Fair's fair. You shouldn't make bets you can't win. And you can't hit the broadside of a barn with that Glock."

We'd been to the shooting range earlier that day and I'd gamed Cillian for all the cash in his wallet. True to form, he wasn't done betting even after taking such a brutal loss.

So when I'd cleaned him out a second time, he'd offered to buy all my drinks next time we went out.

Maybe that'd teach the stubborn bastard not to bet against Artem Kovalyov.

"Fine. You miserable son of a bitch. Where should we go? Decadente? Shangri-La? Oh, how 'bout The Jungle? There's a bottle girl there I've been dying to fuck."

I shake my head. "Nope, nope, and nope."

His scowl deepens. "If you think we're going to The Siren again..."

"That's exactly where we're going."

"You realize that in four fucking months, we've barely been anywhere else?" Cillian points out in exasperation. "Is there something there that you keep going back for?"

"No."

Cillian eyes me closely. "You're a good liar," he says. "But I know you too well."

"It's a fucking *club*, Cillian," I reply. "They've got good whiskey."

"Yeah? And this has nothing to do with—oh, I dunno... some woman you've taken a liking to?"

"Watch it," I warn.

"Don't think I haven't noticed that you've been practically celibate these last couple of months."

Fucking hell. I need to give Cillian more credit. He's a lot more perceptive than I realize sometimes.

I roll my eyes. "You really should focus more on your sex life than mine."

"What's going on with you lately?" Cillian asks. His tone shifts from our normal bro-banter to something more serious. "For real, Artem."

"Nothing," I said, trying not to let my irritation show. "I've just been preoccupied with work."

"Okay, brother. If that's your story," Cillian replies, letting it drop.

The screech of tires on gravel saves me from any further interrogation.

"They're here," I announce.

Two cars drive up at the same time. Standard wannabe-mobster bullshit—windows tinted too dark, no license plates, the backseat jammed with burly enforcers holding guns they barely know how to operate.

Fucking amateur hour.

We have intel that this is the third meeting between the Albanians and the Polish. Neither of the first two received permission from the Bratva, so Cillian and I have been dispatched to remind these bastards of the pecking order in this city.

Meaning: nothing happens without our say-so.

I stay rooted in my seat for now and let it get underway.

It's a pretty straightforward exchange as far as drug deals are concerned. Two men get out from each vehicle and meet halfway.

Some macho banter. Some bullshit posturing. A briefcase changes hands.

That's when Cillian and I get out of the car.

We saunter over, hands in our pockets, making no attempt to conceal our presence.

"What the fuck?" one of the Albanians snarls at his Polish counterpart. "You brought more men? This was not part of the agreement."

"They're not our guys," one of the Polish men snaps back.

"Calm down, boys," I call over. I enter into the circle of light where the two groups are standing. Cillian takes a stance right at my shoulder. "We're not a part of this little business deal you have going. Unfortunately for you."

The two Polish seem to know who I am—I can tell from the horrified look that passes across their face.

They understand that my presence here is not a good sign for them.

They've been muscling in on Kovalyov territory for the past few months. It's time for me to step in and put them back in their place.

"Artem Kovalyov," acknowledges the beefy Polish with the tear drop tattoo beneath his eye.

The mention of my name has the Albanians turning pale.

I see their hands twitch towards their weapons, but no one makes a move to draw their guns.

Wise choice. Maybe they're not as stupid as I assumed.

"You're aware that you're on Kovalyov territory?" I ask lightly.

"It's a private deal, Russian."

I cock my head to the side as I scan their faces. "Do I look dumb to you?" I ask.

When no one answers, I step forward again.

All four men stiffen at once.

"I asked you a question."

"Seems like they think you're stupid," Cillian offers casually.

"No," the second Polish says quickly. "That's not what we think."

"What *do* you think then?" I ask. "Because it sure feels like you think I'm stupid."

The men exchange silent glances, then the beefy Polish snatches the suitcase from his partner and hands it to me.

"The Kovalyov reigns supreme in these parts," he says apologetically. "We won't conduct our affairs… even personal ones on your turf again."

I nod. *Good boy,* I think silently. Cillian takes the suitcase.

"How much is in there?" I ask.

"Five hundred grand worth of heroin."

I nod. All things considered, this is going well. None of these idiots seem to be raring for a showdown.

Which is good, since that would end with their insides splattered all over their outsides.

But part of me wishes they would try something. I'm itching for a fight. For the adrenaline, the rush.

Mostly because it's been four fucking months since I've been inside a woman.

Not ideal. But every time I go to break the dry spell, I see *her* face again.

I see her doe eyes, milky hazel and flecked with green.

I see her trembling lips, full and pouty.

I hear her wild, gasping moans…

And I know I can't fuck another woman when all I want is *her*.

What I really need, though, is a purge. A cleanse of my system. L.A. hipsters might reach for some garbage green juice to accomplish that goal.

But I'm the future don of the Kovalyov Bratva.

The only thing that will make me feel better is *blood*.

Father would be pissed if I cracked heads just for the sake of it, though. So I hold back all the same.

"This is your first and only warning," I announce. "The next time you deal on our turf again, I will take a limb or a life. Your choice. Understood?"

They nod in trembling fear. *Message received,* their terrified eyes tell me.

I turn my back on them and start walking away.

Cillian doesn't say a word until we're back in the car. He throws the suitcase into the back seat and looks at me.

"You didn't throw a punch," he says incredulously.

"I didn't have to."

"Since when have you ever needed a reason to beat some bastard's head in?" Cillian asks.

I think about the fucking son of a bitch who tried to force himself on the girl from The Siren.

I could have killed him. I would have done exactly that, if I hadn't needed to check to make sure she was okay.

But I'd thrown him out of that bathroom with a broken arm and a permanently scarred face.

That gave me at least a little bit of satisfaction.

"I'll fuck up the men that deserve it," I tell him. "Those fuckers out there are nothing but ambitious fools. If they try this shit again, I'll make them rue the moment they chose to disregard my warning. But for now, we have five hundred grand of heroin to resell and didn't even break a sweat."

Cillian shakes his head as though he's trying to figure me out. "Something's different about you, Artem."

I smirk as we pull out onto the road. "You need a woman. Maybe then you wouldn't be so obsessed with me."

Cillian laughs. "You might be right. I haven't gotten laid in almost a week. My balls are full to bursting."

I laugh and shake my head. "Sounds like a personal problem. Drop me off at the mansion before you take care of that, though."

9

ARTEM

It's a short ride to my father's mansion.

As we drive through the security booth behind the iron gates, I can see the lights of the mansion in the distance.

I can just make out the glowing window of Stanislav's study. I wonder if he ever sleeps anymore.

"Any more news about Stanislav?" Cillian asks, pulling to a stop in the circular drive way.

"Fuck if I know. He doesn't tell me anything. I'll catch up with you later."

I give Cillian a parting nod and get out of the car.

Heading inside, I go straight up to Stanislav's study. The door is closed, but I'm not in the mood to knock today. Instead, I push my way in.

I'm expecting to find Budimir in there with my father. But my uncle is nowhere to be found.

I see only a man in a long white doctor's coat standing over Stanislav.

"Father," I say in greeting.

My father's eyes meet mine momentarily. They flash with irritation. I know he isn't pleased to be interrupted.

"Where's Dr. Konstantin?" I ask, sitting down in one of the chairs in front of the massive mahogany desk.

"Off tonight," my father replies. "Dr. Sergei here is stepping in."

The doctor turns to me and gives me a respectful nod. I notice that he's got an IV in his hand and he's checking my father's forearm. His brow is furrowed with concern.

"I apologize, don," Sergei murmurs. "I'm having trouble finding a vein."

Stanislav snatches the IV out of the thin man's hands and flings it across the room.

"Then get out," he says, in a low, dangerous tone. "I feel fine anyway."

"Sir?"

"Now!" Stanislav barks.

The doctor stumbles out the door in terror without another word.

When it swings shut, I fix my eyes on the stubborn old man in front of me.

"That one's not gonna last," I drawl.

"What are you doing here, son?"

"The deal between the Albanians and the Polish is taken care of. They won't be stepping into our territory anymore."

"That news could have waited till morning."

"Why?" I ask. "You never sleep anyway."

He looks older than usual, I realize. And worse. His eyes are bloodshot and his skin sags like it's losing the fight with time and gravity.

"What are the doctors saying?"

He hates talking about it. But some things can't simply be ignored or bulldozed. Even if he wishes otherwise.

"The same old shit," Stanislav replies gruffly. "Bah, the fuck do they know?"

"You've had three teams of doctors. And they've all said the same thing."

"I'll outlive them all," he snorts.

Sometimes, I'm inclined to believe him. My father is as stubborn as they come.

But tonight, I can feel death and sickness looking in through the window at us. It's the same feeling I'd had with Mama years ago. Just before she'd died.

"You need to listen to them. You need to rest more."

"I'll rest when I die," he retorts, "and not a moment before."

"I thought you weren't planning on dying?"

His tired eyes narrow. "Did you come to discuss my health or my business, son? If it's not the latter, then it's time for you to leave."

We stare daggers at each other for a second.

Two stubborn men. Proud men. Powerful men. Neither of us willing to back down.

In the end, I shrug and rise to my feet.

My time as don will come soon enough. For now, I wait.

"Get some rest, Father," I tell him.

Then I leave.

On my way out, I stop by the bar and grab one of the most expensive bottles of whiskey in my father's collection.

I walk out of the mansion, whiskey in hand, and head straight for the garage. A little parting gift from me to me.

There's always two security guards manning the massive garage that resembles a warehouse. They nod respectfully as I sweep past them.

But neither one has the balls to say a thing to me as I grab the keys of Stanislav's favorite Mercedes and get inside.

I tear out of the garage and down the drive towards the black gates. I barely slow as I pass between them with hardly an inch to spare on either side.

From there, I go to the cemetery.

I park the car haphazardly across three parking spots, grab the bottle of whiskey, and clamber out.

It takes me only a few minutes to reach Marisha's headstone. I don't need light to find it. I could walk there in my sleep.

The stone is ivory marble and engraved, but I don't bother reading the words. I know those by heart, too.

I sit down in front of the headstone and twist open the whiskey.

The first drink tastes like heaven. It burns, deep and glowing, the way only good whiskey like this can. Whiskey aged enough to reminisce about the old days.

About the way things used to be.

About Marisha.

The smog hides the stars, making the graveyard so dark I can't see my hand in front of my face.

Out of that darkness, a kind of hallucination appears. Maybe it's just my imagination, or my eyes playing tricks on me.

At first, I think it's Marisha's face. That pale cheek, the light, tumbling hair…

But that's not right. It's not Marisha.

The hair is darker.

The eyes are bigger, more innocent, more pleading.

I'm not seeing Marisha at all.

I'm seeing *her*.

The girl from The Siren.

I'm just drunk enough that I try to reach out and touch her. Like it's real. Like this isn't all some fucked-up trick of the eyes and the alcohol and the remaining adrenaline from the showdown at the docks.

I want to touch that bronze skin again. Taste the sweetness of the girl's lips.

I'm so close.

Almost touching…

Almost there…

And then the shrill ring of my phone scythes through. The vision disappears.

In its place is what was there before—nothing but pure darkness.

"What?" I bark into the phone.

"That's no way to talk to your father or your don," Stanislav breathes wearily.

"I didn't know you missed me so much that you had to call so soon after I left."

"Don't be smart with me, son. I have a job for you."

"No thanks. I'm busy."

"It wasn't a question, Artem. The job is in Mexico. You leave tomorrow. You will need to prepare."

My scornful laughter sounds utterly wrong in the silence of the graveyard. "Is this a fucking joke? I'm not going to goddamn Mexico."

On the other end of the line, Stanislav growls under his breath like the old Russian bear that he is.

"I'm only going to say this once, Artem: do not mess this up. You're going down to Mexico to get something very, very valuable. We cannot afford to lose this. Not after…" He sighs again before finishing, "Not after what happened with you before."

Then he hangs up.

And the darkness descends once again.

10

ESME

THE MORENO COMPOUND, MEXICO

Another day in hell.

At least it's pretty here.

The grand sitting room glitters like everything's been painted in gold.

Every chandelier has been lit. Every surface is gleaming.

Waiters in waistcoats circulate with trays of crisp champagne and five-star hors d'oeuvres.

The guests are dressed for the occasion—although even now, I don't know what that occasion actually is.

The men wear suits and watches worth a mortgage. The women are in cocktail gowns and enough jewelry to fill a museum. Both sexes have applied far too much perfume.

And they won't stop fucking staring.

No matter what I do, I feel their eyes on me. The women are curious, scrutinous, sometimes jealous.

But the men... the men look at me like they want to tear me limb from limb.

I can't stand their stares. After everything that happened four months ago, even a friendly male gaze makes me shiver and twitch.

The piano is my only shield. My only safe space. The one thing that allows me to keep myself from sweating, screaming, panicking.

But I know it won't last. I've been playing for almost a half hour now.

I have shown that I'm an exceptional pianist. I have proved Papa's boasts.

And yet, it won't be enough.

He will want more of me soon.

As my fingers race across the keys, my mind flies back across the weeks and months, back to that one rogue night at the nightclub in Los Angeles.

That memory makes my heart race too.

I still can't believe my luck. Somehow, in my state of flustered panic, I had forced Tamara to her feet and dragged her out of the club and onto the street.

I'd hailed a cab and we'd gone straight to my hotel room, where my guards had been waiting for me.

Apparently, neither one had wanted to get the Miguel treatment, so they agreed to conceal the fact that Tamara and I had given them the slip.

Fine by me.

But even after I had settled Tamara into bed next to me, I hadn't been able to sleep. Not that night. Or the next. Or the night after that.

Sleep's been pretty elusive ever since then, actually.

"Doesn't she play beautifully?"

The voice is soft and low and comes from a few feet behind me. She's not talking to me, though. I can't see who it is, but I imagine her staring at my back, pitying me.

"She's certainly a pretty little ornament," another woman replies to the first. This one's voice is deep but still manages to sound feminine, even sultry.

"Don't be cruel."

"Oh, I'm not being cruel. Isn't that what we all are? Ornaments?"

"Hmph. She just looks very young," the first female voice continues.

"She is. Barely legal."

"It won't stop Joaquin from pawning her off when the time comes. He's the most ambitious man I've ever met."

I close my eyes, trying to drown them both out.

Just breathe, Esme.

That's what Cesar would tell me if he was here. He always knew how to calm me down

So I do that.

For a second, it even works.

The room around me fades. The sound of the guests' voices—all of them speaking pretty lies, laughing at jokes that aren't funny, corrupt men plotting the lives of their wives and daughters without ever consulting the women themselves—all of it recedes into the background.

But as soon as it's gone, something comes in its place.

And just like that, in my mind, I'm back in The Siren's bathroom.

The distant sound of the club's music throbs against the tiled walls. My skin heats up. Sweat breaks out on my forehead.

And there he is.

The man with the dark eyes and the cruel, arrogant grin.

I swear I can feel him touching me. Even though I'm a thousand miles away, it's like he's right here. Between my thighs. Breath steaming against my neck.

I want to stay in this moment. It's the only time in years I've felt free. Like I was in the right place.

But I have to face the facts: I'm not there.

I'm here.

Still stuck in my father's hell.

Something yanks me back to the present moment: I missed a note.

It was a momentary lapse, a tiny mistake, something only I would notice.

But I felt as though the whole room stops what they're doing to look at me. Like the proceedings came to a screeching halt and all those treacherous gazes swung in my direction.

I resume playing, but it's too late. I know what will happen next.

Papa's coming.

11

ESME

I sense him before I see him.

His shadow falls over my keys, blotting out the light of the chandelier. I don't look up to meet his gaze.

"What the fuck are you wearing?"

I tense instantly. My fingers falter again. I miss another note.

"Don't you dare stop playing," he hisses.

I swallow. Where is a dark-eyed savior when I need one?

Far away. Too far to help.

I'm on my own here—as always.

I keep playing like he wants. That's the only way to survive in Joaquin's world.

Obey or face the consequences. No other choices exist.

"That dress is hideous," he continues.

He's smiling the whole time, but his words are pure venom.

"I told you to dress to impress tonight. And you took that to mean that you should dress like a fat old woman whose pussy dried up a decade ago?"

I swallow hard for a second time. It's painful.

I'd picked a billowing lilac dress for the party. It was pretty, but it did little to emphasize my shape. The hemline was long and the neckline was modest.

Of course, I hadn't exactly picked the dress to be modest—though that didn't hurt.

I had picked it because it was the only thing that allowed me to breathe. All my other cocktail dresses had made me feel constricted and claustrophobic. Far too tight, too confining.

"It's Zuhair Murad," I tell him. Mostly because I don't know what else to say.

"I don't give a fuck what it is," he snaps. His smile falters for a split second before it's back in place again. "It makes you look like a forty-year old spinster."

He stands there for a moment glowering, like he can't decide which aspect of my appearance to insult next.

Before he can, someone approaches.

Papa's demeanor shifts at once. Just like that, he's back to being the consummate host. The perfect gentleman.

"Ah, Juan! Allow me to introduce you to my daughter, Esme."

I recognize the man instantly.

Juan Garcia. A local senator with a filthy reputation. His name has been tied to several national scandals in the last few years, each uglier than the last.

He's a stout man, eye level with me in my three-inch heels. He looks even sleazier in person than he did in the tabloids.

Curled mustache. Scraggly beard. Dyed-black hair that's scarcely more than a few wisps like dying weeds on his shiny bald head.

"What a beauty," he murmurs.

He ventures so close that I feel the need to scoot away.

Of course, I know that if I do, Papa will rage at me later for it. So I stay where I am and keep my good-daughter mask on.

"Señor Garcia, it's lovely to meet you," I say, offering him my hand.

He takes it, but he doesn't shake it. He just holds my hand in both of his, one finger rubbing back and forth against my knuckles.

"You make me sound like an old man," he says with a mousy smile. "I insist you call me Juan."

"Juan, then."

He moves even closer to me. My skin crawls.

"I hope to get to know you very well, my dear." His voice is a raspy purr.

And then to my utter relief, he lets go of my hand.

But not before he leans in and gives me a kiss on my cheek.

I imagine a rash erupting where his lips have been.

"I'll be in touch," he tells Papa, before moving across the room.

We stand still, smiling politely until he's gone.

Papa's smile drops from his face as soon as Juan disappears into the next room. He looks at me pointedly, but he doesn't have to say anything for me to get the drift.

That wasn't a casual meeting.

It was a first step towards an arranged marriage.

I feel bile rise up in my throat. The urge to throw up is so strong that it takes me by surprise.

"I just… I feel a little sick."

Papa's eyes churn. "If you embarrass me tonight, girl, you will live to regret it."

I swallow hard and stare right back at him.

We're in a crowded room filled with people he wants to impress. That knowledge gives me a false sense of security. It makes me brave.

That is going to cost me.

"I won't marry him," I say, my voice strong and steely.

He narrows his eyes and moves a step closer. "What the fuck did you just say?"

"He's old and gross," I continue, noticing a few of the women watching us closely. "He's had several wives, children that are older than I am, and if the papers are to be believed, he's sexually assaulted at least half a dozen different women. I'm not marrying him. I'd rather die."

"That can be arranged," Papa says without blinking.

I suck in my breath, but my bravado vanishes.

I need an ally so badly in that moment.

Someone to protect me. To help me find my voice.

Normally, I'd want Cesar. My whole life, he was the wall that kept me safe from Papa's wrath.

But strangely, the man I'm picturing isn't my brother.

It's a dark-eyed stranger with blood on his knuckles and lust in his gaze.

Papa reaches out and takes my hand at the elbow. He digs his nails in and squeezes so hard that a little cry of pain escapes me.

My eyes catch one of the women standing a few feet away. She's older, elegant, beautiful.

For a moment, it seems almost like she's going to intervene. To save me from Papa.

But then her eyes fall to the floor and she turns away.

Nothing has changed. I'm as alone as ever.

"Listen to me, you little whore," Papa snarls in my ear. "You will do exactly what I tell you do to. Juan Garcia is one of the most influential politicians in Mexico. And if our interests are tied to his, our family and the business will be untouchable. So you *will* marry him. You will smile on the wedding day and tell people how lucky you are. And on the wedding night, you will get on your knees and suck his cock like he wants. You *will* make him happy or I will make you very, very unhappy. You understand?"

Silence. Tense and painful.

"You're hurting me, Papa," I whisper. Tears stud my eyes but I refuse to let them fall.

Papa's gaze bores into me. "Do. You. Understand?" he hisses.

I open my mouth—to say what, I don't know—but before I can get the words out, another voice slices in.

"Joaquin? I've been meaning to ask you about these sconces all night. They are fabulous."

I look over Papa's shoulder to see the woman I made eye contact with only moments ago.

Does she know she's saving me? I can't be sure. But I try to send silent gratitude in her direction either way.

My father's smile slides back in place as he releases his hold on my elbow and moves toward her.

I can feel tears welling up more and I know that this time, I can't hold them in any longer.

So I back out of the room as surreptitiously as I can.

The moment the doors close behind me, I lift my dress and run down the hall towards the staircase.

Nausea overwhelms me but I don't stop running until I'm in my room. I make it to the bathroom just in time.

It brings on a strange sense of déjà vu.

Except in this case, Tamara's not the one with her head in the toilet.

I throw up dinner instantly. When there's nothing left in my stomach, I just dry heave for a few minutes until I'm weak and exhausted.

Once I'm done, I wipe my mouth and slump against the cool wall of my bathroom, feeling strangely dizzy.

It takes a while before I start to feel something like normal again.

When I think I can manage it, I get to my feet and remove the lilac dress. I hang it up and walk around to my shelf space where I keep my night clothes.

As I pass the mirror, I stop short, wondering why my body looks so unfamiliar all of a sudden.

Perhaps a little extra weight around my hips? My breasts are maybe a little fuller, too.

Shrugging, I move to my shelves and pick out a soft cotton night shirt.

I'm about to close the cupboard door when something catches my eye.

Tampons.

I don't know why I'm staring so hard. Don't know why seeing my stack of tampons has me feeling sick all over again.

And then my worry starts to crystalize in front of me as I realize something.

I haven't touched my supply of tampons in a while.

It's been so long in fact, that I can't remember the last time I used one.

"This can't be happening," I whisper out loud as my mind scrambles to piece together a truth I don't want to face.

Yes, I'd been feeling different lately.

I'd been emotional.

I'd been eating more.

I'd been experiencing small bouts of nausea.

But all of those symptoms were easy to explain away.

Papa wanted me to marry, my life was closing in around me, it was only natural that I'd feel... off.

But now, all I feel is stupid.

I rush to my dressing table and rifle through the drawers. In the very last one, I find what I'm looking for wrapped in a brown paper bag.

I pull it out gingerly. The pregnancy test is at least two years old.

I bought it right after I was with Mattias, the pool boy. It was the paranoid purchase of a frightened teenage girl—albeit one who knew extremely well what her father would do if she got knocked up.

Now, I get to live that nightmare for real.

I pull out the pregnancy test and rush back to the toilet. The whole time, my heart thunders unnaturally against my chest.

I pee directly onto the stick, taking care to keep my fingers out of the line of fire.

Once I'm done, I kind of stumble to the sink, hoping and praying that my body is just playing tricks on me.

This. Cannot. Be. Happening.

I put the pregnancy test down and start pacing.

The instructions tell me to wait five minutes, so just to make sure, I wait ten.

When the time is up, I turn and face the sink.

It feels like I'm walking to my death.

Three steps.

Two steps.

One step.

My hands grip the edge of the sink but I'm still not looking at the test. I can't bring myself to.

Breathe, Esme. You can do this. You have to.

So I look down.

And just like that, my life changes forever.

12

ARTEM

THE MORENO COMPOUND, MEXICO

The compound is lit up like a jewel.

Guards with automatic rifles patrol the tops of the encircling wall and man each of the two security posts outside the perimeter.

Roving floodlights, cameras at strategic locations, and a swath of clear land so the forces can spot intruders coming from a quarter mile away.

It's Fort fucking Knox.

And I'm about to burn it to the goddamn ground.

I'm lying belly-down on a large hill in a rocky outcrop far enough away from the compound that my men and I won't be visible.

We don't actually have to worry, though.

Not a soul knows we're here.

"What's on your mind?" Cillian asks, as he sits down next to me and passes me a bottle of water.

I crack it open and take a sip, but what I'm really craving is something much stronger.

"Just game-planning."

"The game has been planned for a while now," Cillian says. "There's nothing to think about. Quit overanalyzing."

"Nothing can go wrong. Quit bitching."

"Nothing *will* go wrong," Cillian says. "We're prepared."

"That's not the question. The question is… are *they* prepared?" I point at the top of the compound wall, where a pair of burly men clad head-to-toe in black tactical gear are patrolling.

Like everyone else defending this fortress, they're ex-Mexican special forces, and they've got a lot of motivation to do their job right.

If they do it well, they get paid like kings.

If they do it poorly, them and everyone they love will end up headless in an unmarked grave.

The cartel dons don't fuck around.

"You know what?" Cillian muses sarcastically, stroking the godawful beard he refuses to shave. "They do look pretty determined to keep enemies out. Let's just call the whole thing off and go grab a margarita."

"It's not getting *in* that I'm worried about," I remind him. "It's getting back out."

He knows damn well what's got me keyed up tonight.

A straight-up takedown of the compound would be a cinch. I could pick those bastards off the wall from here myself with a night-vision sniper and have drones dropping bombs smack-dab in the middle of the courtyard while I did it.

I'd probably be able to stroll right through the front door.

But I know that the second the first bullet is fired, every man loyal to the cartel within a twenty-mile radius will come pouring in for backup.

And on top of that... there's the retrieval target.

The retrieval mission that's at the core of this whole goddamn trip.

Part of me wanted to say no. To tell Father to go fuck himself when he explained the details to me.

But the Bratva comes first—always.

And tonight, that means getting what I came for.

"I just sent in a report to Budimir," Cillian tells me. "I told him we're preparing to move."

I nod. "Did he say anything else?"

"He asked about you."

"Which means that Stanislav asked about me."

"This is a big assignment," Cillian points out. "He wouldn't have entrusted you with it if he didn't believe you could handle it."

I glance towards Cillian. I'm grateful that he always seemed to have my back, no matter what.

As much as he annoys the hell out of me sometimes—often, as a matter of fact, and usually on purpose—he's as loyal as they come.

"I appreciate your vote of confidence," I mutter.

He puts a hand on his chest. "Oh, you've got it all wrong—I know you're gonna fuck this up ten ways to Sunday, but Stanislav didn't ask me for my—"

I swat him in the head with a gloved hand as he falls back laughing.

Asshat.

I laugh under my breath and shake my head. Some things never change.

Picking up my night-vision binoculars, I do another scan of the walls. I check my watch as I go.

Everything here works like clockwork. The same patrols, the same lights switching on and off at the same times.

Which means that, in precisely fifteen seconds, a pair of guards holding AK-47s will round the upper west corner.

Three…

Two…

One…

"Hola, amigos," I whisper under my breath as they appear right on schedule.

It's good to have a mission. Something to focus on.

Especially because my attention has been shifting like sand in a hurricane.

It started with Marisha.

With the nightmares.

And then it turned to the brunette beauty in The Siren's bathroom.

But this? Action, a mission, an objective task and only one way to do it—violently?

That's where I fucking thrive.

"What time is it?" I ask.

"Nine-twenty."

I nod. "We move at my command. Are the teams ready?"

Cillian nods. "We've got team one and two at the main entrance, teams three and four on either side of the house at the side entrances and teams five and six right here. All waiting on your signal."

His voice is somber. He may be a jokester through and through, but even Cillian O'Sullivan knows when it's time to shut up and do the work.

And now that time has come.

I look back at my men arrayed in the darkness behind me. They're all geared up with their weapons at the ready.

Each one gives me a curt nod as my gaze passes over them.

Fuck it. Let's go.

I adjust my bullet proof vest and give Cillian a nod.

"It's time."

"Then let's get this show on the road," Cillian says with glee, smacking his hands together.

"Remember," I say to my men, "take no prisoners. The job should be clean. The only one who's going to survive this night is the girl. And she belongs to me."

13

ARTEM

Two dozen men sprint through the night under cover of darkness.

It's quiet out here. Only the sounds of the distant ocean waves and my own sharp breaths.

I have my gun held at the ready. Eyes peeled.

We're about twenty paces from bursting out of our cover. That's when all hell will break loose.

Which means our bombs are going to go off right about...

Now.

A huge, bone-rattling boom erupts. I hear screams of pain, the bellows of dying men. Shrapnel and fragments of concrete explode through the night.

And one by one, the exterior doors of the cartel compound fall clattering to the earth.

I lead two of the four-man teams into the western entrance. Already, the pepper of gunfire has begun.

The eastbound teams have the job of drawing off the bulk of security. All my most bloodthirsty soldiers were assigned that task.

No one leaves alive, I told them in our final briefing before tonight's assault.

The eager grins on their faces told me they understood perfectly.

The men at my side now—Cillian included—are more subtle. The kind of cold-blooded bastards who spend their days raising innocent kids with oblivious wives—and spend their nights slicing throats for the Bratva.

Invisible killers.

My pack broaches the security perimeter. Right on cue, the two point men unleash a quick burst of fire to take out the exterior cameras and floodlights.

Instant darkness.

I give Dimitri, my demo expert, the signal. He runs forward with the breaching charges and plants them against the small iron door set in the wall.

We all take cover a few yards away.

A tiny *boom.*

This door falls just like the rest of them.

We waste no time. Practically the second the charges have detonated, we're already siphoning in through the opening. Guns at the ready and heads on a swivel in case any rogue security notices our arrival.

The hallway is eerily silent, except for the occasional burst of gunfire or dying screams from the far side of the compound.

We're alone...

Until we aren't.

A pair of straggling guards round the corner at a dead sprint.

They hardly have time to come to a complete stop before each of them is sporting a fresh bullet hole in the head.

And we keep moving, running past them and scanning. Always scanning.

"Fan out," I bark. "Check all the rooms."

We move as a single unit, spreading out to encompass the hallway and flow down it with ruthless efficiency.

Fuck, it feels so good to be here again—in the heart of the action.

There are no nightmares here.

No weakness.

Just the purity of might makes right.

Five minutes go by in a flash without any other sign of life. We clear one hallway and then the next.

"Nothing here, sir," the soldiers report again and again as we kick down doors and scour corners for signs of life.

"Keep moving," I tell them. "She's here somewhere."

Soon, we reach a flight of stairs at the end of the hall. I point up, and we keep on flowing to the next level.

The sounds afar have quieted down. No doubt most of the security is dead now.

But that just means we're running out of time. Backup will be here soon—local boys or subsidiary cartels looking to curry favor with the man in charge.

Cut off the head of the snake, get what you came for, and get out—those were my father's final orders as I boarded the plane for Mexico.

And just before I left, he'd added: *But, son... don't forget: a dead snake's venom can still kill you.*

I step past Igor and take the lead once we're on the second floor.

We're walking down a broad corridor lined with pretentious oil paintings when I hear movement coming from one of the rooms down the hall.

I turn to Cillian.

"Take your team to the third floor," I order him. "We've got this."

Cillian nods and takes the rest of his men with him as he heads further upstairs. I continue to move down the hall with the rest of my men.

One door after the next reveals nothing but empty rooms. All devoid of life.

I stop outside the only door that's locked. The handle merely rattles, and when I kick it, it doesn't budge.

Reinforced.

That usually means there's something valuable on the other side.

I raise my gun and start firing right through the wood. It chips apart, splintering until it's nothing but broken shards swinging loosely on its hinges.

The moment I step into the locked room, the two guards hiding in there open fire.

I dive behind a large white sofa that's in tatters now and fire back.

I'm not the only one. My men have entered the room behind me.

Within seconds, both guards are dead and the gunfire all but stops.

Armed guards hiding behind a reinforced door confirm my theory that there was something valuable hidden in here.

The question is... what is that something?

"You gonna come out and face me like a fucking man?" I growl. "Or will I have to flush you out like a rat?"

A few seconds of silence.

The shuffling of feet.

Then, a man emerges from behind a large antique cabinet.

Even in the face of certain death, the son of a bitch holds himself pridefully. There isn't a trace of fear in his carefully arranged expression as he faces me.

I do notice he's holding a gun in his right hand, but it hangs at his side, seemingly forgotten.

He knows damn well that he'll be dead long before he has the time to aim it at my face.

"I should have killed you a long time ago," Joaquin Moreno tells me, his eyes slicing into me like serrated daggers.

"You should have."

"What do you want?"

"I want what you took from me."

"You know I can't give you that," he replies.

The response is almost polite. Damn near apologetic.

But too casual by a long shot.

It wasn't a small thing he stripped away. He took *everything* from me.

Time to return the favor.

"Then you knew I'd be coming."

Joaquin's eyes trail up a little, but his expression still doesn't betray concern. "Get it over with, then. Your daddy will want you home soon, I'm sure."

I snarl in anger. But before I can ask him another thing, he raises the gun.

He's fast, but I'm faster. I shoot him in the chest and he falls back against his white carpet, staining the fabric with thick blood the color of wine.

I grit my teeth and walk up to Moreno's dead body. He wanted a quick death and I just gave it to him.

But I should've made him suffer.

His eyes stare glassily towards the ceiling, a sneer permanently etched onto his face.

"Fucking bastard," I mutter. I spit on his corpse, then turn back towards the hallway to finish the job.

The house is almost completely silent now. I'm two steps outside the room containing Joaquin's dead body when Cillian's voice emerges from the staircase landing.

"Artem!"

I look over at him. "Did you find it yet?"

He waves me over without another word. I go after him, gun dangling at my side.

Cillian leads me to the last room at the end of the third-story hallway. It's ornate and red with a gold doorknob.

Very expensive.

Very feminine.

"This is it?" I ask.

He shrugs. "It's the only one we haven't checked."

I turn to the door, take a deep breath, and give it my best kick.

It explodes inwards. Figures that Joaquin would take the safest room for himself.

I step through the broken shards of the door frame and enter the large, opulent bedroom. I take quick note of the contents—big four-poster bed draped with a white mosquito net like a bridal veil. Mahogany desk, tasteful armchair. A bulletin board brimming with postcards.

There doesn't seem to be anyone inside, though.

I catch a whiff of a perfumed scent. It's vaguely familiar, but I can't quite put my finger on it.

The door to the bathroom is ajar. In the sliver of mirror I can see from here, I notice a flash of movement.

I cross the carpeted floor silently and smoothly, then nudge open the door.

One step inside. My bloody, muddy boots mar the beautiful white tile. This room is so pure, so white, so flawless.

And here I come. The Grim fucking Reaper.

Here to ruin it all.

The anger from killing Joaquin is still roiling in my veins. I feel good, alive, empowered.

Until I see her.

Half-naked and shivering at the foot of the sink. She's folded in on herself like she thinks she can disappear if she tries hard enough.

Dark hair pours in waves over her tanned skin.

And then she turns her face up to look at me with eyes full of tears and I realize something...

I don't know what the fuck I've just gotten myself into.

14

ESME

My first reaction is to laugh.

Because when I see the face of the man who's come to kill me, it confirms what I suspected since the moment the explosions began.

That this is just a horrible nightmare.

It has to be, right?

There's no way it's real. From the second I saw the positive sign on the pregnancy test, I refused to believe any of this was happening.

No baby in my womb.

No soldiers in my home.

I just closed my eyes and stayed curled up in a ball on my bathroom floor. I could hear the distant sounds of guests leaving soon afterwards.

No one came to check on me. No one gave a damn, and for once, I was grateful for that.

The first boom caught me by surprise.

The second made me sit upright.

Then came the gunfire and the roars of men shooting at each other.

None of it could possibly be real. It couldn't be, it couldn't be, it couldn't be.

Even now, as a six and a half foot tall soldier with guns strapped all over his body stands in my bathroom and looks down at me like an angel of death, I refuse to believe it's real.

And for one blissful, beautiful second, I hold onto that denial.

"This is a dream," I mumble.

He shakes his head and keeps staring at me.

"Yes, it is," I retort. "It's a bad dream and I'm going to wake up soon. This isn't happening. The last four months didn't happen. The night we met most definitely did not happen."

"You aren't dreaming," the dark-eyed stranger says.

"Am too."

He sighs in irritation, takes one stride to cross the distance between us, and yanks me to my feet by my wrist.

"No," he repeats grimly, "you aren't. Does this feel like you're dreaming? Do I feel make-believe to you?"

His face is close to mine. Close enough that I can smell sweat, blood, musk, and just a hint of something cool and fragrant beneath it all.

I want to keep living in denial.

But he's right. The man from The Siren is right.

He's very, very real.

Which means everything else is real, too.

The one-night-stand. The pregnancy test. The explosions.

It's all real. It's all happening.

Somehow, I drag my eyes up from the floor to meet the man's gaze. His irises are even darker than I remember. Like pools of oil. Searing right through me.

"Is everyone dead?" I ask numbly.

He nods. "They're either dead already or they will be soon."

I shudder and close my eyes. "My father, too?"

The question is heavy with emotion that I'm too overwhelmed to fully process.

He doesn't blunt his words.

"Yes," he tells me. "Him, too."

I open my eyes and stare back at him for a long time. He watches my face carefully. I'm trying so hard not to cry.

Don't cry, Esme, I scold myself. *Not now. Not in front of him.*

In the end, it's a losing battle. I bury my face in my hands and let loose.

Sobs tear through me as I try and fight for control.

I'm overwhelmed, I'm conflicted, I'm scared but most of all… I'm relieved.

Papa is dead.

And I'm relieved?

That's the first thing that I feel the moment he says the words.

Does that make me an awful person? Does that make a terrible daughter?

I don't know.

All I know is that I can't escape the relief that washes over me when the stranger speaks, confirming what I already know in my heart to be true.

"He's dead," he tells me again, without any emotion or sympathy. Like he knows I need to hear the truth one more time. "I killed him myself."

I stare up at his face. The face that's haunted my dreams these many months.

I never thought I'd ever see him again. I can't figure out what I'm feeling now that he's here in front of me, having just murdered my father, the guards, probably the entire staff.

I want to ask more questions. But emotion clogs up my throat and all I can do is keep sobbing.

Papa hated when I cried. He'd slap me across the face and tell me to stop my whining.

I expect the same from this nameless nightmare figure.

But he does nothing. He says nothing.

He just stands there and watches me cry.

When the tears finally subside, I wipe away my tears and look up at him.

"It's time to go," he says.

His voice is deep, but strangely familiar. I realize I've been hearing his voice in my head for four months now.

I may have forgotten just how piercing those eyes are.

But I remember that voice.

Arrogant as hell. Cold as ice.

Oh, yes—I remember his voice perfectly.

I try not to look away from his eyes, even though I want to. I wonder if he knows the secret I'm keeping with me.

That I'm carrying this man's baby and I don't even know his name. He's just destroyed my home, killed my father.

And he is about to kill me, too.

His hand is still on my wrist. The touch alone is enough to bring me back to the night we met.

I can still feel how his weight nestled between my thighs, pushing into me with forceful passion.

I can still sense the smoky whiskey scent of him flush against my cheek.

I can still remember the way his hands claimed me. Forceful. Irresistible. Dangerous.

This is wrong. He's belongs to Papa's world. He's a monster, too.

He just killed my father. He's probably killed countless others.

I'm next.

My limbs are weak. My mind goes blank. I feel myself losing grip on reality.

All the while, his hands keep me upright.

I wonder how much time has passed since the moment he entered the room.

Seconds? Minutes? Hours?

Impossible to tell. It feels like we've been staring at each other for as long as I can remember.

"It's time to go," he says again. "More troops are probably already on the way."

So he's going to kill me somewhere else, then. He's going to drag out this process. Make me suffer, make me bleed, make me beg.

I knew he was dangerous. From the second I laid eyes on him in that club, I knew it.

Turns out I underestimated by a lot.

He grabs me by the arm and drags me out of the bathroom. My legs move as if independent from my body.

I have no control over my actions right now. I'm in a daze, I can feel it. My head spins madly on and my body goes where he pulls me.

At the threshold of my door, I can see a body. My stomach roils but I manage to keep it together.

The man doesn't stop. He just pulls me down the hall, leading me away from the life I knew one step at a time.

As we move through the house, I feel my body drift deeper into shock. We pass body after body, men with their faces blown off or their heads smashed in.

Blood is everywhere.

If this were a movie, I'd say the set designer needed to relax a little bit. There's just so *much*.

Blood staining sofas.

Blood splattered across paintings.

Blood dying the swimming pool, flowing across the tennis courts, slicked down the banister railing of the staircase as we descend.

I trip several times and only manage to stay on my feet because of his grip on me.

More men with guns join us. None of them say a word.

He moves swiftly through the house, not stopping to talk or look at all the dead.

I'm actually grateful for that. Grateful that I don't have long to linger on the lifeless faces staring at me.

Fernando. Ronaldo. Carlos. Javier. Alejandro.

I don't have to see their faces to recognize my father's guards. Their bodies have fallen to the ground like puppets cut from their strings. Their limbs disjointed and unnatural.

My body stills a little, but he pulls me forcefully forward and we pass them all.

All around the house, more men in black are swarming. They're splashing canisters of liquid on top of everything. The stink of lighter fluid fills my nostrils.

I gasp as I realize what they're about to do—burn everything I've ever known to a crisp.

I want to scream, to stop them, but my voice is lost inside me.

He comes to a stop and I almost ram into him. He doesn't seem to notice as he turns to give orders to his men.

He has a natural authority that's impossible to deny. I see the faces of his men, but I can't absorb any details. Their features all melt together, becoming one. One many-headed, faceless monster smeared in blood from head to toe.

"Any survivors?" he asks one of his subordinates.

"None. We've checked twice now."

I feel his men's eyes flit over to me, but I don't react.

It's not that I don't want to—I *can't*. I feel trapped inside myself, like I'm screaming on the inside but no one can hear.

My fingers twitch instinctively towards my stomach, but I suppress the instinct before I can go through with the action.

They can't know about my baby. None of them.

Especially not *him*.

"Ah, Artem?" someone speaks up.

I flinch. *Artem*. The dark-eyed man has a name.

It suits him. Blunt, brutal, foreign. Explains the faint Russian accent, too.

"What?" Artem barks.

"She's shivering."

I glance up towards the man who's just spoken. He's got shaggy blonde hair, pale blue eyes, the wisps of a patchy beard on his face.

He's tall, built, and tattooed, just like Artem, but there's a boyish innocence about him that Artem does not share.

His words also remind me that I'm standing here in the middle of an army of black ops soldiers sent from god-knows-where to do god-knows what, and I'm very nearly naked. All I've got on is a cotton nightshirt that scrapes halfway down my thighs. Not even a bra or panties on underneath.

Artem doesn't even glance at me.

"I'll bring her something—"

"No," Artem cuts him off immediately. "I'm not wasting time. What she's got on is fine. Make sure the place is burning before you leave. Rendezvous back at the plane."

"Got it," the blond man replies. "Hasta la vista, comrade." He turns to rally the remaining men out of the compound.

Then Artem starts dragging me off again.

We move outside, then deep into the rear garden. Wind slaps at my face. It feels strange. It's strong, too... unnatural.

Then I register sound.

When I look up, I see a helicopter descending from the sky, blotting out what little starlight there is tonight. It lands gracefully in the middle of a broad grassy stretch.

My eyes slide from it to the little parcel of land just a few yards off to the side of the landing site.

Cesar's grave.

I feel life spark inside of me as my voice pushes past all the pain.

"No!"

I wrest my arm free from Artem's grip. He's not expecting it, especially after how compliant I've been up until now, so I manage to slip from his grasp.

But it's a futile effort. He's too fast—I'm still in shock.

He seizes the hem of my shirt before I've even made it a yard clear of him. I hear the tear of fabric and feel the cold breeze from the whirring helicopter blades stream between my legs.

Artem spins me back towards him with a sneer on his face. I see in his eyes what the Boulder Man who tried to rape me must have seen that night four months ago—pure fucking rage.

"I'm disappointed," he snarls. "I thought you'd be smart enough to know not to run."

I don't know why my voice chooses to re-emerge just now of all times, but it does, full of as much acid as I can summon.

"I'd rather be brave and foolish than smart and cowardly," I snap back.

My eyes are still focused on my brother's grave. I can just see it beyond the jet's sleek tail.

"You can be whatever you want," he replies, "but not here and not now. We have business to attend to."

"I don't give a damn about your business!" I scream. It feels so good to speak, to fight back, to resist.

"You've made that clear. And yet, I still don't give a fuck. You're coming."

"I'm not going anywhere with you. You're nothing but a murderer and a monster."

"All true," he nods calmly. "You're still coming with me."

"No," I scream, struggling wildly against his iron grip. "Let me go. Let me go!"

He sighs tiredly, as though my outburst is merely an inconvenient tantrum that he doesn't have time for.

He looks past me and nods to a man standing beyond my line of vision. I feel panic slide up my throat, but it just makes me struggle harder.

My eyes are still on Cesar's grave when I see a glint of something shiny and pointed coming towards me.

I scream as the needle pierces into the flesh of my neck.

No! My baby...

I'm pregnant... my baby...

But I can't find the words.

The sedative works fast. I feel my legs buckle under the sudden invisible weight that compresses down on top of me.

I reach out—to whom, I don't know.

I feel my weight being supported by someone, but my eyes are closing and I'm sinking and all the color is fading from the world.

My last thoughts are scattered fragments of pain and loss.

Cesar... my baby... please, no... I can't breathe... I can't see... my baby. Cesar. My baby.

"I won't let you kill me," I mumble through fat, uncoordinated lips.

The last thing I see is Artem's cold sneer.

The last thing I hear is his laughter.

"Kill you?" he chuckles. "No, darling, we've got something very different in mind."

15

ARTEM

ON A PLANE SOMEWHERE OVER SOUTHERN CALIFORNIA

Her eyelashes flutter slightly as she sleeps.

The sedative worked better than I had expected. She needed it, too.

She was visibly shaken, especially at the beginning when I first stormed her bedroom and found her cowering in the bathroom.

Can't blame her.

Everything she once knew is now on fire.

I'm sitting two seats down from where Esme lies, her chest rising and falling subtly, lost in dreamless, drug-induced sleep.

Esme.

I haven't yet gotten used to saying the name out loud, but it dances on my tongue, waiting to be spoken.

When my father had first mentioned the name during our final briefing in his office a week ago, it held no meaning beyond the facts of who she was.

"Esme Moreno."

"The daughter of Joaquin Moreno?" I asked.

"The same," Stanislav replied. "She is your next mission."

Something in his tone stuck out to me. Extra gravity in my father's voice. Extra importance attached to this mission.

I frowned. "You want me to kill some innocent girl?"

"Kill her? No, Artem, I don't want you to kill her."

He'd paused just then and looked at me over the tops of the glasses he'd refused to wear for the longest time.

Whatever somberness was in his voice was in his eyes, too. They flashed—dark like mine, and just as cold.

Then he'd finished: "I want you to marry her."

Even now, those words echo in my head.

I want you to marry her.

The old man had lost his fucking mind.

Marry this girl? This poor wretch, born in the wrong place at the wrong time to the wrong man?

That's all the proof I needed to confirm that Stanislav's brain was well and truly gone.

But he showed no signs of that. His gaze was level. His voice was calm.

He looked the way he'd always looked—like the don of the most powerful Bratva in America.

I look over at her now.

One petite little girl seems hardly worth the trouble.

We left dozens of dead cartel soldiers behind us in Mexico. As our helicopter lifted out from the garden, I saw the first flames beginning to engulf her father's compound.

By morning, it would all be ash.

And here she is, snoozing soundly. Sleeping fucking Beauty.

I frown. Cillian had pointed out earlier that she was shivering in the cold and not wearing much. It didn't bother me then—I was more focused on getting the fuck out of that godforsaken place.

Now, it does bother me.

I get up and walk towards her. I stand over her and stare down at her body, admiring her beauty begrudgingly.

Who would have thought that fucking bastard, Joaquin, would have a daughter as lovely as her?

She is made of smooth lines and soft edges. She seems slightly fuller than when I last saw her, but I can't be sure.

Either way, it suits her. Softens her. Makes her cheeks rosy against her caramel complexion.

I remove the coat I'm wearing and drape it over her. She sighs a little but she doesn't move.

Even her eyelashes have stopped fluttering now. It's a dramatic shift from the frightened girl I found huddled on the floor of her bathroom.

She still looks just as innocent, though. Just as pure. Just as young.

Looking at her, I get the same feeling as when I dirtied the white tiles of her bathroom with my muddy, bloodstained boots.

Like laying a finger on her—much less claiming her as a wife, the way my father wants me to do—is a crime against something so untouched.

But she has no choice in this.

Truthfully, neither do I.

I find my thoughts drifting to Marisha.

My second wedding will be completely different than the first.

No, this isn't a real marriage. It's nothing more than a political strategy. A power play.

What I had with Marisha was real.

This... this is just business.

Yet, even as the thought crosses my head, I know I'm more preoccupied with this woman than I should be.

I flash back to The Siren, the way her thighs had clenched around me, inviting me in.

The way her hands had fallen over my ass, pulling me deeper, begging me for more.

That memory has haunted my thoughts for four months now.

But I can't afford to be distracted anymore. She was just a random fuck—up until now.

Knowing who she is changes everything.

I make a decision here and now: I won't stain her. And I sure as hell won't let her corrupt me.

It's bad enough that she's plagued my thoughts for months.

But no more.

She's a prop. A bridge from the present to the future.

Beyond that, she means nothing to me.

"Everything okay?"

I turn to find Cillian staring at me. His eyes turn to the jacket I have just draped over Esme, but he doesn't comment on it.

Wise choice—I'm not in the mood for his jokes.

"Everything's fine," I reply gruffly. "Why wouldn't it be?"

Cillian shrugs. "I don't know. You just look…" He trails off without finishing his sentence.

I turn to him with one raised eyebrow. "Are you *trying* to annoy me?"

He throws me a shit-eating smile. "Nope. Just naturally good at it."

I roll my eyes and move down the jet so I can sit down. Cillian follows behind me and takes the seat opposite.

I glance out the window. We're cruising through cotton candy clouds smudged bronze with sunlight.

"How long 'till we arrive?" I ask.

"Couple of hours."

I nod and stare out the window again as though I've never seen clouds before.

I can feel Cillian glancing at me every now and again, but I try and block him out.

The Irish bastard is the closest thing to a brother I have. Which means, when something's up with me, he usually knows.

So, of course, he's onto something now.

But I'm just not willing to talk about it.

I haven't even told him about the fact that I've met Esme before. That I've *fucked* Esme before.

I don't know why I don't tell him, but somehow, it feels like a secret I want to keep to myself.

At least for now.

"It's normal to be nervous, you know."

I turn to Cillian, trying to figure out where his train of thought has landed. "What?"

Cillian shrugs and rubs his knees with his hands like he's trying to get comfortable. "I'm just saying… marriage. It's big."

I scowl. If he thinks he's about to improv as my marriage counselor, he's got another thing coming.

"It's not big," I retort. "Doesn't mean shit."

"Oh, yeah, sure, totally, of course. One hundred percent. Absolutely."

I can feel his incredulity from here.

I sigh and turn to him again.

"This is business, Cillian," I remind him. "This marriage isn't something either one of us asked for. It's not real. It's just… an alliance."

"An alliance?" Cillian repeats.

"Well, a slightly one-sided alliance," I admit. "But fuck, life isn't fair. She should learn that now if she hasn't already."

A slight smirk crosses Cillian's face. "Fair, it is not. I will agree with you there. But as far as forced marriages go… you got lucky, hombre."

"If you say something like 'She's fuckable,' I'm ejecting you out of the plane myself."

"*Fuckable?*" Cillian echoes in disbelief. He disregards my threat completely, as per usual. "Come on, dude, you can't tell me that she's not one of the most beautiful women you've ever laid eyes on."

I shrug my shoulders and try not to glance over in her direction. She's still sleeping soundly. I'm pretty sure she'll stay that way until the plane lands.

"She's just a girl. Same as any other."

"You can lie with the best of them, my man," Cillian says. "But not to me. We've known each other for too long. You and I both know there's something there."

If you only fucking knew.

"Fucking hell," I groan. "What the fuck is up with you today? You wanna talk wedding plans or something? You wanna help me pick out china patterns or floral displays? Is that it?"

Cillian just smiles in his easygoing way, completely at ease.

"Nah, that shit doesn't do it for me," he says. "But I do want to talk about the bachelor party."

I roll my eyes. "Of course you do."

"But, typically, that comes after choosing the best man."

I look at his serious expression with wide eyes and then burst out laughing.

"You are a fucking cupcake," I wheeze.

"I don't know why you're laughing," Cillian scowls. "This is a very serious issue."

I shake my head as my laughter subsides.

"Like I said, this is not a real fucking marriage. It's a business arrangement. She may be my wife soon, but my cock is still destined for every other woman in L.A."

Cillian cocks one eyebrow and looks at me pointedly.

I know damn well what he's thinking.

In the last several months, I hadn't exactly been sticking my cock anywhere.

Well, except for Esme.

But he doesn't need to know that.

"What?" I challenge.

He holds up his hands in surrender. "Easy, tiger," he replies. "I dunno. Maybe this could be something."

"Are you fucking on something? It's a little early to start boozing, Cillian."

He raises a hand like he's swearing an oath. "Sober as the day I was born, chief. Scout's honor. I'm just saying, she's the daughter of a mafia boss and you're the son of a mafia boss. She understands the life better than most. Remember how hard it was for Marisha?"

I squeeze the armrests hard until my knuckles go white.

Her name sends a ripple of pain shooting through me.

Cillian is the only one who's allowed to talk to me about Marisha— mostly because he was the only one with me in the days following her death.

He saw my rage, my pain, my sadness. He suffered when I had so much fury I lashed out.

And he stayed through it. He was loyal. *Is* loyal. I owe him my loyalty in return.

That doesn't mean I like hearing it, though.

"I remember," I nod with gritted teeth.

"She was strong," Cillian continues. "But it takes a different kind of strength to live this life. To be a don's daughter. To be a don's wife."

"You make it sound simple."

"It won't be," he acknowledges. "I'm just saying… it may not be the hell you're imagining."

He brings up a good point. Is "hell" what I'm imagining?

Before I can figure it out, one of my guys ducks in from the cockpit and informs us that we're landing soon.

We buckle in. Half an hour later, we touch down.

I feel a small bubble of relief now that we're back on familiar territory.

The mission went as smoothly as it could have.

But now comes the hard bit.

I walk over to Esme, who's still sleeping soundly. Her breathing is soft and measured.

"Shall I take her in?" Igor asks, gesturing at her.

My immediate instinct is possessiveness.

No one's carrying her out of here but me.

I catch myself before the unexpected anger spills out of me. Instead of saying what I'm really feeling, I just shake my head calmly.

"Go unload the weapons," I order. "I'll take the girl."

Igor nods and disappears to do as instructed. Once he's gone, I turn to Esme.

Bending down, I lift her up into my arms, as gently as I can so that I don't wake her. It's the closest I've been to a woman since…

Since the last time I held her.

Her scent fills my nose. Just the faintest hint of perfume. Sweet, floral, fragrant.

One more thing that getting close to me will destroy.

She doesn't wake as I carefully step down the plane and onto the stairs. But when the first ray of dawn sunlight hits her eyes, she stirs.

Slowly and timidly, her eyes open. She shields her face against the sun and whimpers.

Perhaps Cillian was right. Maybe this won't be as bad as I first feared. Maybe she'll come softly into her new life and I won't have to do terrible things to force her compliance.

I watch as Esme tries to make sense of her surroundings. We're on a private airstrip outside of Los Angeles. California sun shining from a clear blue sky.

I wonder how long it will take her to realize she's never going home again.

Right as my foot hits the tarmac, recognition strikes Esme.

She pales.

"Let me go!" she gasps. "Don't touch me, motherfucker."

She starts struggling immediately, thrashing around in my arms.

So much for coming softly.

But the sedative is still in her system. Weakening her muscles, slowing her reactions.

I sigh loudly and hoist her up over my shoulder like a sack of potatoes.

She screams at the undignified position and starts slamming her delicate little fists against my back.

She's throwing obscenities and insults my way, but all of it just makes me smile.

So much for soft and timid, too. She's a hellcat, deep down. Much feistier than I've given her credit for.

I give her ass a hard smack and she curses me out all over again.

"Act like a fucking brat," I tell her calmly, "and I'll treat you like one."

All she does is scream in response.

16

ESME

The bastard.

The asshole.

The motherfucking murderer.

I claw at his back but I may as well be banging against a brick wall for all the good it's doing.

Artem completely ignores me as he strides across the tarmac towards a huge, sleek vehicle.

The wind bites at my exposed legs and thighs. Whatever poison his goons stuck me with is still clouding my thoughts pretty badly.

Though, not so badly that I'm not pissed as hell.

I may not be capable of fully processing everything that's going on around me in the last few hours. But I'm sure as hell furious that he is handling me like a ragdoll.

"Let me go, asshole!" I scream.

Artem's answer is to open the car door and hurl me inside like useless cargo.

I hit the seat with an *oof*, but the landing is softer than I expect, thanks to the plush leather seats.

I open my mouth to yell some more curses at him, but before I can get my bearings, he flings a coat that hits me square in the face.

Then he slams the door on me before I find my voice again.

The coat is huge and I know immediately it's his. It smells of him—that heady, woody scent that I used to dream about at night these last four months before falling asleep.

I never knew those sleeping dreams would turn into a waking nightmare.

I go to open the door and make a run for it—where I'd run, I have no fucking clue, but I'm sure as fuck not gonna sit here like a good little girl and let him cart me off to God knows where.

But the handle is locked.

I yank at it with two hands. It rattles but refuses to budge.

I scream.

All it does is bounce around the empty vehicle and make my ears hurt.

Fine. New plan.

Glancing up, I see that the keys are in the ignition.

Bingo.

I start to clamber over the divider to get in the driver's seat and put the pedal to the metal. Driving off is better than running away, anyhow.

That plan doesn't last long, either.

I'm halfway over the center console when the back door opens again. Artem sticks his head in, sees me wriggling my way to freedom, and lets out a weary, exasperated sigh.

"Tsk, tsk," he mumbles.

Reaching over, he grabs my ankle and tugs me back into the rear seat.

Once again, I land with an oof.

Once again, he grabs the coat I dropped and throws it in my face.

"Sit down and shut up," he orders.

I get ready to tell him what I think of that particular set of instructions, but before I can find the words, the door on the other side opens and another man gets in.

This one is tall and broad with a shaved head, dark sunglasses, and a gun in a holster at his side. He looks even less friendly than Artem. Like a villainous mob goon straight out of central casting.

The goon looks up at Artem with an arched eyebrow as if asking permission. Artem sighs and waves a hand as if to say, *Go ahead.*

At that cue, the man pins me back against the seat with one meaty paw.

With his other hand, he makes quick work of my buckle. Hardly even notices as I thrash and scream against his hand pressing into my torso.

When the buckle clicks, I realize I'm trapped. All the fight goes out of me and the scream dies on my lips.

"That's a good girl," Artem murmurs when I'm quiet again. "You were starting to give me a headache with all that screaming."

Up front, the car door opens and another suited goon climbs into the driver's seat. He doesn't look back as he starts up the car and we go careening out of the airfield.

"You realize you're abducting me, right?" I ask Artem once we're underway. He's gazing out of the window, ignoring me as I glare at his face in profile. "Which is illegal. Just telling you as a heads up, you know. You don't seem like the type who likes cops."

He doesn't look at me but he scoffs with derision. "I suppose you would know quite a lot about what's legal and what's not."

"My dad was the criminal. Not me."

"True, but you're the one paying for his sins. Doesn't seem fair, does it?"

"You can't do this," I hiss. "Let me go."

He closes his eyes for a moment as though he's trying hard to block me out.

"No," he replies, when he opens his eyes again. "I don't think I will. You may as well just accept the inevitable. Make my life easier."

"I don't give a flying fuck about making your life easier," I snap. Then my curiosity gets the better of me. "What's inevitable?"

I expected him to kill me back in the garden. I was all ready to end my life right next to Cesar's grave.

It'd be kind of poetic, really.

But when I said that, Artem had actually laughed. His final words before I passed out are still seared in my brain, even when the rest of my memories of last night are fuzzy and indistinct.

Kill you? No, darling. We've got something very different in mind.

He turns to me. Something about the expression behind his eyes scares me. I can't pinpoint what it is exactly. But I've met enough bad friends of my father to know true danger when I see it.

His tongue darts out to wet his lower lip. "You'll find out soon enough."

His eyes dip slightly, tracing down my lips, my throat, my chest. My skin tingles. It's almost as though he's touching me.

I tug his coat over myself like a blanket and the moment is broken. He turns away from me again.

"I'm not going to just take this lying down, you know," I announce. "I'm not just going to meekly accept whatever you decide to do to me."

He doesn't answer. Just looks resolutely out of the tinted windows.

I probably should concentrate on where we're going, but I'm too worked up and too scared to focus on details.

"My father has friends," I say, my voice pitching up with hysteria. "They're not just going to accept this. Someone will help me and—"

"Enough!" He raises his voice only a fraction higher, but it feels like he's screaming at me. "That's enough. I want silence now."

"Who do you think I am?" I snarl at him. "I'm not about to follow your commands like some kicked dog!"

Artem sighs and nods once more to the man sitting opposite me.

I whip my head back and forth between Artem and Goon #1.

"What was that?" I demand. "What'd you… what—no…!"

Before I can even finish my sentence, the goon reaches for me with something clutched in his hands.

I scream, but none of the men in the car seem bothered in the least.

Not even when the goon tightens a gag around my mouth.

My scream devolves into a wordless whimper as I'm bound and gagged.

The bindings on my wrists are tight. I strain against them uncomfortably, but it takes just a few seconds of mindless thrashing to realize that they're not going anywhere.

I have to fight back tears as I sink back against the leather seats.

I've lost this fight.

Only now does Artem finally look at me.

Figures—of course I'd have to be bound and gagged before he deigns to spare a real glance in my direction.

I stare straight ahead, ignoring him.

I don't want to give him the satisfaction of seeing my tears.

The car bumps along the road, headed for what I can only assume is a place worse than the one I just left.

I always assumed that my father's death would one day set me free.

Turns out that was just wishful thinking from a girl who was too naïve for her own good.

Papa's dead now—Artem said so himself.

But I'm not free, nor will I ever be if I remain in this toxic world of violence and power. The only way I can be happy, the only way I can protect the child in my womb… is to leave it.

I want out.

I don't know how or when that'll happen. I know it won't be easy.

But I know I have to try.

17

ESME

After a silent half hour of driving, we pull up in front of a mammoth building. I assume that my bindings will be removed, but none of the men in the car with me move to do so.

They just shepherd me out of the car and march me into the building like a prisoner of war.

No one in the lobby dares to look at me. Not the doorman or the concierge or a single living soul.

It's like I don't exist.

Like a bound and gagged girl isn't being dragged through the building in the middle of the morning with a platoon of armed goons around me.

I assume we're going to the massive elevator just next to the concierge desk, but a firm hand on my elbow steers me to the left until we arrive at a smaller, private elevator.

I'm pushed through. Artem steps in beside me. Turning around, I catch the blank gazes of Goons #1 and #2 and their buddies.

I do my best to scowl at them from around the ball gag in my mouth.

Wouldn't want them to part ways thinking we were at the beginning of a beautiful friendship.

The elevator doors close on their stony faces. Good fucking riddance.

I resist the urge to glance at Artem as we rise higher and higher. Can't wait to say good riddance to him, either.

When the doors slide open again, I find myself staring into a lushly carpeted foyer with a gorgeous chandelier hanging over the entryway.

"Go on." He prods me gently in the small of the back

I stumble out of the elevator, hands still cuffed in front of me. Behind me, I hear as a *ping* as the elevator closes and retreats, trapping me inside yet another luxurious prison.

Smart money says those doors open only for Artem. Sure enough, when I glance over my shoulder, I see him tap in a couple of numbers on a security pad next to the doors.

Two-five-three-two-seven.

Was that it? Did I have the code? A brief moment of hope swells up in my chest.

Until I watch him press his thumb against the pad and the hopes curdles into disappointment.

Artem turns to me and reads me at once.

"Did you really think it would be that easy?" he asks in a mocking tone.

The ball gag prevents me from replying, but if I could speak, I'd tell him what I'm thinking: *I can always cut off your finger, you son of a bitch.*

One corner of his mouth turns up in the ghost of a smirk.

"I wouldn't try anything stupid. Follow me."

The penthouse is massive, opulent, and completely devoid of color. Black granite, dark wood cabinets, paintings on the wall that are—I shit you not—just canvases painted delicately in various shades of gray.

It's utterly lifeless.

He comes to a stop a few feet away from a blank bronzed wall that's bare except for the two doors standing right next to each other.

"The one on the right is yours." He points to indicate. "Now, if I untie you, are you going to promise to behave?"

I nod slowly.

He comes forward and reaches behind my head to remove the gag on my mouth first. My lips feel raw and I run my tongue over them.

Artem's eyes flick down to follow the gesture. A sudden twist of tension seizes in my stomach. I don't say a word, nor does he.

But his hand drifts slowly to wipe away a strand of spit from my chin. His thumb is hot and gentle against my skin.

It's a weirdly tender gesture. Possessive, like he's cleaning off something delicate and cherished.

It sends a chill down my spine.

But it's over as soon as it started. Artem blinks and his touch disappears from my face.

He shakes his head subtly and moves to undo the restraints around my hands. When they're gone, I rub my wrists with relief as the blood rushes back to my fingertips.

Then, without hesitation, I slap him hard across the face.

Oh, *hell* yes. That felt so fucking good.

I brace myself for his fury. For a retaliatory slap, a punch, a kick…

But he doesn't move. His hands massages his jaw for a moment before he looks at me.

"Feel better now?" he asks calmly. "Did you get that out of your system?"

That only serves to infuriate me further.

"You may think you're strong and powerful," I spit at him. "You may think you're the boss. But you're not. You're nothing but a boy pretending to be a man."

I see his eyes flash with anger.

I'm not gonna stick around and see what happens next.

Instead, I brush past him and run into the room he said was mine.

I fumble with the lock, my hands trembling. Luckily, it clicks almost instantly. I don't expect that to stop him—no doubt he has a key—but it's just instinct. If nothing else, it makes me feel better.

I back away from the door, breath caught in my throat. He'll be bursting through any second to storm in and teach me another lesson.

Maybe he just went to get something first—more restraints, a belt, a knife.

Hell, maybe he went to get a gun to finish what he started. Why should I trust that he's not going to kill me?

But as the seconds tick past, the door stays shut.

No motion.

No Artem.

Just silence.

Finally, after what feels like a lifetime of standing still, I accept that he's leaving me alone in here—for now.

So I turn and take in my surroundings.

A large floor-to-ceiling window takes up most of the front-facing wall. No balcony, but there's a cushioned window seat bathed in sunlight.

Shelves line the other walls, brimming with books. I meander past, touching the spines as I go.

The center of the wall opposite the window is devoted to a massive king bed with an imposing steel frame looming above it. Still, the room is so big that the mattress seems small in comparison.

I walk over to the window seat. It's large enough to be a bed in its own right.

I sink into the cushions and stare out onto the city.

He's brought me back to L.A.

I recognize the skyline from my last trip… the same one that had led to our heat-filled encounter in the bathroom of The Siren.

Artem had been my hero in that moment. My guardian angel, my white knight.

Now… he's my own personal monster.

The trauma of the last several hours settles over me. My eyes grow heavy, weighted down by turmoil and the last remaining fragments of the sedative I was jabbed with before leaving Mexico…

A small part of my subconsciousness is aware that I'm sleeping when I see my brother standing in front of me.

Cesar looks different than he did in life. Older, but I can't tell why. I guess it's the look in his eyes more than anything.

He reaches for me at the same time I reach for him, but we're too far apart. Our fingers touch nothing but empty space.

He mouths something.

"What?" I call out.

He mouths it again, but I still can't hear what he's saying.

"Speak up, Cesar," I beg. "I can't hear you."

He sighs. Shrugs. Then fades away.

When he disappears, I'm suddenly standing alone in a black fog. The only thing I'm aware of is the little fluttering sensation in my stomach.

I look down and see my belly. My child moves inside me and tears spring to my eyes.

This should be a happy moment.

But it's not happiness I feel.

It's sadness, laced with fear.

Fear that's growing, morphing, intensifying. It climbs up from my belly and into my throat like it wants to choke me out. It's got tentacles on my ribs and they're squeezing so hard that I can't breathe and I'm suffocating and it hurts like I'm being stabbed and oh, God, I'm—

I wake up.

I must've been sleeping for hours. The room is dark and oppressive now. L.A's skyline sparkles proudly down below me.

I turn to the room and wince at the crick in my neck from my awkward sleeping position.

It takes a moment for my eyes to adjust to the darkness.

Which is why I don't see him until I'm on my feet, halfway to the bed.

I gasp and stifle a scream as I freeze in place.

Artem is seated in the leather armchair in one corner of the room. His eyes catch the light of a skyscraper and flash.

"How the hell did you get in here?" I demand, trying to gain composure.

He lifts his hand and dangles a small silver key in the air. "This *is* my home," he drawls. "In case you forgot."

"Don't remind me. I'd like to go back to *my* home now, please."

I don't actually want that, but now is not the time to get into specifics. I'll start with getting away from here and from him. Then I'll figure out where to go from there.

"Your home is a pile of rubble and ash," he says coolly.

"And whose fault is that?"

"Mine, directly speaking. But your father brought that on himself."

"Oh?" I say with an arched eyebrow. "Did I bring this on myself?"

Artem doesn't answer that question. He just uncrosses and recross his leg, still playing with that silver key the whole time.

He doesn't look away from me, either.

"Did you sleep well?" he asks. His voice is so infuriatingly casual.

"Do you even care?"

He just shrugs.

I sit down on the edge of the bed, as far from him as I can manage.

"They were innocent, you know," I say, breaking the tenuous silence.

He raises his eyebrows. "Am I supposed to know who you're talking about?"

"The people you killed," I tell him. "Armando Ayala, Silvio Barrera, Ronaldo—"

"Listing names will not make me care about them," he interrupts. "They were collateral damage. It happens in this business."

I shake my head. "You're a monster."

"I'm not disagreeing with you."

He is so calm that it rattles me.

And then I realize why.

I was never allowed to mouth off or disobey Papa without facing consequences. My whole life, I'd been conditioned to expect pain for the slightest infraction.

I assumed that would happen with Artem, too. He is every bit as dangerous as Papa was. Maybe more so.

Apparently, though, it's a different kind of dangerous.

I felt it once before. Saw it with my own eyes, actually. He'd utterly destroyed the man at The Siren who tried to rape me.

Back then, his violence saved me.

Now, it's about to consume me.

"Stop thinking so much," he says, interrupting my thoughts. "You'll give yourself a headache."

"You didn't have to kill the house staff," I continue, refusing to let him derail my accusation. "They were innocent."

His eyes are cutting. "They were working for a cartel don. None of them were innocent. You can bet they all had a few skeletons in their closet."

"And that means they deserved to die?"

"Sometimes, it's not personal."

"Right. They were just the loose ends you needed to tie up," I mock in disgust.

"That's a lot of judgement coming from the daughter of a man who did horrendous things," he shoots back.

I try not to, but I can't stop the flinch from escaping me. "I can't help who my father was," I reply softly. "I'm not delusional though, I know he was a monster, too. That's how I can tell you're the same."

I glare at him, but he meets my gaze with absolutely zero remorse.

He stands suddenly. I flinch back, even though he's several feet away from me.

He rounds the bed, almost close enough to reach out and touch. But he doesn't stop near me. He keeps going past where I'm seated on the mattress and walks to the window.

He leans against it and crosses his arms over his chest. A beautiful silhouette of a man against the Los Angeles skyline.

I can almost feel that rock-hard chest press against me, my breathing coming in fast, his lips on my neck, his hands dancing up my thigh—

Stop it, Esme. There's no point reliving it. That was all just a lie. A deception. A mistake.

But I can't stop the question from sneaking out of my lips like a thief in the night. "Was I a target all this time?"

"What?" he asks. His tone is genuinely puzzled.

"Four months ago," I say. "In The Siren. Was I just a mark?"

He doesn't look at me. He's not the most expressive of men, but even from here, I can see something warring in his face. Emotions I can't name or describe.

"You were... a mistake," he says at last.

Can he be saying what I think he's saying? That he really didn't know who I was?

I frown, wondering if I should believe him or not. It seems too convenient to have been just a coincidence.

"A mistake. Yeah. It was. That night should never have happened," I say.

I have to fight to suppress the urge to touch my stomach. Where Artem's baby is growing, living.

"That we can agree on," he nods.

It shouldn't hurt me to hear him say that. After all, I was the one who said it first.

But my chest constricts a little anyway when he agrees with me.

All I can do is hope that he doesn't see the hurt on my face.

"I know I'm just an object in this world," I say softly. I don't dare look at him. I keep my eyes on my hands in my lap. "I know I don't mean a thing to you, that I'm just a tool in a big game. And once you've got what you want from me, you'll discard me. I'll be nothing more than the day's collateral damage. But I won't be used. I won't. I just won't."

I half-expect him to laugh at my silly little speech. To mock me, tell me I don't have a choice in the matter.

But he doesn't.

He just stares out the window and takes in my words. The silence makes me aware of other things. His scent. His breathing.

Then he turns and locks eyes with me. He takes two long strides and then he's right there, standing in front of me and looking down at my face.

It's like the night in The Siren, when he set me on the counter. The moment before everything exploded in hot passion.

The air between is charged. The atmosphere prickly with heat.

It's the contradiction that's tearing my brain in two. These opposite but equal memories of Artem.

The night in the club.

The night in my father's home.

He's a savior.

He's a killer.

He's a hero.

He's a beast.

I hate him and yet I'm fascinated to him, drawn to him, both terrified of him and desperate to feel safe in his arms once more.

"I'm stronger than I look," I say softly.

His eyes flicker down over my lips.

"I know."

His jaw tenses for a moment before he turns away from me and walks away toward the teak wardrobe resting to the side of the room. Like he needs space to breathe.

"Get dressed and meet me outside for dinner," he orders.

"What if I don't want to have dinner with you?"

"I'm not going to force you. But even the strongest among us need to eat."

Right on cue, my stomach rumbles slowly. I color with embarrassment, hoping he didn't hear.

"Fine," I say. "Then get out. I need to change."

He stares soberly at me for one more long second. Then he turns and slips out of the room.

The moment the door shuts behind him, I exhale tiredly.

What is it about this man that makes me feel like I'm constantly on the edge of falling?

I open the wardrobe, not sure what to expect.

I definitely don't expect what I find inside: a single dress.

It's sleek, silky, and colored in the palest silver. The hemline is about knee length, but the back is almost completely open except for the thin, barely visible straps that hold it in place.

I'm surprised by how elegant it is.

I'm even more surprised to find that it's in my size.

Had he picked the dress out for me himself?

Like everything else I've learned so far about Artem, it's a baffling contradiction.

18

ARTEM

Back in my room, I stare at my reflection in the mirror and try to convince myself that the raging erection is purely a physical response.

That my desire is related only to the memory of that pussy clamping down on my cock.

Of those lips moaning while she came undone around me.

One goddamn hookup four months in the past shouldn't be doing this to me. It's infuriating.

But sooner or later, it'll pass.

Though, "sooner" would be preferable.

I'm stronger than I look. That's what she said to me.

It took every ounce of willpower I had not to reply with exactly what I was thinking. *I know you are, darling. I know how that body feels in my hands. What it's capable of. And I plan on pushing you to your limits.*

Somehow, I'd swallowed those words—when all I wanted to do was devour her instead.

Next time, I might not be so lucky.

I adjust my suit jacket. After years of hating to dress up like my father always wanted, I'd found myself reaching naturally for it after leaving Esme's room.

It feels… right.

The suit fabric is a deep navy blue, highlighted by the stark white shirt. Both tailored to perfection by the man my father keeps on staff for just that purpose.

I leave my bedroom and walk to the balcony.

I'd had a team come up while Esme was sleeping to arrange a table for dinner. The chef and the waiters are huddled in the kitchen now, putting the final touches on our meal.

I want this night to be as private as possible, especially considering the bombshell I'm about to drop on her.

No one will hear her scream from up here.

I step through the glass French doors.

"Fuck, I could use a drink," I mumble to myself. A bottle of champagne cooling in the ice bucket calls to me, but I ignore it pointedly.

I want my head clear for what happens next.

Instead, I go to the balcony's edge where I can see the city lights below. It's a warm night and the moon overhead is bright and full.

I can practically hear Cillian cracking jokes, even though he's not here.

When the moon hits your eye like a big pizza pie, that's amore…

"Shut up," I growl under my breath.

The bastard is miles away doing fuck knows what, and irritating me anyways. Son of a bitch.

Sighing, I turn my back to the skyline and look once more at the dining arrangements.

The table is set for two. A cream-colored tablecloth sweeps close to the floor and the silver cutlery reflects the candlelight.

Smells waft out from the open kitchen window, mouth-watering and fragrant.

It's romantic. Elegant. Refined.

What a bunch of bullshit.

In truth, it's all merely a façade, a mockery that I don't think Esme will appreciate.

I don't know what has led me to tell her *this* way, but a part of me wants to parcel out the bad news by wrapping it in nice things.

As if I give a fuck what she thinks about all of it. About any of it.

As if her opinion matters in the slightest.

"Fancy meal for a prisoner," says a voice from behind me.

I turn, more startled than I'd like to admit.

And I almost suck in my breath at the sight of her.

Esme looks like a mirage. An ethereal fairytale come to life.

The pale silver dress I picked out for her clings to her graceful curves. She's kept her hair loose and it falls over her bare shoulders with careless ease.

She looks cautious as she steps out into the balcony, but by the time she settles into her seat, she has her features carefully composed once more.

Her eyebrows rise before she turns her gaze to me. "All this for me? You shouldn't have."

I don't miss the sarcasm, but I choose to ignore it for now.

The erection that was driving me insane when I got dressed hasn't gone away. In fact, it's gotten noticeably worse.

"I like my guests to be comfortable," I reply from where I'm standing.

She scoffs. "Now I'm a guest? That's news to me. I don't usually sedate my guests on their way over."

I cross the open balcony and settle into the chair opposite of Esme.

"Call yourself what you want. It makes no difference to me. It doesn't change what happens next, either."

She quirks an eyebrow. "What happens next?"

I grin wickedly. "Dinner."

She rolls her eyes and turns her attention to the floral centerpiece at the middle of the table. It's a bouquet of pale roses with sharp thorns on the stems.

I should've had them removed. They send the wrong message.

I'm not trying to seduce the woman—I'm trying to break her.

Though, sometimes, there's a fine line between the two.

"Hungry?" I ask.

"Ravenous."

I smile and raise a hand. Almost instantly, two waiters in crisp suits appear with our first course. They set down two steaming bowls of lobster bisque in front of each of us and a basket of freshly baked focaccia.

"Lobster bisque with cognac marshmallow and a brandy reduction," one of the servers informs us.

Then the other one picks up the bottle of champagne and prepares to pour it in the waiting glasses.

Suddenly, I raise my hand to stop him. I don't know why, but I have a strong urge to avoid alcohol.

That's odd. I've drank almost every day since Marisha died.

But just like that, something in me has shifted.

"None for me," I tell the waiter. "Esme?"

She flinches when I say her name. But then she glances at the waiter and shakes her head. "None for me, either."

The waiter dips his head toward her and backs away, leaving us to the fragrant soup.

"Afraid it will loosen your tongue?" I ask.

She eyes me. "I don't know what drug you stuck in my neck earlier," she says. "I don't want to mix it with anything."

"Just a mild sedative. You can drink if you want to."

"Your 'mild sedative' messed me up bad. I'm gonna pass on the bubbly, thanks very much."

I shrug. If she doesn't want to drink, I'm not going to push her.

I watch as Esme dips forward and breathes in the bisque as though she can't stop herself any longer.

It's probably been a while since she's eaten. She must be starving.

Without waiting for permission, she plucks a spoon from the table and takes a sip of the soup.

I suppress a smile. Her tongue runs across her bottom lip and then her eyes rise to mine.

"Are you going to stare at me all night?" she asks. More like demands, really.

"Maybe."

She rolls her eyes again and returns to the soup, pointedly ignoring me.

A few minutes later and her bowl is dry.

She reaches for a piece of the bread and sits back in her chair, gazing out at the open sky, still avoiding my eyes.

"Do you really live here?" she asks after a moment.

"As opposed to…?"

"You stole me from my house. Maybe you stole this house from someone else."

I chuckle. "Yes, I really live here."

"Hmph." She looks around, chewing sloppily on her bread as if she knows that the rude table manners will piss me off. She's right about that, but I let it pass.

I know she knows better. She's just trying my patience.

I won't let her get to me that easily.

"If I ask you a question, do you promise to be honest with me?" she asks suddenly.

"I suppose I can agree to that," I say. "On one condition. One rule: no talking about the past."

She frowns. "The past is kind of relevant."

"Usually, when people say they have one condition, it's not up for negotiation."

She wrinkles her nose. "Fine. But will you promise to be honest with me?"

"I'll try."

She nods. One lock of dark hair falls over her face and she brushes it back absentmindedly. "What is it about this life that's so great?"

Of all the questions I expected from her, that wasn't it.

I stare at her for a moment, gathering my thoughts.

What's her angle here? What's her play? What's the subtext?

But her expression remains quietly curious.

Maybe there is no underlying question. She genuinely wants to know.

I consider it for a moment. In the end, I decide to answer truthfully.

"Power."

"Power," she repeats. "Over what?"

"Over anything I want," I answer. "Over everything. That's what makes it power."

"So you just like being in charge?"

I hesitate. They are simple questions, so why am I struggling with the answers?

"I never had a choice."

Her eyes go wide for a moment. She looks like she's about to smile but then she turns her head to the side and her dark hair falls over her face like a curtain.

I dislike not being able to see her, but I wait patiently until she turns to me again.

"We all have choices," she retorts.

I shake my head. "Not me."

Something in her face shifts. Softens.

"Yeah," she says in a near-whisper, "me neither."

Another moment of silence passes. Esme's gaze is soft, unfocused. When she speaks again, she does so without looking at me.

"If you did have a choice, what kind of life would you pick?"

Before I can answer, the waiters appear again and remove our empty bowls.

I've only taken a few bites of my soup but I wave for him to take it away, with my eyes staying trained on Esme.

The second course is crab ravioli dressed in a brown butter sauce. It smells amazing, but Esme looks at me pointedly. She's still waiting for my answer.

"I don't know."

"You don't know," she asks, "or you don't want to tell me?"

"I was born to this life. Groomed for it," I tell her. "It's all I've ever known. It's all I ever will know."

Her face looks strangely sad. Pained, almost. I almost don't catch her next words.

"He used to talk like that, too."

I frown. "Who?"

She lifts her eyes and shakes her head. The sadness and pain I saw vanishes at once. Fire returns to her face.

"No one," she says. "Never mind. Out of curiosity, exactly which band of criminal assholes do you belong to?"

I steeple my fingers. "You tell me."

She screws up her eyebrows in concentration. "Definitely Russian," she replies carefully, "based on the accents I heard from you and some of your men. I'm just not sure which Russian mafia family… There are a few in L.A., right?"

"There *were* a few in LA," I correct her, with some satisfaction. "But not anymore."

She thinks for a moment, then snaps her fingers. "The Kovalyov Bratva."

"*Bravo.*" I applaud mockingly for her.

She puts her fork down as though she's just lost her appetite. I notice her body kind of tense, like she is curling into herself.

"You've heard of us, then?" I ask.

"I know the name. Not the details. I've spent my whole life avoiding the details, actually."

The puzzle pieces are starting to fit together. "You don't like this life."

"I *hate* it," she says passionately, her eyes flaring up, turning her hazel irises gold. "How can you like a life where you have no freedom, no voice, no *worth*?"

I see the desperation in her face. She just wants to be seen. Acknowledged. Valued.

Being with me is going to break her heart.

"Being a woman in this world doesn't make you worthless."

She throws her hands up. "Sure, if you're a woman with no morals who loves the violence and the men who commit it. Those are the women who embrace this life, who become a part of it. That's not what I want. That's not who I am."

"Sometimes, you don't have a choice. You do what you must."

"No, sometimes the people around you don't *give* you a choice," she snaps.

Esme seems to sober up a second later. She takes a deep, shuddering breath. I can see that she's trying hard to keep her emotions in check.

"Why am I here, Artem?"

Is that the first time she's said my name?

It fuels a reaction so strong that I find myself leaning forward and gritting my teeth together.

Why the fuck do I like it so much? Why the fuck does hearing my name on her lips make me hard as a rock?

I strain against my pants and remind myself that she needs to be told about what's coming for her. For both of us.

"You're going to be my wife," I say. A flint of ice slips into my tone. "You may as well just accept that now."

She freezes. Goosebumps let loose on her arms.

I want to reach out and touch her. To run my fingers over her skin.

But it's an impulse I push away immediately.

I promised myself that I would not cross that line with her.

I wouldn't ruin her with my bloodstained hands.

This is an alliance, I'd told Cillian. *Nothing more.*

Did I still mean that?

"You're really not going to kill me?"

I shake my head. "No."

"So, you abducted me to… marry me?" she asks. "Really?"

"Yes."

"Because you think claiming me as your wife will deliver you my father's contacts."

"You catch on fast."

"That's no guarantee," she says quickly.

"No, but it's a step in the right direction," I tell her. "And I can be very persuasive."

She looks up toward the moon. I can see her eyes are bright. Almost teary.

But when she looks back at me, they're dry once again.

She looks so fucking beautiful.

"And then what?" she asks.

I frown. "What do you mean?"

"You force me to marry you, you take control of Mexico, my father's stooges offer you their fealty," she narrates. "And you'll have what you want: power."

"Yes."

"And once you have it... what happens to me?"

That's the million-dollar question.

"Nothing happens to you," I tell her. "I don't plan on murdering you once I have control of Mexico, if that's what you mean."

Is that true? I don't know. I don't fucking know.

"So we're just supposed to stay husband and wife... forever?"

"However long that lasts, yes."

She shakes her head and sighs. "And I suppose you will continue to fuck whomever you want, whenever you want."

It's not a question, so I don't bother answering.

"And I'll be expected to be the loyal wife, waiting home patiently for my dear husband to return from screwing his latest whore," she continues. "Am I right? Did I get all those details correct? Or am I allowed to go have fun, too?"

The thought of another man putting his hands on her sends waves of fury rippling through me.

I feel my fists clench in response.

"No other man will touch you as long as I'm your husband."

She looks at me with a pitying expression. "You're really just like him. My father."

I don't like that one bit.

"I'm not like anyone," I snap. "I'm my own man."

But Esme shakes her head and laughs right in my face. "Oh, yes. Yes, you are. You're cut from the exact same cloth and you don't even know it. And just like him, you are utterly clueless."

I narrow my eyes at her. I know I shouldn't ask, but I can't help myself.

"Is that so?"

"It's all about possession with men like you," she says. "But even if you possess something, that doesn't make it real. You can put me in a room and lock me up. You can force yourself on me and take my body, you can marry me and call me your wife, but you will never truly possess me. Not in any way that matters."

Her tone is biting. Her expression fiercer than I've ever seen.

She's glowing so brightly that she outshines the fucking moon.

What angers me more than anything… is that she's right.

And all my strength, all my power, all my wealth cannot change that.

Part of her—her heart, her soul—can't be taken. Can't be claimed.

It can only be given.

She can tell that she's struck a chord. Her eyes light up even brighter and she leans forward.

"And you hate that, don't you?" she presses. "You fucking despise that you can't just snatch that away from me and make me yours. This isn't your first time trying, is it?"

She shakes her head as if answering her own question and licks her lips greedily. "Is this what you do? Kidnap women, marry them, and then lock them away for the rest of their lives? I bet you've done this before, haven't you? If that's the case, I'd rather you kill me. I won't be your newest fake toy wife."

I see Marisha's face in my mind's eye instantly.

I'm already on the edge of anger.

Esme's words push me over.

She stiffens when she sees my expression change. She knows she's gone too far.

"I think it's time for you to go back to your room," I say coldly.

Her eyes widen for a split second. "Why?"

"We had one rule. You broke it. Dinner's over."

"You can't just send me away!" she balks. "I'm not some little kid getting put in timeout."

I seize her wrist and yank her close to me. My plate goes clattering to the floor and splinters, but I don't give a fuck. My eyes are locked on Esme.

"Let's get one thing very clear," I hiss right in her face. "I can do anything I want to you. The sooner you get over that fact, the easier this will be for both of us."

I hold her a moment longer, close enough to feel her breath plume on my face. My anger is simmering, boiling.

Then, suddenly exhausted, I let her go.

She collapses back in her chair, eyes wide.

I raise my hand. "Guards!"

Esme's head snaps to the side the moment I call for them. Two of my men storm out onto the balcony and go right for her.

Before they can grab her, Esme pushes her chair back violently and backs away from both of them.

"Don't you dare touch me, you pigs."

They look at me.

I nod.

And without another word, they scoop her up, one grabbing her arms and the other her legs.

She screams and thrashes. Her hair flays wildly and that silver dress sparkles in the moonlight with every twist of her body.

"You bastard!" she yells as they carry her away.

I just sit where I am, breathing heavily.

Esme is strong, but I'm stronger.

And I *will* break her. That's a fucking promise.

19

ESME

When I wake up the next day, I'm still wearing the silver dress from the night before.

Apparently, I was too busy crying myself to sleep to remember to take it off.

I'd like to go back to sleep, as a matter of fact. But the sun coming through the massive wall of windows has other ideas.

As does Artem's house staff.

The door bursts without so much as a knock. I immediately scramble back against the headboard and cover myself with the comforter—not that that provides much in the way of protection.

I'm expecting Artem again.

But it's not him.

It's one of the sour-faced guards who manhandled me back into this room last night after Artem abruptly decided our romantic rooftop dinner had reached its conclusion.

"What do you want?" I hiss at him.

He looks at me with a blank expression on his face. Something tells me he's not exactly a rocket scientist.

"You are to get ready," he tells me in a subtle Russian accent. "Your car arrives in one hour."

I frown. "Where am I going?"

The guard's answer is to turn his back on me and leave just as unceremoniously as he entered.

"Where's Artem?" I yell to his retreating back.

No answer to that, either.

The door clicks shut.

"Thanks a lot, Mr. Talkative," I grumble when I'm alone again.

I thought I locked the door the previous night, but either the lock is fake or everyone and their freaking mother gets a key to my room.

Feeling deflated and angry all at the same time, I walk into my en-suite bathroom and fill the tub with steaming water.

Then I strip out of the dress and clamber in. I wince as the water bathes my aching muscles. Those guards were not exactly gentle last night.

The tub is set right next to another massive window that looks over L.A. As I sit and soak, it feels like I'm floating in the sky, gazing down at the rest of the world.

I might even be able enjoy the moment—if thoughts of last night would just stop plaguing me.

Artem had answered the big question: *If you're not going to kill me, what do you want?*

The answer was somehow stranger and more horrifying than I could've ever imagined.

Marriage.

He wants me as his wife. Willing or unwilling, fake or not, he doesn't give a shit.

He just thinks I'm his golden ticket.

Which means I've gone from living in the clutches of one bad man who wants to marry me off for empire-building purposes, right to another.

The only difference is that this new bad man wants to marry me off to himself.

I shudder. How am I supposed to wrap my head around this crap?

I'm so confused that it makes my brain hurt. I'm trying to battle with the voices in my head, but even they don't seem to agree.

Mostly because of this: a part of me is attracted to Artem.

It's crazy to think that. I don't dare voice the thought aloud.

But I can't deny it. It's true. That arrogant tilt to his lips, the wicked strength in his body, and those dark eyes that consume me with every glance…

It's… a lot. That's all I can really say about it.

So it's safe to say that part of me is curious about the man beneath those harsh, beautiful features. About what makes him tick. What kind of soul there is—or if there's a soul in there at all.

Curious, yeah. That's a good word. Maybe even… hopeful?

But another part of me is desperate to get away from him.

He's not going to be different.

He's not going to love or respect you.

He's going to use and discard you. And your child will grow up the same way you did—caged and lonely.

My hands flutter over my stomach.

The baby is his—there is no doubt of that.

But revealing that secret to Artem would bind me to him so completely that I'd never be able to escape.

I try and sort through the jumble of uncertainty in my head, but even after my skin has turned pruny, I can't seem to find clarity.

These dilemmas will take more than one bath to resolve.

Giving up, I get out of the tub, wrap a towel around my body and another around my hair, and head back into the bedroom.

I stop short when I realize a new outfit has been placed on my bed. A black cashmere blouse with an elegant V neckline and an ivory midi skirt that complements it perfectly. At the foot of the bed awaits a pair of Louis Vuitton heels.

Just like with last night's clothes, everything is in my size.

That's a little unnerving. To be fair, all of this is a little unnerving.

But what choice do I have?

I put on the clothes because I have nothing else to wear and turn to check my reflection in the mirror that's been set into one of the doors of the wardrobe.

And again, just like last night, the effect is flawless.

The outfit definitely flatters my figure. I look chic, elegant.

But mostly, I'm relieved to see that my pregnancy isn't evident at all. My hips seem a little wider, and perhaps my belly isn't as flat as it normally is, but those are small details that only I'm able to notice, and that's because I'm looking close for any sign of change.

With any luck, it'll be a long time before I have to figure out how to hide a growing baby bump.

When I walk out of my room, I come face to face with the same two guards from the night before standing on alert at the corner.

They both turn blank eyes to me. Neither one says a thing.

Does anyone around here know how to use their words?

"Where's Artem?" I ask.

"Breakfast is waiting in the dining room," the taller of the two guards says instead of answering my question. He has light brown eyes and a crew cut that makes him look older than he probably is. "Your car will be here in twenty minutes."

I scowl in irritation and turn left to a huge kitchen with—yet again—an exceptional view of downtown Los Angeles.

A table off to the side has already been laid with an assortment of different breakfast foods. Sausages, croissants, bagels with cream cheese and smoked salmon, jams—the works.

My stomach rumbles. But it's not this food I crave.

It's the memory of breakfasts I haven't had for years.

I miss those quiet summer mornings with Cesar. When he'd wake me before anyone else in the house was up and persuade one of the more lenient security guards into taking us into town.

We'd hide in a corner booth and eat hot tortillas, freshly caught fish, eggs that had been laid that very morning.

Life was simple then.

It's not so simple anymore.

Truthfully, it hasn't been simple for a long time.

I take a quick glance around, but there's no one else in the kitchen. Fine by me.

I sit down and help myself to a blueberry muffin that's softer than a cloud. When I finish that one, I grab another.

I eat until I'm full—crumbling all the empty muffin wrappers together so I can lie to myself about what an embarrassing amount of food I just took down.

I'm drinking juice when the guard with the crew cut walks in.

"Your car is here."

I sigh and get to my feet. "And where the hell am I going?" I demand. "Or am I not permitted to know that either?"

"Mr. Kovalyov left this for you," Crew Cut says. He passes me a folded note.

The second guard thumps in carrying a huge duffel bag.

"Is that where you're going to stuff my body once you've murdered me?" I ask pleasantly.

Neither one cracks a smile, so I roll my eyes and open the note that Artem has left for me. His writing is aggressive yet sleek. Captures his personality perfectly.

He doesn't bother with pleasantries, either. That's also right on brand for him. No *"Good morning, Esme,"* or *"Hello, captive."*

Just this:

I want you to go shopping today. The driver knows where to take you. You will be accompanied by Leo and Vlad the entire time. I've attached a list of items you will need. See that you get them all. If you don't, then I will be forced to choose for you. Vlad will take care of payments with the contents of the duffel bag.

I glance at the duffel bag and then at blue-eyed Vlad. "Open the bag," I tell him curiously.

To my surprise, he starts to unclasp the buckles and unzips it. This is the only instruction he's followed to date.

When he does, I see stacks of crisp hundred-dollar bills stuffed inside. It's packed to the gills—which means there's probably tens of thousands of dollars in that one bag alone.

I let out a low whistle.

Vlad doesn't seem to care one way or the other, though. He just zips up the bag and gestures me out of the apartment.

Apparently, he has exit clearance, because his fingerprint opens the elevator doors. The three of us get into it.

"One happy little family," I mutter sarcastically under my breath.

My jovial bodyguards don't even blink in response.

20

ESME

The car waiting for us outside Artem's condominium building is a luxury sedan limo. Papa used to own a similar one a few years back.

When I duck inside, I find a fully stocked minibar in the center console and a pair of designer sunglasses on the seat next to me.

Vlad and Leo get in the seats up front, leaving me to enjoy the rear compartment in silence.

I sit quietly as we drive through the streets of LA. When we finally come to a stop, Vlad gets out first and opens the door for me.

I step out onto the bright streets of Rodeo Drive right in front of a huge and intimidating Armani store.

"Go on," he tells me. "We wait here."

I find myself moving forward into the store.

The whole place drips of money and luxury. The floors are exquisitely carpeted, the air is perfumed, and the salespeople look like runway models.

In comparison, I feel like a hag.

The woman who walks up to me is a foot taller than I am in her six-inch heels. Her blonde hair is tied back in a sleek bun and the stunning ombre wrap dress she's wearing complements her slender frame.

"Welcome to Armani, ma'am," she says with a tight smile. "How can I serve you today?"

As ridiculous as it is, I find myself freezing up with self-consciousness.

The truth is I've never done much shopping. Deliveries of clothes came into my father's compound regularly, but I never went out to purchase them myself. Strictly one way traffic.

So now, I'm overwhelmed and out of my depth and my mouth is opening and closing like a fish that's flopped its way onto dry land.

"Ma'am?" the woman says with a touch of concern.

"I... um... came to... shop," I say awkwardly, mentally cringing at myself.

No shit, Sherlock. So did everyone else here. That's why people go to stores.

"Of course, ma'am," the saleswoman says, taking my pathetic answer in stride. She's polite, but there's nothing warm about her. "Is there anything in particular you're looking for?"

"Umm... I have a list," I say, pulling out Artem's list and looking through it.

I feel one of my guards step forward as I'm busy trying to read the first item on the piece of paper.

"Mr. Kovalyov sends his greetings," Leo tells the gorgeous blonde.

Instantly, her perfectly arched eyebrows shoot to the top of her Botox'd forehead.

She turns to me with the brightest smile I've ever seen. "You're a friend of Mr. Kovalyov's? Well, we're honored that you chose to visit our establishment. Please, ma'am, come this way. I'm Yvonne and I'll be happy to assist you today."

Suddenly, she is all warmth and radiance as she leads me through the massive store towards a private dressing room at the back.

My guards retreat back outside while I trail along after Yvonne, still feeling very much out of my element.

The dressing suite is a big circular space, complete with a silver-grey sofa and a coffee table bearing buckets of champagne on ice.

"Would you mind if I looked at the list?" Yvonne asks.

I hand it over with relief. She scans it quickly and nods.

"Wonderful," she says, passing the note back to me. "Why don't you make yourself comfortable and I'll be back with some options for you?"

I take a seat next to the champagne and marvel at how quickly things had changed once Artem's name got dropped.

I'm willing to bet that's going to happen in every store I visit today.

A few minutes later, Yvonne walks back in, followed by several men pushing garment racks.

I stare at the four separate garment racks in the dressing room with me. One rack holds evening gowns. Another has cocktail dresses. The third has simpler, day-to-day looks along with skirts and blouses.

"Once you're done selecting your top choices from these options, we can bring in the rest," Yvonne tells me enthusiastically.

I frown. "There's more?"

"Oh, there's so much more, ma'am," Yvonne says with a grin.

She's not kidding. I spend the next two hours trying on different clothes.

Most are mind-bogglingly beautiful. All are mind-bogglingly expensive.

I feel like I'm trapped in some perverse Cinderella story.

Except that in this version, Cinderella is being forced to marry the prince, who's more brutal than charming and she also happens to be pregnant with his child, though she's keeping that from him, even though they already had sex in a club bathroom months ago and then parted ways without exchanging names, and that would've been the end of it but then he came charging back into her life to murder her father and burn down the only home she's ever known...

So, on second thought, maybe not so Cinderella-y after all.

"Ma'am, may I pour you a glass of champagne?" Yvonne asks, cutting through the dark bend my thoughts were taking.

"Uh... no, thanks."

She raises her eyebrows as though I'm the first client ever to turn down champagne. I probably am.

"I'm... on a cleanse?" I offer, though it sounds like I'm asking her a question.

She brightens and nods. "Of course, ma'am. Can I get you anything else? A mocktail, perhaps, or fresh juice? Whatever you need, just say the word."

"I'm not hungry, but thank you," I reply nervously.

She gives me a strange look but she covers it up with the same false smile she's been wearing for the past two hours. "Not a problem. Allow me to bring in our next selection of outfits for you."

I sigh and slump down in the closest chair. I'm exhausted already.

Half an hour later, I finally leave the store with a few items ticked off the list Artem gave me.

But I'm nowhere near complete.

Crew Cut and Blue Eyes—I keep forgetting which one is Vlad and which one is Leo, and they're not particularly eager to remind me—take me to five more stores down Rodeo Drive.

In each store, it's the same song and dance. The only thing that changes is that I start dropping Artem's name before his guards do.

The reaction is consistently amazing. Salespeople transform before my eyes the moment they hear who's sent me.

Their austere smiles turn warm, they become more talkative, and their only concern is keeping me happy.

They shower me with compliments the entire time we're together, fawning over everything from my hazel eyes to my hourglass figure.

They're so effusive that it's hard for me to believe any of them.

But I don't deny that, for the first few hours, it is fun.

Each store offers me a selection of food and beverages as I try on their clothes. I always turn down the champagne, but I accept the delicate little finger sandwiches and petit fours.

And yet, when I walk out of the Prada store in the early evening, I'm exhausted, hungry, and most of all, thirsty.

Do people in L.A. drink champagne instead of water, I wonder?

"Is that it?" I ask Crew Cut. "Am I done for the day?"

"There's one more place that Mr. Kovalyov wants you to visit," he replies soberly.

Knowing it would be pointless to argue, I get in the car and we're off to yet another designer store.

When I step out of the car, however, I freeze in front of the store's elaborate façade.

The mannequins in the store's display window are wearing the sexiest lingerie I have ever seen. Straps in places I didn't know straps could go. Sheer fabric over bits that I'd always thought were meant to be covered.

I blush before I manage to get ahold of myself.

It's just clothing, Esme.

I glare at Blue Eyes, who's not even looking at me.

"Is this it where I'm meant to be going?" I ask.

"Yes."

That's when I start to get mad.

Gritting my teeth in anger, I practically march into the store, indignation coursing through me.

Artem has some nerve, expecting me to whore myself up for his pleasure. He thinks I'm going to come back to his penthouse all dolled up in this shit?

I glance over at a bejeweled thong and shiver.

Not in a million fucking years.

But when I walk further into the store, I find myself stopping and glancing around with grudging admiration.

Their pieces are certainly sexy and very beautiful.

I end up in a dressing room again. This time, the saleswoman is a tall, statuesque red head named Monica.

Despite my annoyance, I can't help but try a few of the pieces she suggests for me.

Some are subtle—black silk teddys with intricate details across the breasts.

Others are more risqué—sheer bras with body harnesses.

And there are other options that actually make me blush, like the selection of crotchless Ouverte briefs and strap thongs that reveal more than they hide.

After I've tried on a few pieces, however, I wave them all away and shake my head.

Something has just occurred to me.

A way to take a little bit of control back for myself.

Monica's lovely, charcoal-ringed eyes go wide with disappointment as she glances at me.

"You don't like anything, ma'am?" she asks.

"Actually, I think every piece you've shown me is gorgeous," I tell her. "But it's not what I'm looking for."

She looks at me with confusion. I just give her a smile, refusing to explain what I mean. "I think I'd like to take a look around the store myself."

I walk around for about fifteen minutes with Monica tailing me the entire time.

Until I turn and see a mannequin a few feet away from me and my eyes light up.

"That's it," I say, pointing. "That's what I want."

"Uh… are you sure, ma'am?" Monica asks, clearly surprised.

"I'm sure," I say with a wicked smile. "Very, very sure."

Gilded Cage

Ten minutes later, I walk out of the lingerie store feeling as though I've finally got one up on Artem.

It's probably only a temporary high, but I'll take my wins where I can get them.

There's one other thing left on my own personal agenda, though.

Before I get into the car, I turn to Crew Cut.

"I want to stop by a pharmacy."

He frowns. "Why?"

My eyes flare wide as I stare him down. "Would you like me to give you a detailed explanation of my lady problems?"

He looks instantly uncomfortable. I have to resist the urge to laugh.

It's the most expressive I've seen him all day.

"Okay, we'll stop by a pharmacy," he nods. "But you have only ten minutes."

When we get to the pharmacy, I hurry inside as Blue Eyes stays by the entrance. Thankful to have gotten a few moments of privacy, I steal towards the pharmacist's counter and stop in front of the portly older woman behind a glass partition.

"What can I help you with, dear?" she asks without so much as looking up at me.

My fingers shake just a little, but I ring them together and force them back to steadiness.

I need to do this.

But I absolutely cannot let Artem find out.

"Um… I just need to know… what do I take for a healthy pregnancy?"

21

ARTEM

ARTEM'S OFFICE

I close the page on one file and reach for the next one just as Cillian appears at the door to my office.

His brow furrows.

"Can I help you?" I drawl.

"According to the boys, you've been here all day."

"And that's cause for concern?"

Cillian steps into my spacious office and crosses the room. He rests his hands on the chair opposite my desk but he doesn't sit down.

"It's not like you to spend the day at the office," he says. "Much less spend it doing paperwork. Can you even read?"

"Fuck off," I mutter.

He's not wrong, but I need the distraction. There's a certain dark-haired temptress at home who was making it very difficult for me to control my baser impulses.

It doesn't help that I know exactly how giving into those impulses would feel.

Last night after dinner, my cock had risen with my anger. I'd been forced to jack off to the memory of our night together in The Siren. I was disgusted by how irresistible the temptation was.

"Anyway, someone needs to do it," I say dismissively. "And I know you're not much of one for administrative tasks."

"And someone will," Cillian replies. "I just never expected *you* to be that someone. Especially considering you have a fiancée at home waiting for you."

I raise my eyes to him. "Don't do that."

"Don't do what?" he asks innocently.

"Don't pretend that this is anything like a real relationship," I say. "She's not my fiancée. She's not my anything. And she's certainly not waiting for me."

"And thus we've arrived at the heart of the issue. You're avoiding her!" he announces triumphantly. He looks way too pleased with himself.

Sometimes, the fucker knows me a little too well.

"I had work to do," I say gruffly, looking down at the open file without actually seeing anything there.

"Sure you did," Cillian nods. "And I'm not Irish."

I crack a smile and lean back in my seat. "I haven't managed to beat that out of you yet, huh?"

"Never," Cillian scoffs. "My family and country may have turned their backs on me, but I'll never turn my back on them."

"They lost a good man the day you left Ireland."

Cillian smiles. "But you won because of it."

I roll my eyes while I chuckle, but I can already sense Cillian moving off the topic of his complicated past. We don't go down that road too often. It holds a lot of hard memories for him.

"So… how has it been going, with Esme?"

"We're back to that topic, are we?"

"It's just a question."

"Doesn't have to be."

"Tough shit."

I sigh. "It's fine."

"You told her about the marriage?"

"I did."

I know that my short answers are probably revealing more than I'd like, but I can't bring myself to elaborate.

How can I explain to Cillian when I barely understand what's going on myself?

I've battled half the day trying to get her out of my head. Every time I close my eyes, I keep seeing her in that sexy silver dress, her shoulders on display, her face natural and glowing like she was the fucking moon.

And then I picture fucking her until we're both ragged and spent.

"And?" he prompts.

I rub my temples. I can feel a headache on the horizon.

"She was so happy that she dropped down on her knees and gave me a world-class blowjob," I drawl. "How the fuck do you think she reacted?"

Cillian shrugs. "Hey, there are quite a few ladyfolk out there who'd love to be trapped in a forced marriage with you."

"Yeah, and I'm sure you're one of them."

Cillian laughs. "Do you think the reason you're trying to avoid her is because you're attracted to her?"

I narrow my eyes at him. "I never said I was trying to avoid her."

Cillian rolls his eyes and sighs. "Fine, whatever. You don't want to talk about her, that's fine. Let's change the subject."

"I'd love to."

"…to your bachelor party."

I groan and curse in Russian. "*Passossee mayee yaitsa*, are you fucking serious?"

"That's why I'm here in the first place," Cillian tells me. "I'm here to wrangle you and bring you in. We can even go to The Siren. I know how much you love that club."

I tense slightly, searching his face for clues.

But there are none. He still doesn't know why I'd been frequenting The Siren so often the last several months.

Which means he doesn't know that my interest in The Siren has disappeared now that Esme has re-entered the picture.

"I'm not in the mood for a club tonight, Cillian."

Cillian's smile drops instantly. "Well, too fucking bad! You don't have a choice. This bachelor party is happening. And if you wanna call it off, you'll have to go down and tell Budimir and the boys yourself."

I raise my eyebrows. "My uncle is downstairs?"

"Big time," Cillian nods. "You wanna tell the second biggest boss in this business that he's not gonna get to party because you're on the fucking rag?"

"Right, because my presence is essential for Budimir to enjoy himself. He owns half the clubs in the goddamn town. He can party whenever he wants."

"Don't be a prick," Cillian says. "Just come to the club with us. We'll drink a little, dance a little, fuck a little, and then it'll be over and you can be a boring celibate married guy if you want. Okay?"

The corner of my mouth twitches up in a smile even as I exhale frustratedly. "Jesus. Fine. You're in a goddamn *mood*."

"Yes!" Cillian smiles, punching the air. "Let's get going."

I stand and reach for my jacket. Cillian turns and whistles slowly as I put it on.

"Fucking hell, now *that's* a jacket. No way you picked that shit out yourself."

I grin. The jacket is one of the flashier ones I own, but it works. Fine leather in a deep rust red hue and flawless craftsmanship with every stitch.

Not every man could pull it off.

But I'm not every man.

Cillian and I take the elevator down to the lobby. When the doors open, there's a huge crew waiting for me on the other side, with my uncle heading the pack.

He throws his arms open when he sees me, a tilted smile on his chapped lips.

"It's time to say goodbye to the days of whoring and drinking, my boy," he tells me as I walk towards him.

I smirk at him. "Is that so? I wasn't aware that whoring and drinking put a stop to anything. As I recall, you've been married three times and nothing ever stopped for you."

Budimir laughs and shrugs. "Your father and I are Kovalyov men," he says. "Our appetites are tremendous. One woman will never be enough for us."

He claps me on the back but it feels almost like a rebuke. I know he's referring to the fact that during my marriage to Marisha, I was faithful only to her, something that my uncle had never truly understood.

"As I'm sure you will never be enough for any woman," I bite back, softening my words with a smile.

My uncle just laughs it off and pushes me towards the waiting procession of vehicles outside.

Budimir, Cillian, and I get into one of the SUVs together and head off towards the Siren.

I'm not thrilled about going there, but I figure Cillian has made plans and I don't want to disrupt them.

More to the point, I just want to get through this night as fast as possible so I can be done with it once and for all.

"So," Budimir says, giving me a salacious smile, "how's the girl?"

I don't love the way he says "girl," but I need to project an attitude of indifference where Esme is concerned.

Though, I'm not sure if that's more for my sake or everyone else's.

"I don't give a fuck," I answer.

Budimir chuckles. "I would have thought you would, especially after everything I've heard about her."

My eyes snap to his face immediately. "Which is what, exactly?"

Budimir shrugs. "That's she's quite the beauty," he says innocently. "And that she's got a tight little ass on her, too."

I grit my teeth and try to pretend like it doesn't bother me that all my men have obviously been ogling my woman.

That thought stops me in my tracks.

When did I start thinking of Esme as *my* woman?

"I think you need to get laid tonight, Uncle," I say, trying to steer the topic away from Esme.

"You're right about that," he nods. "It's been almost a week since I've had new pussy."

Cillian and I exchange a glance. We're used to Budimir and his insatiable appetite. But sometimes I wish he traveled in his own circles instead of ours.

The Siren is packed when we arrive, but of course we stride in without a problem.

Glass tables bearing bottles of expensive whiskey beckon under the lights. There's enough alcohol to kill an army of elephants.

My uncle slaps me on the back and grins. "Whiskey for the whiskey man," he jokes, steering me towards a bottle. "My treat."

I give Budimir a grateful nod for arranging the display, but I refrain from telling him that my desire for alcohol has dwindled significantly in the past few days.

The whole entourage moves forward, each group taking a table and helping themselves to a drink.

I stand back, feeling strangely removed from everything and everyone.

"Come on, brother," Cillian says, coming up next to my shoulder. "Try and enjoy yourself tonight."

I just nod and take a seat at a booth next to my uncle.

He's already pouring himself a drink, his eyes trained on the dance floor a few feet below us, where a group of young women are dancing.

His eyes linger on their asses, their breasts. He's not subtle—but his position in this city means he doesn't need to be.

I look at the women. It's easy to see why Budimir is watching them. They're young, sexy, definitely looking for attention.

But that's the very reason I turn from them.

Because they aren't *her*.

Though I can't help but notice they are dancing in the same spot where I first noticed Esme.

That image is stuck in my head. Her eyes had been closed, her head tilted back, her hair flowing around her shoulders as though she were in freefall.

She hadn't been concerned about being noticed, which was exactly what was so fucking beguiling about her.

"See something you like, Artem?" Budimir asks, drawing my attention back to the present.

"Not really."

"That's okay," he replies with a wink. "I have a few other surprises planned for tonight."

I have to suppress a sigh, but I don't need to ask because I have a good idea about the kind of surprise that Budimir has in mind.

Strippers.

Hookers.

Drugs.

Drinks.

Everything our money and power can get us, in quantities that would kill lesser men.

None of it is appealing in the least.

I wonder what Esme is doing right now. She spent the whole day shopping on Rodeo Drive.

A part of me secretly wishes I had been with her.

I relish the thought of sitting there while she parades in front of me in outfit after outfit, her body on display for me to admire.

To look at her and think, *I own that now*.

Something about the feeling that image provokes is unsettling.

I pull out my phone and check the live security feed of my penthouse. All I have to do is type in my password and I can see exactly what's going on in my apartment at any time.

I had three extra cameras installed in Esme's room before she arrived. It was just a precaution, but now I'm glad I did.

I see her sitting at her dressing table brushing out her hair. She looks tired, reserved.

She's wearing a long silky robe that covers her body entirely. Not an inch of skin to be seen, and yet she still looks like a fucking dream.

"What are you doing?"

I close the feed before Cillian can lean in and see what I'm up to.

"Nothing," I say quickly. "Just… work."

"It's your bachelor party, Artem," Budimir booms. "Put your fucking phone away! I'm going to make a toast."

A full glass is shoved in my hand and Budimir raises his already half-empty glass. All around us, his entourage does the same.

"To my nephew! May your new wife's pussy be as tight and beautiful as the rest of her."

My fingers clench around the glass I'm holding. I set it down quickly before I break it.

Everyone else drinks, so I'm hoping no one notices that I don't.

Unfortunately, Budimir doesn't shut his fucking trap once the toast is out of the way.

"Here are some words of advice, Artem," Budimir tells me. "Never forget who or what she is. Don't be fooled by her pretty face either, or the sweet nectar between her thighs. She'll seduce you like the whore she is, but she's never going to be loyal. Women don't know the meaning of the word."

I can feel the vein in my forehead throb.

"What makes you think she's a whore?" I growl before I can stop myself.

Budimir cocks one eyebrow. "She's a Moreno, isn't she?"

"After we're married, she'll be a Kovalyov."

"Grow up, boy," Budimir says, with a wave of his hand. "Taking a name doesn't make it your own. Do you really think she will forget that you murdered her father and destroyed her home? You're not marrying her to play house—you're marrying her to build an empire. She is and always will be expendable to you."

I can feel my temper flare with every word he speaks. I need to keep my feelings in check, but I keep seeing red.

It doesn't help that Budimir still does not fucking stop talking.

"But it doesn't matter what she feels inside," Budimir continues. "To the rest of the world, she must be a dutiful Bratva wife. And if she misbehaves, you can simply fuck her into submission."

My fists clench together.

"And if you don't have the stomach for that, tell me and I'll do it for you."

It takes all my strength not to upend the table and punch Budimir in his saggy fucking face.

"You, Uncle?" I manage, as calmly as I can. "I'm surprised your cock even works at your age."

He chortles, but it cuts off a little too soon to be real. He searches my face.

"Touchy touchy, Artem. I meant no harm. I didn't realize you had developed... feelings for the woman so soon."

I scoff. "I haven't," I lie. "But I *have* claimed her. She is mine and no one else's cock gets anywhere near her."

Budimir bows his head, concealing his eyes from me for a moment. "As I said, I meant no offense. I'm just a tired old man out past his bedtime. In fact, I think I'll take my leave now."

He puts down the glass in his hand as he stands and offers a quick bow.

Then he's gone, leaving behind only a ridiculous wad of cash—par for the course when it comes to dear old Uncle Budimir—and a whiff of foul Russian cologne. His men file out behind him.

I frown, surprised by Budimir's abrupt departure and the manner in which he left.

But I'm not upset about it. I have no interest in enduring any more of his advice tonight.

"Well, you sure know how to kill a party," Cillian teases, moving to fill the seat that Budimir just vacated.

"It was that or I was gonna punch him in the face," I tell him. "This was the better option."

"Whatever you say, bossman," Cillian smiles. "Now that the old coot is gone, we can let loose."

22

ARTEM

Cillian and I spend the next hour in the booth shooting the shit. That is, until the women show up and capture Cillian's attention.

I, on the other hand, am not keen to entertain their advances.

Or anyone's, really.

So I sit where I am, smoking and brooding and generally trying not to think of Esme, which of course means she's the only thing I think about the entire time.

The party dies down slowly, as my men either go off to fuck the hooker of their choice or just drink and snort themselves into oblivion.

Cillian disappears for a bit with a voluptuous blonde.

When he returns, he has the biggest smile on his face.

"I take it she was a good lay?"

"Fucking hell, man, the sounds she made," Cillian sighs. "Even when I stuck my cock in her mouth... You wanna try her? Name's Ivory."

I roll my eyes. "I'm not taking your sloppy seconds."

"Mate, she's a fucking hooker," Cillian points out. "That ship has sailed."

"Cillian, I'm sorry, man, but I'm just not in the mood tonight," I say, unwilling to pretend any longer. "The night ends here for me."

"You serious?"

"Yeah. Thanks for the party, though." I stand, ready to duck out immediately. "You should stay and sample the rest of the goods."

"Jesus, fine," Cillian says, standing himself.

"What are you doing?"

"I'm coming with you."

"You don't have to—"

"I know, I know," he says, cutting me off. "And yet, I am. This party's pretty much over anyway."

I shrug. He's a grown man. He can make his own decisions.

The two of us make our way out of the club.

The line has long since vanished and the streets are practically empty. Since all our men are too drunk to drive, Cillian tries to hail a cab, but I stop him.

"Forget it," I say. "Let's just walk home."

"You sure?"

"Fuck it. It's a nice night."

"As you wish, your highness. It's your night. We'll do things your way."

We start walking, ears still pounding from the club. It really is a nice night. Clear, warm, quiet.

"What're you eyeing me like that for?" I ask Cillian after a while. "Feels like you're about to knock me out and steal my kidneys or some shit like that."

Cillian shakes his head. "That's one snazzy fucking jacket, man."

I laugh. "You wanna try it on?"

"Fuck yeah I do. Hand it over."

Still laughing, I remove the jacket and pass it to him. He pulls it on and laughs triumphantly. "Well, do I look like a fucking don now, or what?"

"You need to work out more, man," I snort. "You don't fill out that jacket like I do."

"Asshole. You're never getting this shit back now."

We turn into a narrow alleyway so that we can cut across to the other side of the street. It's only a block or two from here to my apartment building.

That's when I hear two voices.

"... quickly... which one...?"

"...said it would be the one in the red jacket!"

Then, before either one of us can react, I see a tire iron swing out of the shadows and crash against the back of Cillian's head.

It makes a sickening *thunk*. Cillian crumbles to the ground.

Fury burns through me as I whip around and grab the arm that holds the tire iron. I pull the son of a bitch out of the shadows and twist his arm before crashing it down against my knee.

The crack of bone snaps through the air, followed by an agonized scream.

I hear the second mugger curse in a panic, but I don't allow him the opportunity to run. He's holding a tire iron of his own, but there's also a dagger in his other hand.

I headbutt him into a wall, snatch the dagger out of his hand, and stab him in the stomach in one smooth motion.

He lets out a pathetic little squeak as I bury it to the hilt. Blood oozes out, hot and thick.

I sneer at his wide, fearful eyes before he drops to the ground.

Then I turn to Cillian, who's clutching the back of his head. His fingers come away sticky with blood.

He groans and rolls over to look at the limp, unconscious bodies of the two attackers.

"That's a fancy knife," he says with a pained whistle.

"Probably stolen," I answer. "Come on, let's go. Before we draw attention to ourselves."

I help him to his feet. He's breathing heavily, but he'll be all right.

"Jesus," Cillian mutters, as we walk out of the alleyway, trying to look calm and unflustered. "Fucker packed a punch."

"You gonna be okay?"

"Yeah. But your jacket nearly got me killed."

I frown. "Huh?"

"Right before they attacked," he explains in a wheeze. "They said, 'the one in the red jacket.' Leave it to me to pay attention to the details." He stops, shrugs out of the jacket, and hands it back to me. "You can have it back. I don't like red anyway."

"Not interested in being the don anymore?" I ask, half-amused and half-concerned.

"I never was," Cillian sighs. "Another reason my family kicked me out of Ireland."

"I thought they kicked you out of Ireland because you killed a politician's son?"

"Fucking hell, I just got whacked in the head with a fucking tire iron. Do we really need to dig into my personal history right now? I could have brain damage."

I grin. "How would we ever be able to tell?"

"Fuck off," he mumbles, but he's chuckling.

I'm laughing, but I am worried about the damage that initial hit has done to his head. He seems fine, but you can never be too sure.

"I'm calling the doctor. We need to get that wound checked out," I tell him. "No arguments."

"Fine," Cillian concedes. "You fuss like my grandma."

"You're welcome by the way," I prod. "You know, for saving your life."

Cillian sighs dramatically. "You're not going to let me live this down, are you?"

I shrug. "Story of my life. I'm always saving your ass."

23

ARTEM

"Well, Doc?" Cillian quips. "Will I live?"

Dr. Sokolov is on call for the Bratva twenty-four-seven. He's a second-generation Russian immigrant who's pushing sixty and trying to turn back the clock.

His blonde highlights catch the unnaturally bright lights of the medical room that's been built into the back of his sprawling Beverly Hills home. He's been in the Bratva's employ for almost two decades now.

Judging solely by the pricey furniture we saw on the way in here, it's going pretty well for him.

"You'll live," Sokolov says mildly. "I just need to put in a few stitches."

"Gently, please," Cillian says.

"Don't be a bitch," I scold him.

Sokolov grabs his head and pushes it front facing. "No moving. No talking, either."

I catch Cillian's eye from where I'm sitting in a nearby armchair. "Do you need me to hold your hand?"

"I had to drink for you and me both since you were being a baby tonight," he retorts. "Can't feel a thing."

"Ah, the beauty of youth and alcohol," Sokolov chuckles. "Don't worry. I'll clean you up and finish the stitches. Shouldn't take more than half an hour or so."

"You don't need to stay," Cillian tells me. "Contrary to what you might think, I don't actually need you to hold my hand."

"I'm not convinced," I smirk.

Cillian flips me off. "For real. I'm good. Fuck outta here."

Grinning, I grab my jacket. "Okay then. Call me tomorrow and let me know how you're doing."

"If you insist, Pops," Cillian replies, with that shit-eating smile of his.

"So much for the hooker in a sexy nurse costume I was gonna send over to your place as a get-well-soon present." I get up and make for the door. "Make sure those stitches hurt when you put them in, Doc!"

I call a Bratva car to pick me up and drive me back to the apartment.

Esme's probably asleep by now. I tell myself that my need to check on her is purely business, nothing more.

But I don't even sound convincing. Not even to myself.

When the elevator doors open to my penthouse, I notice the lights are still on in the sitting room.

I move forward and turn the corner. The room kind of melts into the background as my eyes focus on the woman lounging on the sofa with her legs kicked up.

She straightens up a little when she sees me and flips her dark locks for effect.

"There you are," she says, with a raspy familiarity that doesn't immediately register. "I've been waiting all night."

I stare at her, confused by what I'm seeing. Esme stands slowly, a wicked little twinkle in her eye as she gives me a smile that makes my cock twitch.

It would have been completely hard by now...

If it weren't for the fact that she's wearing the ugliest lingerie I've ever seen in my life.

As though she knows what's running through my head, she fingers the frilly fabric that ends just below her pussy and gives me an elaborate twirl.

"What do you think?" she asks, as though it's a serious question. "You like it?"

It looks like a moomoo with sporadic cutouts dipped in neon green paint and sewn together by a whole factory's worth of baby doll frills. And then there's the purple leopard print patches...

I'm literally speechless.

What kind of sick fuck can take something as sexy as lingerie and make it... *this*?

I can tell that Esme's enjoying the moment. She picked it out for this exact purpose, I'm sure.

Trying to fuck with me. Get inside my head. Seize back control of whatever you'd call this dynamic between us.

She's made one mistake, however.

She let me see the fire in her eyes.

That's what does it for me. What's always done it for me.

Bare-faced, bright-eyed, she looks as sexy as she did the night I met her at The Siren.

If I block out that disgusting lingerie and focus only on her face, I'm as hard for her as I've ever been.

"Well?" she pushes.

I cock my head to the side. I know I need to be very careful. More careful than usual, even.

Because when it comes to Esme Moreno, I'm not as in control as I like to be.

"You chose that for me?" I ask faux-innocently.

"I did," she murmurs, her eyes flashing dangerously, despite the smile she wears. "I thought it was important you see me in this."

"Oh? And why is that?"

She comes forward, moving gracefully despite the ugly thing she's wearing.

She stops only inches from me. Her perfume fills my nostrils, and it only serves to make my cock harder than ever.

She's at least a head shorter, but by the way she's looking at me, you'd think she was twice my height.

Gazing right up into my eyes, she lets a teasing smile play across her lips. Subtle, tempting, delicious.

Then the smile drops off her face and her hazel eyes turn gold with anger.

She hisses, "So you know that I'm not your fucking china doll."

There it is, I think.

The fire.

The fury.

Fuck—I love it.

"Who the hell do you think I am?" she continues.

The sexy whisper is gone. Her voice is rising into a fever pitch now.

"How dare you send me off to a fucking lingerie store to tart me up like one of your whores? You're not the boss of me, Artem Kovalyov. You're not *anything* to me. You may command every brainless puppet in this city, but I'm not one of them. I'm not your little fuck doll and you don't get to dress me up like one."

I just stand there, still as a statue, and watch her rage at me.

My eyes land on her lips first. I fucking love the way she says my name—I don't even care that it's in anger. Honestly, that makes it better.

Her cheeks burn red with fury. Her eyes sizzle with passion.

And my cock is so damn hard that it's fucking painful.

"Did you hear me?" she asks. "I'm not your goddamn fuck doll!"

I stare at her full breasts rising and falling with exertion, baby doll frills moving right along with her.

In the end, that's what does it.

That's the straw that breaks the camel's back.

I can't abide the sight of that horrendous piece of filth anymore. I just want *her*—bare, beautiful, bitchy as hell.

I snatch her hand from her side and yank her towards me. She stumbles in shock and lets out a delicious little gasp as she falls into my torso.

The desire to be inside her is so intense that I have to fight hard not to fuck her right through her hideous lingerie.

But first, I need to teach her a lesson.

"Let go of me!" she snarls as she struggles against my hold. "I told you, I'm not your doll."

But my grip on her is viselike. She can barely move.

Fear snakes across her tone, but I catch something else, too. Something familiar.

She wants me.

Just like I want her.

"You are what I say you are," I growl at her, my voice low and heavy with lust.

I push her back to arm's length, grab two fistfuls of the green material, and rip it right off her.

She gasps again as the teddy comes off in one clean tear, leaving her standing before me in nothing but a pair of sheer panties.

Her hands scramble to cover her body. It's futile, though, and she knows that.

"Don't," Esme says. Her voice trembles.

But we're long past that.

I peel her hand off her, exposing her breasts.

They're even more glorious than I've imagined. Perfect full globes, high and perky with taut little nipples that are as hard as I am.

She moves backwards. "Don't do this, Artem," she tells me, as her back hits the wall.

She shouldn't have said my name. That only stokes the fire more.

"Me?" I shake my head. "You're the one that did this."

I corner her at the wall and put both my hands on either side of her head, trapping her.

I'm desperate to touch her heaving breasts. My tongue yearns to lick across one of those pink nipples.

But even that doesn't feel like enough.

I want more of her.

I want all of her.

I want to lick her from head to toe and fuck her until I can't thrust even one more time.

If I don't bury myself in Esme Moreno right this goddamn second, I'm going to explode.

I go straight for her panties. Knocking her other hand out of the way, I rip them once, twice, until they finally surrender and tear apart.

So close. Only a few more layers left between us.

I press closer, letting her feel my hardness.

She's completely bare now, naked and vulnerable, and I'm still fully dressed.

But her eyes are bright and filled with a strength that belies her tiny frame.

"You can take my body," she says. "But you'll never have *me*."

I narrow my eyes. "We'll fucking see about that."

That makes me pause for a moment.

I know what she expects me to do next.

She expects me to pull out my cock and fuck her senseless—at least until I get mine.

She expects me to be rough, selfish... angry.

So I'm going to give her the exact opposite. A lesson she'll never forget.

She thinks I'm just going to pillage her and leave her ruined? Well, yes, I am—but not that fast. Not that sudden.

No, this is going to be a long, slow burn. Torturously slow.

It'll be a lesson she never forgets.

I lean in, pressing my chest against hers. Her hands hang at her sides, limp and slightly shaky.

She's trying not to engage, not to touch me. She thinks she can remain removed from whatever's about to happen.

That choice went out the window a long time ago, though.

My tongue slips out and tangles with her ear. She starts wriggling underneath me, still refusing to touch me.

I smile as I hear her breathing get heavier, more labored. She's got to fight me as well as her own desire now.

Her nipples pierce through the fabric of my shirt. I'm confident that she's already wet, but I can't wait to find out any longer.

I place my fingers between her breasts and she shudders.

Just a little.

Just enough.

Then I trail my touch down her flat belly, towards her trembling thighs.

My hand settles between them and pushes them apart. It doesn't escape my notice that I don't have to push very hard.

Esme's eyes still flare with anger, but her body betrays her at every turn.

"You know what?" I ask, my breath slick against her soft skin.

"What?" she bites back.

"I think you're full of shit."

Her eyes go wide with anger. But she doesn't move.

"I think you *want* to be my fuck doll," I continue.

I want to piss her off. To push her over the edge and make her feel what she makes me feel.

"I'm *nobody's* fuck doll," she seethes.

"Wrong," I say as my fingers run delicately up and down the insides of her thighs.

Then I move in for the kill, brushing like a whisper over her pussy lips. She shudders and gasps, and for a moment, her eyes close.

"I own you."

And then I push two fingers inside her.

Her eyes fly open. She stares into my face with shocked awe. Utterly wordless.

I could come just looking at her. The way she stands there, open-mouthed and gasping...

Just as I'd suspected, she's wet. Soaking wet, in fact.

But not yet wet enough for me. I want her so wet she's dripping down my hand.

I push my fingers deeper inside her. She moans and her hands shoot forward and cling to my shoulders.

"St—stop.." she gasps.

I don't pull away. "Say that again," I tell her. "And this time, mean it."

"I, uh... fuck... I do..."

I chuckle darkly as I keep plowing into her wetness, savoring the feel of her juices slicking my fingers.

She's trembling now, her pupils dilated, and she's trying so hard not to moan a second time that she's actually biting her bottom lip.

"Like I said," I whisper in her ear, as I continue finger-fucking her, "I own you, Esme. You're my dirty little fuck doll, aren't you, *kiska*? Come on now, moan for me. Moan like you want to."

She bites down on her lip harder and shakes her head.

I just smile.

Esme is stubborn, even when she's at my mercy. I should be annoyed by that, but I can't help admiring it.

I want her so fucking bad that the desire to just pull my cock out and take her against the wall is a never-ending temptation.

But I want more of this, too. More torturing her with her own desire.

I want to see her lose control at my hand.

I want to see her come with my eyes clear—without the distraction of my own imminent orgasm.

I can see little pearls of perspiration start to form on the skin just above her breasts. As I continue to delve into her, I drop my head down and lick the sweat right off.

A startled little moan escapes her lips before she clamps them shut again. Fueled by that sound, my tongue wraps around her plump, pink nipple and I start sucking hard.

And that's when she starts to truly lose it.

Her mouth falls open once more with a little pop and I feel her fingers entangle in the hair at the back of my head.

But she's not trying to pull me off her.

On the contrary, she's trying to hold on for dear life.

Desperate to ride out the storm.

Her breath comes out in gasping bursts and I take advantage of her vulnerability as I slip a third finger inside her. I can feel her tighten around me, as her juices start slipping down my fingers onto my hand.

"Oh… oh, God… fuck…"

I release her nipple and look at her face. It's flushed, uninhibited. She looks dazed, disoriented.

Utterly at my mercy.

"Yeah, you like that, *kiska*?" I rasp, looking her right in the eye.

I'm sweating through my shirt now. I wish I was as naked as she is, but I can't bear to withdraw my hand right now, not even for a fraction of a second.

Not before she comes.

"You're my slutty little fuck doll, aren't you?" I continue.

Her gaze burns into me. She's unable to stop me, and I know she doesn't really want to, but she's not going to give me what I want, either.

At least, not willingly.

"Fuck. You," she breathes.

I grind my fingers deep inside her while my thumb lands on her clit. I circle fast, teasing her until she's shuddering against me, her breasts sweaty and heaving, one leg raised high so that I can reach her better.

She's laid open for me, but I can feel her still holding something back. One last shred of resistance.

"Come on, Esme," I growl in her ear. "Come on my hand. Come on my hand like the fuck doll I know you want to be."

Then I bore down on her clit and she screams, her back arching as she explodes over my hand.

And it's beautiful.

Absolutely fucking beautiful.

I pull my hand out of her and wipe it against my pants before I reach to start unzipping myself.

The time for games is over. I need to be inside her now.

I've suppressed the urge to burst for too fucking long.

But then I look up and catch her expression. Her cheeks are rosy, her lips slightly parted, her hair a wild sweaty mess that's pasted against her shoulders.

She looks so fucking satisfied.

She also looks so fucking sad.

That stops me in my tracks.

"Is this what you like?" she asks softly. Her voice barely rises above a whisper. "Having a helpless woman at your disposal? Forcing yourself on a woman who can't refuse?"

Her words send a jolt stinging through me.

I feel my cock deflate.

The desire coursing through my veins hits a wall suddenly and I feel my hands fall to my sides.

"Go," I growl. "Now. Get out of here."

She stares at me for a moment. Trying to figure out if I'm serious or not.

Then she slides out from underneath me and runs for her bedroom.

A second later, I hear the door slam shut.

I lean my forehead against the wall, the same one I had just made her come against.

And then I send my fist slamming into it.

Now, I've got a raging hard-on *and* bruised knuckles. I ignore the pain lancing through my hand and head straight for my bedroom.

I discard my sweaty clothes and without so much as sitting down, I start masturbating furiously, my head swimming with thoughts of Esme.

I relive the moment when I saw her breasts for the first time.

I relive the moment I sucked her nipples until she moaned and grabbed my hair.

I relive everything, again and again, until hot seed shoots out of me.

Only then can I breathe again.

The relief pours through me. Like I've purged her—fucking *finally*.

But that lasts for hardly a few seconds before it sets in again—the hunger. The burning, aching need for more of what I've just barely tasted.

That pisses me the fuck off.

I walk into my bathroom and turn on the shower. I step inside, and cold water assaults my body.

I welcome the prickly pain.

I stand there for a long time, trying to get her out of my head.

But twenty-five, almost thirty minutes later, I'm still consumed with thoughts of her, and only her.

"Fuck!" I yell to the empty cavern of my bathroom. My roars echo until they fade away.

I have to find a way to deal with this massive need inside me.

I have to fill it with something other than Esme.

Because I know now, without a doubt, that something terrible is happening.

And I need to fucking end it.

24

ESME

I wake up the next morning, heart still hammering.

It had taken me hours to fall asleep and I still wasn't able to escape the dreams that plagued me.

"Nightmare" is the wrong word though.

More like a fucked-up fever dream. Part delicious, part horrifying.

I can still feel it all—everything that happened.

Artem's brutish hands on my body, gentle despite their size and strength.

The way he pinned me to the wall, taken what he wanted despite my feeble, dishonest protests.

I wish I had been stronger.

I wish I had fought harder.

But my body wanted him—even if my mind and heart didn't.

Liar.

I try and shake the self-made accusation from my head.

No, it's not a lie—I definitely do *not* fucking want Artem Kovalyov.

I'm just... confused.

I've spent four months fantasizing about this man. Is it any wonder I'm taking some time to adjust to the reality of him?

Fantasies are powerful things, especially for women like me who've spent so long living with no other means of escape.

But I'm ashamed of how much I gave him last night. Far more than I should have.

My body was laid out for him like a gift, my desire for him pooling between my thighs and running down his fingers.

And those fingers... I didn't think it was possible for a man to bring a woman to climax that way.

Yes, I'd seen it in movies and read about it in books, but it had always seemed like one of those scenes that were titillating more than realistic.

It felt like he had taken my body hostage. And when the orgasm had finished ripping its way through me, I was left breathless and scared and hungry for more.

And his face... that all-consuming, powerful, desirous expression he wore the entire time his fingers were inside me...

It was the sexiest thing I'd ever seen.

But perhaps the most shocking thing about last night was the fact that something I said had actually gotten through to him.

"Is this what you like?" I'd asked. *"Having a helpless woman at your disposal? Forcing yourself on a woman who can't refuse?"*

I saw his hunger extinguish instantly. The craving slipped off his face and left him bare and angry.

He had let me go and I had run, but even then, as I'd scampered back to my room, I wasn't sure if safety was what I really wanted or if it was just what I was *supposed* to want.

I sigh deeply and sit up. I'm still naked and reluctant to take a shower.

I tell myself it's not because I want the scent of him on me.

In order to prove that to myself, I get up and soak in the tub for twenty minutes.

When I move back into my bedroom, I pick ripped black jeans and a white cashmere sweater, two purchases from yesterday's shopping spree.

I'm just finishing dressing when there's a knock on my door and Crew Cut walks in with his usual sour expression.

"Your car will be here in twenty minutes," he says, like a programmed robot. "Breakfast is in the kitchen."

"Where are we going today?" I ask him. "More shopping?"

He doesn't bother replying. Just walks away.

I curse at his back and head into the kitchen. I'm not hungry, but I know it's important for me to eat. For my unborn child to eat.

So I sit at the table alone, eat a croissant, and wash it down with some cold milk. I take my vitamins discretely back in my room, then head to the foyer by the elevator.

Blue Eyes and Crew Cut are waiting for me. For the first time, I notice that both are in their usual suits, but they seem somehow dressier than usual.

"What's with the ties?" I ask when I spot the difference. "Is that a pocket square?"

Of course, neither one answers me. And when we walk out of the building, I'm more than a little surprised to see the stretch limo waiting for me.

"What the hell is this for?" I say to no one in particular, even as I get into the limo.

The drive is about fifteen minutes. The whole time, I try and figure out where I'm going that would require such a fancy ride.

Another question keeps nagging me, but I refuse to ask either one of my personal goons this time.

Where's Artem?

It's not until the limo stops in front of a grand cathedral that realization finally dawns on me.

"Oh, my fucking God."

Today is my wedding day.

Panic is the only thing I'm aware of. Like getting sucked under a huge wave in the ocean, it's all I can sense.

Then my door is pulled open and I start shaking my head.

"No," I shriek. "No! I'm not getting out. This can't happen!"

My bodyguards exchange a glance. Clearly, they're prepared for just such a reaction.

They move in on me as a single, emotionless unit.

I scream and kick and try to escape their claws. But I'm no match for them.

They succeed in dragging me out of the limo while I curse their mothers and spit at their faces.

"No! You can't do this!" I yell. "If Artem is such a strong fucking man, tell him to get out here and do this himself!"

Neither Blue Eyes nor Crew Cut seems inclined to do that.

Instead, Crew Cut grabs a hold of me and hoists me over his shoulder. He carries me into the cathedral, downstairs to a bottom level of the building, and into a corridor lined with rooms.

Blue Eyes opens a door for his comrade. I'm carried inside and deposited unceremoniously onto a soft sofa that cushions my rough landing.

"You fucking bastards, both of you!" I rage at them.

My bodyguards don't respond as they leave the room without a word.

Only then do I realize that I'm not alone. Not by a long shot.

In fact, there's a whole team of people in the large, carpeted room with stone walls that looks like something out of a medieval fairytale.

"Who the hell are you?" I demand.

An older woman with dark, curly hair steps forward, her expression sympathetic and almost apologetic.

She gives me an awkward smile. "I'm Alice," she says. "And this is my team. We've been hired to get you ready today, love. We'll need to start with your hair and makeup."

I blink at her, trying to wrap my head around the absurdity of the situation.

Is everyone just gonna pretend that I'm not being forced into marrying a Russian mobster?

"I don't want to do my make-up," I say. "I don't want to do my hair. I don't want to get married!"

Alice looks at the four people standing behind her, then back to me again. She kneels in front of me so that we're at eye level.

"Ma'am, I understand all that. But like you, we don't have a choice."

The way she says it, her tone dripping with fear, makes me pay attention.

Alice and her team are not at fault here. They are merely doing the job they've been hired for.

Or maybe they haven't been hired at all.

Maybe they're here because someone, somewhere made a deal with the devil and now it's payback time.

Maybe she's as trapped as I am.

"Please, ma'am," Alice continues. "If you struggle, it will be harder for all of us. The Bratva are dangerous men. If you stop fighting them and just accept your fate, things will go easier for you. For everyone."

Her tone sobers me and I find myself nodding, despite myself.

I don't want to accept anything. It's not in me to just accept being dealt a bad hand. I will always be searching for a way out, a means to escape.

But I know I have to be smart about it.

It may take time—but when it finally happens, I'll need it to work.

"You can call me Esme," I tell her softly.

She gives me a smile and leads me to the elaborate dressing table that's been set against one of the stone walls.

Alice and two other women get to work on my makeup. I just sit there and let them do what they want.

Looks like you're a doll after all, Esme. Nothing but a pretty little doll for men to dress up and move around as they please.

I swallow the tears bubbling up inside me and focus on Alice. She has a beautiful face, classical features, and sad, narrow eyes. She's probably in her fifties, but she's aged naturally and that makes her look younger.

When the other girls move to the other side of the room to do God knows what, I turn to Alice.

"What do you know about the Bratva?" I ask.

"Nothing good," she murmurs. "They're hardened men, ruthless and calculating. Trust me, it's better to submit than to fight. There is no such thing as mercy where the Bratva are concerned."

She doesn't tell me how she knows all this. I don't ask. Something tells me I won't like the answer anyway.

25

ESME

An hour later, Alice stands up and looks at me with satisfaction.

"There," she says. "You're perfect."

I turn back to the mirror, really looking at myself this time.

Alice has done an amazing job. She's kept my makeup natural, matching my skin tone perfectly. She's highlighted my eyes with bronze and charcoal eye shadow, and teased out my eyelashes so that they look much longer than usual. My lips are nude with only a slight hint of pink and my cheeks glow with just the faintest touch of rouge.

Thin braids frame my face and sweep into a delicate knot at the back of my head. The knot is clasped in place by a wreath of seed pearls that twist in and out of the bun, along with the braids.

Only a few stray locks of hair have been kept lose, a deliberate choice to frame my face and add to the romantic, dreamy feel of my bridal look.

"You're a vision," Alice says like a proud mother.

The funny thing is, I actually believe her.

"Now, it's time to put on the dress."

The moment she says those words, I go pale.

It just feels too real. Too much.

The reality of what I have to do next settles over me like a weight I can't move.

"No," I say softly.

"Esme, love, I know this is difficult…"

"I can't put on a dress," I say, dangerously close to tears. "I… can't get married."

Alice grabs my hands and gets ready to say something.

But before she can, the door bolts open. Alice jumps to her feet and backs away, releasing my hands as she turns to Crew Cut and Blue Eyes.

"She's not ready yet," she stammers.

"It doesn't matter," Crew Cut tells her. "The ceremony is about to start."

"You can't make me do this," I say, getting to my feet.

For the first time, Crew Cut meets my eyes.

"If you don't do it yourself," he tells me, "we'll be forced to get involved. Do you want us dressing you?"

My heart thuds unevenly in my chest. I know what will happen if I fight them. They've made that more than clear.

"Get out," I spit at them. "I'll be out in fifteen minutes."

The moment the door closes, Alice's team rushes forward with the dress. I try not to stare at it too much, but I can't help but notice that it really is a beautiful gown. Made of silk and chiffon, its A-line skirt is simple and classic and its bodice is worked with the same seed pearls that have been woven into my hair.

Once the dress is on, something is attached to my head and the veil is inserted right after.

I don't bother looking at myself in the mirror.

I don't care anymore.

"Are you ready?" Alice asks.

"No," I whisper. "But as everyone keeps reminding me, I don't have a choice."

Alice reaches out and squeezes my hand. "I'm sorry, love."

That's the last thing she says to me.

Then it's time to go.

26

ESME

I walk out of the room and out to where Crew Cut and Blue Eyes are waiting for me.

They lead me down the corridor, up the stairs, and into a huge space that's hundreds of feet high.

The ceiling is adorned with mosaic, tilework, and the most beautifully intricate paintings I've ever seen. But I allow myself only one glance before my eyes turn to what's before me.

The pews of the church are packed. I recognize precisely none of the faces that are crowded into the pews. There are a few women here and there, but it's mostly men—big Russian mobsters in their fine suits who look me up and down with lust.

I glance behind me but my bodyguards have disappeared into thin air. I'm standing there alone, dressed to the nines, about to walk down the aisle to…

Artem.

I see him at the very end of the aisle, standing next to a minister who doesn't really look like a minister.

I look down instantly. My heart beats furiously. Like it is trying to tell me something.

This is really happening. You can't escape it.

"Start walking," someone hisses at me.

I don't see who and I don't turn to look behind me.

I just start walking, trying to push back tears.

I will not cry in front of them. In front of any of them.

Everyone stands as I walk past. I'm amazed at the level of dedication to this farce. It's almost enough to make a girl feel like she's really getting married.

You are *getting married, Esme.*

Okay, fine, it's real, but it still isn't a true marriage.

The walk down the aisle is lonelier and more isolating than I could have imagined, but when I make it to the end, my eyes nonetheless search for the one face that's familiar to me.

I hate him, but for some reason I need to see him.

The man who stole me and murdered my father is dressed in a smart black suit. He's nearly clean shaven—only light stubble lines his square jaw.

His dark eyes are hooded, but they drink me in the same way they have since the moment we met.

He looks like a modern-day Adonis. Even if I hate to give him that much credit.

I realize that I've stopped moving only when someone pushes me towards the raised dais. Artem leans forward and takes my hand. He pulls me up next to him and then drops my hand almost immediately.

We turn to face the minister, who gives me a smile that's almost kind.

Then he starts talking and I block him out.

I can only hear my own thoughts—panicked, scared, and uncertain. But for some reason, a part of me has resigned myself to my fate just as Alice advised me to do.

I stand there like a statue as the minister says all the typical things you would hear at a real wedding.

When he asks me if I take Artem as my lawfully wedded husband, I don't even know if I answer out loud.

Maybe I do.

Maybe I don't.

This is all such a fucked-up nightmare that I'm not sure what's real and what's fake anymore. What's inside my head and what's actually happening.

Besides—no one in the cathedral gives a fuck either way.

This is happening whether I like it or not.

At some point, Artem takes my hand and slips a ring onto it. I stare at the gorgeous Princess cut diamond that reflects the sunlight streaming in through the stained glass windows above.

And then the minister speaks with finality.

"I now pronounce you man and wife," he says, in a low rumble. "You may kiss your bride."

The veil that's given me some small degree of protection through the entire ceremony is whisked over my head and then, all at once, he's kissing me.

I gasp as his lips thunder down on mine with furious possession.

I'm vaguely aware of clapping and whistling from the crowd, but all I can really absorb is this kiss.

I try desperately to pull up some kind of resistance to him, but it melts into dust when his lips coax open my mouth and his tongue slips inside.

My head spins for a moment, but he's holding me close and I know there's no chance that I'll fall.

Artem Kovalyov will never let me go.

He's the one who started this kiss and he's the one who ends it. He pulls back, leaving my lips raw and stinging as he looks down at me.

Then he leans in and whispers in my ear. Something in Russian.

"*Teper' ty moya navsegda.*"

"I don't know what you just said," I manage to stammer. It still sends a chill down my back all the same.

One corner of his mouth goes up in a dark tilted smile.

"You will soon enough," he rasps.

Then he hooks my hand around his arm and we move down the aisle to thunderous applause.

As we walk towards the cathedral's entrance, I'm able to take in more faces, people I wasn't capable of noticing before.

Like an older gentleman in a sharp black tux, insulated by a ring of the largest men I've ever seen.

It takes me only a second to figure out why he looks familiar.

He must be Artem's father.

The two don't exactly look alike, at least not physically. The familiarity is more in their mannerisms. The hooded, dangerous look burning in their dark eyes.

I expect Artem to stop, but he doesn't. He keeps walking past everybody until we emerge into the bright sunshine.

The limo is waiting for us at the steps of the cathedral. Artem walks me all the way down and opens the door for me.

I get inside, but he doesn't follow me.

For one moment, I actually think he's going to shut the door in my face and send me back to the apartment by myself.

Some fucking wedding day.

But then he ducks down and looks at me, framed by the car door.

"I have to speak to my father," he tells me. "It'll only be a moment."

He shuts the door. I sit there in the limo, trying to process what just happened.

I'm *married*.

Legally speaking, I'm a married woman now. That seems like it ought to be top of mind.

But strangely enough, I'm more preoccupied with what Artem said to me. The words he whispered in my ear.

Acting on impulse, I press the button to bring down the partition separating me from the driver.

The chauffeur glances back at me with surprise. Nervousness, too, like he's afraid of being caught talking directly to me.

I don't explain myself. I just repeat the words that Artem said to me back in the cathedral.

"Teper' ty moya navsegda." I say, enunciating as carefully as I can. "What does it mean?"

He raises his eyebrows and there's a second of silence.

"Tell me," I order with a confidence I don't really feel.

He licks his lips and sighs before saying, "It means, '*You're mine forever now.*'"

I hold the driver's pitying gaze for just a moment.

"Thank you," I say as I put the partition back up.

It takes everything I have not to scream.

27

ARTEM

"Congratulations, son."

Stanislav's face remains impassive even as he shakes my hand. His skin has a sallow complexion to it today but I refrain from asking about his health. He'd never forgive me if anyone overheard it.

Budimir and Cillian converge around me, saying more of the same. I accept their congratulations with a nod of my head.

"Don't look so somber, boy," Budimir says. "With a bride like that, you should be grinning from ear to ear."

"He is right to be cautious," Stanislav interrupts. "She may be your wife now, but she's still an unknown quantity. If she compromises our mission, then she will be terminated."

He says it coldly, his eyes flickering over to the limo where Esme is waiting for me.

I feel a surge of anger, but I bite it down.

This was always the plan. No sense in getting riled up about something I can't change.

So I just nod again. "I'll watch her."

"I'm sure you will," Budimir says salaciously.

I turn away from all of them and move down the stairs towards the limo. Cillian is the only one who comes with me.

"You are one lucky bastard," he tells me. "She looked like a fucking treat up there on the altar."

I scowl. "A treat that might kill me, you mean."

"Some treats are worth choking on, my friend," Cillian retorts with a wink. "Just… one bite at a time, you know?

"That's exactly what I plan on doing."

Cillian grabs my hand and pulls me in for a brotherly hug. Then he claps me on the back. "Enjoy your honeymoon. Don't break the bed."

"Stay out of trouble while I'm away," I tell him.

Cillian shrugs. "I'll do my best. No promises."

Then I duck inside the limo.

I glance towards Esme as we pull away from the cathedral, but she's not even looking at me.

She's sitting on the other end of the seat, as far away from me as she can manage, and staring out of the tinted windows.

I can't see her face at all. I'm sure that's not an accident.

I glance out the window myself. If she wanted to be left alone, then I'm happy to give her space. Fussing over her feelings is not my fucking job.

If she has issues, she can handle them herself.

Only when we come to a stop on the wide, open tarmac of the Bratva's personal airstrip, does she look toward me.

"Where are we going?"

"We're going on our honeymoon. Where else?"

She clenches her jaw. "I didn't agree to that."

"Do I look like I give a damn, princess?"

Before she can ask me anything more, I get out of the car, leaving her to maneuver out of the limo in her billowing dress on her own.

I'm halfway across the tarmac by the time she manages to unfold herself from the car. Against my better judgement, I glance back to see how she's doing.

Wind tugs against the folds of the skirts. Her hair has come loose from its bun, unruly locks whipping around in the harsh breeze.

She looks like my perfect fucking wet dream.

"I'm in a wedding dress," she snaps at me from where she stands a few yards away.

"You know what? I did notice that. Been meaning to say something."

"I can't travel in a wedding dress."

"There's a full wardrobe on board for you," I tell her.

"Oh."

I turn back and board the waiting plane.

Esme makes it on a few moments later. She looks pissed off—that's not new, though. Nor totally unexpected.

In comparison to how poised and polished she looked walking down the aisle, she looks wild now. Hair messy. Dress slipping off one shoulder. A high blush in her cheeks and that never-ending fire in her eyes.

I think I actually like this look better.

The stewardess, a leggy blonde with too much makeup, takes Esme to the back of the jet where her wardrobe awaits.

A few minutes, the blonde emerges alone.

"Your wife is changing, sir," she says, her words coated with honey as she stares at me appreciatively. "I'm Svetlana. Please don't hesitate to ask me for anything you might want. I'm here to service your *every* need."

She even licks her lips. "Piling it on" doesn't do this justice—she's throwing herself at me like a dog in heat.

The old Artem might've taken her up on it. Would've bent her over the teak dining table in the middle of the plane, hiked that navy pencil skirt over her hips, and fucked her senseless until the cabin reverberated with her moans.

The new Artem doesn't consider it for the slightest of seconds.

"Thank you," I say curtly. "I'll let you know if I need anything."

"Please do," she replies, leaning in a little and offering up her cleavage to me. Her manicured nails graze my forearm. "I just want to make sure you're completely and totally satisfied during your journey."

"I said I'll let you—"

"Ahem!"

We both turn towards Esme. She's standing a few feet away, her eyes tight with annoyance as she glances between me and the slutty stewardess.

She's swapped out the wedding dress for a sunflower yellow lounge dress with little cut outs along the bodice. Her dark hair compliments the color perfectly, as do the flecks of molten gold in her hazel eyes.

"Please," she says, in a snippy tone as she passes between us, "don't let me interrupt you."

The stewardess gives me an apologetic smile and heads towards the cockpit. For the rest of the flight, she brushes against me every time she passes. I ignore it each time.

Esme, on the other hand, picks a seat as far from me as possible and stays there. I can only see the back of her dark head, but I can see from the stiff posture of her back that she's tense.

Possibly even a little jealous.

Like her wild hair, I think like that, too.

She's hotter when she's angry.

28

ARTEM

I manage to sleep for a bit. When I wake up, we're about to land.

Everything goes smoothly as we touch down. When the hostess informs us that we've just arrived in Hawaii, I see Esme's eyes go wide with surprise.

She hides it as soon as she sees me looking. Doesn't want me to notice her genuine interest.

Suppressing a smile, I disembark. Esme follows behind. We take a car to the private ferry and ride the boat to Kauai, where our private mansion awaits.

Esme continues with the silent treatment the whole time.

Fine. She wants to be a brat? So be it.

I intend to enjoy myself.

I decide to just ignore her completely. Once I'm settled in, I change into a pair of black swimming trunks and head down to the pool.

It's a beautiful day to do nothing. Moments like this are rare in a life like mine. Since birth, I've spent most of my waking hours fighting and working for the Bratva.

So when the chance comes to laze in the sun, I take it.

Out of the corner of my eye, I spot Esme making her way to the pool. She's wearing a long, sheer white cover-up, but the moment she hits the pool deck, she discards it.

My eyes bulge when I see what she's got on underneath: the skimpiest bikini I've ever seen.

It's comprised of a thong bikini bottom and a bikini top that has hardly enough fabric to cover her nipples. The electric blue stands out sharply against her tanned skin like it's glowing.

She walks around the deck towards me. Confident. Alluring.

And for the life of me, I can't look away.

She seems to be aware of my attention because she's definitely doing her best to put on a show.

She sinks gracefully into the deck chair next to me and starts rubbing sunscreen on her soft caramel skin.

I watch her as my cock jumps to life. A few minutes later, she's all oily from the lotion and I'm struggling not to touch myself.

"Would you mind getting my back?" she asks suddenly, offering me the sunscreen lotion.

I raise my eyebrows. "You sure about that?"

She makes a big show of looking around the rest of the serenely empty pool deck. "Well, there's no one else here to help me," she says innocently.

I have to suppress a smile as I take the lotion and squirt some onto my hand.

She's a cunning little vixen, I'll give her that.

I really hadn't expected this move from her. I expected her to rage and storm, curse me and spit in my face.

But this kind of manipulative play? It's out of left field.

I'm used to waging war with my guns and fists.

Esme is ready to do it with her ass and tits.

That's not a war I'd be upset about losing.

I apply the lotion to her lower back. Her skin is warm and soft to the touch. I take my time, moving my palm in broad, slow circles up the sides of her torso. It takes a huge effort not to squeeze a handful of her ass.

I move higher towards her shoulders blades, but she shifts and stops me.

"Wait."

Propping herself up, she reaches behind and undoes the tie on the back of her bikini top. Her face is perfectly calm as she sighs and lies back down, cheek on the chair.

"That's better," she says dreamily. "You can keep going."

I know she's playing a game. And she knows that I know. But fuck—this is much more challenging than I would've predicted.

My cock is now painfully stiff and my jaw is clenched.

I make quick work of the rest of her. When I'm done, I snap the cap back on and hand it to her.

"Gracias," she murmurs in that sexy Mexican accent. Her eyes flutter closed.

I lie back in my deck chair and try to calm myself down. It takes a full fifteen minutes for my erection to go down. When I happen to glance over and catch another sight of her ass tanning in the Hawaiian sun, it resets the clock.

Fuck this. I'm not sitting here and letting her screw with my head this way.

So I head for the kitchen, craving something sweet to drive out the image of my tongue pushing deep inside Esme's pink little pussy.

I rummage through the refrigerator and the cabinet, but nothing is appealing. Not when what I want—what I *really* want—is right out on the pool deck.

Waiting for me. Tempting me. Daring me to devour her.

I look back out the huge living room windows to where she's lying. No—she's sitting up now, actually.

And as I watch, she unscrews something, tips the contents into her hands, and throws them into her mouth.

I drop the pitcher of sangria I'd been holding back on the island countertop with a harsh clank and storm outside.

"What the fuck was that?" I demand.

She looks up at me in surprise. "What was what?" Her voice is still sugary sweet. Innocent as could be.

Fucking liar.

"You know damn well what I'm talking about."

"You need to relax."

She goes to push her designer sunglasses back up on her nose, but I snatch them off her face and hurl them into the pristine blue water behind me.

"Do not ever tell me to relax," I snarl.

Her face freezes. Not with fear, but with anger.

She puts her feet on the pavement and rises to her full height. "If you're going to freak out about me taking fucking *vitamins,* then this marriage will be even shorter than I expected."

Then, with one final searing glance into my eyes, she sidles past me and goes inside, switching her hips with every step.

"Not a chance, *kukolka,*" I rasp to myself when she's gone. "You're mine until the day we both die."

29

ARTEM

Esme stays in her room for the remainder of the evening.

When dinner time comes around, she asks one of the house boys to bring her up a tray of food.

The disappointment I feel is palpable and unwelcome, but I decide to leave her be on the first night. If she doesn't want to eat with me, I'm not about to force her.

Still, it's a long night. I end up masturbating twice before I can finally sleep.

I wake up the next morning, wondering how Esme is planning on avoiding me today. My cock can't take this kind of tease and denial much longer before I do something rash.

I'm finally starting to understand the term "blue balls." It isn't exactly a phrase I'm overly familiar with. Not until Esme Moreno came into my life.

When I get downstairs, I find Esme in the breakfast nook eating eggs on toast. She's wearing a pair of denim cut-offs and a bright pink bikini top underneath a sheer white t-shirt.

"You're up early," I say, sitting opposite her as I help myself to hot coffee from the pot.

"You're up late," she counters without really looking at me.

I grind my teeth together as my patience wears thin. She's already on her bullshit today.

I can't handle that right now. I need to get out a little, feel the wind and the sun on my face. I need open ocean.

"I'm going sailing," I tell her, getting up from my seat abruptly. "If you want to join me, be by the boat dock in fifteen minutes. Otherwise, I'll see you when I see you."

∽

Exactly fourteen and a half minutes later, she steps onto the boat dock with a small tote bag slung over her shoulder. She's got sunglasses on, but when she approaches the sailboat I'm on, she removes them and squints up at me.

"I was expecting a smaller boat," she remarks.

I smirk. "Then you don't know me very well."

"Go big or go home, huh? Am I supposed to be impressed?"

I lean in and offer her my hand. She hesitates for only a moment before she takes it and lets me guide her on board.

The boat has a lower deck equipped with a bedroom, bathroom, a small storage compartment, and a refrigerator that's been fully stocked.

I don't bother with a tour, though. I figure she's been on boats like this plenty in her life. After all, she was the daughter of a don.

I cast off and get us moving. The wind picks up, and soon, we're sailing away from the dock towards open ocean.

She moves gingerly once we really get to cruising. That's all it takes for me to realize that she doesn't have much experience with boats.

"You're not going to throw up, are you?" I ask.

"I just… need to get used to this," she replies, sitting near the gunwale beside me.

Her hair whips chaotically around her face but she makes no move to tie it up. Instead, she closes her eyes and keeps them closed for several long minutes.

When she finally opens them, she's smiling.

"Okay, I'm used to it. This is amazing."

Her soft grin is genuine, glowing. And I find myself smiling back in exactly the same way.

Fuck me.

The woman has a strange, hypnotic hold on me—that is, when she isn't trying to fight me at every turn.

We cruise along peacefully for almost an hour. I strip my shirt off and work on the sails. The simple physical labor is relaxing. Like meditation.

Pull this.

Tighten that.

Everything does what's expected of it.

Unlike my new wife.

I catch Esme checking me out a couple of times. She tries to pretend like she isn't, but the blush on her cheeks betrays her every time.

I take my time with the sails for her benefit, flexing my muscles and moving closer to her than I need to.

It's payback for the stunt she pulled yesterday.

Two can play at that game.

We don't talk much at all, but for some reason it doesn't seem to matter. The silence is comfortable.

When we circle back around, the island comes back into view, but I stop the boat again within swimming distance.

"Why are you stopping?" Esme asks.

"I want to take in the sun here."

She frowns. "I've had enough. I want to go back."

I stare at her. So much for this dreamy summertime world where my wife doesn't fight me every chance she gets.

We're back to harsh reality now.

"It's not time yet. We'll go back when I say so."

She narrows her eyes. I see that familiar fire flare again. I'm ready for her to start arguing.

Instead, she turns from me and clambers onto the boat's bow.

"What the fuck are you—"

Before I can finish my sentence, she's diving right into the ocean.

"God*dammit,*" I curse.

I rush to the edge, ready to jump in after her when I see her resurface.

She doesn't look troubled in the least. Her hair floats behind her in the water as she glides seamlessly along the gentle wavetops in a smooth breaststroke.

She doesn't look back. Not even once.

I'm left on the boat, staring at her and shaking my head in a mixture of awe and frustration.

Nothing is easy with this girl. Can't even take a fucking boat trip without a blow-up.

30

ESME

The swim back to the island leaves me feeling both exhilarated and exhausted.

On one hand, fuck Artem. It felt good to turn my back on him and dive into the water.

He's so hellbent on controlling me. On keeping me where he wants me, when he wants me there.

I've spent a lifetime doing that with Papa. Now that my father is dead, I won't ever let myself be chained down like that again.

But in the bigger scheme of things, I don't have much of a choice. Like it or not, Artem is a mob boss. There's no place I can go that he can't come find me and drag me back kicking and screaming.

So for now, running isn't an option.

I have to find smaller rebellions.

I had planned on going straight up to the house when I got to land, but my legs and arms complain, so I sit on the beach near the boat dock and stare out into the horizon.

Several little rays of sunlight have managed to break through the riot of clouds above. It's as picturesque as I've ever seen. True paradise.

And yet my eyes keep darting back to the sailboat bobbing just out in the harbor.

Even from here, I can make out his silhouette.

Even from a distance, it's impressive.

It had taken all my willpower not to gawk at him open-mouthed when he'd been moving around the ship, adjusting the sails.

Everything from his tattooed chest to his washboard abs screamed of strength and power. Everything he did forced me to squeeze my legs together against the rush of desire.

I was trying to be subtle, but I'm pretty sure he caught me staring at him a few times.

It's the strangest situation of my life—which is saying a lot.

Legally speaking, we're married, right? But I don't feel married to him so much as I feel possessed by him.

I can be rooms away, not with range of hearing or seeing. But he's still in my head—always—his dark eyes piercing through the mask I've spent so many years perfecting.

There's something else that's been swimming around in the back of my consciousness, too. A feeling that's new and unfamiliar.

Jealousy.

When we'd been on the plane, I had heard the stewardess talking—no, *flirting* with him—I had felt a sharp pang of jealousy so acute that I couldn't even deny it to myself.

It infuriated me that she would throw herself at Artem like that. I mean, I had walked onto the jet in a fucking wedding dress!

But that's insane. I don't give a shit who Artem flirts with. Who he sleeps with.

Better her than me...

Right?

I push the memory from my head. There's no point obsessing over something I have no control over.

Frustrated with myself, I stand, dusting the sand off my shorts, and head back to the house and up to my room.

My bikini top is dry already from my few minutes in the sun, so I keep it on, but I shimmy out of my shorts and exchange them for panties and a wrap-around skirt.

It's getting dark and the house has lit up, casting a warm glow on the floral-patterned walls.

I haven't really explored the mansion much, mostly because I've been so aware of Artem, trying to avoid him and my own complicated feelings for him.

Now, though, I take the time to move through the large open spaces, noticing little details that had evaded me before. Wall sconces like fanned-out palmetto leaves. The delicate linens of the white couches sprawling in all the wide open spaces, inviting me to nap endlessly.

It's truly a beautiful place, inside and out. I could wander around in here forever.

But when I come across a grand piano in a room overlooking the ocean, I know I'm not going any further.

I move across the room as though I'm in a trance and sit down in front of the sleek black instrument. My fingers are already twitching, desperate for the catharsis that playing has always brought me.

I touch one key. It rings out beautifully into the warm silence of the empty house.

And then I'm off. Another note, another, each flowing into the next like the waves on the beach. I'm creating music, losing myself to the melody.

Forgetting who I am. Where I came from. Why I'm here.

I close my eyes and sink into the music.

And for a moment, it feels good.

But it doesn't last long.

Because Artem's face appears suddenly in my mind's eye. Jolts me back to reality.

I have to face the truth: there's no "losing myself" from this mess. There's no easy escape button.

If I want out, I have to get *myself* out.

If not for my own sake, then for the sake of the child in my womb.

I open my eyes again with a weary sigh. It's getting dark. I can't see the boat out on the harbor anymore.

But when I turn my head to the side, I realize why.

Because Artem is here now.

He's leaning against the open doorway that links this room to the kitchen. Arms crossed over his bare chest, dark eyes locked on me, and the faintest ghost of a smile playing across his lips.

I gasp. The melody dies at once with a harsh clang.

"Jesus!" I exclaim.

He doesn't move. Just keeps staring at me calmly, a muscle twitching slightly in his jaw.

"How long have you been standing there?" I demand. "You scared the hell out of me!"

His eyes dip down to my breasts. The bikini top I'm wearing suddenly feels like a negligent wisp of fabric that serves no purpose. I might as well be naked.

"When did you learn to play?" he asks, ignoring my question.

"I started when I was four. My father flew in an instructor from Italy."

"That's young."

"I was lonely. The music made me less lonely."

The moment the words are out of my mouth, I regret them. But it's too late to recant them.

He moves closer and sits down on an embroidered sofa chair adjacent to the piano. "What else did you do?"

I frown. "What do you mean?"

"Apart from playing the piano, what else did you do to fill your time growing up?" he asks.

I'm so taken back by his interest in my childhood that I answer honestly. "School."

"Joaquin sent you to a school?" Artem asks, surprised.

I shake my head. "I was home-schooled. That teacher was from Switzerland. The tennis coach was from France, in case you were wondering. The sewing teacher was Canadian, the cooking teacher was Spanish, and the man who taught me to shoot guns was just like you."

"He was Russian?"

"No, he was an asshole."

To my surprise, he laughs at that. I expected a harsher reaction.

"So you cook, you sew, you play piano. The perfect little housewife."

I search for mockery laced in his tone, but there's none. That's surprising, too.

He's right, of course. It's why Papa raised me the way he did. *To maximize my value,* as he would say.

"I guess that was what I was groomed for," I concede. I pause, then add, "Maybe my father knew that I would end up as nothing more than a mindless doll trapped in a life I didn't ask for."

Artem doesn't so much as bat an eyelid. "There's nothing about you that's mindless, Esme."

I glare at him, trying again to search for subtext in his words.

But as before, he looks and sounds completely sincere. As open and honest as he's ever been.

Maybe this is just another mind game he wants to play with me.

"Do you think flattery is going to make me forget that you forced me to marry you?"

"I wasn't trying to flatter you at all," he replies. "I was merely making an observation."

"Oh yeah? And what else have you observed about me?"

"Apart from the fact that you're stubborn and frustrating as fuck?" he asks conversationally. "I'd say you're not as confident as you appear to be."

I laugh scornfully. "You don't know a damn thing about me."

I hate that he can be so fucking calm, while I feel like I'm about jump out of my skin. Even now, he looks at me without giving anything away. It makes me feel like I'm close to tears or tearing my hair out half the time.

"Perhaps. It doesn't have to be that way."

"I'm not like the women you're used to, you know," I tell him, trying to get to a place where I feel like I'm solid ground.

"Oh?" he asks, raising his eyebrows. "And what women are those?"

"Women without a moral compass. Women who care about money and power."

"You don't care about money or power?" he asks.

I know already that he's trying to lead me into a trap but I can't help walking into it anyway. "No, I don't."

"That's because you've always had it." He runs a hand through his thick hair absent-mindedly.

"Okay, yes," I admit. "I was raised in luxury, I had everything money could buy. Except my freedom. Ask me if I'd trade it all to be free. I would—in a heartbeat. And as for power… money or not, I've never had any of that."

"Your father protected you—"

"No," I correct, "my father *controlled* me. I wasn't allowed to go to a normal school with other kids because he didn't want me to be influenced by ideas other than his. He didn't want me meeting boys or having a life of my own. I was raised in a cage, and I thought when my father died, I would be free from it. But here I am again, right back where I started. Same bird, different cage."

He looks at me in a measured way, but I can tell he's purposefully keeping his expression vague.

I hate that I can't tell what he's thinking.

I hate that I'm giving him so much…

But I can't seem to help myself.

Now that I've started talking, it's hard to stop.

"At least when I was growing up, I had my brother," I whisper, stumbling over my words just a little. "I had someone to rely on and talk to. He really loved me. Protected me. And now... now I don't even have him."

Something rages in Artem's eyes for a moment. A flicker of something that I can't put a name to. He sits forward a little, his gaze slipping from my face for a few seconds before he brings it back to me again.

"You two were close?" he asks.

I tense up.

I shouldn't have mentioned Cesar at all. It's too personal a topic to discuss with Artem. Especially when I've already let him in far too deep.

So I turn away from him and try to breathe through the aching hollowness in my chest.

"He's been dead a long time now," I say numbly. "Another reason I hate this world."

"Another reason you hate *me*."

It isn't a question, but I feel the need to respond. "You're just like my father—"

"I'm *nothing* like your father, or your brother," he snarls, with a whiplash of anger so fierce it has me cowering back for a second.

At least, until my own anger surges up to meet his.

"Then you're delusional. You crave power and position just like they did," I snap. "They did whatever it took to get what they wanted. I loved my brother, but I knew he did horrible things to people who didn't always deserve it. He killed men and women, he bought and sold drugs, he tortured innocent people to get information they didn't have. And you've probably done the same and worse. You can pretend all you want. But you're no different from them, or any other man who willingly chooses this life."

He stands abruptly. I stand, too.

My skin is hot, but I don't know if I'm feeling desire or fear. Sometimes it feels like the two things are one and the same wherever Artem is concerned.

He crosses the space between us in one stride and looks down at me, leaning in a little so that he's all I can see.

"How long are you going to keep this up?" he demands.

"Keep what up?"

"This tough woman front. Fighting me every step of the way."

I narrow my eyes at him and jut my chin out. We're inches apart but I can already feel his heat encroach into my space. His smell—salty, masculine—flows into my nostrils and overwhelms me.

I raise my gaze defiantly to his face.

"Until you let me go."

He stares at me for a moment, conflict raging behind his eyes.

Which begs the question... what is Artem Kovalyov conflicted about?

"That's never going to happen," he says softly.

"You don't know what it's like," I say bitterly, unable to keep the words inside me any longer. "You've always been in control of your life. Every choice you make is your own. But me? I have no voice. I have no independence... I'm passed around like... like..."

I choke on the last word and I stop short. I don't know how to go on. How to put it in words what it's like to hammer at the bars of this invisible cage day after day after day.

He'll never understand it.

Artem hasn't moved but I know he's still looking at me.

Then I feel his hand under my chin, forcing me to face him again.

He doesn't say anything. Just looks at me, as if that is enough for him right now.

"Some things are out of our hands," he replies cryptically.

"What does that mean?"

"It means that I didn't have a choice either," Artem replies. "I married you because my father needed me to. Because the Bratva needed me to. What I wanted didn't matter. It still doesn't. It never will."

My heart constricts uncomfortably. This is not the first time he's hurt me, but it's the first time he can see exactly what he's done.

"Let me go," I whisper.

He shakes his head. "No."

"What do you want from me?"

He contemplates for a moment before he sighs and answers, "I don't fucking know."

And then, before I can truly process what he's just said, his hand snakes around the side of my neck and pulls me against his chest.

His lips slam down on mine in the next breath and I feel the brokenness inside me sigh with relief.

It takes me a beat to realize that this kiss is not like the other ones we've shared.

This one is… gentle.

Tender.

Sweet.

Even when my lips part under his, our tongues meet with intense and passionate friction, our bodies melting together until we're wrapped up in each other's arms.

I don't even try to resist this time. It's almost as though I've been walking around like a zombie these last couple of days and this kiss is slowly bringing me back to life.

I want his fingers inside me again.

I want his breath on my nipples, teasing me to another orgasm.

I'm desperate for release, for a respite from the constant worry, stress, and fear.

His hands stroke across my naked back, playing with the string of my bikini top. One light pull and it will fall away, leaving me bare and ready for him.

As if he is reading my thoughts, he unburdens me of the bikini top and it falls to the floor between us.

One of his hands closes over my breast while the other lands on the small of my back, pulling me closer into his groin.

I can feel his erection pressing against my thigh and it makes me dizzy with need. I want to reach down and feel his erection, but we're pressed so close together that there's no space for my hand to slip through.

Then his lips leave mine and fall on my neck. I can feel the intensity build and I know we're about to have sex.

I know I shouldn't be encouraging this. As a matter of fact, I should be pushing him off me.

But there's no denying how much I want him now.

An involuntary moan escapes my lips. "Artem…"

I feel him stiffen, his lips still pressed against the nape of my neck.

Then, without warning, he pulls away and drops his arms from around me.

I'm so shocked that I can only stare at him, waiting for an explanation. His eyes are hooded, his thoughts shielded from me.

It makes me want to scream. He wanted me—I know enough to know that—so why had he stopped?

I want to know, but I don't want to give him the satisfaction of asking.

So I stand mute, confused, and watch him move for the door.

At the threshold, he stops and looks over his shoulder at me.

"You know, this doesn't have to be as bad as you're making it out to be," he says quietly.

Then he leaves, melting into the shadows.

He doesn't show up for dinner that night.

When I go to bed alone, I'm still thinking about his parting words.

Still thinking about the look in his eyes when he said them.

31

ARTEM

LATE THAT NIGHT

My phone starts ringing. Unknown number. Unblockable. Untraceable.

I sigh.

Can't avoid this one.

"Hello, Father," I answer.

"You don't sound like a happily married man."

Immediately, I notice he sounds different than he had when I left him not so long ago.

Less gruff. Far more tired.

"I didn't know you had my happiness in mind when you cooked this plan up."

"No," he agrees. "But I did hope you might find some measure of happiness with the woman. She is a rare beauty."

"She doesn't want to be married to me."

"As if that matters."

I exhale. I'm exhausted with this conversation already.

I can hear Esme's voice in my head. Can see that sad, lost look in her eyes.

She didn't say as much, but I saw it in her face. She needed me to understand where she was coming from.

She needed *someone* to understand. Anyone.

Even someone she hated as much as me.

"Doesn't it?" I ask. "Can a marriage be happy if one of the two people involved is not?"

"I wasn't aware you were concerned for the girl's happiness."

His voice breaks a little, but it's not the connection. There's something gravelly in his tone that shouldn't be there.

I wanted to ask about his last doctor's appointment but I know how that conversation would go. He'd just get impatient with me for asking, avoid my questions, and then change the subject.

I'm not in the mood for that song and dance.

In fact, I'm not in the mood for this call at all.

"Why did you call, Father? I'm assuming it's not to provide marital counseling."

He hesitates. "There is something I've been meaning to discuss with you."

"If it's about work, I'd rather wait until I get back to discuss it," I snap at him. "One fucking week off shouldn't be such a big ask."

I feel like I've been rung dry after that encounter with Esme. I don't have space in my head for anything else.

"This is important, Artem," Stanislav replies.

"Everything is important in your eyes. Is it urgent?" I ask.

There is a prickly silence. He's frustrated with me.

Well, the feeling is fucking mutual.

"Very well," he answers. "We will discuss this when you get back."

"Don't wait up for me."

The line goes dead.

I discard my phone with relief.

I feel a pang of guilt. I shouldn't have been so curt with him. As gruff as he is, he's still my father. He helped mold me into the man I am today. I'm grateful for that.

But Esme has worn my patience thin. And yet, now that Father has agreed to leave me alone for the rest of this trip, where does my mind turn to?

Right back to her.

I can practically still feel her beneath my hands. Her body as soft as silk but firm with those runner's muscles. Her eyes like beacons drawing me closer.

And the scent of her—that sweet, floral smell that draws me close and tempts me to stay there forever…

Fuck.

Before I can finish reliving the memory, my phone rings again. Cursing under my breath, I pick up without checking who's calling.

But it's not Stanislav phoning back like I expect.

Instead, it's a bright, cheery voice that makes me roll my eyes.

"Hey, buddy, miss me?" Cillian chirps.

"Not even a little bit," I say, though I'm grinning just a little.

"How's the honeymoon going?" he asks, getting right to the chase. "Have you consummated your marriage yet?"

"None of your fucking business."

"That's a negative, ghostrider," Cillian fills in for me. I can picture that stupid, lopsided grin on his face that makes him look like a human golden retriever. "How tragic. I should have given you some tips before you left. Practice unrolling a condom on a banana, that kind of thing. Pull up the Wikipedia page on female anatomy so you know where to put your dick."

"I'll come to you next time I need tips on how to leave a woman dry and unsatisfied."

"Please!" he scoffs. "Women get wet just looking at me."

"Women over sixty don't count."

"Fuck you," Cillian laughs, before his tone irons out into seriousness. "But, honestly, how's it going?"

I pause. How *is* it going?

I genuinely have no fucking clue.

We've been on this island a little while now and we still have a week left. That's enough time to fuck each other senseless or stab each other bloody.

I can't tell which outcome is more likely.

"Wow. If it's taking you that fucking long to answer, I'm guessing it's not going so good?"

"It's... complicated."

"Because you *have* fucked her?" Cillian asks. "Or because you *haven't*?"

I roll my eyes. "Why is everything about fucking with you?"

"It used to be the same with you..." he points out, "...before."

"I'm not the same man I used to be," I say simply. "I haven't been since Marisha."

It's as honest as I've been about that in a long time.

"Until recently," Cillian corrects.

I frown. "What?"

"I don't know," Cillian muses vaguely. "There's just something different about you lately. You seem less... pissed off. I think that happened around the time we stormed the Moreno compound."

My frown deepens. I know what he's trying to imply.

But I'm not taking the bait.

"Have you been keeping out of trouble?" I ask instead.

"Trying to change the subject?"

"Ah, the Irishman's not as stupid as he looks."

Cillian laughs. "I'm actually on my way out. Checking out this new club in town with the boys. Need to stop and get condoms. I have like ten on me, but I don't think that'll be enough."

"You know you don't have to wear a condom when you're masturbating right?" I tease. "Especially not ten. Probably not good for blood flow."

"Asshole."

Laughing, we say our goodbyes. I hang up and turn off my phone.

But the moment the silence settles over me, I find myself—yet again—slipping back to thoughts of Esme.

I strip off my clothes and lie down on the bed, naked and tense as fuck. As my thoughts linger on Esme's face, it takes only seconds until I'm hard.

I need a release, especially after what almost happened between us.

We were right on the edge together. Right on the cusp of falling into a mess we'd never get out of.

If I'd stripped her down and fucked her on that piano she had played so well, she wouldn't have stopped me. She might've done what she'd done that night in bathroom at The Siren: begged for more, harder, faster, deeper.

So close to happening. So *fucking* close.

I saw the disappointment in her eyes when I'd pulled away, but something in me had struck a brick wall back there.

She's conflicted. She's wary of me. She doesn't want this life.

That much has all been made very clear.

And as for me... I brought one woman into my world before. She died because of it.

I always swore I'd never make that mistake again.

I place my hand around the shaft of my cock and start massaging a little, imagining that it's Esme's hand around me.

That's not enough, though. That's just a fucking tease. A first taste.

My fantasy builds. I imagine her bending over me, her sexy little mouth parting slightly to take in my tip between those plump, perfect lips.

But even that fantasy crumbles almost immediately. Nothing is fucking satisfying about lying here alone with my hand on my cock when Esme was in the next room.

"Goddammit," I growl up at the dark, silent ceiling overhead.

I abandon the sexual fantasy altogether and just picture her standing in front of me. I see what I always notice in her—the dark waves of her hair, the fire in her hazel-gold eyes, the defiant fullness in her bottom lip.

Sweet. Wild. Beautiful.

That's what I want.

I jerk off to that image, thrusting up and down on my cock with increasingly violent movements until I burst over the sheets.

For one second, I'm purged of the never-ending desire.

A second later, as always, it's back.

"Goddammit," I say for a second time. "God fucking dammit."

32

ARTEM

I move to the bathroom and wash my hands as I stare at my reflection in the mirror.

I look like an addict in withdrawal. Like I'm craving something.

No prizes for guessing what "something" that might be.

I splash cold water onto my face and move back to the bedroom. I've just pulled on my boxers...

When a scream explodes through the quiet night.

My mind goes blank for a second before I jump right into action mode.

I snatch my gun from my bedside table and rush out of the room, straight towards Esme's where the cry came from.

The screaming is getting louder, more panicked.

My mind goes blind with fury.

This can't be happening.

Not again.

Not to her.

For the first time since Esme has come into my life, I see Marisha's face clearly. But it's not an image I welcome.

It's the image that's haunted my nightmares for far too long.

In this memory, Marisha is lying on her back in a pool of her own blood. Her eyes are open, but she stares unseeing at the ceiling above her. Mouth parted, frozen in the middle of forming unspoken words that would haunt me for the rest of my life.

I failed Marisha.

But I won't fail Esme.

I slam open her door and rush into the room with my gun at the ready, looking around for the intruders.

I freeze when I realize there are none. No one else in the room but Esme.

But she is thrashing around wildly in her bed, still screaming at the top of her lungs, her face locked up in fear.

Her eyes are closed, though.

She's having night terrors, I realize, as I click the safety on my gun and set it down on a table by the door.

I move forward. Esme continues to writhe on bed as if she's possessed.

She's wearing a soft cotton slip that's drenched with sweat. Her hands scrabble to grip at the sheets.

"No!" she screams. "Please… no, no…"

When I touch her, she bolts upright and starts fighting against me as though I'm her attacker. I grip her tightly, trying to get her to stop thrashing around.

"Esme," I say calmly. "Esme, calm down. You're having a nightmare. It's just a nightmare."

"No, please… let me go."

"Esme!"

Her eyes fly open and find mine, but I can see by the glassiness in her gaze that she's still not fully awake or fully aware.

"I'm scared," she gasps, looking right at me.

"I know," I tell her. "But you don't have to be. I'm here."

She squints. "I know you," she mumbles. "I… Do I know you?"

She's not herself at the moment, so I don't try and explain anything to her. I just pull her to me.

She comes willingly. Her arms go around my neck and she presses into me like a child seeking comfort.

"Esme, *vse budet horosho*," I whisper into her ear. "*Ya zdes. Ya zdes. Ya zdes.*"

Everything is going to be okay.

I am here.

I am here.

I am here.

She burrows in deeper against my neck. I savor the feel of her in my arms like this. It's foreign but it feels right.

She's still shivering, so I lie down, taking her with me and then I bring the sheet up and over to cover us. She curls gratefully into my embrace.

Her screams quiet to infrequent whimpers, and then to the soft in-and-out of sleep breathing.

I stay perfectly still for a long time. I don't want to leave her.

And then she turns around in my arms so that her face is only an inch from mine. Her head rests against my arm and one hand falls over my chest.

Only then does she finally settle for real.

Tangled up in the sheets with our legs entwined, this infuriating girl cradled in my arms—it is the most intimate I've been with a woman in years.

I feel so fucking exposed.

I've already given Esme too much power by letting her inside my head. And yet, it crosses my mind that power in a relationship seems suddenly overrated.

That's the most fucked-up part of all of it.

She's making me question everything.

I need to clear my head.

I need to get control of this goddamn situation.

Or else, I'm going to come undone.

I can already feel it happening.

33

ESME

THE NEXT MORNING

I wake up feeling strange.

I had nightmares last night. I was panicked. Scared.

I remember feeling so desperately alone that I felt as though I was drowning in it.

And then... it had just stopped. Like someone had pulled me out of those dark waters.

Was that real? Was any of it?

I glance around the room, but nothing seems different.

I look at the bed, but the chaotic spread of the sheets doesn't give me any clues.

As I sit up however, Artem's scent floods my senses. Instinctively, I stop, close my eyes, and breathe it in.

That is definitely his scent—musky, woodsy. All raw sex appeal and quiet strength.

I wrack my brain for snippets of memory that can give me a better idea of what exactly had happened last night, but I keep drawing blanks.

It's all just messed up. Fuzzy.

I get out of bed and stretch. My hands fall impulsively onto my belly.

I can feel my body changing slowly and I know it's only a matter of time before I start showing. I'm extremely lucky that I've managed to conceal my pregnancy for this long.

But I'm running out of time.

I walk to the window and stare out at the ocean, hoping for answers to magically appear. My eyes land on the lone figure sitting on the beach with his back to me.

Artem.

A sudden thought catches me off guard.

He deserves to know I'm carrying his baby.

The plan was never to tell Artem, but somewhere along the way, that has obviously changed.

He means… *something*.

I wish I knew what.

My heart stumbles a little as I realize how familiar he has become to me. He's more than just the stranger who taken me on the bathroom counter of a club. More than just the man who killed my father and destroyed my home.

He's no longer just a hero from a twisted, sinful fantasy.

Nor is he the villain from a nightmare.

He's both.

He's neither.

He's everything.

He's nothing.

I force my eyes away from him and head into the bathroom to shower. When I step out, I change into a light floral dress before making my way downstairs.

The house is empty and I find myself longing for company. Which is why I start walking along the beach, straight to where Artem is sitting.

He's in the same position, eyes trained on the horizon. Either he doesn't notice me coming or he doesn't care. Whichever it is, he doesn't look up until I'm close.

I sit down next to him, keeping a modest foot between us. The sand is cool between my toes.

Artem acknowledges my presence with a sigh and nothing else.

"You've been out here a long time," I say eventually, admiring the blue-green hues of the ocean.

"You've been keeping track?"

I turn my gaze to his face, marveling at the classical beauty of his profile. His dark eyes look elsewhere, filled with secrets that don't include me.

That's when I notice the bottle sitting next to him. Alcohol of some kind, and judging by how much of it is empty, he's consumed a lot of it.

But he doesn't seem drunk. He's as steady and frigid as ever.

And every bit as frustrating.

"Artem?"

He turns to me, his eyes grazing over my features, before slipping away again.

"Yeah?"

"Were you with me last night?"

"Why? Did you dream about me?"

"Artem."

Nothing. A long, drawn-out silence. I think he's going to just ignore me, until...

"I heard you screaming," Artem says softly. "I thought someone had broken in, but you were just having a nightmare."

I nod. "You calmed me down."

"I tried," he says. "You settled after a while."

"What did you do?"

"What?"

"I asked what you did to settle me."

His eyes flicker to my face again. My body heats up. I remember the feel of him suddenly. How his arms wrapped around my body like a blanket. I remember feeling safe, protected... content.

"I held you, Esme."

My lip is trembling for some reason. I rest my chin against my folded knees to stop it.

"Thank you," I whisper.

He nods. Silence laps over us for a few minutes and there's only the sound of waves before us and birds flapping around in the sky above us. The wind nips lightly at my hair.

It's a beautiful day.

"How long have you had night terrors?" Artem asks, breaking the silence.

"It started after my brother's death," I reply carefully, amazed that I'm okay sharing this with him. "I had them for about six months after his funeral and then… they kind of stopped."

He reaches for the bottle beside him and lifts it straight to his lips. He takes a swig and sets it back down in the same place. The smell hits my nose a second later: whiskey.

"Until now."

"I dreamed he was trying to hurt me again," I tell him, trying not to stare at the bottle.

He stiffens instantly, his biceps flexing under the white t-shirt he's wearing. "The fucker from the club?" he asks.

I glance down at my hands. "No," I answer. "Not him."

"Then who?" Artem asks, as his knuckles go white.

My voice is soft and pitiful, even to my ears. But there's anger in it too. So much anger. A lifetime of anger.

"My father."

One corner of his mouth goes up but he doesn't allow himself to smile. I continue as though he hadn't interrupted me.

I don't know why I'm even telling him this, but there's a strange unspoken truce that exists between us this morning and it makes me feel brave.

"Right before we… uh, met," I tell Artem, "Papa caught me sneaking off the compound. He didn't like that. He slapped me. Told me what I meant to him, what he was going to do with me now that I was old enough to whore out. It wasn't nice, in case you were wondering. I think he got skipped when they were handing out textbooks on how to be a good father."

I have to pause, swallow, and steady my suddenly trembling hands before I keep going.

"And then he hurt someone I cared about. He hurt them really, really badly. That was worse than the slap, I think."

The anger is back in Artem's eyes. He's like still water, except I know that no matter how tranquil he appears to be on the surface, there's something lurking beneath the calm.

"I wish I'd known," he says, in a low, dangerous voice.

"Why?" I ask. "What could you possibly do? You already killed him."

For the first time, he meets my gaze and holds it, direct and piercing as ever. "I would have made sure his death was slow and painful."

I wish that answer didn't make my heart hurt in a completely different way.

"Why does it always have to end with death?" I whisper.

He frowns and tilts his head to the side. Like he didn't expect me to say that.

"You hate it, don't you?" he asks.

"Of course I hate it," I snap. "It's all just death and pain and loss. Violence followed by more violence. How can you experience anything real, anything pure, anything beautiful, if you're surrounded by so much ugliness all the time?"

His brow furrows deeper as he considers my words. It hits me that this is the first time we're really talking to each other. This is the first real conversation we've had that's not combative or manipulative.

"Beauty can exist," he says at last.

"How?"

"Didn't you say you loved your brother?" he asks.

"I still do," I tell him. "Love doesn't stop when you lose the person."

I see sadness flood across his eyes. I wonder who he has lost. It's clear there's a void inside him, a pain he's trying to cover.

But I can see it now. Clear as day.

There's a broken heart inside this beast.

"That love you feel for your brother," he says softly. "That's the beauty that exists in our world."

"It's not *my* world," I correct quickly. "I want no part of it."

"I used to feel that way, too."

"Really?"

"You look surprised," he observes.

"I am," I nod. "I just… you… um…"

He smiles this time. "Yes?"

I sigh. "I guess it just seems to me like you were made for this life. My brother wasn't. He had to try very hard to be the man my father wanted him to be. But it didn't come naturally to him."

"And you think it comes naturally to me?"

"Well… yes."

His answer is a smile. I can't quite read it.

"Am I wrong?"

"Maybe I'm just that good an actor."

I frown. "Maybe, but I don't think so. You just have a natural authority. The night you stormed the compound and took me, you looked like you were in your element."

His face clouds over only for a moment. "I wasn't aware you were taking in much that night."

"I wasn't," I admit. "But when I look back on my memories, I realize I've noticed more than I thought I did."

"You started crying when I walked in and found you," he says suddenly, as though the question has been nagging him since that day.

I nod.

"Why?"

I close my eyes, thinking of that horrific moment before I laid eyes on Artem and realized he was the man from The Siren.

"I thought I was dreaming at first. Or hallucinating," I say slowly. "And then... I just felt... relieved."

"Relieved?"

I nod. "I thought I was free." A deep sigh ripples through me. "I was wrong."

At that, I can feel a gulf open up between us again.

Yes, we have a temporary truce going at the moment. But my words have opened up the questions that remain unanswered.

How long will this last?

How long *can* it last?

At the end of the day, he stole me and made me his. I should hate Artem Kovalyov with every fiber of my being.

And yet, I don't want this conversation to end.

The secret I'm holding in my belly sits there in the space between us. I wonder how he would react if I just told him right now. Would it hurt him or please him?

I don't know which option I'd prefer, to be honest.

But the moment I think of telling him, my throat constricts with fear and I know that I'm not going to.

I can't.

Not now.

Not yet.

"I'm not a monster, Esme," he says. "I know it may not seem that way to you right now, but you'll see in time."

"*In time,*" I repeat. "You really expect us to go on like this? Stay married, play the part of a loving, married couple, even though we're anything but?"

"Other people have done it," he says with a shrug.

"You don't strike me as the type of man who'd force himself on a woman. I know real fucking well what that kind of man is like, and you're not it."

He chuckles. "I think that's the first nice thing you've ever said about me."

I laugh bitterly. Then, before I lose my nerve, I say softly, "I never did thank you."

He sets down the bottle without taking a swig.

"For what?" he asks.

"For saving me from being raped," I reply.

It's the closest we've ever come to discussing it—what happened between us at The Siren. Maybe on some level, we've both been avoiding it this whole time.

Like we just agreed to leave that past behind us.

As if the people who consumed each other with passion in that nightclub bathroom and the people here on this beach aren't one and the same.

Artem nods, accepting my thanks without a word.

"Did you really not know who I was?"

"I didn't," Artem replies. "That's the truth."

I nod, but his eyes still bore into me.

"Do you believe me?"

It's not a question I expect from him, but I understand in that moment that it does matter to Artem that I believe him.

Perhaps it even matters that I *trust* him.

I hesitate. "Actually… I do."

He nods like he appreciates that.

My eyes fall to the whiskey bottle next to him. "How much have you had to drink today?" I ask.

"Not as much as usual."

I raise my eyebrows. "What's the usual?"

"Why do you care?" he asks, but his tone is not combative. It's like he genuinely wants to know.

"You're the one who keeps insisting we're married," I counter. "I'm playing my part. *Nagging wife.*"

He almost smiles at the joke. "I like whiskey." But his shrug is too practiced, too casual. He's used this lie before.

"No one likes whiskey that much." I pause, then charge forward. "You wanna know what I think?"

"I have a feeling you're about to tell me regardless."

I ignore that and continue. "I think you're self-medicating."

"Is that your professional opinion, Dr. Moreno?"

"You were different when we first met. Or maybe I was just blinded by your strength, the natural power you have," I say. "But now I can see past it."

He tenses a little and his forehead creases. I know he doesn't like that, but I keep pushing forward anyway.

"You are strong. You are powerful," I say. "But you use it as a shield to hide the pain you feel."

"You don't know that," he says sharply. "You don't know me."

"I do," I nod. "Sometimes, when you think no one's watching you… you look the way I feel."

He glances at me and I know immediately that I'm right.

"Who did you lose, Artem?" I ask gently.

He takes a deep breath and shakes his head. "I'm not going there."

"Why?" I demand. "What are you afraid of?"

"Because I established a rule, remember?" he growls. "No talking about our pasts."

"Seriously?" I say. "That's a ridiculous rule, especially given the situation we're in."

"It stands."

I cross my arms and stare Artem right in the eye. "Then we have a problem," I tell him.

"Oh, yeah? And why's that."

"Because I refuse to accept that rule."

The sunlight hits his face at just the right angle, illuminating one dark eye and turning it into shining obsidian. He looks magnificent, ferocious—and haunted.

In a way, it breaks my heart. But he's just so damn infuriating that I can't show him that sympathy just yet. We're so close to… to something. A breakthrough, maybe. So I just stare at him angrily, arms crossed over my chest.

This whole morning has been strangely revelatory.

I've realized that I can talk to Artem.

When we're not fighting, it's easy and natural between us. I'm pretty sure he feels the same way. Why else would he be finally showing signs of opening up to me?

Still, talking about his past seems damn near impossible. He doesn't share that part of him. Not even with me.

Until—maybe—now.

Or maybe not.

I sense him closing up under my scrutiny. His expression turns stony, though I swear I see the flicker of emotions raging deep inside him.

"Too fucking bad," he tells me.

I narrow my eyes and shake my head. "You were the one who forced me to marry you," I say. "I deserve to know who you are."

"You might not like what you hear."

"Maybe I won't," I agree. "That's a distinct possibility. But I might understand more than you think."

"How could you possibly?" he asks. "When you have so much disdain for my world?"

"Because like you said, it's my world, too. I was born in it. I grew up in it," I say. "Because, despite wanting something different, your world is the only one I've ever known. I may have been a bystander, but my brother wasn't. I knew what he went through to feel like he could be don one day."

His face twitches strangely the moment I mention my brother. I don't know what to make of that.

Like he's hiding something from me.

Something I don't know.

"Who did you lose, Artem?" I ask again.

The answer rises to his lips. I can see it right there. Right on the verge of being spoken.

So close…

But the words don't come out.

Maybe some pain is too deep to ever see the light again.

Instead, Artem reaches for the whiskey instead and takes a long draw. When he puts the bottle back down, he looks even more troubled than he did when he picked it up.

I understand that reaction instinctively. He thinks the alcohol will save him from facing his trauma. Thinks it will quiet his demons, blunt his pain.

But for some reason, it's not working today.

Part of me pities him for that. It can't be easy to live with grief constantly threatening to tear you apart. Everyone needs a coping mechanism.

But the bigger part of me wants to tear that mechanism out of his hands and make him reveal his pain to the light. To me.

That's the only way anyone can ever heal.

"Tell me their name," I say softly. I sidle a little closer to him.

He stiffens.

"I've lost too many people to name," he rumbles.

"That's a cop-out and you know it."

"It's all I'm giving you."

I sigh tiredly and stare out at the ocean for a while. This man is so fucking frustrating. My hair flutters in the wind, long dark ribbons tossed across my face.

"What are you thinking about?" he asks after a minute has passed.

"Just wondering if things would have been different if my brother were here."

"Meaning what—he could have saved you from me?" he practically snarls.

I don't cringe back from the venom in his words the way he thought I might.

Instead, I just nod. "Maybe."

"Then you're more naïve than I thought."

That gets the reaction he wanted. A pang of hurt lashes through me. I pull my knees up to my chest and wrap my arms around them for what little comfort I can find.

"You didn't know him," I say in a whisper.

"I didn't have to," Artem growls back.

"Meaning what?" I snap, throwing his own words back at him. I keep my features calm but I can't keep the undercurrent of fury out of my voice. "You would have killed him like you killed my father?"

I thought I wasn't moved by Papa's death. That maybe I was even happy he is gone. *"Relieved"*—wasn't that the word I'd used?

It's not until this moment that I realize it's much more complicated than that.

I hated my father. A part of me was scared of him—rightfully so.

But he was the constant presence in my life that had been snatched away in the same kind of violence that had taken my brother.

Artem stares at me. Like he's weighing what to say next. Whether to keep lying, keep hiding…

Or to finally start giving me answers. The truth I can handle. The truth I deserve.

"Yes," he says quietly. "I would have killed him like I killed your father."

"Or maybe he would have killed you."

"Is that what you dream of at night when you get into bed?" he demands. "Do you want to see me dead?"

I suck in my breath. "That's not what I said."

"It was implied."

I get up suddenly and brush the sand off my legs. Then I look down at Artem where he sits hunched over on the white beach.

"I'm not like you," I hiss at him. "I don't wish death on anyone. Even people who may deserve it."

Then I turn away from him and start walking down the beach, my feet displacing little tufts of sand with every step.

I hear motion behind me, but I don't look back.

Until, a second later, Artem seizes my arm and whirls me around.

I spin fast and stumble into his chest, but the contact just pisses me off further, so I place my hands on his torso and shove him away from me as hard as I can.

"Don't touch me!"

"I didn't mean to upset you," he murmurs.

"Bullshit," I retort, and I hate that my voice trembles as if I'm close to tears. "Everything you do is to upset me. You're addicted to your fucking power games."

"Esme—"

"No!" I scream, trying to shake off his hand. "I wish that you'd just leave me alone!"

"Do you?"

The question slices through the air between us and lingers there.

I stare at him, forehead wrinkled in confusion. "I... what the hell does that mean?"

"It means that I can see through your tough façade, Esme Kovalyov," he says, deliberately using the name I now bear as his wife. "You want to hate me, but you don't. You can't."

I swallow hard. He struck a nerve. I should go. Should turn my back on this son of a bitch for good.

"I..."

My words break off in a whimper. The sound of my own grief, my rage, my despair, my desperation... it all reverberates inside me like a dull echo.

I feel so powerless. More so than ever.

I can't even fight back against my own emotions.

I raise my eyes, searching Artem's face like there are answers written there. But all I can see is confusion.

"It was that night at The Siren," I whisper. "That night... it messed with my head. It's still messing with my head. I thought you were someone different."

"You thought I was your knight in shining armor," he guesses correctly. "But it turned out I was just another monster."

I cover my face with both hands for a moment. He twitches forward like he wants to peel them away. Before he can, however, I remove them myself and fix him with a gaze that's equal parts desperate and defiant.

"Are you, Artem?" I ask in a muted voice. "Are you a monster?"

"Aren't we all? At the end of the day, we're all just beasts."

That's a coward's answer. He knows it. I know it.

I want more truth.

"And what kind of beast are you?"

"The kind that would die to protect you."

Then he crosses the space between us and pulls me to him, his mouth slamming down on mine with the intensity that's been building between us for weeks.

I let out a strangled moan, but my hands are already on him, clawing at his shirt. My body pushes up against his as his fingers tangle in my dark, velvety hair.

Together, we pull his shirt over his head, discarding it in the sand at our feet. My eyes scour over his body with naked longing, fingers trailing over his pecs and then his abdomen with deliberate sweeps.

Then I dip further down and reach for the swell of his erection. I brush over it a few times, teasing him, working him up until his hands are on me again, tearing at my clothes as if they'd personally offended him.

The dress I'm wearing comes off easily. I'm wearing only a thin black thong on underneath. Artem's cock throbs in my grasp at the sight.

He reaches around me, squeezing my ass as his other hand gropes my bared breast. My nipples are achingly hard, and when he leans down to take one in his mouth, sucking and pulling at it with his tongue and lips, I let loose a frantic gasp.

We collapse to the sand together, our bodies entangled and desperate to be joined.

Artem slides my thong down my thighs, spreads my legs, and feasts his eyes on the slit between my legs.

I don't look away. Don't even blink, like he owns my very gaze, as he moves down my torso, pushes my thighs wider, and then runs his tongue over me.

It feels like fucking heaven. Salvation. Redemption.

I moan loudly, my back arching against the sand as my husband starts eating me out like he's been starving for a year, for a lifetime.

But it's not enough. I need more.

I need all of him.

I scrabble at his shoulders with my fingertips and he responds at once. Pulling himself up, he settles over my body, pressing his chest down into mine.

We've never been skin to skin before and the sensation leaves my mind numb for a second before another wave of desire jolts us both into action.

"Please..." I whisper in a strange, husky, desperate voice.

In response, he spreads my legs more with his hips and I widen for him. He looks like a dream, framed against the sky with wild, sandy hair and those dark eyes staring down at me like a promise of what's to come.

He places the tip of his cock at my opening and moves it up and down my lips while I writhe underneath him.

My hands flutter at his waist, trying to spur him into me. I can't wait a second more to be filled. Claimed. Owned. Loved.

"Please..." I gasp again.

But he waits more, and more, and more. Prolonging the moment. Building the anticipation.

It's exquisite torture.

"Artem!" I moan.

And just like that, he crosses the final distance.

He thrusts into me and I'm so wet that he glides inside easily. He presses himself in me balls deep and holds for a second, letting me savoring the feel of him being inside me again after so long.

I squeeze tight around him, heels hooked behind his lower back, as he starts pumping into me. I want to go slow, build momentum gradually, but my mind is a blank that's taken a back seat at this point.

My body is in control.

And my body wants him to devour me whole.

He leaves a wreath of kisses along my neck and down along my breasts, and all the while, he hammers into me, until all I can hear is the slapping sound of flesh on flesh while water laps at our feet.

I can feel my orgasm approaching rapidly as I start to clench even harder around him. My breathing gets heavier and my moaning gets wilder.

My nails dig into his back, but if Artem cares, he doesn't say a word. Just drives harder, drives deeper, increases the tempo of his thrusts until he's ramming into me like a man possessed.

Like *I've* possessed him.

And then, three thrusts later, I explode on Artem's cock with his mouth on my nipple. My body is wracked by wave after wave of the most intense sensation I've ever felt. Like electricity is surging through me, raw and uninhibited.

Artem doesn't wait a second longer for his own release.

He erupts deep into me. I want it. Want this. Want him. More than I've ever wanted anything in my life.

Surge after surge, each one ebbing out after the last. I take them all, still twitching from head to toe like a live wire.

When there's nothing left in him, he collapses against me, sweating and breathing heavily. My fingers trace light patterns along his spine.

After our breathing returns to normal again, he rolls off me onto the warm sand that blankets the ground beneath us.

I turn my head to the side and find him looking at me, his expression a mixture of too many emotions to untangle.

What the fuck was that? I wonder.

It felt like more than sex.

I wish I knew what to make of that.

34

ARTEM

She sits up a little and supports her body with one elbow against the sand. Then her hand lands on my chest and she finds my eyes again.

"Do you want to get breakfast with me?" she asks.

I nod, not trusting my words right now.

We get up and dust ourselves off. Sand clings to every crevice on my body but I don't care.

That was so fucking worth it.

I pull just my shorts back on, leaving my shirt off for convenience and when I turn, Esme's bending over to retrieve her dress.

The sight of her ass in the air in front of me is enough to get me hard all over again, but I curb the impulse so that I can admire her for a moment.

She stands back up with her dress in hand and turns. When she realizes that I'm watching her, a blush rips across her face and she drops her eyes.

"Can you stop staring please?"

I smile. "Not a fucking chance."

She rolls her eyes, but there's another blush just underneath it. She finally manages to get her dress back on—without a shred of help from me—and then we make our way back to the house.

Our feet sink into the fine sand as we walk and Esme bumps into me a little. I reach out to steady her.

But afterwards, I find it difficult to pull my hand away.

So I don't.

My fingers snake down to find hers. I can feel her surprise, her hesitation, in the tense way she's grasping my hand back, but a few seconds later, she relaxes and returns pressure.

When we get up to the house, Esme turns to me, and there's a bright hopefulness in her eyes that I haven't seen before.

It makes me feel hopeful, too.

"There's sand *everywhere*," she says, and we both burst out laughing. Her hand stays clasped in mine. "Can you give me a few minutes? I want to shower before breakfast."

"Of course," I nod, releasing her fingers reluctantly.

She gives me a thoughtful parting smile and heads upstairs. I watch her go, memorizing the way her hips sway ever so slightly when she moves.

I go to the kitchen and check my phone resting on the island. I frown when I see that I have four missed calls from Cillian as well as a text.

Artem, call me as soon as you get this message.

He probably just wants to tell me about the threesome he scored last night or something equally idiotic. But with Esme still showering, I decide to humor him.

I dial his number. He picks up on the second ring.

"So how big were the tits?" I tease. "I'm sure some kind of Guinness World Record, right?"

He doesn't laugh.

"Oh, so it's a *bad* morning-after report," I continue. "You ended up with someone's granny? Did she at least bake you some—"

"Artem," my best friend interrupts in a voice I've only ever heard from him once before—when he found me after Marisha was killed.

Dread pools in the pit of my stomach at once.

"What's wrong?" I demand hoarsely. "What's happened? Tell me what the fuck happened."

"Artem, my brother…" Cillian says again.

There's no trace of laughter in his tone. Just pain and sorrow.

"If you don't fucking spit it out—"

"Your father is dead, Artem."

I grip the phone a little tighter. That can't be right. I must've misheard him. Because if Stanislav is dead…

"You're the don now."

35

ESME

The water feels amazing against my gritty skin. I wash off the last remnants of sand and step out of the shower.

Once I've toweled off, I stare at my naked body in the mirror. Almost four months in, my pregnancy is still not too obvious, but I'm seeing more and more changes with each passing day.

Belly not as flat. Hips a little wider. Are my breasts bigger too?

Maybe. I can't quite tell if it's all real or just my mind playing tricks on me.

The idea of telling Artem about the baby feels right all of the sudden. Like it's so obviously the perfect time.

Just the thought of sharing this with him actually has me smiling like a loon, of all things.

I might actually be going insane.

Or not. Or maybe insane in a good way. Who knows anymore?

All I know is that something significant has shifted between us. It's been a slow burn these last few days but last night was a turn in the tide.

And then this morning was—well, to beat the metaphor to death, this morning was a tidal wave.

A blush taints my cheeks. I wrap the towel back around myself, even as my mind is still racing with the images.

Artem on top of me, his cock poised between my legs.

Artem's lips on my neck as he shoved into me with the kind of power that I didn't think any man possessed.

Artem's eyes, the way he had looked at me as we coasted down from our peaks.

What strikes me most about what we just shared—it wasn't just hot sex.

It wasn't just great sex.

It was *tender* sex.

He held me, he caressed me, he looked me in the eye.

In that moment, I didn't feel like I was his captive. And I certainly didn't feel like I was being forced into anything.

No. In that moment, as crazy as it sounds... I was exactly where I wanted to be.

Which is why the idea of telling Artem about the baby is almost... exciting.

I'm still nervous, still unsure of what his reaction might be. But there's something damn near fateful about it. Maybe it's meant to be?

Trying not to smile like an idiot, I walk back into my room to dress.

And come to a screeching halt when I see Artem in there already.

My smile dies instantly. He's rifling through my drawers in a fury and shoving all my clothes back into the branded suitcases some unseen housekeeper had packed before our departure to come here.

"Artem, what are you doing?"

All the joy I felt a moment before evaporates into thin air when he turns to me.

His eyes belong to a stranger.

They're dark, of course, like always.

But dark in a different way. Haunted, maybe. Like he's not really seeing anything in front of him at all.

His face is cold, cut from stark lines that remove any trace of softness from his features.

"We're heading back," he replies, flat and hoarse. It's a stranger's voice in a stranger's face.

I feel a chill ripple over my skin.

"Now?"

"Now."

He clamps my suitcase shut and glances unfeelingly at the towel around my chest. Not an ounce of the warmth or passion that was burning up there just a few short minutes ago.

"Put on some clothes and meet me downstairs. I'll send someone to collect the suitcases."

Reeling from the mental and emotional whiplash, I grab his arm as he passes by me.

"Artem, what the hell is going on?"

He stares down at me. I see a blip of emotion flash across his eyes.

A second later, they're dead again.

"Just get dressed," he repeats.

He rips his arm from mine and leaves the room.

What changed so fast?

My hands fly to my stomach as I try to process Artem's sudden personality change. The man puts Dr. Jekyll and Mr. Hyde to shame. "Hot and cold" doesn't even begin to cover it.

It's like we went from the core of the sun to the depths of Antarctica in the blink of an eye.

As numbness slips into my bones, I dress in a daze and walk downstairs to find Artem on the phone.

He's talking in low, guttural Russian that has my hair standing on end.

Bratva business—it has to be.

I stand rooted in place and watch him for a moment. He hasn't seen me yet.

But I see him.

I see the man he thinks he wants to be.

The man he thinks he *has* to be.

This is the Artem who stormed the Moreno compound, killed my father, and abducted me.

The gentle man who held me through my night terrors, who made love to me on the beach this very morning…?

That man is gone.

It's the loneliest feeling in the world.

I choke back a sob, but Artem hears it anyway. He mutters something quickly in Russian before hanging up and turning to me.

"Come on," he orders. "We don't have time to waste."

He doesn't wait to make sure I'm following him. He charges ahead, leaving me to trail along in his wake.

We get into the waiting car and drive to the ferry. From there, we head to the airport, where the Bratva's private jet is waiting. Men stand outside the plane in black suits like funeral ushers.

It feels like I'm being pulled back into the same sunken nightmare world I just left.

The men stand a little straighter when they see Artem coming.

"Don Kovalyov," one says to him with a bow as Artem passes by.

Don?!

I suck in my breath as I begin to piece together what's happened.

Something has happened to his father.

And now Artem has inherited the Bratva throne.

I stare at my husband's back as he climbs the steps to the jet, but my legs feel cemented to the ground.

"Ma'am?" says one of the men. I don't even know which one is talking to me. "You have to board."

My stomach sinks. We had been doing so well. Finding common ground, rediscovering a connection that had sparked the first time we'd met in The Siren months ago.

I'm carrying his child, but I hadn't realized until just now how much I had been banking on our temporary truce turning into something more permanent.

It's like my heart is breaking all over again. It freezes me in place.

Suddenly, I feel a shadow fall over me.

I look up. Artem is standing in front of me, glaring down at me with impatience.

"What is wrong with you? We don't have time for this."

I stare at his face, trying to find any trace of familiarity in his features, but he looks so different.

And then I realize why: he's wearing a mask, too.

The cold, hard mask of a Bratva don.

The same one that Cesar had tried wearing every so often.

But it had been different with Cesar. His mask hadn't fit quite so well. His mask was chipped at the edges, riddled with fissures of doubt and uncertainty.

Artem's mask is so perfect that I can't see past it.

"I want to go back to the beach," I whisper in a voice so low that the wind carries my words away.

"What?" Artem barks.

I flinch at the harshness of his voice. "Never mind," I mumble. "Nothing."

He wraps his hand around my arm in a vise grip and tugs me up the steps of the plane himself.

I go silently, suddenly so tired that I'm actually glad for the support.

The moment we're on the plane, he drops my hand. The doors close behind us.

Artem walks to the furthest end of the plane, leaving me to find a seat at the front. I sit and close my eyes, trying to picture the ocean, trying to imagine the feel of the sand beneath my feet again.

But I can't.

The images from this morning feel like a daydream. A childish one at that.

At some point, we take off. And at some point, I fall asleep, though I don't really know how. Maybe my brain and body are just so tired from everything that's happened. From my life being upended again and again and again. Like all systems are shutting down to protect me.

But even sleep can't keep me safe.

My dreams are plagued with images from my past.

I see my father.

I see my brother.

I see my unborn child.

I see all the people I've lost, staring back at me through the walls of a new gilded cage.

Just like always, I'm the one trapped on the inside.

36

ESME

I wake up when we touch down, but before I can get my bearings, I'm ushered off the plane and pushed towards a black sedan by more faceless men in suits.

I turn, expecting Artem to follow behind me. He doesn't even look up before stepping into a second black sedan parked behind the first.

Someone shuts my door. Moments later, we pull away from the plane and cruise onto the streets of Los Angeles.

I recognize the building we pull up in front of. It's Artem's apartment.

I recognize the two men waiting on the sidewalk, too.

If they recognize me, they don't show it. Crew Cut and Blue Eyes say nothing as the driver opens my door and helps me out.

They still don't say anything as I approach. They just turn and lead me inside—one in front, one behind, as always.

We take the private elevator up to the penthouse. It's so eerily silent that I want to scream, to shout, to fight. I want somebody to say something to make it all make sense.

But it's just quiet.

So fucking quiet.

The moment the elevator doors open, I rush through the foyer and head straight for my room.

Slamming the door behind me, I throw myself down on the bed and cry for the lost hope that I allowed to blossom the last few days.

I was a fool for thinking that this relationship—if you could even call it that—could be salvaged.

That it was anything other than a beautiful lie.

∼

Half an hour later, I hear a knock on the door. I sit up, my eyes puffy and swollen from all the crying.

I don't particularly care about my appearance as I walk to the door and open it angrily.

"What?"

Crew Cut stands there, holding a tailored black outfit.

"Your car arrives in half an hour," he tells me. The same way he always has—in a flat, toneless monotone. Like this day is no different from all the days before it or all the days I have left in this hellhole of a life.

"Where am I going?" I demand. "And don't even fucking *think* about not answering me."

"Don Stanislav's funeral," he replies. Nice of him to answer for a change.

But that gives me pause.

For some reason, I hadn't even thought about a funeral for Artem's father, much less attending it. No one has even confirmed to me that that's even what happened, although I can connect the dots myself.

Numbly, I accept the outfit he's holding out to me. He turns and leaves without another word.

I let the door swing close, then I walk back to the bed and lay the outfit on top, smoothing away the wrinkles as I think.

Could I get away with not attending the funeral? The thought of standing next to Artem and putting on a brave face for the men in his organization makes me nauseous.

But the moment I think it, I know it's a stupid idea.

Artem would force his bodyguards to drag me to the cemetery kicking and screaming.

Even if he didn't, I'd no doubt pay for it later.

That was how it had always been with Papa, too. If I did anything to displease him, he would make sure I was punished when the time came.

The punishments differed depending on his mood. Sometimes, it was mental manipulation. Other times, it was physical.

Personally, I preferred the physical punishments. A punch, a slap. One time, he pressed his smoking cigarette butt into the soft skin just above the crook of my elbow.

Those things hurt, but I could disassociate from them. And afterwards, it was over.

What I hated were the mind games.

Those kept me up at night, praying for an end to the turmoil inside my head.

And now here was Artem, proving to be a master at the same tortures.

I was right about him. He's just like Papa. They're one and the same.

I take out the outfit out from under its protective plastic wrap. It's a smart black dress suit from Gucci. As with everything Artem has ever bought for me, it's flawlessly classy and absurdly expensive.

I try it on. The numbness spreads through me again.

When I turn to my reflection in the mirror, I realize that my stomach is pooching out just a little. The obsidian black of the dress helps to hide it well, and it's only noticeable when I turn sideways.

But still, it serves as a reminder. The clock is ticking and my time is running out.

Thankfully, when I pull on the matching jacket that goes with the dress, my tiny little baby bump all but disappears.

I breathe a sigh of relief. Today of all days is not the time for this baby to make itself known.

I choose a pair of black heels from my existing wardrobe and sit in front of my dressing table, trying to figure out what to do with my face.

My eyes are still puffy, my cheeks stained with dry tear tracks.

Sighing, I go into the bathroom and wash my face first and tie my hair up into a loose bun at the back of my head. Then, I apply a little foundation, some mascara and add a dark lip to finish.

That's as much of an effort as I'm prepared to make.

When I walk out of my room, my bodyguards are waiting for me.

We go downstairs as a silent unit and get into the same black sedan that brought me here from the airport.

When we turn into a quiet cemetery, I sit up a little straighter.

"We're not going to a church first?" I ask.

No one answers me.

I fall back against my seat, frustrated and sick of resisting the urge to rest my hand against my belly.

The cemetery is quiet and empty when the car pulls in.

But then we turn a corner and I see the number of cars converging through the narrow roads. They all look the same—dark, anonymous, luxurious.

Mobster cars.

My heartbeat ratchets up as our vehicle pulls to a stop. I just sit there with my hands in my lap until my door opens.

"What do I do?" I ask Crew Cut as he shuts the door once I'm out of the car.

He looks at me with an expression that I'm almost convinced is sympathy, although I'm probably just projecting my own anxieties onto the same blank look he always wears.

"The family is gathering over there," he says, gesturing with his chin. "We'll take you."

It's not really what I meant. I was half-heartedly hoping he'd crack into a big, sympathetic smile, sweep me up in his arms, and tell me to go live free as a bird with my baby somewhere far away from here.

Wishful thinking, obviously. I wonder if Crew Cut even knows what a hug is.

I follow him and Blue Eyes across the cemetery to the crowd gathering around an open grave.

A coffin sits off to the side of the pit in the ground. One glance tells me that it's the expensive kind.

My bodyguards flank me, but I feel utterly alone as I continue the walk towards the crowd. Eyes settle on me, piercing and suspicious.

"Esme."

I look up hopefully.

But it's not Artem who's spoken my name. It's the blonde, boyish friend of Artem's I've seen a few times before.

He gives me a sympathetic smile—real sympathy, not my imagination projecting onto Crew Cut's blank canvas of a face—and offers his elbow to me.

Instinctively, I take it. He leads me towards Artem, who's standing at the head of the open grave.

My husband doesn't even look at me.

Clenching my jaw, I turn my eyes to the coffin. It's a deep, elegant rust-brown that manages to glint even in the muted sunlight. The golden handles seem to glow.

I stand beside Artem like the dutiful wife Papa had always expected me to be. The others gathering around glance at me—some with open dislike, others with tempered curiosity. They're all dressed well in dark, expensive fabrics.

And they have piercing eyes. The kind of eyes used to seeing straight through to someone's soul.

I want to shrink back, turn around, and hide in the car.

But for some reason, Artem's presence is the one thing that keeps me standing.

He's shrouded in darkness, his expression shadowed and steely. I would have thought I'd shrink away from him, too, but instead I find myself wanting to reach out.

To take his hand and give him the comfort I never got when Cesar died.

My hand twitches towards his, but I can't bring myself to do it. Not because I don't want to, but because I'm scared that he'll pull away from me.

Before I know it, they start lowering the coffin into the grave. No one has spoken any prayers or anything, and I'm pretty damn sure none of these people are priests, so I'm not sure if we arrived too late for the formalities or if the people in this world just don't give a shit about sending off the dead with respect.

Whatever the case, the coffin descends slowly into the shadowy pit.

I glance at Artem. His expression hasn't changed since I arrived.

"Are you okay?" I whisper to him.

He doesn't bother responding to me. His eyes remain fixed on his father's coffin.

Only once it's lowered all the way down does he move forward to grab a fistful of dirt from the pile at his feet.

He extends his fist over the gaping hole and releases the red earth over the final resting place of the man who raised him.

It feels like an intensely private moment. Not meant for my eyes.

I look away, embarrassed to be caught watching.

And when I do, I spot a man in the distance.

Unlike everyone else at the funeral, he's not well dressed.

And unlike everyone else, his eyes aren't trained on the coffin.

They're on Artem.

I start to mumble, "Who is—"

That's when the first gunshot is fired.

37

ARTEM

What were his last words to me?

What were my last words to him?

I can't for the life of me pull them from the depths of my memories.

All I remember is that when he had last called me, I'd been distracted and impatient, desperate to get off the phone so that I could obsess about the dark-haired temptress sleeping one door down from me.

My eyes flicker over to Esme, who's standing next to me, mute but watchful.

I can't bring myself to meet her eyes. To face this new reality.

Becoming don will change everything for me.

Which means it will change everything for her, too.

Before, Stanislav ran things. Now, I do.

That means the life he had will now be mine. It's a life I know Esme wants no part of. She's made that very fucking clear.

The question is… since when did I start caring what Esme wants?

You're a cold bastard.

She deserves better than that.

Marisha deserved better, too.

I release the dirt. It falls through the air in slow motion and lands on top of my father's coffin.

Next to me, I see Esme frowning out of the corner of my eye. Her gaze is fixed in the distance.

I start to follow it, to see what she's looking at. And at the same time, I hear her say, "Who is—?"

The next thing I hear is the blast of a gun.

The bullet whistles past my ear, an inch away from ending my life. It strikes a bodyguard standing a few yards behind me.

He hits the ground without so much as a whimper.

Dead.

I don't think. I just act.

What did my father always teach me to do in a firefight?

Grab what matters and take cover.

So that's what I do.

Esme is next to me. She's cowering low, her knees in the dirt and her hands covering her head.

I grab her arm. She gasps and tries to fight back before realizing it's me.

"Artem!"

I don't have time to reply. For the first time in my life, I'm running away from the fight instead of towards it.

Instead, I pull her to her feet and try and shield her with my body as we run from the burial site.

People scatter to the wind like flailing ants.

A fresh cacophony of gunshots is fired.

Esme stumbles, but I keep her up and moving, sprinting towards the black gates at the perimeter of the graveyard.

I sense more attackers coming before I see them. Grabbing Esme, I yank her into my body as I turn, my gun at the ready.

I fire off three shots and two of the men tailing us take hits. I'm pretty sure I've killed one, but the other is still alive, screaming with agony as the blood spurts from his abdomen.

Esme shakes against my chest but I don't have time to make sure she's all right.

I just need to get her out of here and somewhere safe.

We step onto the cemetery streets just as more men converge behind us. I pull Esme out of the line of another gunshot and fire back with three rounds.

The shooter drops to the floor but there are still two others coming.

"Get behind that car!" I order Esme, pushing her behind a blue Lexus.

Her hand clings to my arm in hesitation, but I look at her urgently.

"I will protect you," I promise her. "But you've got to listen to me."

She nods and ducks behind the car for cover. I go straight for the pair of men who've come for us.

I fire as I run, forcing them to go on the defensive. When I get close enough, I shoot one right between the eyes and plunge my fist right into the second attacker's face.

He falls back and cracks his skull hard against the asphalt road, blood pooling at the back of his head. His eyes stare up at me, dazed.

I make sure to look him square in the eye when I shoot him in the face.

I spot another shooter behind a tree and take cover behind a silver Prius before I start shooting again. The tree gives him too much coverage, but he keeps shooting until he's clean out of bullets.

As he stumbles to reload, I stand, aim, and shoot him in the thigh that's just barely sticking out.

He hits the ground with a scream. I growl with satisfaction.

I'm about to call for Esme when I hear her scream.

"Artem, watch out!"

I whirl around—just in time to avoid a swinging fist from a man dressed like he's attending the funeral.

I grab his arm before he can bring it down on me and twist it around. He tries to reach for his gun with the other hand, but I break his elbow and smash his face into the back of the Prius, leaving his blood smeared across the trunk.

Before I can catch my breath, I feel a grazing pain at my back. A shot —not a direct hit, but enough to draw a pained bellow from my lungs and send me to my knees.

Fuck.

There's one too many.

And I'm a little too slow.

I pivot and try to stand. Ready to fight back, even as I know that the odds aren't good.

But fuck this son of a bitch if he thinks I'm going to go down easy.

He's got a dark bandana tied around his jaw so all I can see is laughing green eyes and thick eyebrows. The man lines up his gun, with me square in his sights.

This is it.

This is how it ends for me.

I'm too close to dodge, but too far to stop him.

I'm staring death in the barrel.

But before he can pull the trigger, there's a blur from off to the side.

And Esme appears out of nowhere with a banshee scream.

She claws at the man's face with her nails and angry red claw marks blaze across his cheek. The man roars in surprise and pain. I'm so overwhelmed with pride that I don't act as fast as I normally would.

That is, until I see his eyes turn wild with rage as he turns his violent attention to my wife.

It's all the opening I need.

Before he can touch her, I've fired five times, getting him twice in the stomach, twice in the heart, and once right between the eyes.

I hear Esme gasp. Her eyes go wide with horror at the recognition of what we've done to his dead, mangled face.

But we don't have time to panic. I grab her and force her gaze away from him.

She's breathing heavily, her eyes are panicked and anxious, and I can sense she's close to falling apart.

"Look at me!" I roar. "Just focus on me. I'm right here. You're with me."

She nods slowly, the panic in her eyes receding a little. I take her hand again and we run from the cemetery quickly, leaving a litter of bodies in our wake.

When we hit the street nearby, I discard my blood-stained suit jacket behind a hedge and hail a taxi.

I can't afford to go back to find my men right now. Nor am I willing to wait for a Bratva car to come pick us up.

I have to take care of Esme first.

We only have to wait a minute before a cab stops for us. I get Esme inside first.

I don't know who did this. But when the time is right, I plan on finding out.

And when I do, they're going to rue the fucking day they decided to cross the Bratva.

38

ARTEM

I give the taxi driver an address close to the nearest Bratva safehouse and we head off.

Esme looks visibly shaken, hands trembling, though she's trying hard to hide it.

I reach out instinctively and take her fingers in mine. She looks at me gratefully, but her face still carries the remnants of fear.

Neither one of us talk while we're in the cab. We get out on the corner of a nearly abandoned residential area. It's a three-block walk to the safehouse, but I'm still worried about Esme. She looks ashen-faced and her body keeps trembling sporadically.

"It's a short walk," I tell her. "I can carry you."

She shakes her head firmly. "No. I'm fine. I'll walk."

The safehouse is settled on the edge of the suburban street. It's a small, two-bedroom house with a backyard and minimal furnishings. Completely innocuous.

I punch in the code to unlock the key box and retrieve the key from inside it. Then I open the front door and let Esme in.

It's quiet and musty inside from months of disuse. I leave the lights off.

I take Esme's hand and lead her upstairs to the bigger of the two bedrooms. She stares at the walls, the lights, the furniture, as if she's never seen any of it before.

She only reacts when I gently remove the jacket she's wearing.

"What are you doing?" she whispers.

"Checking for wounds."

"I'm not hurt."

"I'm going to check anyway."

And to my amazement, she lets me. I slowly unzip the black dress she's wearing and peel it down her hips.

My touch is gentle, careful. All the adrenaline from the fight has concentrated on this moment. Like the slightest wrong move will ruin everything.

Esme seems like she's scared to breathe too loud. She doesn't move or speak or even blink. Just lets me undress her a little bit at a time.

When she's standing before me in her black lace bra and panties, I circle her slowly. Her skin is as soft and caramel as it's ever been. Every inch still sweet. Still beautiful. They didn't get to her. They tried to kill me, and that's expected, that's fine, that's just the nature of being the don.

But God help them if they so much as scratch my wife.

"You're fine," I rasp quietly once I've finished my examination.

"Are you?"

"Those fuckers couldn't shoot for shit," I growl. "I'm fine."

"That's not what I mean," Esme says. "You buried your father today. And you didn't even get to bury him properly."

My chest constricts. "I'm fine," I repeat gruffly.

I move to turn from her.

But she grabs my hand before I can go.

"Stop," she says, with such natural authority in her voice that it takes me by surprise. "Look at me, Artem."

I freeze. Then, with a sigh, I turn to face my wife.

"Why do you think showing vulnerability makes you weak?" she asks me.

"You don't want to see my vulnerability."

"You think it'll scare me off. Make me fear you. Or worse—pity you."

I look her square in the eyes. My silence serves as my answer.

She reaches out and places her hand on my chest. I can feel myself gravitate towards her, like she's a magnet drawing me closer.

Sighing again, I lean in and rest my forehead against hers.

"Tell me honestly now," she whispers. "What do you need, Artem?"

I think about it for a millisecond at most.

But I already know the answer. It coats my tongue like a prayer.

"You."

She cups my face with her palm and then her lips reach up to mine.

They linger softly for a second before I grab her and pull her into the circle of my arms.

My hands float over her body and land on her ass.

I grip her firmly and lift her up, tucking her legs around my hips, and then I carry her to the waiting bed.

We sink onto the soft covers together, her hands wrapped around my neck as she continues to kiss me. I strip off her panties and bra delicately.

When she's naked, she removes her hands from around my neck and reaches for the buttons of my shirt. She goes slow, her eyes thick with lust and something deeper as she removes each button and pushes it off my shoulders.

My shirt hits the ground and she reaches for my pants at once. I'm so hard that it takes some maneuvering to get them off.

When I'm naked just like her, she wraps her hand around my girth and strokes slowly, her eyes fixed on my face.

She rubs me slowly as I pepper her neck and breasts with kisses.

I'm ready to enter her, but when I go to spread her thighs apart, she pushes me off her.

"What is it?" I ask, frowning.

She doesn't answer.

Instead, she twists around and pushes me onto my back.

And then she straddles me.

She looks so fucking sexy, so confident, so powerful.

A queen.

My queen.

Her breasts push together as her hands run down my torso. My cock is pressed against her slit and pre-cum gleams on the tip.

I expect her to lean in and kiss me, but instead, she sinks lower down my body and licks the drop of pre-cum away.

I moan as her fingers play with my balls while her tongue flicks over my cock, teasing and massaging in circular motions.

Once she's done playing with me, she slips the tip of my cock into her mouth and I close my eyes involuntarily.

It's the first time her sweet, wet little mouth has been wrapped around my cock and it's even more transformative than I could have imagined.

She takes her time, sucking slowly on my cock while her hand works the base. Then she starts picking up speed, and I feel myself slide deeper and deeper into her mouth.

When I hit the back of her throat, I moan with pleasure, my body wrung tight with desire as she swallows my cock.

I can feel my orgasm start to peak, but I don't want this to end. I want it to stretch on and on until I forget my own fucking name.

She takes me right to the edge, devouring me whole, stripping away my pain and my past, until there's nothing left but the two of us, holed up in our little bubble.

I think she's going to suck me off until I explode, but then she pulls her mouth away with a soft pop.

Before I can recover, she's straddling me again.

I watch my cock sink into her pretty little pussy.

I grab her hips as she rides me hard, her boobs bouncing in my face.

I grit my teeth and slam my hips up into her until her back arches and she starts moaning.

She keeps moving, too, creating delicious, wet friction between us until I'm close to losing control of my own orgasm.

Esme is right there with me.

"Artem, you're going to make me come," she whimpers as she rides me, her hair flying wildly against her face while drops of perspiration glitter on her breasts.

I slam into her.

One, two, three hard thrusts.

And then I feel her blow up, her body shivering as the orgasm washes over her.

I let myself go in the second after her.

And in that sweaty, passion fueled moment, I do forget my own name. But the name of this woman—my captive, my wife, the last thing my father ever gave to me—remains on my lips.

Esme.

Esme.

Esme.

39

ESME

When I wake up, I'm alone.

I reach out and touch the other side of the mattress. Even though it bears the indent from Artem's body, it's cold, too.

Wherever he went to, he's been gone for a little while at least.

There's a cold draft blowing from somewhere unseen. The thin sheet on the bed isn't enough to warm me, so I get up and look around for my clothes.

I see them folded neatly on a chair at the corner of the room by the window.

I pad over and slip on my bra and panties. I'm reluctant to put on the black dress again, but I have nothing else to wear.

There's a delicious soreness between my legs. And an emptiness, too.

I'm already longing for Artem, desperate for him to fill me again, make me come again.

Going down on him was probably the single most erotic moment of my life. With him in my mouth, it was like I could play his body like a piano. Coax moans and growls from his mouth. Makes his hips twitch and demand more, more, more from me.

And I wanted to give it to him. I wanted to give *myself* to him.

So I did. And he gave himself right back to me. Until we both went tumbling over the edge together and fell asleep in one tangled, sweaty mess.

I hear murmurs just outside the bedroom door. I recognize Artem's deep, authoritative voice. There's someone else out there with him, too.

I open the door and peek outside. It's still too dark in the predawn hours to see anyone, so I step out into the narrow landing and walk down a little to the closed door of the room adjacent to this one.

I think about knocking and walking in, but I don't know who he's with and I don't want to interrupt.

I'm about to go back to the bedroom and wait for him to finish his conversation—when I catch my name.

"…Esme…"

I freeze.

It's wrong to eavesdrop. Artem is the don now, and practically the first hour on his watch was marred with a vicious ambush. I'm sure he's busy as hell.

But I can't help myself.

I inch closer, unable to turn away now. I press my ear to the door and realize that the voices are coming through clearly.

"…we're trying to find out…"

I pick up the distinct Irish accent and I realize that Artem's in there with his blonde friend, the one who'd offered me his elbow at the funeral.

Cillian, I recall with a ping.

"... motherfuckers thought we'd be vulnerable at the funeral... We're going to hit back... fucking hard. How many men did you pick up?"

"There were no survivors," Cillian replies. "There was one we caught alive, just barely. He drowned in his own blood before we could get anything out of him."

I cringe at the gory details. But the two men are as calm as if they're just discussing the weather.

"Were they marked in any way?" Artem asks. "Any identifiers? Tattoos?"

"I checked every body and weapon myself," Cillian says. "There was nothing, which was obviously deliberate. Whoever mounted the attack didn't want it to be traced back."

"We have many enemies. The question is, is it an old enemy or a new one?"

There is a beat of silence. I can imagine Artem's stoic face, his dark eyes scouring the unseen possibilities, vowing to get revenge.

It's not in his nature to let things pass. And even I have to agree—this brazen assault demands some kind of response.

But the implications terrify me.

I would've thought I'd be used to this. I'd glimpsed some of what Papa had done to enemies over the years. What he'd done to his own men, even.

The memory of Miguel bound and beaten on that chair swims behind my eyes. I'll never forget the horror, the pain in his eyes.

Papa had never been afraid to hurt people when it suited him.

But it didn't bother me the way this does. This feels... realer, somehow. Maybe it's because I know how much tenderness Artem is capable of.

He has a soul, somewhere deep down inside.

The men who attacked won't care about that. They'll kill him in cold blood if they can.

They'll kill me, too.

I'm Artem's wife. That makes me a target.

And it does the same to the baby in my womb.

I plug back into the conversation when I hear Cillian speak.

"How is she?"

"She's okay, I think," Artem replies. "Better now. She's got fight in her."

"Yeah, it certainly seems so," Cillian agrees. "We can move her to another safehouse. This one isn't secure enough."

"She's sleeping now. I don't want to disturb her. She's been through enough." Artem sounds exhausted.

"Mhmm."

"What?" Artem's tone is impatient, but Cillian chuckles.

"Nothing. Just making observations."

"If you have something to say, fucker, say it to my face."

I smile. I haven't really seen him interact with anyone this way. There's a familiarity, a brotherly bond that's evident between the two of them even though I can't see either one.

"I'm just saying, you seem very protective of her," Cillian points out.

"She's my wife."

The words make my heart flutter like a lovestruck fifteen-year old. They're possessive, and they ring with sincerity.

With truth. With feeling.

The men shuffle around. For a few seconds, I can't hear a thing.

"What?" Artem asks suddenly. "What's that look on your face?"

"I was just wondering whether or not you've told her yet."

A long, drawn-out silence makes me nervous again.

Told me what?

"No," Artem sighs.

The denial sounds hollow and ugly. My nerves ratchet up a notch.

"I'm not gonna tell you what to do—"

"Then don't," Artem barks, before he breathes deeply. "Shit, I'm sorry, Cillian. I… I know I need to tell her. But…"

"You don't want to hurt her."

"She's been through enough," Artem says again. "This will break her. She loved him."

She loved him.

My mind races through the possibilities.

What the hell is he talking about?

I already know he's the one who killed my father. He told me himself the night he burned my world to ash.

Which means…

"She needs to know if you're trying to build something real with her," Cillian says softly.

"I know she does," Artem says after a small pause. "But if I tell her, it'll destroy any chance we have together. There's no coming back from that."

My body goes cold. A part of me wants to turn around and run back to my room. Pretend I'd never heard that. Pretend that my mind isn't already leaping to the one inevitable conclusion that remains.

But as my hand flutters over my belly, I know that I have to put my unborn child first. And that means finding out the truth about its father.

About the sins of his past.

About the blood on his hands.

"It may," Cillian concedes. "But if she finds out before you tell her, it definitely will."

"Fuck." Artem's voice is low but there's no mistaking the frustration in it. "How do I even start?"

"Explain the circumstances to her."

Artem lets out a low laugh that's completely devoid of any humor. "Trust me, the circumstances won't fucking matter. I killed her brother. That's all she's going to remember."

I almost gasp.

The sound punctures my throat but I manage to hold it in long enough to push myself away from the door.

I killed her brother.

Artem killed Cesar.

Artem. Killed. Cesar.

My husband murdered the only other person who ever really loved me.

Pain branches through my body like a lightning bolt and I cringe against it.

But it's not just a figment of my imagination.

It's real pain.

I grab the banister of the staircase and stagger my way back to the bedroom. My stomach twists like I'm going to vomit, but there's nothing in there to come out.

Another lurch of agony. Sharp. Brutal. Sudden.

I trip. Try to grab the side table, but my aim is off and instead, I knock off a vase of flowers. It crashes to the floor like a peal of thunder.

Shards scatter across the hardwood. My vision is blurring, darkening at the edges.

The pain is everywhere. Head to toe, heart and soul. So much of it.

The door behind me opens. I gasp again, turn, and see Artem standing on the landing.

He looks at me with concern that I no longer believe.

His dark eyes are merely a pretense, a facade I couldn't see past because of my romantic, naïve fantasy of who I thought he was.

He's not a special kind of monster. He's not the beast who will protect me, like he said he was.

He's just a nightmare come to life.

He reaches for me. "Esme!" he says, panicked.

I shake my head frantically and try to scramble back away from him.

But the pain twists my vision until all I can see is spots of light floating in front of my eyes, bathing everything in strange, confusing stripes.

It feels like I'm falling.

Maybe I am falling, but I don't care anymore.

The light fades into darkness.

The world slides out of focus.

I'm left alone with only my memories for company.

~

Many Years Earlier

"Esme?"

"I'm not talking to you, Cesar!" I pout, turning my back to him.

He chuckles under his breath as he runs up to me. "Are you mad at me?"

"Yes!" I spit like a little brat.

"Why?"

"You told me you'd take me to Tulum with you."

"I tried, little bird—"

"I'm not a little bird!" I snap at him. "And you promised!"

"It was a good thing you didn't come, little Esme," Cesar tells me, putting his fingers under my chin and pushing my face up to meet his eyes. "It was... not what I expected."

I frown, noticing for the first time the expression my brother is wearing. In only six days, he has aged a decade, it seems. His eyes are dark and sunken. New lines mark his face.

"Cesar... what happened?"

He shakes his head. "Papa showed me some things."

"What kind of things?"

He hesitates. "Scary things," he says eventually.

His eyes are turned inward like he's remembering what happened in Tulum.

Whatever he did.

Whatever was done to him.

I don't understand what he means by that, but I'm afraid to ask because if I do it'll just prove that I'm too young to be told certain things.

And I don't think I'm too young anymore. I turned seven last week. It was a big deal.

"Scary?" I repeat.

Cesar nods as he swallows hard. "I don't think I'm cut out to run the business, Esme," he admits quietly. "I... I don't really want to."

"So tell Papa," I urge him. "He'll understand. Tell him you want to be a doctor instead."

Cesar shakes his head. "I can't do that, little bird," he says. "Papa will never understand. Not like you do."

I feel proud of that. I wear his compliment like a badge of honor.

Cesar and I share a bond that no one else can touch. Not even Papa.

"Maybe I can talk to Papa," I tell him.

Cesar smiles but it doesn't reach his eyes. "No. I appreciate you offering, but it won't make a difference."

I'm secretly relieved. Papa scares me, and I prefer avoiding him even on the best of days.

But I still need to know.

"Why won't it make a difference?"

"Because this was never a choice," Cesar tells me. "It's not about what I want. This is about duty. I am Papa's only son and I have to be ready to take over after him. That's just how things are done."

Again, I don't understand, but I don't ask him to explain either. Papa doesn't like when I ask too many questions, and it's made me self-conscious about my curiosity.

"Don't worry," I tell him, hoping my words make sense. "One day, we'll run away together, just you and me. You can be a doctor and I can be a flight attendant."

Cesar balks with laughter. "A flight attendant? Is that what you want to be, little doll?"

I glare at him, offended that he would laugh at all. "Yes! They visit so many different places and I want to travel to every country in the world."

He considers my answer and his laughter dies slowly. "That's a good ambition," he says. "I hope that one day you'll travel far away from this place."

"I will," I tell him with a smile. "And you'll come with me."

His expression grows sad, but he takes my hand and kisses it softly. "Wherever you go, I'll be watching over you."

"I don't need you to watch over me," I say imperiously. "I can handle myself."

He laughs softly. "I believe you, little bird," he nods. "You were always the stronger of the two of us. You should have been the heir, not me."

"I will be," I nod. "Then you don't have to be. Then you'll be free to be a doctor."

Cesar smiles. "You'd do that for me?"

I squeeze his fingers as tight as I can. "I'd do anything for you."

40

ARTEM

ONE DAY LATER

"Don Kovalyov?"

It takes me a moment to realize the man is talking to me. I'm still unfamiliar with the title.

Igor is standing off to the side of the hospital bed, wearing an expression that's a cross between discomfort and sympathy.

I ignore him and turn my attention back to Esme.

She's been lying in the same bed now for almost twenty-four hours. She hasn't woken once.

I reach out and push back her matted hair. Her skin is sallow and she looks so tiny amongst the tangled sheets. Is it possible for someone to lose weight in so short a span of time?

I glance up at the IV that's hooked up to her hand, feeding her energy and nourishment directly so that she can take her time waking up when she's ready.

Except that she doesn't look close to being ready to becoming conscious.

It's started to grind on my soul.

What the fuck happened in the safehouse? I'd been talking to Cillian in the second bedroom when we'd heard a crash.

I'd bolted into the hallway to find her crouching there, pale and wide-eyed, with broken ceramic and glass scattered around her feet.

She'd looked at me as though she couldn't recognize me and in the next second, she'd lost consciousness.

I was close enough to catch her before she hit the ground.

But since that moment, she hasn't opened her eyes.

Cillian and I rushed her to a private facility that the Bratva uses when we want privacy and a medical staff that doesn't ask the wrong kind of questions.

"Don Kovalyov?" Igor repeats.

"What?"

"Your uncle is on the phone for you."

I don't take my eyes off Esme. "Tell him I'll call him back."

Igor nods and backs out of the room just as two nurses walk in. I turn to the blonde one holding the clipboard.

"Well?" I ask.

She looks at me without giving anything away. "The doctor will be here in a moment to speak with you, sir." She moves forward to check Esme's IV.

She's the only nurse who doesn't seem completely intimidated by our presence here. An impressive feat, considering there's an entire contingent of Bratva soldiers outside the facility, four armed guards stationed outside Esme's private room, and two more in the room at all times.

I know my wife is strong. I've seen her fire. I've felt it.

But I can't stop worrying until she opens her eyes and tells me she's going to be all right.

That's another wife you stand a chance of losing.

I push away the unwelcome thought, trying to get ahold of myself.

It's not just Esme I need to worry about. I have an entire Bratva under my control, not to mention an unknown enemy out there, waiting to finish what the bastards started.

I can't afford to remain stationary at her bedside.

And yet, this is the only place I want to be.

"Artem?"

I turn at the sound of Cillian's voice.

"Yes?"

"Budimir has been trying to get a hold of you," he tells me.

"Well, he can fucking wait," I hiss.

Cillian walks to the opposite side of Esme's bed so that I can't avoid looking at him.

"She's going to be okay, Artem."

"We don't know that."

"She had a panic attack," Cillian continues. "The attack on the funeral must have shaken her worse than we realized. She's not used to this. Not the way we are."

"But I should have realized."

"You were dodging bullets and fending off enemies," he reminds me. "How could you have?"

"I mean afterwards," I explain. "When we were alone together."

But that's exactly what has me so fucking pissed off, not to mention confused.

Esme seemed fine when we'd gotten back to the safehouse. Fine enough, at least. She'd taken everything in stride.

She was fucking phenomenal through the whole damn thing, and afterwards, she'd been the one to initiate sex.

So what the fuck had gone so wrong between then and the moment I'd crashed into the room to find her staring at me, dazed and glassy-eyed, like I was some fucking freak?

"Artem, I know you're worried about her," Cillian says. "But we need to have a meeting. This situation needs to be dealt with."

I nod. I know he's right. He's my best friend for a reason.

"Set it up," I tell Cillian. "But first, I'll speak with Esme's doctor before I leave."

I sense Cillian is about to say something else, but he stops himself at the last moment. A call comes in on his phone and he glances at it before looking up at me.

"Budimir again?" I guess.

"Yes."

"He's been trying to find leads on who launched the attack," Cillian tells me.

I grunt. It strikes me that Budimir and I will be working together a lot more going forward. He has decades under his belt working alongside my father, and now he will serve me.

My whole life, I've never spent much time thinking about the pecking order. I always thought my stubborn father would outlive us all.

"I'll call him soon," I tell Cillian. "I want him to brief you, too."

Cillian narrows his eyes at me.

"What?"

"I hope you're not thinking what I think you're thinking."

"What am I thinking?" I ask.

"Budimir is your second, Artem," Cillian tells me. "I can't be."

"I'm the fucking don now—"

"And what? You think that makes you invincible? You think that means you can do anything you want?" Cillian hisses. "You are one man, Artem, and there will be those that are loyal to you. But there will be as many, if not more, who are loyal to your uncle. Alienating Budimir by putting me above him will not ingratiate you to the men who have sworn fealty to him. It's a bad idea."

Cillian's right about everything, but I still feel a twist of anger when I think about the fucking politics of being don.

I'll have to exercise qualities that I'm not even sure I possess. Diplomacy was never one of my strengths.

"Budimir is an old man now," I point out.

"Exactly, which means he has decades on you," Cillian retorts. "Decades building contacts and strengthening alliances. You need your uncle and he's been working for you this entire time. Don't insult him by turning to me before you turn to him."

I nod, unable to deny the wisdom of his words.

"In any case, the Bratva will never accept an Irish outcast into the fray."

I frown. "They've done that for years," I point out.

"Sure, when I was merely your well-meaning sidekick," Cillian says, with his trademark smile, though his eyes are sad. "They're going to be less accepting if I'm advising the Bratva in a leadership position."

"Fine," I growl. "I see your point."

"Happy to be your voice of reason."

"And as always, the pain in my ass, too."

Cillian chuckles and glances at Esme with a sigh.

"She really will be all right, Artem," he tells me.

I badly need to hear that, but I still have trouble believing. The way she looked at me in that safehouse hallway still haunts me.

"I'll leave you two be." He steps back around her bed and exits the room, clapping me on the shoulder as he goes.

A moment later, the door opens and Dr. Sussman walks in. He's a short, fat man with a bald patch and grey whiskers. His looks don't inspire confidence, but I've seen firsthand what he's capable of.

"Evening, sir," he says with a cool, detached tone. "I've been briefed on everything. I'll just do a small examination now and let you know where we stand."

I nod and place Esme's hand back against her stomach. My gaze lingers on her face for a moment before I walk around her bed.

"You can stay for the examination," Sussman tells me.

"I have a call to make," I tell him. "I'll be back in soon."

Then I head out of the room. It's crowded outside with all the guards I've stationed to protect Esme.

Cillian's off in the corner talking to someone on the phone. Probably coordinating with our men outside the facility to lockdown a meeting spot.

I pick up my phone and call Budimir, who picks up on the fourth ring.

"Artem, my boy."

"Sorry I didn't return your call sooner," I tell him. "I was—"

"With your wife," Budimir finishes for me. "Yes, Cillian told me. How is she?"

"Honestly, I don't know."

Budimir makes a sound that's meant to be sympathetic, but it sounds more like he's trying to cough up a hairball. Sympathy is not among his finer qualities.

"Those bastards really took us by surprise," he scowls. "But we won't be caught off guard the second time."

"There's not going to be a second time," I vow through gritted teeth. "The next time there's an attack, we're going to be the ones to launch it."

"Spoken like a true don," Budimir says approvingly. "Your father would have been proud."

I bristle against the words. We're already talking about him in the past tense. It feels somehow like a betrayal.

"No, he wouldn't have," I counter. "He would have criticized every single decision I'm making."

There's a low chuckle that confirms the truth of my words. "That was his way of making you better."

"Fat lot of good that did him," I snap back.

"I've been searching for clues, Artem," Budimir continues. "Trying to find out who was behind this attack."

"And? Any leads?"

"A few. All unsubstantiated for the moment, but I'm following them through."

"You'll let me know the moment you know anything."

"Of course," Budimir assures. "You are the don now."

The title feels strange coming from my uncle's lips. I hang up and take a deep breath before walking back into Esme's room.

Dr. Sussman is writing down something on a notepad, which he then passes to the blonde nurse.

"Well?" I ask, more gruffly than I intended.

"You have nothing to worry about," Dr. Sussman says with a small smile. "Your wife will recover. She's young, healthy and strong. I think perhaps she's been under a lot of stress lately. That, combined with the stress of pregnancy…"

The stress of what?

"…might have exacerbated her anxiety. But you have nothing to fear: the baby is perfectly healthy as well."

What the fuck is he talking about?

I stare blankly at the doctor, trying to reconcile what he's just said with my reality.

I shake my head, trying to convince myself that I've misheard him.

Esme isn't pregnant. She can't be.

"Did you just say… baby?" I ask.

"Yes, I've checked both their vitals," Dr. Sussman explains with a pleasant nod. "A strong heartbeat and vitals all look flawless. A healthy little bean."

He must notice the horror in my expression then, because his smile sours to a frown.

"Forgive me, Mr. Kovalyov. Have I said something wrong?"

"How far along is she?" I demand, my eyes narrowing.

Fury rises up in my belly. Hot and vicious.

Esme lied. She hid things from me.

A baby.

A child.

An heir.

Dr. Sussman glances at the chart in the nurse's hand and then back at me. "Uh… four months," he reads. "Just about."

Four fucking months.

There's no way Esme didn't know she was pregnant for that long. Which means that she knew and she didn't tell me.

I tighten my hands into fists.

All the questions I've been asking myself for the last twenty-four hours dissipate completely.

Now, there's only one left…

What else has my wife been hiding?

41

ESME

I know it's a nightmare, but I can't wake up.

I'm strapped to a chair in the middle of an ocean of darkness.

In the distance—footsteps. Heavy. Plodding.

A man emerges from the swirling shadows. It's the son of a bitch from The Siren. The one who tried to rape me.

He's back and uglier and twice as big as before.

Twice as hungry. Twice as cruel.

"No one is coming to save you this time," he rumbles. His face splits in a sickening grin. "You're all mine for eternity."

Then, moving impossibly fast for a man of his size, he shoves a knife between my ribs.

I gasp.

Pain explodes.

The bastard grins. Vanishes.

Leaving me slumped forward in the chair. Unable to do anything but writhe with pain and scream into the empty void around me.

Then—more movement in the black beyond.

And Cesar steps forward into my line of vision.

He smiles sadly. That tousled black hair that would never lay straight looks the same as it always did. The same as it did the day he left and never came home.

My dead brother walks over, kneels next to me, and strokes the back of my hand.

"Hello, Esme," he murmurs.

"You left me," I whisper. The knife in my ribs hurts so bad. "You promised you wouldn't, but you did. Look what happened now."

"I know, little bird," he says. His eyes are full of tears. Mine are, too. "I didn't have a choice. I'm sorry."

"That's enough," another voice says. Sharp, cruel, and horribly familiar.

A new man joins us.

"Papa," I breathe.

My father ignores me. He sets a hand on Cesar's shoulder and pulls my brother to his feet.

"She's a lost cause," he mutters. "A whore for the Russian. Do what must be done."

Cesar nods. Dutiful as ever.

Slowly, he pivots to face me again.

"I'm sorry, little sister," he says in a voice so low I can barely hear it.

Then he pulls a knife out of nowhere and stabs me in the chest.

I scream, so long and loud that I nearly shred my own eardrums. Cesar lets his hand fall, but he leaves the knife buried in me.

Then he too turns and leaves.

It's just Papa and me now. He's staring down at me. His mask is off—there's no hiding the bubbling malice in his brown eyes.

He despises me.

Or maybe something worse, actually.

Maybe he just doesn't care about me at all.

"Papa, please, no—"

But he's already doing it. Already plucking a knife from his hip and plunging it into my thigh.

I scream again. My throat is raw from it.

Papa is leaving. He doesn't look back.

I don't know how long I sit there with a waterfall of tears pouring down my cheeks. Seconds or centuries—I can't be sure.

But some eternity later, one more man comes forth.

Artem.

He looms over me, eyes dark and stormy. I know deep in my bones that this is it. He's going to finish what the others started.

"You lied to me, darling," he whispers.

"No," I gasp. "My baby… Our baby…"

Panic rises in my chest. My heartbeat is hammering against my ribs. I try to move away, to run, but I'm trapped in this chair. Strapped down. Can't move.

And I realize suddenly that I can't scream anymore, either. It's like I'm underwater—I open my mouth but no sound comes out.

I'm drowning in this darkness, in these shadows, and Artem comes closer and closer, and that knife of his touches the soft curve of my throat and there's nowhere to run, nowhere to hide, no one to help because my husband killed the only other man who ever tried to protect me and if I don't have one or the other of them than I don't have anyone and so all I can do is scream and scream and scream as Artem takes one final look in my eyes and then he tugs his jagged knife across my throat.

Blood spurts.

Artem laughs.

And everything turns to darkness.

42

ESME

I sense voices all around me. Some calm, others panicked.

I hear the shuffling of feet and the beeping of monitors.

I feel whispers at my ear and warm breath on my cheek.

I try to open my eyes, but my eyelids are impossibly heavy. It takes all my effort just to lift them a tiny crack.

I manage to catch quick, blurred glimpses of white walls. Bright fluorescent lighting. Snatches of rushed, whispered conversations.

"… she's stable… so is the baby…"

"She'll wake up when she's ready…"

The echoes of Artem's voice from my nightmare are still ringing in my head.

Wait, no.

That's not the nightmare.

That's the living, breathing man.

"I'll be back," he says.

He's here, in this room with me—wherever this is.

I open my eyes a tiny bit again and catch sight of his shoes across the room.

A scream rises up at the back of my throat, but I swallow it down. My brother's murderer is standing just a few feet away.

I want to curse him. Spit in his face. Cause him just a fraction of the pain he's caused me.

I let my eyes fall closed before anyone notices I'm awake.

I hear more murmured voices. The shuffle of movement.

He's leaving.

A door on the far side of the room opens. I risk a peek. It's a little easier to open my eyes this time. Enough that I can make out some more vague details of where I am.

There are two armed guards stationed on opposite sides of the room, one near the window and the other near the door.

"Olezka. Sacha," Artem says to them. His tone contains harsh, confident authority. "I need to step out for an hour. Two at the most. You both are to remain here with my wife. Do not let her out of your sight. If you so much as blink too long, I'll have your heads on a platter. Is that understood?"

The way he talks about me makes my stomach churn.

My wife.

Just a possession. His property.

I've only ever been a pawn in a game to him.

"Yes, Don Kovalyov," his sheep bleat without inflection.

I'm only a pawn in a game to them, too.

A pretty bird in a gilded cage.

But not for long.

As soon as Artem leaves, I'm getting out of this fucking room.

Out of this fucking city.

Out of this fucking life of crime and violence and murder and hatred.

I won't be caged anymore.

How exactly I'm going to manage that is still up in the air.

Artem said he'd be gone for an hour or two. That means a clock has begun—because I intend to be gone by the time he gets back.

When I hear the door click shut, I risk peeking out through my half-closed eyes. There's no one left but my two stone-faced guards.

Now what?

I spend the next few minutes peeking around. Subtly, though, so my guards don't notice I'm awake and call Artem to come back.

I'm definitely in a hospital room of some kind, although it seems somehow cozier than any hospital room I've ever seen. Maybe it's just some sort of private, rich people hospital that only men like Artem have access to.

The guards are both armed with massive automatic rifles, which also seems like it is some kind of healthcare faux pas. Not to mention total overkill for one pregnant girl in a hospital bed.

Beyond that, there's not much to check out. The window in one wall just looks up at empty blue sky. Occasionally, a machine beeps.

A few minutes go by like that. Just scouting and brainstorming.

At the end of that window, my plan consists of... jack shit.

If I so much as twitch wrong, the guards will notice. And there's no telling how my body will respond if I try to just sprint for freedom.

Not to mention the fact that there's still an IV needle jammed into the back of my hand.

Think, Esme. Think.

A ringing phone interrupts before any good ideas strike.

The guard by the window pulls out a cell phone and starts talking in fast Russian. Something about his tone seems weird, almost conspiratorial, but I can't put my finger on it.

The guard hangs up and says something to his colleague. Their voices are gruff, giving their accents a sinister edge.

Then, to my amazement, they leave my room.

I open my eyes slightly and check to make sure I'm alone.

Is this a test?

A moment later, I decide—fuck it, I don't care. If it's a test, then I'm failing with flying colors.

I open my eyes all the way and sit up.

Wasting no time, I yank the IV out of the back of my hand. I hiss at the stab of pain and press down the bedsheet to stop the blood from bubbling up through the injection point.

Then I swing my legs off the bed and gingerly put one foot on the ground at a time. I move slowly, making sure I'm steady on my feet before I start walking. I don't want to faint or lose my balance before I even get out of this room.

Next on the agenda—clothes or shoes, if I can find them. This lilac-green hospital nightie is good for showing the world my ass and not much else besides that.

Scouring the room, I locate a thin cupboard in the corner next to the window. I go straight for it and throw open the doors to find a folded pair of my jeans, a t-shirt, and a sweater.

Obviously, Artem had a few of my things brought here from the apartment.

I discard my hospital gown quickly and pull on the jeans first.

I've just put on the t-shirt when I hear footsteps approaching my room. Panicking, I stumble to the window and peer outside.

The window looks out onto a narrow balcony that's obviously used for maintenance, but if I can get out onto it, I'll be able to shimmy down to the proper balcony on the lower floor and keep going like that until I'm on the ground.

Of course, my whole plan teeters on whether or not this window is locked.

I'm just about to try the window when the footsteps get louder. I freeze, my eyes turning towards the door as I wait to be discovered.

Oh, God...

And then whoever is outside my room keeps walking right on past it.

Pulling myself together, I remember to breathe as I turn my attention back to the window. I say a silent prayer and push it open.

Relief floods through me when it swings wide without a problem.

Scratch that—it gets to about a thirty-degree angle before it gets stuck.

"Fuck," I mutter under my breath. "Fuck, fuck, fuck…"

I hear more voices congregating outside the room. If I don't get out now, I can kiss my chances of escape goodbye.

And I *have* to escape. There is no way I can stay.

Not now, knowing what I know about Artem. About what he's done.

I have to protect myself.

But more importantly, I have to protect my baby.

Drawing strength from that, I put all my strength against the window and push as hard as I can. The window moves two more inches but I keep pushing anyway.

I need at least another inch or two if I'm going to be able to get out onto the balcony.

The voices get louder, but I drown them out.

"Come on, come on, you fucker…" I growl. "I've almost got you…"

The window shoves open several more inches.

Hell yes.

I have to resist the urge to scream out in celebration.

That'll do the trick.

I slip out of the window and land with a thump onto the tiny little balcony. My heartbeat is so loud I can hear it thundering in my ears as I survey the drop.

The series of balconies that make up the building's back façade allows me the perfect irregular ladder to climb down.

I take a step forward as the cold metal of the balcony grills prick at my soles, and only then do I realize that I'm barefoot.

There were shoes in the cupboard next to my jeans, but in my panic, I hadn't put them on.

Stupid, stupid, stupid.

But there's no going back now.

I start my descent.

43

ARTEM

"I'm not fucking leaving her, Cillian," I growl into the phone.

Cillian just sighs from his end of the call. He's been doing a lot of that lately.

I remind myself that he's only trying to help. I can't afford to be distracted.

Not with a threat this big looming.

But the anger that's been boiling in my veins since the moment the first shot was fired at my father's funeral refuses to go away.

It simmers just under the surface. Ready to explode at any moment.

"I understand you're worried about Esme, brother," Cillian says. "But this is important, too. I would argue it's *more* important."

I bite back my retort. "Where are you now?" I ask instead.

"The warehouse down Weston," he replies. "It's only ten minutes or so from the clinic. It shouldn't take that long."

"Fine. I'll see you soon."

I hang up.

It takes everything I have to resist my urge to turn back into Esme's room. To stare at her body again, the way I've done for hours and hours since we arrived here. Since I found her haunted and slumping into blackout.

Was that a bump in her belly? I couldn't be sure.

But the doctor said a baby was in there. He has no reason to lie. I have no reason to doubt him.

Which prompts another question: is it mine?

Four months ago, Esme and I had crossed paths in the bathroom of the Siren. There is a fairly good chance the child she's carrying is mine.

But just because the timing's right doesn't mean anything. There could have been other men.

My blood just boils even hotter at that thought. The idea of another man with his hands on my wife makes me unreasonably murderous. I can taste the bitter metal of fury on my tongue.

Why should I care? She lied to me. She's a liar.

And yet I do care.

It's the most frustrating fucking merry-go-round of circular thinking I've ever experienced.

I can't keep her.

I can't let her go.

With another heavy sigh, I turn my back on Esme's door and stride down the broad well-lit hallway.

Through the glass entryway doors, I can see my SUV waiting for me to take me to the meeting point that Cillian has arranged with Budimir.

I'm about three steps shy of breaking out into the Los Angeles sun when I feel a hand grab me by the back of the shirt collar and yank me into an empty room.

My reaction is immediate.

I seize the wrist of whoever the fuck is attacking me and rip it backwards. As I'm spinning around, my other hand finds the man's throat. We go crashing to the ground together.

Our combined bulk careens into a shelf of some kind filled with cleaning supplies. Bottles of bleach and a pair of mops smack down on top.

I wrestle for control. Hands on his windpipe, crushing, squeezing the life from this fucking—

"Get off of me, you fucking moron," hisses a familiar voice.

I stop, release. "Cillian?"

He sits up and wheezes. One hand rubs at the throat where I was just about to strangle him to death. My fingerprints are bright red on his pale skin.

"Well, I'm sure not the goddamn tooth fairy," he grumbles.

Still seated on the cold tile floor of this supply closet, I slump back against the wall.

"What the hell is wrong with you?" I demand. "I thought you were at the warehouse on Weston?"

"Lower your voice," he snaps. He leans forward to peer through the slightly ajar door. "Did anyone see me grab you?"

"I don't fucking—"

"Good." He pulls the door closed. It plunges us into semi-darkness. Just enough light filters under the crack for me to see his bright blue eyes.

In all the time I've known him, I've never seen Cillian O'Sullivan fear a single thing.

Until now.

Now, he looks downright fucking terrified.

"Listen to me and listen to me closely, brother," he says. "We don't have much time."

"You're going to lecture me on time?" I interrupt. "Whoever attacked us could be coming back anytime now. We have no intel, we have no plan, we have no—"

"They already came back."

I freeze. "What?"

"We were looking in the wrong place for answers, Artem. Looking out when we should've been searching in."

"Why the fuck are you still speaking in riddles? Talk straight to me, man!" I bellow.

He winces like something is physically paining him. His eyes fall to the ground between us before he sighs and fixes his gaze on me once more.

"Budimir," is all he says.

I blink. "Budimir what?"

"Budimir has taken over."

Silence. Footsteps shuffle past outside the door. I hear a gruff male voice—is that Olezka?—calling my name.

"Artem? Don Artem?"

We don't move a muscle or dare to breathe. Eventually, his footsteps fade away.

When he's gone, Cillian grips my forearm. "He's been planning this coup for a long time. The meeting you were about to go to is a trap. He was never going to let you walk out of there alive."

My head is spinning. "You're not making any sense."

Cillian runs a frustrated hand through his hair. "While you were in the safehouse, he called a meeting. Demanded loyalty from the rank-and-file. Accused you of treason, too."

My throat constricts with rage. "Treason?"

"Against the Bratva. He's saying you killed your father. You staged the shooting at the funeral."

"You can't be fucking serious."

"He has nothing," Cillian tells me. "But he wants his takeover to appear legitimate. If he comes across like a rebel, it's going to cause friction. Make the Bratva look weak, you know?"

I don't even know what to say. All I can think about is wringing the light out of my uncle's beady eyes.

"Artem, we have to get out of L.A. immediately."

Those words snap me back to the present.

"What do you mean?"

"We can't fight your uncle like this," Cillian tells me. "We don't have the men or the resources. He's issued a kill order on you. And on me."

"He did all of this," I whisper numbly, mostly to myself. "Everything he's accusing me of. He killed his own brother. Tried to kill his own nephew."

Saying the words out loud makes them easier to process. Forces me to accept the cold reality.

It's like a slap in the face.

But I can handle a fight, even if the deck is stacked against me. There's a simple clarity in facing down an enemy. There's a sense of finality to it.

Either you win or you die.

"He's going to pay for this," I growl under my breath.

Cillian's hand lands on my shoulder. "We will make him pay together, brother," he assures me. "But in order for that to happen, we need to lie low for a while. As long as we're in this city, we're sitting ducks. Budimir's men are everywhere."

The words themselves make me sick. *Budimir's men?*

No, those are *my* men. My father's men.

How fucking dare he take what's mine?

"Any motherfucker who supports this coup will pay with his life," I snarl.

"Yes, they will," Cillian says with a nod. "But there are many who are still loyal to you. They're targets too now, which means they've gone into hiding. We need to rally, find our allies and then—when we have a plan, when we're stronger—then we can attack."

He's right about everything, but the idea of running doesn't sit well with me.

I wasn't made to run.

I was made to stand up and fucking *fight*.

"Artem," Cillian's voice cuts through my conflicted thoughts. "I know you better than anyone. We've grown up together, we've been through dark times together. I know what you're thinking… you want revenge."

"He opened fire at my father's fucking funeral!" I yell, but Cillian doesn't so much as flinch back. "He's trying to kill me. He's trying to kill you. He's betrayed the Bratva and he's been planning this for a long fucking time."

"I'm not arguing his crimes," Cillian says in his most measured voice—although I notice that the angry vein in his forehead is throbbing. "But I am advocating for our lives. If we stay and fight now, we *will* lose. To have any hope of taking back control of the Bratva, you need to get out of this fucking city. We have to play the long game here. Not just for yourself. For everyone in your care. You're the don, Artem. You have people to protect."

I hate this plan. But it's the only real option.

Cillian is right—I owe my loyalty all the men who have gone into hiding rather than betray me.

They've chosen their true don over their own sense of self-preservation.

They've chosen me over my uncle.

And I have a duty to prove to them that they had made the right choice.

I have someone else to protect, too.

I swallow the metallic fury in my throat and croak, "Fine. We'll leave. But first, I need to go and get Esme."

"Let me get her," Cillian says. "You need to leave now."

"Not without my wife," I growl.

"I will get her out—"

"No!" I bark, my tone harsh. "This is one thing I have to do myself."

Cillian's eyes go wide as he realizes how deadly serious I am. He can see that I'm not going to budge on this so he drops it immediately.

"Fine then. You can use the—"

My phone rings. I glance down at the screen. It's the clinic, weirdly enough. They must've thought I'd already left the building.

I pick up immediately. "Yes?"

"Sir? Mr. Kovalyov? I'm Nurse Louisa…"

"Is she okay?" I ask, already impatient with her nervous energy. "Did my wife wake up yet?"

There is a long, pained pause on the other line. It takes my full effort not to bellow.

"Tell me," I say through gritted teeth.

"Sir… she's gone."

44

ARTEM

My blood turns to ice at once.

The first thought in my head is that Budimir got to her first. I want to fucking break something.

Why am I crouched in a fucking janitor's closet instead of protecting my wife? Protecting my *child*?

"What the fuck do you mean she's gone?" I snap into the phone.

"I, uh… There were some men who came," she stammers. "They were trying to get into her room. They had guns, sir, and I didn't know what to—"

Fuck. Fuck. Fuck.

"They pushed past me and got into her room but…"

"But what?" I growl. "But *what*?"

She sounds like she's on the verge of tears. "When they walked in… she was gone, sir. She had run."

"How?"

"She pushed open the window, sir, the one that leads to the maintenance balcony."

"Where were my guards?" I demand. "The ones I left in her room?"

"They left," she replies.

"They… left?"

"And then they came back with more men, sir."

She's a blubbering mess now. It's one thing to run a private clinic that sometimes caters to the city's nastier elements. It's another thing to have murderous troops storming down your hallways and hunting your patients.

But I don't have time to cater to her emotional breakdown.

"I… don't they all… work for you, sir?"

Fucking hell.

Not anymore, it seems.

"Does anyone know you've called me?" I ask.

"No, sir."

"Good. Let's keep it that way," I reply. "Forget my name. And go home. You're not safe here."

I hang up before she can answer.

"Artem?" Cillian asks, his eyes pierced with worry.

"Budimir's men are here," I tell him. "But Esme was gone by the time they'd got to her room."

"Gone?" he asks, his expression falling flat.

"I don't have the answers," I snap, furious that I have to admit that at all. "I just need to fucking find her."

I get to my feet and I'm about to charge out of the closet when Cillian grabs me again.

His face is solemn. "Artem... we may have to leave her. Budimir won't hurt an innocent woman."

I look over my shoulder and glare at him. "She's my wife, Cillian. I'm not leaving her."

"Artem—"

"She's fucking pregnant!" I yell, the words ripping from me before I can stop them.

Cillian looks at me in shock. There's two seconds of silence and then his hand falls from my shoulder.

"Pregnant," he says with a look of amazement in his eyes. "Not how I expected you to ask me, but yes, I'll be the godfather."

In spite of everything, I laugh.

This fucking idiot is my best friend?

There's no one else in the universe I'd rather have at my side in this war.

"Come on, brother," he says to me with a grim set in his jaw. "Let's go find your woman."

45

ARTEM

I peer out into the clinic hallway. The coast is clear.

Carefully, the two of us step out. Cillian starts to head back towards Esme's room, but I grab him.

"They said she went out the window," I point out. "That means she's outside somewhere."

"Then she could be anywhere, Artem."

"She can't have gotten far. She's been laid up in a hospital bed and sedated. She's going to be disoriented and weak. That's going to slow her pace."

I have no idea if that is true or not, but I'm counting on it working in my favor. Every time I think of Budimir getting to Esme before me, my stomach turns to black bile.

That is not a fucking option.

"But you're right about one thing," I continue.

"I'm right about everything," Cillian jokes with a hollow laugh. "Which thing in particular are you talking about now?"

"We don't know which way she went. So we need to split up. Cover more ground. You get us ready to escape the city. I'll find Esme."

He shakes his head at once, just like I knew he would. "No way. We're sticking together."

"Not this time, brother."

"You can't do this alone," Cillian says.

"It's better that I do," I reply. "She's my wife, and in any case, it makes more sense. I'm going to look less suspicious walking around by myself."

Cillian narrows his eyes at me. "Have you looked at yourself in the mirror lately? Shit, *I'd* arrest you on suspicion of something, and I'm the best friend you've got."

If the situation weren't so fucking heightened, I might have smiled. "Don't worry about me," I say. "I can handle myself."

Cillian grumbles in frustration, but he knows I'm right. The sooner we find Esme, the sooner we can escape Budimir's trap. Every second he spends arguing with me could be the difference between life and death.

"Fine. We'll meet tomorrow," Cillian says. "We need to figure out our plan."

"You're staying in the city?"

"As long as you're here, I will be, too," he replies soberly. I can tell from his tone that he isn't going to budge on that.

"Fine," I nod. "Find a phone. Make sure it's untraceable. Send me a place and time for tomorrow and I'll be there."

To my surprise, Cillian steps forward and embraces me. "Take care of yourself, Artem," he whispers in my ear. "I mean that."

"You do the same," I tell him. "You're ugly enough without a bullet hole in the face."

We both laugh as we separate. It's the kind of parting I never thought he and I would share.

The kind where you don't know if it may be your last.

We exchange one final nod. Then I spin on my heel and push through the front doors.

I take stock of my surroundings. There's a park just a short ways down the block lined with trees. When I step around the side of the building, I see a dirt path leading from the fire escape Esme climbed down. It leads off into the shrubbery.

That's as good a place to start as any.

I break out into a jog—just as I hear the jangle of the front doors opening again. I hurl myself behind a bush and peek back over my shoulder.

Borya and Evgeni are standing out front, chests heaving from exertion. Both hold pistols in their hands.

Looking for me, no doubt.

My blood boils at their betrayal. They were part of the older contingent of Bratva men. Had served my father for decades.

And yet, they'd turned before my father was even cold in the ground.

They'll pay for that.

As I watch, they clamber into an SUV and peel away with a screech of tires.

Carefully, I slink back away from the sidewalk under cover of the trees. I find the dirt path again and turn the corner, only to come face to face with—

"Olezka."

The guard's eyes go wide the moment he sees me.

He reacts instantly. His hands flies to the gun at his hip, but I move faster. I launch my body into his in a full-on football tackle.

He stumbles backwards and rams into a thick tree trunk, abandoning his reach for the gun.

Then I grab him by the neck and snap his head back against the tree like a rag doll.

There's a nasty crunch. When his head lolls forward, I can see blood smeared on the bark.

He struggles, so I land a punch right on his jaw. His eyes swim out of focus for a moment before they're back, still determined and ready to fight.

But this motherfucker couldn't beat me on his best day.

And today is most certainly not that day.

I punch him again, then I grab his shirt collar in both hands and headbutt him hard in the nose.

Another crack.

Another groan.

Another spurt of blood.

His head is drooping forward uselessly on his thick neck, but he's still awake. I pin his throat to the tree with my forearm.

"You motherfucker," I hiss. "Where's Esme?"

I lean in, putting pressure on his neck long enough for him to start spluttering desperately, before I release just enough for him to be able to reply.

"I will not speak," he rasps.

Bad decision.

I pull out my blade and run his stomach through. He pales when I pull the dagger out and force him to look at his blood gleaming against the shiny steel.

"One more time," I hiss. "Or there will be much more of this on the ground soon. Where is she?"

"*Urgh*... I don't fucking know," he burbles. "We were instructed to fan out and look for her."

"Were you working with Budimir this whole fucking time?" I ask.

I'd trusted this fucker to protect Esme while I'd been gone. Of course he'd walked away the moment I had left.

"I had to choose a side."

"Well, you chose the fucking losing side, asshole," I snarl. "Budimir's gonna be pissed when he realizes you had my wife unconscious on a bed and you still managed to lose her."

"The bitch woke up and—"

I don't let him finish his sentence. One quick slice of my blade across his throat finishes the son of a bitch for good.

He slumps to the ground.

But I'm not done with dear old Olezka.

I slit open the shirt he's wearing. Using his chest as a canvas, I carve out a little message for my uncle.

I work fast and messy. Olezka won't care anymore.

When I'm done, I stand up and look down at what I've written. The blood clots under the light filtering down through the trees, but it's clear as fucking day.

Tvoi dni sochteny.

Your days are numbered.

"That's a fucking promise, Uncle," I whisper to the corpse that chose him over me.

I wipe my blade on the leg of Olezka's pants and sheath it. Then I turn and keep running.

I don't know why I think I can find Esme before Budimir does, but instinct is telling me to keep walking, keep searching.

She's out there. She's close.

I'm glad she ran. It's the only thing that saved her from Budimir's men.

But a sudden thought gives me pause.

Esme doesn't know about Budimir.

She doesn't know that he's after me—and by extension, after her.

But she escaped anyway.

Which begs the question... who is she escaping from?

46

ESME

A few people glance at my bare feet as I walk past them, but I ignore the stares and keep going.

It isn't until I've walked out of the park, down a few alleys, and fifteen minutes into the heart of L.A. that I realize I don't actually know where I'm going.

After all, who do I have left to run to?

Ghosts.

I have only ghosts.

I try and shake the morbid thought from my head. But it refuses to budge. My stomach roils with hunger and my body aches as it withdraws from the drugs that have been pumped into my system since I collapsed in the Bratva safehouse.

I know I need to get off the streets as fast as possible, but my head keeps running in circles, making me even more tired, even more confused.

I end up sinking onto a bench by the side of the street, looking up at a massive billboard of a scarlet-lipped model in black lace lingerie.

I shouldn't stop. I should keep moving. Artem could be anywhere.

But I'm just so, so tired.

The billboard model stares at me seductively, her lips parted ever so slightly.

She makes me feel… unsettled.

Probably because she's completely and utterly dead in the eyes. It scares me how much I relate to that expression.

"I have to get indoors," I mumble up to her. As if this 2D bimbo gives a shit about me, or about anyone. "Somewhere safe and hidden, so he doesn't find me." My stomach rumbles again. "Preferably somewhere with food."

She doesn't even blink.

With a sigh, I let my gaze fall from the billboard to a coffee shop nestled across the street.

There's a couple sitting at one of the outdoor tables. They lean in towards each other, foreheads pressed together and dreamy smiles on their faces, oblivious to everything around them.

A fat piece of cake sits between them on the table.

Red velvet, unless my eyes deceive me. The things I would do for a single bite…

Out of nowhere, a prickly sense of unease skims over my body. That "someone's watching me and they don't have good intentions" spidey sense that every woman in public knows all too well.

My first thought is laced with panic.

It's Artem.

He's found me.

I whirl around one hundred and eighty degrees.

Sure enough, there's a man behind me.

Tall. Broad. Dark-haired and—

Wait, no. His hair is too shaggy and the wrong shade of dark. And Artem Kovalyov would never be caught dead in a pinstripe suit that faded and old.

But I don't let my guard down just yet.

The man's weathered face is kindly, but just because he doesn't look the part doesn't mean he's not dangerous.

"Here you go, hon," he says, stretching his hand out towards me.

I flinch back, wondering who he works for, already planning which direction I'll dive if he tries to grab me.

That's when I notice the five-dollar bill in his outstretched hand.

I look up at his face and realize he's giving me a sympathetic smile.

He thinks I'm homeless.

I'm so shocked by this realization that I actually reach up and take the money.

"Thank you," I whisper automatically, not sure why the gesture touches me as much as it does.

"Go get yourself a nice warm meal, dear," he tells me. Then he walks away.

A bubble of laughter rises to my lips. I must look like a real pile of flaming garbage if kind older men are out here dispensing cash to wretches like me.

I bury my head in my hands as the laughter takes me over. It's the kind of laughter that only comes to those who have nothing left to lose. Desperate, heaving laughter.

I let it run through me like a storm. When it's gone, I look up at the coffee shop again. Maybe I'll go get a piece of that cake with this five bucks.

The remnants of the laughing tears stain my eyes.

So when I first see him, it's too blurred, too much of a fragmented mosaic to seem real.

But then I wipe the tears away and it all resolves into perfect clarity.

There he is.

No false alarm. No mistaking the man.

I'd recognize those dark eyes in a room full of shadow.

The taint of furious betrayal lingers in the lines of Artem's mouth. He's standing on the opposite side of the street in a dark coat that acts as camouflage. Even from here, I think I can see blood on his hands.

What has he done to find me? Who has he hurt to track me down?

And what will he do when he closes the final distance?

The traffic on the road is light. It's not going to take much for him to cross.

That means I have to go—right fucking now.

I dart up from the bench, still clutching my five-dollar bill, and run down the street without looking back.

My legs still feel drugged and heavy, but the adrenaline is loosening them up considerably.

The cold pavement slaps at the soles of my feet but I don't let that stop me, either.

I don't slow down.

I don't look back.

I just run.

I turn the corner, sprint down an alleyway, and find myself on a broader street with grotesque-looking signs outside its shops.

A left turn leads me into another alleyway, this one narrower than the last. I run down it, realizing that I've made a huge mistake by veering away from the crowds of the busier L.A. roads.

Another turn.

Dead-end.

I stare in disbelief at the brick wall at the end of the trash-filled alley. I can barely breathe. Panic squeezes my lungs, but I don't have the option of stopping here.

I turn, stumble...

And that's when I run right into Artem's broad chest.

I bounce off, but he grabs me before I fall to the concrete. His hand locks around my wrist so tight that it nearly cuts off my circulation, but I still struggle to get free, as useless as that effort is.

"Let me go," I spit, trying to summon up every last lick of bravery I still possess.

Artem tows me towards him until my face is only inches away from his. His eyes burn with an urgency I don't quite understand.

He doesn't look angry so much as... determined.

"What the fuck are you doing?" he demands. "It's me."

"You?" I hiss. "You are nothing but a murderer. A liar and a murderer."

He looks down at me with something like confusion. "You know what my world requires of me," he says softly. "I never lied to you about that."

I shake my head, all the while trying to pull my hand out of his grasp. He shakes his head in frustration as his eyes flash dangerously.

"Fucking hell, Esme!" he yells, pulling me back behind a dumpster so that we're out of sight of passing cars and foot traffic. "Calm the fuck down. You're disoriented and confused, but I don't have time to explain anything to you now. We have to get out of the city."

"Oh, I plan to," I scowl. "But not with you."

"Goddammit," Artem says, "you don't understand what's happening. You're not safe here. You're not safe alone. You need me."

I laugh at that. Right in his smug fucking face.

Does he really think that line is going to flip a switch and persuade me to run into his arms?

I need him?

No. Hell no. I absolutely do not.

"Get your fucking hands off of me."

His eyes narrow viciously. That familiar burst of anger that has come to be so familiar to me burns in his eyes.

He's about to say something, but I'm done talking and I don't want his explanations clouding my already clouded brain.

So I do what Cesar told me to do an eternity ago—back when I was still naïve enough to believe there was such a thing as heroes.

I swing my knee up hard, straight into Artem's crotch. He could have avoided the hit easily if he had been prepared for it.

But for once, I succeed in taking him off guard.

He grunts, more in shock than in pain, but it distracts him enough that he releases his hold on me.

I don't hesitate—I turn tail and run as fast as I can.

"Esme!" he yells after me in a pained roar.

It amazes me that even now, after everything I've learned about him, I desperately want to turn back. I desperately want to risk one last glance at him.

But I don't.

I suppress the desire and turn into a bustling L.A. strip mall that allows me to blend into the crowd.

I slip through the crowd as fast as I can, ignoring all the people I elbow or push aside to get around them.

An exit spits me out a few blocks away. When I emerge on the side street, I hail a cab and get into it with cautious relief.

Something occurred to me while I was running.

I have one more place to go.

47

ESME

It takes twenty-five minutes to get to the east side of Los Angeles. I wring my hands nervously as I stare at the meter going up, up, up.

The moment the driver comes to a stop in front of the building, I lean in a little and give him my best smile. It might've worked better if I didn't look so ragged that someone had already mistaken me for a hobo today.

"Umm, so I have only five dollars on me—"

He turns to me, his happy-go-lucky grin dropping like a hot potato. "You fuckin' kidding me, girl?"

"It's been a rough day," I say, by way of explanation. *If only you knew the half of it,* I want to add. "But I'll get you the money. My cousin lives in this building."

The driver peers through his window, examining the building as though it's my last credible witness. "Seems like a nice building. Even got a doorman."

"See?" I say. "I swear, I'll be back with your money."

He narrows his murky blue eyes at me before pulling out his phone and handing it to me. "Call your cousin and tell her to come out here with the money. I let you go up in there, I ain't never gonna see you again."

Relieved that I remember Tamara's number, I take his phone and dial in her number. She doesn't answer for the longest time.

I start to panic. If she doesn't answer, I'll be stranded somewhere else with a pissed-off cabbie ready to beat my head in.

Just as I'm trying to figure out my back-up plan, she picks up and I sigh inwardly.

"Hello?"

"Tamara! Thank God. Where are you?"

"Oh my God… Esme?"

She sounds shocked to hear from me, and honestly, who can blame her? I haven't been in contact with her since days before the compound was attacked and destroyed by Artem and the Bratva.

"Where are you?"

"Um… I'm in my apartment. Where are *you*?"

"Outside your apartment," I reply without explaining. "I'm in the cab parked outside the building. I need to pay for my ride and I only have five dollars on me."

"Oh… oh," she says, sounding shell-shocked.

"Tam? Can you help?"

"Right, right… I'll be down in two seconds."

I hang up and hand the phone back to the driver. "She's coming down."

He gives me a sheepish smile. "Sorry, but can't be too careful, ya know," he says. "I've been fooled by a pretty face before."

"I understand."

"The prettier the face, the more careful you gotta be," he continues. "My old man used to say that all the time. And you've got one of the prettiest faces I've ever seen."

I give him a tight smile and look out the window just as Tamara rushes out of her building with a couple of dollar bills clutched in her palm.

"There she is," I say, before jumping out of the cab.

Tamara looks at me like I have a second head sprouting out of my neck before hurrying over and paying the driver. Then she grabs my hand and pulls me back into her building.

The moment we step into the elevator and the doors close, she turns to me.

"What the fuck?!" she breathes.

I shake my head. "Where do I even start?"

"How about you start from the beginning?"

She reaches out and wipes something off my cheek. I turn my head to the side and catch my reflection in the mirrors that hang on either side of the elevator walls.

It's enough to make me want to scream.

My eyes are huge and bloodshot, my cheeks look like they've hollowed in, and my hair is a dirty, matted mess that clings to the side of my face.

I'm half a ghost myself.

The elevator doors open on the sixth floor and I follow Tamara down the broad corridor, around the corner, and into her apartment.

I stop one step over the threshold. Tam realizes I'm frozen in place and turns around to face me.

"Esme?"

I don't trust my voice. She wants an explanation for why I'm showing up at her doorstep unannounced and broke, looking like hell warmed over. She wants to know what happened. She wants me to start from the beginning.

But what was the beginning?

Was it when Artem had stormed the compound and murdered my entire household?

Was it when our paths had first crossed at The Siren four months before then?

Was it the day I was born into this horrible world?

I see the concern in Tamara's eyes, pure and honest. That's what unravels me.

I open my mouth to explain, but only a sob comes out.

And then I'm crying—full, hacking sobs that double me over and drain the breath from my lungs.

Tamara's face crumples as she moves towards me and wraps her arms around me.

"Hey," she says soothingly. "Hey, chica, it's okay."

My whole body convulses while I cling to her. "No, it's not… It's never going to be okay again."

I lean against the only family I have left, desperate for the warmth and comfort of someone familiar. She sinks to the floor with me and holds me until my sobs subside.

Only then does she pulls away, though she keeps both hands on my shoulders.

"I'm sorry," I hiccup.

Tamara's eyes are conflicted as she looks me over. It's like she's trying to figure out how to *not* break me.

It makes me realize that I hadn't been thinking clearly when I'd decided to come to her apartment.

I've endangered Tamara now by coming here.

The blade edge of clarity cuts through my fog and my stomach twists in knots.

"I should leave," I start to stammer. I try to struggle to my feet.

"What are you talking about?" Tamara asks, with a frown.

"I need to leave, Tamara. There are men looking for me. Bad men." I'm stumbling over my words as I move back towards the door.

Tamara grabs my arm and pulls me to a stop. "Esme, you have no shoes on."

I look down at my bare feet, covered in layers of dirt and grime and oozing cuts that I haven't had the luxury of noticing until now.

"It's not safe for me here."

"You can't leave!"

Startled, I look at her with raised eyebrows and she gives me a quick smile.

"Don't take this the wrong way honey," Tamara says. "But you look like hell."

A burst of laughter escapes from my lips. Tamara's smile irons out a little. "Come on... let's get you a nice, hot shower. Afterwards, when you're ready, we can talk."

"Okay," I say in a small voice. I don't have much willpower left to argue.

I let myself be led to the bathroom, where Tamara helps me out of my clothes and into the tub. She puts on some music and places a fresh towel on the railing next to the tub.

"I'll go see what I have in the fridge for you," she says as she backs out of the bathroom.

I sit in the tub and soak for fifteen glorious minutes until I've washed off the anxiety and sweat of the last several hours.

Bit by bit, my muscles unclench. And when I empty the tub and watch the dirt of the last few days whisk away down the drain, it feels like I'm letting some of the fear go with it.

It takes the edge away, but it's nowhere near a cure-all.

I may be clean now, but I'm far from safe.

Reluctantly, I get out of the tub and towel myself off. When I walk back into Tamara's bedroom, I find a fresh pair of jeans and a white silk blouse laid out on the bed for me.

I dress and comb out my hair, vaguely aware of Tamara's voice coming from the kitchen. She's on the phone, but her tone is hushed, so I have no idea who she's talking to.

She hangs up, picks up a small tray, and walks around the kitchen island towards the room. I duck back inside and wait for her on the bed.

"Hey, you," she says, as she enters. "Feel better?"

"Marginally," I acknowledge just as her phone pings again.

She ignores it and sits on the bed next to me. "There wasn't much, but this should hold you over until I can order some real food."

The tray is filled with crackers, cheese, and grapes. There's also two full glasses, one with orange juice and another with water.

I grab the water first and down it within seconds. Then I reach for the crackers and cheese as my stomach churns desperately.

"Sorry," I tell her. "This ain't gonna be pretty."

Tamara laughs distractedly as her phone pings twice more. She pulls it out and checks the screen, but she doesn't respond. She just sets the phone aside and looks back at me.

"So…"

Before she finish her sentence, her phone pings for a fourth time and she sighs and rolls her eyes.

"Do you need to get that?" I ask, wondering why she's being cagey with her phone.

Tamara is usually an open book, which is why it's obvious when she tries to hide things.

"No," Tamara says with a wave of her hand. "I'll get to it later. Just another boy who's obsessed with me. Nothing new."

I smile. That is definitely nothing new.

"Seriously, if you need to take it, I can wait," I assure her.

"No, no," she says. "This is more important. Now, are you ready to talk, chica?"

I swallow crackers and cheese and take a sip of the orange juice.

"You're not going to believe me if I do."

She grins wickedly. "Try me."

48

ESME

I tell Tamara everything. From the assault and subsequent hookup in The Siren bathroom when she was passed out in the stall to the attack on my family compound.

The only thing I leave out is the fact that I'm pregnant.

For some reason, I cling to that information, guarding it like a precious stone. I know I can trust Tamara, so I'm not sure why I hesitate, but I have so much else to tell that I don't dwell on it.

By the time I'm done, I feel like I've been talking for as long as I can remember.

"Artem brought me back to L.A.," I continue. "And then... well, he married me."

"He *what*?" Tamara asks. Her eyes go wide, but not just with surprise. There's another emotion in there, too—something I can't put my finger on.

"It was a marriage of... convenience, so to speak," I explain, trying to pretend like that admission doesn't hurt me deeply. Like that little spark of hope I'd been nurturing never existed.

"Did he force himself on you?" Tamara asks. "Because so help me God, if he did, I will slice his cojones…"

I start to fumble for an answer, but before I can, Tamara's phone pings again.

Honestly, I'm glad for the distraction. I really don't want to get into the weeds of my relationship with Artem. It is—*was*, I correct mentally—too complicated, too confused, too filled with betrayal and regret for me to wade through by myself, let alone share it with someone else.

"Sorry," Tamara says, picking her phone up again. "I'll only be a few minutes."

Weird of her to walk away to answer a call from some thirsty boy. Tam never cares about that kind of thing. "Kiss and tell" is her middle name.

But if she has gotten shy since the last time I saw her, that's okay. I'm too tired to care one way or another.

I start eating the grapes, and now that the edge of my hunger has been sated, I feel a little more balanced, a little more capable of clarity. I can hear Tam pacing on the balcony outside and whispering rapid-fire.

She comes back in a few moments later. As soon as she sees me, she smiles. But again, there's something in her face—an edge, a shadow—that troubles me.

"Sorry about that."

"Tam," I ask, "is everything all right?"

"Of course," she says, with so much surprise that I find myself wondering if I'm just being paranoid. "Everything's fine. It's just…"

"A guy."

"Right. A guy."

"I've never seen you pay much attention to one man for too long," I say. "Is this one different?"

She lets out a burst of laughter. "This one is definitely different."

"Is it serious?"

Tamara nods. "He wants it to be," she replies. "I just... I'm not so sure about him."

"Hence the texts and calls," I nod.

"Right," she replies. "But enough about me. I can't really deal with him right now. Not when my cousin needs me."

I smile, feeling a warmth in my chest that I haven't felt in a while. She sinks to her seat next to me and tucks her toes under my thigh.

"I can't imagine what you've been through these past several weeks," she says. "You're like, my hero."

"It's been difficult," I admit. It feels good to be honest. I've spent so many long days and nights putting on a brave face to spar with Artem.

Being truthful, being vulnerable—it's a welcome change of pace.

"How did you get away from that bastard?"

It takes me a moment to realize that she's talking about Artem. I jolt at the curse, but when you look at it from Tam's perspective—he kidnapped me, killed my father, burned my house down, forced me to marry him... "bastard" starts to feel very appropriate indeed.

So why does it bother me?

Because he's more than that to me.

"His father died," I murmur. "And we were ambushed at this funeral."

"No way."

"We got to a safe house and... and..."

My words stall as I realize that I don't want to explain the next part to her.

I don't want to relive the moment that broke my trust in Artem. Mostly because, while it *did* break my trust in him, it hasn't succeeded in breaking my desire for him.

I still want him.

I still miss him.

That's the thing about falling—there are some cliffs you can't climb back up from.

"Esme?"

I glance at Tamara. She's staring at me curiously. "Sorry. I'm just a little tired, that's all."

"Of course," she nods. "You look like you could use a nice, long sleep."

The thought of a warm bed beckons me, but despite my exhaustion, I don't think I'll be able to sleep.

"I wish I could. But I have to get out of here, Tam," I tell her. "I don't want to put you at risk, too."

She waves away my concerns. "I can handle myself. That door triple locks, baby. You think your Russian boy toy is the first crazy motherfucker that's tried to bust in here? Nuh-uh." She grins, then her expressions softens into sympathy. She reaches out and brushes back a lock of my hair. "I just want you make sure you're okay, honey."

My hand lands over my belly subconsciously, but I move it away before Tamara zones in on the gesture.

"I think you need to stay here with me, at least for a day or two," she says. "You need a plan and a destination. Once you have that, then you can leave if that's what you really want."

I smile at her, incredibly grateful for how supportive she's being. "I can't thank you enough."

Tamara gives me a sad smile as she reaches out and takes my hand. "Don't thank me yet, cousin."

"You let me in. That's enough."

Tamara actually looks a little emotional as she leans in and hugs me tight. When we pull apart again, my eyes are wet, too.

"I'm glad you came to me," she says. She squeezes my hand and gets to her feet. "Why don't you go to my room and get some sleep? I'm going to pop downtown and grab us some real food."

"You don't have to do that," I protest.

"You look half starved, Esme," Tamara insists. "The least I can do is send you off with a full tummy."

I smile and nod. "Thanks, cuz."

"Of course," Tamara chuckles with a wink.

I stand up as she grabs a light faux-fur jacket and her bag. I walk her to the door, but at the threshold, she whirls around suddenly and pulls me in for a hug that I don't expect.

"What was that for?" I ask with a confused smile.

Tamara shrugs. "For my peace of mind."

I watch as she sashays out the door and down into the elevators before turning and locking the door behind me. She wasn't kidding —there are three top-of-the-line locks on the door.

I'm half-asleep and getting sleepier with every step towards Tamara's bedroom. I'm hoping for a few uninterrupted hours of no-dream slumber before I have to face tomorrow.

Before I have to decide what to do with the rest of my life.

I collapse gratefully onto the mattress. It feels like a cloud. Tam-Tam is not one to skimp when it comes to her beauty sleep.

I've just settled in between the soft cotton sheets when the subtle chime of the doorbell interrupts my peace and quiet.

Tamara must have forgotten her wallet.

Grumbling, I get up and drag myself to the door.

I'm so sure it's Tamara that I don't bother checking to make sure. I undo the chain, the deadbolt, and the backup lock, and pull open the door.

But it's not Tamara.

It's not Tamara at all.

49

ARTEM

Esme tries to slam the door on me, but I move fast, blocking the door with my foot.

She yelps in fright as I shove my way inside the apartment.

The door swings shut and clicks behind me. Esme backs away like a cornered animal, her eyes twisted with fury and fear.

It's unsettling for me to see her look at me this way.

It's like she's not seeing me at all, but a monster with two heads that's hellbent on devouring her whole.

I'd been hoping our alleyway encounter was nothing more than a half-delusional reaction to waking up in an unfamiliar clinic after a traumatic experience.

But I can see now that it wasn't a reaction at all.

Something has changed since the funeral.

"Esme," I say as gently as I can manage.

She doesn't answer.

Every time I move forward, she takes a step back, as though she has to maintain a five-foot distance between us at all times.

I start to say her name again, but she cuts me off. "Don't," she hisses.

I hold my hands up. "I'm trying to talk to you."

"Well, I'm done talking to you," she snarls at me, her eyes flashing like a viper's. "Everything you've ever said to me was a lie."

I frown. "You're confused," I tell her. "You're not thinking clearly."

"Don't do that," she says, her tone is as steady as mine. "Don't make me out to be crazy or irrational. Don't you dare belittle my feelings because it's more convenient for you to pretend that *I'm* the problem."

"I didn't think there *was* a fucking problem."

My voice comes out harsher than I intended. Esme flinches, but she stands her ground.

I take stock of her. I have to admit—she looks a lot better now than she did on the streets a few hours ago. She's dressed in jeans that are sinfully tight and a white blouse with thin straps that shows off her delicate shoulders and sharp shoulder blades.

Her hair is bouncy and fragrant, and her face has been wiped clean of the sweat, dust, and chaos of the streets.

As pissed as I am right now, I'm also incredibly relieved that she seems to be in one piece.

Unfortunately, I don't think the feeling is mutual.

"Esme," I say with frustration, "we can't stay in the city."

"There is no 'we' anymore, Artem," she snaps. Her eyes burn softly with hurt. "I want you to leave."

I grit my teeth. "I'm not going anywhere without you."

"Too fucking bad! Because I'm not going anywhere *with* you."

"Fuck!" I roar, resisting the urge to put my fist through the nearest wall. "Would you mind telling me why the fuck you're acting like a madwoman right now? I'm the same man that took you to the safehouse after the funeral. So what the fuck changed?"

I see tears turn her eyes into shimmering pools of gold. She blinks and a single teardrop falls free, creating a jagged line down her cheek.

My fingers ache to reach out and wipe that tear away.

Instead, I clamp my hand into a fist.

"You want to know what changed?" she asks softly, taking another step toward me.

We're standing close together now, her body is only inches from mine. Her breasts rise and fall with the heat of her emotion. It takes all my self-control to keep from grabbing her.

"Because you killed him," she continues without waiting for me to answer. "You killed my brother."

The words fall from her lips like wilted petals. Each one heartbreaking.

I draw a slow, shuddering breath.

So she'd overheard. She must've been awake when Cillian and I were talking. Of all the ways for her to find out, this is the worst.

At least it explains everything. Most of all, it explains the haunted look in her eyes just before she passed out at the safehouse.

She was looking at me and she wasn't seeing the man who kept her safe from killers at that funeral.

She was seeing the man who'd ruined everything she ever loved.

I lift my eyes to Esme's.

I will not shrink from this.

I owe her my honesty. It's all I have left to give.

"Yes," I whisper.

I see her hand fly up towards me. I could dodge the slap or snatch it out of mid-air.

But I do neither.

I stand still and accept it. My face jerks to the side when her palm makes contact with the side of my jaw.

It's a faint sting. Hardly enough to register—physically, at least.

But in some ways, it's the most agonizing thing I've ever felt.

"You bastard," she spits. "You fucking bastard."

I say nothing.

Esme is shaking her head. She takes one slow step away from me, though her eyes never leave mine. "You lied to me."

"I never lied to you." It's a cop-out, but I have to say something. I can't stand the way she's looking at me. The hate, the burning fucking rage in her eyes. "I just didn't tell you that part of my past."

"It was *my* past too!" she screams. Her tears are gathering faster now. "He was *my* brother and I loved him."

Her love for him is the only thing that prevents me from telling her everything.

It's the only thing protecting her from the truth of what happened all those years ago.

"I can't change what happened, Esme."

She stills for a moment, her eyes fluttering to me as tears glisten like frost on her long eyelashes. "Even if you could change what happened… would you?"

Fuck me.

Of all the questions she could have asked, did she have to ask that one.

I could lie. Smooth all this over. If she just knew the story…

But I won't.

I can't.

"No," I admit. "I wouldn't."

Her face caves in. I take a step towards her, my hand outstretched, but she flinches away from me like I'm the devil.

"Don't you dare touch me," she snarls through her tears. "Don't fucking touch me."

"There's a lot you don't understand, Esme," I tell her, hoping her anger and pain won't drown out my words. "You don't know the reasons why I did what I did back then."

"I don't care," she cries. "I don't care about your *reasons!*"

"You might one day."

That makes her stop in her tracks, her expression teetering between bewilderment and fear. It takes a lot to keep my eyes from dropping down towards her stomach.

For some reason, I'm reluctant to bring it up. Reluctant to pull the veil back and hear why she concealed the pregnancy from me.

What if I'm not the father?

"You're just trying to confuse me," Esme accuses, cutting through my thoughts. "You're just trying to justify what you did."

"I'm not," I say. "I'm not justifying anything. I killed your brother and I'll freely admit that. I'm not the hero in this story, nor will I ever be. But that doesn't make me the villain, either."

"Doesn't it?" she asks. "Isn't murdering another human being without reason or compunction the very definition of being a villain."

"Life is not a fucking fairytale, Esme," I growl. "Everything isn't always black or white. In fact, nothing is. Your brother wasn't a fucking saint—"

"Don't you *ever* talk about my brother!"

Her body seems to fold in on itself, as though she's trying to protect herself from my words. As though each word I say is a new and deadly weapon hurtling towards her.

"I will explain it all to you one day," I promise her. "I'll tell you the truth."

"I don't think you know the meaning of the word," she bites.

"Truth is a matter of perspective, too," I concede, with a shrug. "So I can only offer you my truth. That's all I have."

"Why can't you tell me now?"

"I'll tell you when the time is right."

Her eyes flash at my words and dart around the room as though she's looking for a way to escape.

"Fuck you," she hurls at me.

I shake my head. "Stop acting like a little girl."

"Don't call me that."

"Then stop acting like one."

"I'm not going anywhere with you, Artem," she says, her lips curling derisively around my name.

I growl low, furious and frustrated in equal measure. I understand she's processing a lot right now, but I don't have the luxury of being patient.

"You don't have a choice," I tell her. "There's a hit out on my head. Yours, too, most likely. My uncle has taken over the Bratva, which means we have only a limited amount of time before his men find us."

Panic darkens her features for a moment, and she looks at me with something close to concern. She drops her head.

But when she looks back up again, the concern is gone, replaced by an emotion she wants me to see.

Scorn.

"I told you before," Esme says, her tone soft. "There is no 'us.'"

"You're wrong about that," I say in a low voice. "The moment I claimed you as my own on that altar, you became mine. It became 'us.'"

"No," she says, shaking her head. "No, no, no—"

"We have to get out of this city, Esme," I interrupt. "I swore on that altar to keep you safe. Let me do that."

"I plan on getting out of this city," she says. "But not with you."

"You won't get far without me."

"Why?" she snaps. "Because I'm helpless without you? I've got news for you, motherfucker. I don't *need* you. I don't need anyone."

"You're delusional if you believe that," I say. "The only way you're going to live is if you come with me."

"Why would I go anywhere with someone I don't trust?" she asks. "Why would I go anywhere with someone I hate?"

I look her dead in the eye and laugh. Her anger turns confused for a moment before it snaps back again.

"What's so fucking funny?"

"You don't hate me."

Her eyes go wide with rage. "Is that what you think?"

"It's what I know," I tell her. "The person you really hate right now is *yourself*."

"Fuck you," she snaps, screwing her nose up with indignation as she tries to writhe out of the trap that I'm laying for her.

"You know it, too," I reply, backing her into a corner. "Which is why you're not looking me in the eye right now."

"Oh, yeah?" she says, taking the bait and meeting my gaze to prove how wrong I am. "And why the hell would I hate myself?"

I wonder if she expects me to falter, to hesitate. To hit her with another lie.

But I know I have the upper hand here.

Because this time, I'm the one bearing the truth.

"Because," I say, as my hand darts out and grabs her by the throat, pinning her back against the wall, "you know I killed your brother. But you want me anyway."

Shock flares up in her hazel-gold irises. I see only an iota of denial before it's overpowered by self-awareness.

And that is all the confirmation I need before I slam my lips down on hers.

Her body freezes in shock, taken aback by the sudden assault. A gasp escapes from between her lips, sharp and sudden.

I crush her against the wall with the entire length of my body. She's tense from head to toe. I can feel her hesitation, her desperation to resist—but her inability to commit to denying me.

She pulls her lips from mine for a moment. Her breathing is heavy, laced with lust, but she still tries.

"Stop... Please, stop."

I know why she's asking. She doesn't actually want me to stop. She wants me to help her lie to herself. To keep up this charade that she really does hate me. That she really doesn't want me.

But that would rely on me being willing to let her live those lies.

And I'm not fucking willing.

"You want me to stop?" I ask.

She trembles, swallows, and tries to nod. It's hardly convincing.

I wind my fingers through the roots of hair at the back of her head. Leaning close enough that I can count each splash of gold in her eyes, I touch my forehead to hers and whisper the last words needed to destroy her resistance.

"Then make me."

So I close the remaining distance and begin to retake what's mine.

50

ARTEM

I suck her bottom lip between my teeth. It draws a sharp moan from her. That's the sound I was missing, so sweet and innocent that my cock stiffens immediately.

She grinds her hips into mine and mewls.

But some part of her is still trying to hold back.

Still unwilling to give everything up to me.

I'm going to fuck that out of her.

One way or another, she's going to have to confront her feelings for me.

Right.

Fucking.

Now.

I move my head to the side, deepening the kiss and forcing a cry from Esme that sounds like a cross between a moan and a plea for help.

I run my tongue along her full bottom lip, nipping it lightly as my cock hardens to rock against her thigh.

I'm prepared to pry her lips open if necessary, but they part for me willingly, allowing me access to her sweet mouth. She tastes of fruit and nectar, and I drink it all in as our tongues entwine together.

My hands release her and move down, tracing the perfect lines of her petite hourglass shape. I unbutton her jeans and rip them down. They fit her like a second skin, but they're no match for me, for my desire.

She doesn't complain at the rough treatment. If anything, she just moans louder. She clings to my neck and steps out of the jeans.

I note the blossoming wet patch on her panties as I slide back up her body to tower over her again. Grabbing the bottom hem of her shirt, I pull that over her head and throw it aside.

Her breasts look fuller somehow, but I'm pretty sure my knowledge of her pregnancy is forcing me to notice the little differences that escaped me before.

She's still trembling, still tense, and I know she's battling an internal conflict as my hands move to cup her breasts.

Don't worry, I want to whisper. *That won't last much longer.*

But I'm too busy pulling her nipple into my mouth to bother saying that out loud. There's too much of her body left to explore. To reclaim.

I circle the peaked nipple with my tongue as my hand slides down her stomach to the trembling moistness between her legs.

I move aside the thin white panties that cover her slit and slip my finger inside her. She's wetter than I anticipated and I can't help relishing the surge of excitement that sends through me.

I explore the folds of her wetness while my tongue laps eagerly at each nipple. Esme's head is lolling backwards and little moans escape from between her parted lips with each new sensation.

I could spend years like this. Tonguing every inch of my wife's naked body. Listening to her cry out again and again.

But we don't have years.

We have hours at most. Minutes, more likely.

And I intend to spend them doing much more than kissing.

I sink quickly to one knee, tear Esme's flimsy panties down her thighs, and toss them over my shoulder. In the same motion, I pull her hips towards me and run my tongue between the silky folds of her pussy lips.

Esme doubles over and seizes onto my head, a tremor leafing through her body like a fault line.

"Artem!" she chokes out.

She wants mercy.

But I have none of that to spare.

I grab her leg and hike it over my shoulder so I can delve deeper. I start licking her folds, pushing my tongue inside only long enough to make her desperate for more. When little beads of perspiration start to dot her skin, I roll my tongue around her clit and suck hard.

"Fuck... Artem!"

My name tears from her lips again. She tries to swallow it back in underneath another moan, but it's too late for that. It's far too fucking late now.

My cock throbs painfully in my pants, but I ignore the ache and focus on the taste of Esme. Her pussy is sweeter than her fucking mouth and she coats my tongue with a salty nectar that leaves me hungry for more.

When both her hands wind through my hair and her moans start getting violently uninhibited, I know she's close to the edge.

The sadistic part of me wants to draw it out longer. To prevent her from coming until I give her permission to do so.

But the hedonist in me wants to be inside her now.

I want those sweet juices dripping off my cock.

I reach up with one hand and squeeze a nipple while I bare down on her clit with my tongue. She writhes with pleasure as the orgasm ripples through her body, clutching my head between her thighs to ride it out.

She's still gasping for air when I stand up and start removing my pants. She slumps against the wall and I see her knees shake, but I grab her just in time.

"We're not fucking done yet," I tell her.

Her eyes go wide for a moment but I can't mistake the expression this time.

I've seen real, unbridled desire enough times now to know when I'm staring it in the face.

This is real.

I pull off my shirt and Esme's eyes zone in on my chest. I follow her gaze, realizing that she's staring at the sweat that clings to my muscles. Or maybe she's staring at my tattoos.

Either way, whatever she's seeing is turning her on. Her irises dilate further and a new shiver travels across her breasts, hardening her nipples all over again.

She places a hand on my chest as if to push me away, but she doesn't put any pressure on me. Her eyes dip down to my cock, which is standing at attention between her thighs.

I stare at her challengingly, daring her to stop me.

When she doesn't, I move in on her, grabbing her ass and using her firm cheeks to hoist her up so that she can wrap her legs around my waist.

The moment her back is pushed up against the wall, I shove my cock into her hard. She cries out, not having expected the first thrust to be so brutal.

But I'm done being gentle now. I'm going to fuck her into submission, fuck her into accepting her fate, into facing her true feelings for me.

No more clothes.

No more lies.

No more secrets.

Just this—me and her. My wife and I. "Us"—no matter how many times she tries to deny that such a thing exists.

She's so wet that I slide in and out of her easily, ramming my hips into hers so hard that the entire apartment echoes with the harsh slap of flesh on flesh. Her tits bounce between us and her head arches back, bumping against the back of the wall.

But she hardly seems to notice the pain. If anything, she savors it.

Her hands are slippery against my shoulders but she holds on tight anyway, her pussy clenching every time my cock disappears inside her.

My balls slap against her ass and she cries out in harmony with the sound. Her body is already riding a wave that started with her last orgasm, so it takes only a few more minutes until she's ready to come again.

I can feel my own orgasm on the brink of unleashing. I increase the tempo of my thrusts.

She curses again, a long string of Spanish under her breath, barely intelligible.

I respond by ramming into her so violently that her eyes roll back in her head.

I watch her lose herself in the moment. Her hatred dissolves. There's only the next thrust, and the next, and the next. That's all that matters anymore.

And then there's the final one. The one that undoes both of us completely.

Perfect. Wet. Deep.

Esme's fingers dig into the arch of my shoulders as she explodes on my cock. I let myself go, too.

I erupt inside her and on the last thrust, I stay buried to the hilt as I go still.

We stay like that for a long time. Trembling with the force of what just tore through us. Her heartbeat thuds erratically underneath me.

Eventually, I slip out of her, forcing yet another curse from her lips, and then I carry her wordlessly into the next room. I sit down on the white sofa, keeping her cradled on my lap.

Neither of us have said a word yet. But I know she's already thinking of putting distance between the two of us.

She shimmies off my lap. When she stands, I see my seed slide down her inner thighs. It makes me smirk with satisfaction.

Esme sees my expression and scowls. She stands in front of me, stark naked and as beautiful as a goddess. Fire in her eyes, just the way I like it.

I want her to stand there forever.

But the more my eyes travel over her body, the more self-conscious my little bird becomes. She walks to the wall against which we just fucked and picks up her clothes.

She puts them back on, ignoring me pointedly. When she's done, she picks up my clothes, strides back over, and dumps them in a heap on my lap.

"We shouldn't have done that," she says sourly.

"You could have stopped me any time," I tell her. "You just didn't want to."

Her eyes flash with anger, but I can see it's directed at herself this time, not me. "Artem—"

"I know about the baby," I interrupt.

Her mouth pops open in shock, her eyes flash to me, all confusion and vulnerability. Then realization washes across her expression and she sighs.

"Of course," she nods. "They would have done tests at that clinic."

"Four fucking months, Esme," I say, in a low, dangerous voice. "You knew for that long."

"Yes, I knew," she says unapologetically. She crosses her arms under her bare breasts. "I was trying to protect myself. I was trying to protect my baby."

I hear the flare of possessiveness in her tone. It doesn't escape my notice how one hand slides down to her belly and rests there protectively.

"When did you find out?" I ask.

"A few months after The Siren."

My heart stills for a moment. "So... the baby is mine?" I ask cautiously.

Her eyes go wide at the question. I realize it hasn't even crossed her mind that I might assume the baby was someone else's.

"You're the only man I've been with since then," she hisses venomously. "And for a long time before that, too, if you really wanna know."

I sink back into the couch and contemplate that. It makes me strangely happy to know that. To see that beautiful, fiery body and know it's truly mine.

"Okay," I say. "I believe you."

She seems satisfied enough with that. Nodding, she wraps her arms around her body, like she's trying to comfort herself.

"I don't know what to do," she admits softly.

"Then you're in good company."

She laughs bitterly. "Does your uncle really want you dead?"

"Yes." I nod. "I think he was hoping to get rid of me at the funeral, but that didn't work out quite like he wanted."

"You're leaving L.A.?" she asks.

"Only with you."

I had hoped we'd turned a corner in the last half an hour, but I can't be sure anymore. She's still holding her cards pretty close to her chest.

"You better put your clothes back on," she tells me, gesturing to the pile she dumped on my thighs.

"Does that mean you're done fighting me on this?"

She groans with frustration and throws her hands up in the air.

"I don't know," she says. "I don't know anything anymore."

"We don't have time for you to fucking find out, Esme," I growl as I stand up and put my pants back on. "We have to get out of this fucking city! Trust me on this—you don't want to be a prisoner of the Bratva."

She pales at that.

I reach out to her, grabbing her arm and forcing her to face me. "Esme, I *will* protect you. You and the baby. You just have to trust me."

I see the doubt in her eyes then. I want to pretend like it doesn't cut to the fucking core of me, but it does, and I'm just gonna have to deal with that.

I hear my father's voice in my ear, the Russian rasp that's already growing hazy in memory.

Trust takes decades to build and moments to shatter.

"We have to leave," I repeat for the thousandth time.

"I have to wait for Tamara," Esme says, shaking my hand off. "I need to say goodbye first. She risked everything to take me in and—"

Tamara.

I had watched Esme's cousin leave the apartment with her head turned down towards her phone.

"Actually, it's been over an hour," Esme says, frowning. "She should have been back here by now."

My body stiffens with alarm as I grab my shirt and pull it on.

"Where did she go?" I ask.

"She said she was gonna get us some real food," Esme replies. "She was a little distracted, though."

"Distracted?"

Esme frowns. I can see her trying to catch up with my train of thought. "Um, well... there's a new guy in her life. She was just preoccupied with him, I guess."

"Did you hear her speaking to him?"

"On the phone," she says. "A couple of times."

"What did she say to him?"

"I... what does it matter?" Esme asks. "She wasn't lying to me."

"What did she say to him, Esme?"

She flinches a little. "I... I didn't actually hear what they were talking about. She wasn't talking too loud."

"Fuck," I groan, kicking myself for being a fucking idiot. "Fuck!"

"Artem, what's wrong?"

I grab her hand and pull her towards the door. "We have to get the fuck out of here right fucking now. We've been here too damn long."

"Artem!" Esme cries. There's fresh panic in her tone. "What are you talking about? Tamara has nothing to do with any of this. She's my cousin. She *helped* me."

I move quickly into the kitchen, with Esme following behind me, and pull out the sharpest knife I can find. I hand it to Esme, who takes it with wide-eyed disbelief.

"You don't know my uncle, Esme. He can make people do anything he wants," I tell her.

I know I'm frightening her, but she needs to be frightened now.

Our lives might depend on it.

"Come on. We've been here too long already."

I grab her free hand and pull her towards the door.

That's when I hear it—thundering footsteps.

Heavy, angry footsteps.

The kind made by dangerous men with violent intentions.

Esme hears it, too. She freezes in place, her skin flushing with adrenaline and fear.

I have just enough time to push her behind me before the door blasts open.

51

ESME

Artem shoves me behind him just as the door blasts apart.

Bratva soldiers pour into the apartment with guns raised, barking orders in Russian that I don't understand.

"Esme!" Artem roars. "Stay down."

The Russian continues, loud and grating. I hear a scream that sounds distinctly female but I have no idea where it's coming from.

Had I just screamed? Was that me?

I find cover behind the white sofa and peer from around it. I can't see Artem, but I can see two of the Bratva soldiers crowding the doorway.

They're dressed in all black, with masks covering their faces, revealing only their eyes.

I don't even know if Artem has a gun on him. Does he have any weapons on him at all? He'd passed me a knife in the kitchen, but—

I look down only to realize that I'm still clutching the knife in my hand. My palms are sweaty and the hilt feels lose in my grip. My own heartbeat pounds in my ears, drowning out everything else.

Breathe, Esme. Just breathe. Don't leave Artem out there alone.

Two of the masked Bratva soldiers stride towards Artem at the same time. It strikes me as strange that no one has used a firearm yet, but in the next second, I realize why.

This is bad guy versus bad guy.

No one wants to bring the police down on this situation.

The moment a gun goes off, the people in the neighboring apartments will be dialing 911.

Artem's eyes are trained on his assailants as they charge at him. He doesn't move until the last second—not until the lead soldier is right on top of him.

Then he moves, faster than I would have thought possible.

He ducks under the soldier's raised arm, punches him in the gut once, and then goes for his face.

He lands one elbow to the face before grabbing the soldier by the neck from behind and slamming him against the same wall he fucked me against.

His movements are fast and confident. His eyes never veer from his target.

It looks almost like a choreographed fight scene—except that Artem's the only one aware of the moves.

Luckily for us, Tamara has a narrow entryway to her apartment. Only a few soldiers can fit in at once.

With the first soldier down, two more approach, stepping over their comrade's limp body.

I feel the panic return. I've seen Artem fight enough times now to know that he would win in a fair fight easily.

But now he is dealing with two trained assassins, both of whom look as tall and as large as him.

And then a flash of movement to the corner reveals a third Bratva soldier pushing his way in.

I don't know when I make the decision but suddenly, I'm getting to my feet, knife clutched in hand. In front of me, the fight is starting already.

One of the soldiers manages to get in a punch. Artem stumbles back as blood trickles from his nose.

Taking advantage of the defensive position Artem's been forced into, the second soldier swoops in and punches him in the gut. The third soldier moving forward, victory already written in his beady eyes.

"No!" I scream. "Artem!"

All three masked men turn to me, giving Artem time to gain his footing once more.

He grabs the first soldier, shoves him against the wall, and stabs him in the heart with a knife I didn't know he had.

The moment the blade sinks in, he's already moving, ripping it out and throwing it end-over-end through the air at the creeping soldier who's decided I'm the better target.

The man sees it at the last second and starts to duck, but it still slices open his cheek. He roars in pain as blood sprays on Tamara's white couch.

Artem moves towards me to intervene, but his path is blocked by the second soldier, who lunges at him.

The last thing I see is Artem being thrown against a thin wooden console table before rough hands latch onto my shoulders and I'm being lifted into the air.

That's when I remind myself that I have a weapon in hand.

I'm not defenseless.

I can protect my fucking self.

Kicking into survival mode, I bring the blade down blindly. It makes sickening, squelching contact, and a moment later, the masked soldier cries out in shock and pain.

He drops me like a hot rock. I land on my hands and knees. The pain of the fall radiates through my joints.

I try to scramble to my feet, but before I can get far, the man's hand grabs my left ankle and he pulls so hard that I'm getting a face full of carpet again.

I try and kick him off me, but he's fighting hard, even as blood spurts from the puncture wound in his thigh.

"Come here, you fucking bitch," he snarls. The whites of his eyes are huge and terrifying.

I can hear the commotion of another fight in the room next to this one, and I hope that Artem has the upper hand now, but I can't be sure and I have to get away from the attacker still attached to my leg.

All the while, I can feel a strange pulsing in my stomach.

As though my body's trying to remind me that it's not just me I'm fighting for.

I twist around so that I'm on my back against the floor and kick as hard as I can. My foot careens into his face and he recoils backwards with a pained grunt, giving me enough time to get to my feet.

But in the chaos, I've lost track of the knife. It's definitely not in my hand anymore.

I search the floor desperately. I don't have long. Without the knife, I'm screwed.

"I will fucking kill you," he growls at me. "Come here."

"In your fucking dreams," I say. I'm shocked at how confident I sound.

He tries to lunge for me again but the wound in his leg stops him short and he clatters to the ground.

I run around the couch, my eyes darting between my attacker and the floor.

Where the fuck is that knife?

I see it glinting by the door that leads to the balcony and I jump towards it.

"Stop!"

The fury in the soldier's voice forces me to a standstill.

When I look up, he has his gun out and pointed at me.

"I'm not playing this fucking game anymore," he hisses. "You take another step and I'll shoot."

"Will your boss be happy about that?" I ask.

I honestly don't know if Artem's uncle will care either way, but these men broke in here today with the intention of taking me captive.

If the end goal was to kill me, I was fairly certain I'd be dead by now.

"He'll deal with it," my attacker spits. "What's one more dead whore?"

I cringe at his words, disgusted and terrified in equal measure. Then I hear the cock of a second gun.

My eyes dart to the entrance of the room. Relief floods through me when I see Artem standing there, his eyes honed on the masked man opposite me.

"Move the fuck away from her right now," Artem commands.

Blood spatters the front of his shirt and there's a spray of it that's landed across his face in a Picasso-like flourish.

"Is that you, Mischa?" Artem asks, his tone conversational.

"It's not personal, Artem."

"Like fuck it isn't," my husband hisses. "You chose the wrong side."

The soldier breathes shallowly. "Your uncle is a powerful man."

"No, my uncle is a traitorous motherfucker," Artem fires back. "My father was the powerful man."

"And look where that got him," Mischa retorts. "*Dead.*"

I expect Artem to explode at that, but he remains stationary, totally calm.

"I am my father's son, Mischa. Remember that when the life is draining from your body."

"Today is not the day I die."

Artem laughs, dark and cold. "There was a reason I told you to stay away from casinos, old friend," he says. "You were never good at gambling. Now put the gun down."

"You first."

Artem narrows his eyes and I recognize that his patience is drawing to its edge. Mischa seems to sense that, too, because he darts towards me suddenly and before I can react, he has his arm around my neck and he's using me as a human shield.

I stare at Artem, whose expression has turned to thunder. His lips curl up over his teeth like a wild beast.

"I *was* going to give you a quick death," Artem says.

Mischa laughs scornfully. "Now maybe I'll give your woman a quick death instead."

We both realize at the same time that that was the wrong fucking thing to say.

I jab my elbow into Mischa's thick torso. The unexpected pain causes him to drop his gun.

At the exact same time, Artem explodes forward with vengeance written on his face.

Seeing him coming, Mischa pushes me to the ground. The man's gun hits the floor at an angle and it fires.

The bullet careens across the air and hits the window overlooking the balcony. Glass shatters around me. I put my hands over my head to shield myself from the falling debris.

When I look up, I see Artem and Mischa on the floor, both men struggling to get the upper hand. Punches exchanged. The meaty *thwack* of fists meeting faces.

I stumble to my feet, trying to get my brain to stop panicking. The gun is just a few yards away. I scramble for it, but just before I'm close enough to reach, Artem's boot comes swinging around and kicks it under the couch.

The brawling men tumble into me before I can get out of the way. Combined, it's like being hit with a wrecking ball.

I hit the floor with an *oof*. My skull cracks back against the hardwood. I see stars.

Another crash sounds through the air. I'm aware of screams and running footsteps coming from the apartments around us.

It takes a moment for my vision to clear, but when it does, I turn my head and see something shining just out of reach.

The knife.

It's still slick with the blood from Mischa's leg. I pick the dagger up with shaking hands just as Artem rams Misha into the television. It hits the floor, explodes.

Mischa snarls something in Russian, but Artem doesn't bother to respond.

Then Artem makes a mistake that turns the fight against him.

He looks for me, checking to make sure I'm all right, but that one second of distraction costs him.

Misha punches him in the face and sends him stumbling to the ground. Before Artem can get his bearings, Misha jumps on top of him.

The snacks I ate earlier rise in a wave of nausea.

Move, Esme. Do something before it's too late.

My feet move forward and it feels as though I'm watching myself from a distance.

I raise my hand high. Then I plunge the knife into Mischa's side, just above his hip.

He stops mid-punch as his body goes limp. He turns his neck to the side and catches sight of me.

He's stunned. As if, despite everything, he didn't really think I could do it.

He thought I was weak.

That's what makes me draw the blade out of him, cock it back, and stab in one more time.

This one goes right in his chest. Unlike the first time, the blade doesn't go in smoothly. I have to push. I have to put some force into it, but I manage with a little effort.

And once I've started, I can't stop. I keep stabbing him.

Even as his blood sprays across my face.

Even when he stops struggling.

Even when the life has long since left his body.

I realize suddenly that my throat is raw and I'm screaming, "I'm not weak, motherfucker! I'm not weak!"

Only Artem's voice jolts me back to reality.

"Esme."

I stop. I stare at my hand, suspended in mid-air, the blade of my knife dripping with blood that looks too red and thick to be real.

"It's okay now," he says gently. His hand reaches for mine.

He plucks the blade from my clenched fingers and throws it to the side. His hands come around my shoulders and he pivots me around to face him.

He looks so unbelievably calm that for a moment I wonder if I've dreamed the entire nightmarish fight.

But then my eyes zero in on the blood dripping from his face and clothes. I look down at my own hands that is splattered with the same ruby red.

It doesn't feel real. None of it.

"Come on, Esme," Artem says softly, as he pulls me through the destroyed living room. "It's time to go."

He pulls me to my feet and loops an arm around my waist to keep me up. I feel nauseous again, but I hold it down as we make our way over the dead bodies of the soldiers and out of the apartment.

We get to the corner of the hallway and turn towards the elevator lobby.

And then we both freeze in our tracks.

A fifth Bratva soldier stands in front of the elevator doors. This one is dressed like all the others, but he has removed his face mask to reveal heavy-set features, dark, bushy hair, and unsettlingly light eyes.

And he's got a gun held against Tamara's head.

52

ESME

My cousin's face is screwed up in terror, her eyes wide, panicked, and brimming with tears. She's mumbling under her breath, begging for her life, her eyes darting between Artem and me.

The soldier keeps her body in front of his. His arm is clenched around her neck, while his sweaty hands grip and regrip the gun pressed to her temple.

"Leonid," Artem says, making sure to position himself right in front of me. "I'm not surprised."

The man's face contorts into an ugly sneer. "Take one more step and I'll blow her fucking brains out."

"No!" I cry at the same time that Tamara lets out an anguished shriek, more tears flying down her cheeks.

"Shut the fuck up," Leonid huffs, tightening his grip on Tamara's forearm.

She trembles, crying unintelligibly, her face paler and more desperate than I've ever seen it.

I still can't quite wrap my head around the fact that she sold me out. But even that doesn't make me enjoy the sight of her like this.

"I mean it," Leonid says. "I will kill this bitch if you try anything."

Artem is quiet for a second. Then he shrugs. "Kill her."

Tamara whimpers at his words. I reach for Artem's arm in horror, but he pushes me back roughly.

"Let us walk out of here," Artem counters, "and I'll let you live."

"You're in no position to bargain," Leonid snarls.

"Oh, I'm not bargaining," Artem replies. "I'm walking out of this building either way. You on the other hand have two options. Resist and die or move aside and live."

"Cocky bas—"

Before he can finish the insult, Artem is in motion.

He hurls the dagger that I used to kill Misha.

It flies through the air and hits Leonid right between the eyes. He drops to the ground instantly, taking Tamara down with him.

Her screams penetrate the air, but Artem drops to his knees and slams his palm over her mouth.

"Enough. That's enough, you're all right."

Tamara starts sobbing uncontrollably as I run over and kneel down beside her. I can see the dagger protruding out of the dead man's forehead.

But I don't look any closer.

I don't want the nightmares.

"Tamara," I say, grabbing her hands. "Tamara…"

I don't know what else to say apart from that. The idea of comforting her now feels strange and unnatural somehow.

Probably because I can't seem to reconcile the cousin I knew and loved with the woman who ratted me out to a killer.

Her eyes find mine. I see the shame and guilt written across her tear-stained face.

"Oh, Esme… Esme, I'm so sorry. I'm so sorry," she sobs. "I didn't want to… but he… He threatened to kill me. He told me that if you ever contacted me, I was to inform him immediately. Esme, I'm so sorry."

I hold her hands tightly, marring her pale skin with the fresh blood that's all over me.

Our eyes meet. I wonder if I'll ever see her again.

"Esme…"

"We have to leave now," Artem interrupts, grabbing me and pulling me to my feet, breaking my hold on Tamara.

She stares up at us with a shell-shocked expression on her face.

"You're going…?"

Sirens sound in the distance.

Artem's right. We have to go, but for some reason, my legs aren't budging.

"Esme," Artem growls again.

"I can't just leave her." I'm staring down at Tamara and seeing only the bright-eyed little girl I once knew.

"You have no choice," he snaps, pulling me towards the stairwell next to the elevators.

"The police…?" I whisper.

"The police are the last of our fucking problems," Artem says. "Another contingent of Budimir's men will be on their way by now."

"Esme!" Tamara cries out hysterically.

Even as Artem pulls me along, I crane my neck back to stare at her.

"I'm sorry," I say, a tear slipping loose from my left eye. "I'm sorry, Tamara. I have to go."

She says my name one more time. It's pitiful. Heartbreaking. Her voice teeters on the brink of collapse.

Then the door shuts and she disappears from my line of vision.

I don't have time to think as Artem pulls me down the staircase, to the ground floor of the building. He stops at the last landing. There are two doors, placed on opposite ends of the landing.

One leads into the building's lobby. The second leads to the back alley.

He pulls me into the alley. The smell of putrid food and urine fills my nostrils.

I expect him to keep moving, but he pulls me to a stop in front of him and pulls out a handkerchief of all things, from the back pocket of his trousers.

"You own a handkerchief," I say, before I can stop myself.

"You really wanna talk about that now?" he asks as he rubs down my face first and then his own.

It does little in the way of making us both presentable. We still look like we've exited a war zone. But it's better than nothing.

"That's the best I can do for now. Keep your head low and keep pace with me," Artem instructs as we make our way down the alley.

There's chaos churning all around the building. People are milling about the street and looking up. Some are even taking pictures. I realize that there's glass on the sidewalk, a result of the broken window in Tamara's living room.

"Head down," Artem tells me. We turn the corner of the alley and walk purposefully in the opposite direction from where the crowd is forming.

I keep my head down like he said, but I can still feel eyes on me. Even with Artem's hand around me, keeping me steady, I still stumble.

Fatigue, fear, and the trauma of the last few hours was making me sluggish. I look ahead and see a corner.

Instinctively, I force myself to move faster. I tell myself that if we can just round that corner, we'll be okay. We can walk away from here and it'll be as easy as hailing a cab and getting as far away from this city as possible.

Still just a little girl. A little girl who believes in fairytales.

I make the mistake of looking up. I watch a woman pass by us. She's curly-haired and spectacled and her eyes go wide as she takes in the blood staining the front of my white blouse.

Of course—it had to be a white blouse.

"Keep walking," Artem orders. "Don't look back." His voice is growing more urgent.

I realize a second too late that his body has gone taut once more.

Someone has eyes on us.

Someone knows who we are.

Danger, my body instincts warn me, at the same exact time that Artem hisses, "Run!"

My heart feels like it's going to beat right out of my chest as we sprint into a run that has the blood rushing back to my ears.

We whirl around the corner, causing a couple to break apart as we push between them. Someone screams, someone curses, but we don't stop—we just run.

Behind us is the hard thumping of running feet. Three people, maybe more.

But my only focus is on Artem's hand in mine.

He doesn't let go of me and I'm secretly grateful. Without his momentum pulling me forward, I don't know if I'd be able to move at all. Or if I'd just stand still and turn to embrace the oncoming death machine.

We turn another corner. People see us coming and flee in every direction but closer. That's when I notice that Artem has pulled out his gun with his free hand.

Even as he runs, he twists around and fires twice at the masked men on our tail. They fire back.

More screams. More glass shattering. More bystanders cowering in fear.

An old woman doubles over to protect her dog.

A young man presses his girlfriend up against a wall to keep her safe from the wild bullets.

So many innocent people brushing up against this sick, twisted world of ours. Getting stained by it. Hurt by it.

None of them will ever be the same.

My mind takes snapshots of the chaos we're causing as we run, but I can't process anything more. I have to save the rest of my energy. I need to convince myself that my lungs aren't going to give out on me a few seconds from now.

Suddenly, a dull blue Toyota careens around the bend, taking a turn so sharp that for a moment, I think it's going to tip over.

But the car veers back into place with a metallic thump. It screeches to a halt right in front of Artem and me right as we were about to race across the street.

It's all over. Oh, God, it's all over.

We're trapped.

But before the panic can truly set in, I see the driver lean across the car's center console to push open the passenger door.

I catch a glimpse of shaggy blonde hair and ocean blue eyes.

"Get in!" he yells at us.

I hesitate, mind too slow to process this unexpected turn. But Artem pulls open the door to the back seat and tosses me inside.

The door slams. The engine revs. It all happens so fast that for one fear-stricken moment I think Artem has been left behind.

But when I look back up, I see him sitting in the passenger seat, next to the blonde man who appeared out of nowhere to save our asses.

Cillian. His name is Cillian.

Then I collapse against the back seat, put my hands on my stomach, and close my eyes. It's not quite relief that I feel as the car flies through the streets of LA.

But it's close.

53

ARTEM

I look at my wild-eyed best friend, who's grinning like this is all fun and games.

"You're not going to let me live this down, are you?" I ask soberly.

His grin ticks one notch wider. "Story of my life. I'm always saving your ass."

Nothing worse than having your own words thrown back in your face.

We both burst out laughing.

In the back, Esme is baffled.

But what is there else to do besides laugh?

Reality settles back in quickly as I take stock of the situation. We're well and truly fucked.

We're together, though. At least we're all together.

Two miles in, we ditch the Toyota for a meek white hatchback that's parked between two suburban neighborhoods.

Esme stands back and watches closely as I hotwire the car, but she doesn't say a word when I open the door for her. Her eyes flit to Cillian, who shrugs and smiles. Then she gets into the backseat with a sigh.

The fatigue is evident in the slump of her shoulders and the dark circles around her eyes. I want to check in with her, ask her how she's doing, how she feels, but the questions sound so stupid even in my head that I stop myself from asking.

Obviously, she's had better days than this one.

Once we're in the hatchback, Cillian drives at a normal pace through the heart of L.A. to the very edge of the city.

Soon, the large corporate buildings and fancy apartment complexes give way to smaller, more run-down structures.

I glance back to check on Esme and find that she's fallen asleep with her head resting against the window. I resist the urge to reach out and touch her.

"She asleep?" Cillian asks, breaking the silence that has plagued us since jumping into the getaway car almost an hour ago.

"She's fucking exhausted," I confirm. "And who can blame her? The fucking bastards almost had us."

"You shouldn't have been in that building at all," Cillian says disapprovingly.

"Thanks for the heads up, Mom."

"You know I'm right."

I do, but my defensiveness rears up anyway. "Esme was in there. I had to."

"You could have at least told me what you were doing," Cillian continues. "We could have come up with a smart plan. Or a plan, period."

I glare at him before sighing and relaxing. "You saved our lives, so I'm gonna let you get away with that."

Cillian smirks. His eyes fall to the rearview mirror. "She definitely doesn't look pregnant," he says.

I glance back at Esme. Her position looks uncomfortable but she's so tired I doubt it even matters.

He's right, though. She looks the same as she did in that bathroom at The Siren.

Or maybe not. Maybe there's something—a new line in her jaw, a flush to her skin—that signals what's happening inside of her.

I can't tell. Can't decide. I still haven't figured out what to think about it.

"Where exactly are we heading?" I ask Cillian instead of ruminating more.

"I found this motel at the edge of the city," he replies. "It's not exactly the Ritz, but it's a popular destination for families with kids. I figured it'll provide you two with some coverage while you take a beat."

"How much of a beat?"

"A day, tops," Cillian says. "I wouldn't hang around longer."

A day is enough. It will give Esme some time to rest and it will give me some time to figure out my next move.

Cillian turns left at a crossroad, and we drive down about a mile before veering onto a gravel driveway that leads to a monochrome building two stories high.

"Not the Ritz" would be an upgrade from this shithole.

In fact, "rotting cardboard box" would probably be an upgrade from this shithole.

But it'll do for now.

I get out and survey the place. It's a smaller motel than most, probably about twenty rooms in total. There's obviously a pool out back around the building, because I can hear the sounds of shouting and splashing. Definitely sounds like a family with kids.

"I'll go and get the keys," Cillian says. He trots off, leaving me with the sleeping Esme.

Her face is more or less clean of blood, but there are dried smatters of it on her hands, as well as large swirling stains on her clothes. I'm sure I look just as bad, if not worse.

Thankfully, it's dark, so no one's going to see the state that either one of us are in.

Cillian arrives a few minutes later. I open the back door and lift Esme out. I expect her to wake up, at least stir a little, but she doesn't.

If her breathing wasn't even and consistent, I would have checked to make sure she was okay.

Cillian leads the way to the staircase at the corner of the building. I follow him up, cradling Esme in my arms.

Our room is the fourth one down. Cillian opens it for me.

The room is predictably mundane and small, but the bed is at least a queen. The covers have an unnecessarily bright, floral pattern with stains I'm not interested in exploring further. Directly opposite to the entrance door is another one that leads to a little private balcony overlooking the pool.

Cillian pulls the covers of the bed away on one side to reveal clean white sheets underneath. I set Esme down gingerly on the edge that's closest to the window and straighten up again.

When I turn around, Cillian is looking at me with raised eyebrows.

"What?"

"You don't exactly blend in," Cillian points out. "Big fuckin' oaf."

"Does the blood stand out a little?" I ask sarcastically.

Cillian rolls his eyes but chuckles lightly under his breath. "I'm gonna go and get you two some clothes," he says. "We passed a twenty-four-hour department store about a mile or two back. I shouldn't be long."

I nod gratefully. Cillian leaves, pulling the door shut quietly on his way out.

I walk into the bathroom, which is so small that I have difficulty maneuvering. But I find two small hand towels under the sink and an empty toothbrush holder that I fill with water before walking back into the room.

I peel away Esme's clothes, one by one. The pants come off first, and then her white blouse. I leave her panties on, but I remove her bra and place it on the bedside table next to the night lamp.

Then I dip the first towel into the water and start massaging her body as gently as possible. She stirs a little when I put pressure on the dried blood caked around her arms, but she settles back into sleep when I pull away.

She's as beautiful and as tempting as ever, but I tamp down the desire. Need to try and focus.

Once I've managed to get all the blood off her, I bring the covers back over her, shielding her body from view.

She looks much more comfortable now, or maybe that's just what I want to believe. I throw the blood-stained towels straight into the bathroom trash, along with Esme's clothes.

Then, leaving the door wide open so I'd know when Cillian comes back, I strip down and get in the shower. The water is cold but I welcome it.

I need the icy bite to wash this fucking day off me.

I stand there for ten minutes before I finally turn off the flow. Wrapping a towel around my waist, I step out just as Cillian comes in through the front door.

"Spare me the gun show," he says with an obnoxious eye waggle at my bare chest. "I've seen the tats before and I'm not impressed."

"Shut up and give me the clothes, wise ass."

He tosses a plastic bag of clothes to me. I step back into the bathroom and shrug into a pair of boxers and a white t-shirt.

"There's stuff in there for Esme, too," he calls from the main room. "I was just guessing on sizes and shit."

"Should be fine." I smell fresh bread and my stomach churns with hunger. "You brought food?"

"Meatball subs," Cillian replies. "And beer."

"I fucking love you."

"Wow, you must really be hungry."

"Starving."

I step out of the bathroom and reach for the bag with the subs, but Cillian pulls them out of my reach with a grin.

"You wanna say you love me again? I'd like to record it."

"Fuck off," I laugh. "Let's sit on the balcony and eat these. She needs the rest."

Nodding, Cillian heads straight for the balcony. I lag behind to fish out a navy-blue t-shirt with a round neckline. Then I walk over to Esme and pull back the covers long enough to slip the t-shirt on her.

She mumbles in her sleep before turning on her side, a sigh emanating from her slightly parted lips.

My hand reaches out before I can stop it and my fingers trail over her perfect lips. I let myself stare at her for another minute before tearing myself away.

I head out to the balcony where Cillian is waiting for me. It's only big enough to accommodate the two fold-out chairs and the tiny round table that sits between them.

"I don't bite," Cillian says, patting the empty seat. "Much."

"That's the lamest dad joke I've ever heard."

"How long 'til you start cracking those?" he asks.

I shake my head. "I'm too hungry for that conversation, man. Give me the motherfucking sub."

Laughing, he hands me my sandwich and a cold beer. I take a long swig, realizing that it's been days since my last drink, and even longer since my last drinking binge.

That's a little unnerving.

I set the bottle down and reach for the sub. The first huge bite is heaven-sent. The second is pure crack cocaine.

"Fuck," I say, looking down at the sub. "This might be the best thing I've ever eaten."

"Might be the last thing you ever will eat if you keep taking bites like a goddamn horse."

"Good point," I mumble, taking another generous mouthful.

We sit in silence for a while, eating and drinking until the subs disappear and our beers come down to the outdoor temperature.

I look down at the pool, which has long since been empty. The water looks calm and still, like a glowing blue mirror.

"I should leave soon," Cillian says after some time has passed.

I turn to him. "You can sleep at the foot of the bed. I've always wanted a dog."

"No, man," he replies without laughing, shaking his head. "I mean, leave this motel. We shouldn't be travelling together at all."

"Fuck that. We stick together."

"We've both got targets on our backs, Artem," he replies. "So does Esme. There's no fucking way staying together is the right thing to do, and you know that, too."

I sigh. I do know that.

Cillian claps a hand on my shoulder. As chummy as ever, as if this was all a fun field trip instead of what it is—fucking betrayal.

"We'll get some snazzy flip phones," he says breezily, "so you can call me whenever you need a good laugh."

"Can't fucking wait," I grumble.

"That's the spirit. Mr. Optimism, Artem Kovalyov, ladies and gents."

He's laughing, but his eyes are sad. He knows what's at stake. There's a very real chance that, if things go badly, we're close to the end. Splitting up could mean we'll never see each other again.

I refuse to let that happen.

"Where will you go?"

He hesitates.

"No, you're right," I say. "Maybe it's better if you don't say."

"Safety first, you know? Just in case one of us gets caught. If we don't know where the other one is at, can't give up the location, right? Keeps us both safe. Lord knows your pain tolerance ain't shit."

I laugh. "Let's just not get captured."

"Deal." Cillian leans back in his fold-out chair, his eyes fixed on the pool. "It's fucking ironic," he says in a quiet voice that's weighed down with old memories.

"What is?"

"Just, you know… life," he says with a shrug. "When I left Ireland, I resolved to leave this kind of shit behind. I figured it had screwed me over enough times, and cost me everything in the process. I told myself I was done."

"And then you met me," I chuckle.

Cillian smiles. "I gave fate the middle finger and boarded that plane to L.A., and I guess in a way, you were the middle finger that fate gave back to me."

I roll my eyes. "Geez, fucking thanks for that."

He laughs easily. "Hey, man, I'm not complaining. I know now—this is the only kind of life I could have lived."

"You think?" I ask. "You don't think things would have been simpler if you'd just taken some run of the mill, every day job, found a nice Irish girl, and settled down?"

"Oh, life would definitely have been simpler," Cillian agrees. "But I'm not convinced I would have been happy."

"You would have been bored out of your fucking mind."

Cillian raises his beer to toast to that. "I was made for this life," he says. "Just like you were."

I'm not sure why, but his words make me feel strangely uneasy.

I sit with the feeling for a moment—before I realize it might have something to do with the brunette beauty sleeping on the other side of this wall.

"I spoke to my ma the other day," Cillian tells me. "Kian's being groomed to take over."

"Kian?" I ask, in confusion. "I thought Sean was the older one?"

"He is," Cillian nods. "He walked away."

I whistle low. "Bet your old man had a fucking conniption."

"That fucker," Cillian says. His tone is light, but I can see the resentment in his eyes. "He's used to being disappointed by his sons. I still remember the look on his face the night he bailed me out of jail."

"Wasn't a warm fatherly hug, I imagine."

Cillian's gone down memory lane. "'A smart man knows his place.' That's what he told me through the bars of my jail cell," Cillian tells me, his eyes far away. "'A smart man knows not to fuck with men above his station.'"

"Fuck."

He runs his hand over his face. "I didn't even know that the fucker I fought with was some politician's son," he whispers. "All I saw was some entitled motherfucker who put his hands on my woman after she'd asked him not to. I told him once nicely—he flipped me off. The second time, I wasn't so nice."

I know the story. He told it to me once, about six months after we'd first met, but he had kept the details vague and I hadn't pried.

He had been defending a girl he was involved with, but this is the first time I've heard him refer to her that way.

My woman, in that possessive tone that tells me she meant more to him than he had ever let on before.

"Fucker's still alive to this day, you know," Cillian says, turning to me.

"Yeah?"

"Still on a ventilator," he tells me. "Still being fed through a tube. Way I see it, that's a good thing. He'll never be able to touch another woman without her permission again."

"Did your old man know that?" I ask.

Cillian snorts. "'Course he fucking did. He told me I should've just let him fuck Saoirse."

"You've never told me her name before," I say without looking at him.

He's quiet for a second. "Yeah, well, I promised myself that I'd never say her fucking name again."

I venture, "You loved her."

He nods slowly. His eyes are unfocused like he's seeing stuff that happened years ago, decades ago, instead of this crummy, empty motel pool. "There are days I think I still do."

"What happened to her?"

Cillian shrugs. But I see how heavy his shoulders are, how tense they remain when they fall back down again.

"She didn't want to deal with the fallout," he replies. "I was the son of a small time don who turned a powerful politician's son into a vegetable. There was too much politics for her to deal."

"Politics?" I repeat. "It was personal."

"Apparently not for her. After Dad bailed me out and told me that I had to leave the country immediately, I went to see her before I went to the airport."

My head jerks towards him. This part he'd definitely never told me about before.

I sit quietly, waiting for him to continue the story.

"When she opened the door and saw me standing there, she paled so much she looked like a fucking ghost," Cillian says. "That should have been my first clue."

"You went to say goodbye?"

"I went to ask her to come with me," Cillian admits. "She looked right through me for a moment, and then she shook her head. That was it. She didn't fucking say a word. Just shook her head. I didn't realize her love was fucking conditional. I didn't realize her love was weak."

I say nothing. I don't think Cillian even knows I'm here anymore. He's lost in his past.

"I turned and walked away from her. I wish I can say I didn't look back," Cillian sighs. "But I fucking did. She had wild red curls and the bluest eyes you ever saw. She stood at that doorway and watched me drive off."

"Do you know what happened to her?" I ask.

"Lives in Dublin," Cillian replies. "Married some fucker a few years after I left."

"Cillian...?"

His eyes pull away from the still water of the pool and turn to me.

"We've known each other a fucking life time," I say. "You've never told me the whole story. Not like that. Why now?"

He attempts a smile that falters slightly. "We're in deep shit right now," he says. "Guess I was reminiscing about the last time I felt this way. I figure if I don't make it through this shitstorm, I want you to know my whole story."

The words are ominous.

"We've been through shit storms before," I remind him. "We made it through those and we'll make it through this."

"We weren't fighting against Budimir Kovalyov," Cillian points out.

"He hasn't earned his reputation," I say, my tone going flat with loathing. "But I'm about to earn mine. After I'm through with my uncle, no one will ever dare cross the Bratva again."

He smiles. "If anyone can take on the old fucker, you can."

"*We* can."

We lapse into a deep silence, each pulled in to our own thoughts. Even the sweat on our beers has cooled now.

I glance back towards the bedroom, where I can see Esme through the half-parted blinds.

She's still lost in sleep, her back to me.

"So... Esme's pregnant huh?" Cillian asks, breaking the silence.

I was wondering when he would broach the subject. It's not like we'd had much of a chance to discuss it up until now.

I nod.

"You found out from the clinic?"

"Fucking felt like I was punched in the stomach," I reply with a glance at him. "She's four months along."

Cillian turns to me with a startled expression. "What the—"

"The baby's mine," I say before he can ask.

"Um, brother, I know your math has never been very good but—"

"Shut the fuck up," I say, suppressing a laugh. "I never told you about the first time Esme and I met."

"The first time?" Cillian says, frowning. "What the fuck are you talking about? Did you get it in with her while the rest of us were shooting guards in that fucking cartel compound?"

I shake my head. "It was months earlier… in The Siren."

"The Siren?" Cillian repeats, just before his eyes go wide with realization. "That's why you were so obsessed with that place!"

"I wasn't fucking 'obsessed.'"

Cillian smacks his knee with his hand and laughs. "Well, fuck me," he exclaims, shaking his head. "What are the fucking chances?"

I nod, still amazed by the coincidence.

"So she would have been pregnant when we stormed the compound?"

"She was."

"Fuck," Cillian says, drawing out the word. "And she didn't tell you?"

"Not a fucking word."

There's three seconds of silence. I look at him strangely.

"What? You've got that fucking look in your eye. I hate that look."

"Artem… you're in love with her."

I bristle at his words, feeling strangely exposed by them. "Fuck off."

Cillian laughs. "Why do you bother lying to me?" he asks. "I know you too well."

"I think it's time for you to go," I say, but my tone is clearly teasing.

We're both laughing, but Cillian runs a hand through his hair and straightens up. "I really should get going. We've been sitting here for hours."

We stand up together and quietly make our way through the room to the other side of the motel. Esme's stirring a little, trying to find a comfortable position.

When Cillian and I step outside the room, I see the white hatchback parked down below, half-shrouded by darkness.

"Cillian…" I say, as he turns to me.

"I know, brother," he interrupts. "Stay safe. Stay smart."

I nod. "Contact me when you establish a safehouse. I'll do the same."

He offers me his hand and I clasp it hard, pulling him to me for a hug. When we pull back, I feel the seriousness of this parting settle over me. The second time in just a few days we've done this, and it hasn't gotten any easier.

"This is just another fight we're gonna win," I tell him. "The stakes may be higher, but the outcome will be the same."

Cillian nods without a single shred of doubt in his eye. "See you around, brother."

He stops at the staircase and turns back towards me.

"Oh and Artem?"

"Yeah?"

"Congrats," he says with his signature carefree smile. "You're gonna be a dad."

I smile and watch him walk down the stairs and across the lot to the hatchback. He gets in and, with a wave, drives off into the night.

54

ARTEM

I suppress the unease I feel after parting ways with Cillian and head back into the room.

Esme is sitting up, looking at me with a half-dazed expression that makes me pause.

"Artem?" She sounds worried.

"You're okay," I say, as I walk to her bedside. "You're safe now."

She rubs the sleep from her eyes and looks down at the unfamiliar t-shirt she's wearing. "I'm not wearing any pants."

"You were covered in blood and sweat," I tell her. "I cleaned you up as best I could."

"Oh," she says. "Oh."

Before I can second-guess the instinct, I place my hand on hers. She glances down for a moment and then lifts her eyes to mine.

"I think I need a shower," she tells me, her voice still a little hoarse with sleep. "Not that you didn't do a great job or anything.

"No hard feelings," I laugh. "There's a towel in the bathroom and a fresh set of clothes in the bag if you need it."

I offer her my hand and help her out of bed. She walks slowly towards the bag on the floor, as though she's still trying to get her bearings. She picks it up, but instead of looking inside, she pauses, then turns slowly to face me again.

"Artem?" Esme says, her voice shaking a little.

"Yes?"

"I don't want to be alone."

I walk to her immediately, take her hand and pull her into the tiny bathroom. She pulls off the t-shirt and then slips off her panties.

I try and control my desire as I see the soft V between her legs and the glorious swell of her breasts.

She steps into the shower and turns the water on, gasping as a cold spray assaults her skin.

I see goosebumps prickle along her arms and breasts, but she doesn't try to get away from the steady stream of water. She just stands there, much like I did, and grits her teeth until her body acclimatizes.

Unable to keep my distance any longer, I strip naked and step into the water with her. I reach out and touch her body, wiping away the last remnants of blood and sweat. She turns into my arms instead of shying away from them.

My fingers linger over her breasts, her thighs, the firm roundness of her ass, but she doesn't say a word through any of it.

When my hand lands on her stomach, I keep it there, trying to sense the swell of a child… *my* child, inside her.

She's gazing at me with eyes that are heavy with conflict and uncertainty, but her hands trail over mine before she reaches for the soap and shampoo. She shampoos her hair, while I lather her body with soap, straining against the erection that presses up between us.

I'm pretty sure she can see it too, but she doesn't say a word.

Once all the soap has been washed away, she turns the water off while I grab the towel and dry her off slowly, carefully.

Her dark hair clings to her face and neck, framing her hazel eyes and the lingering flecks of worry that clings to them still. I reach for a clean t-shirt but she squeezes past me, her wet hair falling down to her middle back as she walks naked to the bedroom.

I leave the bathroom to find her standing next to the bed, one hand placed over her stomach protectively. She glances at me with wide, fearful eyes.

"Esme," I say, moving closer to her.

"Artem," she answers. My name comes out in a sob.

She starts trembling slightly as she reaches for me. I encircle her in my arms and pull her close.

I hold her until her trembling stops. Then I drop a kiss on her head. She looks up at me, her eyes full of questions.

In response, I bend down and press my lips to hers.

I want to comfort her, to take her mind off her fears, if only for a moment. But she clings to my kiss as though I've just thrown her a life jacket.

Her lips part almost instantly and I feel her tongue in my mouth, grappling with mine with increasing desperation. My hands slide down her back and fall over her round ass. Her breasts press against my chest, her nipples already hard, begging to be sucked.

She pulls away from me abruptly, but the look in her face is pure fire. One thin finger reaches out to stroke my hard erection.

It turns into her wrapping her whole hand around me like she's sizing up my thickness. Her lips part in unconscious desire.

Then she puts her hands on my chest and pushes me back onto the bed, though she never lets go of my cock.

I stare at her in amazement, taken aback by the unexpected control she's exerting. I'm so fucking turned on that my cock keeps twitching urgently every few seconds.

I expect her to get on top of me, but she sidles down my body and settles between my legs, kneeling at the foot of the bed.

Never breaking eye contact, never releasing my shaft, she brings my tip to her lips and then sucks me in.

I groan as her sweet, wet tongue laps at me, sucking slowly as though we had all the time in the world.

"For fuck's sake, Esme..."

With one hand teasing my balls, she takes me deeper into her mouth until her saliva starts trickling down my cock. She starts sucking harder and I groan again with pleasure as my cock hits the back of her throat.

When she pulls her mouth off me with a wet popping sound, I'm panting hard, craving the bliss that's waiting between her legs.

As though she's read my mind, she hops up along my body and straddles me. My cock lines up with her glistening slit and she rocks back and forth a little, rubbing herself against me and driving me mad with want.

Then, all at once, she sits on my cock, slamming herself down on me with a force that draws me upright to meet her with a savage, sloppy kiss.

She rocks on top of me easily. Every pull and push is seamless and smooth. It's a steady grind, an endless ride of blissful friction, of skin on skin, of breath mingling between our faces as we kiss and gasp and stare so deep into each other's eyes that the boundaries between us dissolve.

My wife rides me until her hair is all but completely dry and flows down her back, dark and lustrous.

When her movements slow, I grab her by the waist and roll over with her, taking back control. She shrieks in surprise, but the first thrust takes her breath away.

She wraps her legs around my waist, her hands clinging to my shoulders as I fuck her slowly.

I've never been able to look a woman in the eye when I fuck her. It's too personal. Too intimate.

But with Esme, it's easy, natural, irresistible. I *want* to see her emotion. I *want* to witness her pleasure.

And when her pussy walls start constricting around me, I see exactly that.

I know she's close to orgasm. So I increase the tempo of my thrusts and drive her home. She screams softly as she comes, her hands wrapped tight around my neck while her body shivers with the aftershocks of pleasure.

I give myself a minute longer and then I release inside her. It lasts forever and a day. Again and again, each wave nearly as strong as the last.

Until finally, there's nothing left in me.

I roll off her and we lie next to one another in silence. Our breath cascades back down to normal.

Eventually, Esme turns to the side and props herself up on her elbow as she looks down at me.

"So," she says, "we should really talk."

"Okay."

"About that handkerchief you keep with you…"

I stare at her for a moment and then burst out laughing. She joins in and the tenseness of the previous moment breaks.

"Is that the first thing you thought about when you woke up in a strange motel room?" I ask.

"Maybe," she says with a mischievous smile. "It just took me by surprise."

"So when you have to sneeze…?"

I roll my eyes. "I use tissues," I reply. "I'm not a fucking Neanderthal. The handkerchief is just an old habit."

Truthfully, it started years ago because of Marisha, but I still kept up the practice for her. Call it a tribute of sorts.

"Right. Old habit."

"Besides, you never know when you might need to impress a beautiful woman," I add.

Esme grins wider. "It worked."

I press a kiss to her forehead. She moves closer and settles her head down against my chest.

"Artem," she whispers after a few easy quiet minutes have passed, "what are we gonna do?"

"Hey," I say. "Look at me."

She lifts her head off my chest and gazes at me with trusting eyes.

"For now, we're safe," I tell her. "The rest, we'll figure out in the morning, okay?"

She nods slowly. "Okay. I trust you."

She settles back against my chest and I wrap my arms around her. It takes only a few minutes until she's falling back into sleep.

It takes me a little longer, but when my eyelids finally shut, I don't stir until the morning comes.

55

ESME

It's still dark outside when I wake up the next morning. I sit up in bed and let the covers fall away from my naked body.

I reach out instinctively for Artem but my hands find only the soft emptiness of the mattress.

I look around the room for him.

But I'm alone.

With my heartbeat ratcheting upwards, I get off the bed and rifle through the bag at the foot of the bed for clothes. I have no choice other than to pull on the one pair of panties I have, but at least there are other fresh clothes in the bag.

I find a pair of drawstring shorts and a grey t-shirt that's soft and comfortable. My hands are shaking as I pull them on.

Crazy thoughts are running through my head. Did Artem leave me here alone? Did he get snatched in the middle of the night somehow?

I've just pulled on the t-shirt when the door clicks open and I turn to see Artem walking into the room. I let out a deep breath, feeling stupid, and sit down on the edge of the bed.

"Good morning, Sleeping Beauty."

He looks like a dream in a simple white t-shirt. Those fucking arms.

Last night's sex is still top of my mind for me. Not to mention all the confusing feelings that always come with Artem's presence.

But it's easy to forget about those things when he smiles gently. That mob boss mask I saw at the funeral is gone now. *"Don Kovalyov"* has left the building.

Standing in front of me is just… Artem.

"I brought coffee," he says, offering me the Styrofoam cup in his right hand.

The smell of fresh coffee makes my stomach lurch with longing. I accept it gratefully.

"Thanks," I say before taking a sip.

It tastes more like the Styrofoam it came in than the rich goodness I was used to drinking at breakfasts in Artem's penthouse.

"This is coffee?"

He chuckles. "I'd call it more of a coffee-like substance. We can stop at a diner on our way out of L.A. if it's not good enough for your highness."

I grumble, but I don't have much of a choice. "Where exactly are we going?" I ask him.

"That's what I'm trying to figure out," Artem says with a sigh. He sinks into the armchair shoved in one corner of the dingy motel room. "We can't stay anywhere close to Los Angeles. Budimir will be searching for us all along the West Coast. We need to put some real distance between us and them."

My mind pings with an idea, but I'm not sure Artem's going to be too happy about it.

I decide to suggest it anyway.

"What about Mexico?"

"Mexico?" he repeats, his brow knotting together.

A small part of me is craving a familiar landscape, some place surrounded by mountains and trees.

Not to mention, it's the perfect hideaway.

"I know a place," I tell him. "A secluded little hunting lodge in the mountains. Up near a peak called Picacho del Diablo."

"Devil's Peak," Artem translates.

"Uh-huh," I nod. "It's virtually abandoned up there. It's the perfect place for us to lay low for a while."

Artem thinks it over for a moment, before turning to me with a curious expression on his face. "How do you know about it?" he asks.

I had hoped he wouldn't ask me that question, but I'm not about to shy away from it now that he has.

"Cesar used to go there sometimes. When he needed to get away from it all."

My brother's name—and all the baggage that comes with it—fills the space between us and the silence grows weary and itchy with heat.

Then Artem nods. "Okay."

"Okay?" I repeat. "As in, yes?"

"I don't have any better ideas. A mountain lodge in a different country checks all the boxes for now."

"Right. Great. We'll be there by tonight then, I think. It's like a three-hour drive at most."

He shakes his head.

"No?" I say. "Why not?"

"We can't risk taking the straight route. We'll have to take the long way."

"Which is?"

"Backroads only. Stop often. Double back when we can. Zig zag all the way down to the border."

I swallow. "That sounds awful."

He laughs. "We'll be stuck together for a while. Got a problem with that?"

"Several," I retort, but I'm smiling.

"File them with Human Resources then," he says. He points towards the trash can in the corner of the room. "The suggestions box is right there."

I promptly chuck a pillow at his head.

"We can make it to Joshua Tree by tonight," Artem says. "Then make our way to Devil's Peak from there. We'll be surrounded by mountains tomorrow."

I nod and push myself off the bed as Artem picks up the only bag we have.

"Ready?" he asks.

I nod. "As ready as I'll ever be."

Then we head out of the motel room and downstairs to the lot where the cars are parked. I realize that I haven't seen Cillian since yesterday.

"Where's Cillian?" I ask, stopping at the foot of the stairs when I realize that I don't see the white hatchback in the lot.

"He left late last night while you were sleeping," Artem tells me. "The black car's ours."

He leads me to a black sedan that manages to be both boring and sensible, which is probably the exact reason why he picked it in the first place. He throws our one bag into the back seat and we get into the car.

"Where'd you pick up this one?" I ask.

"A few miles out from here, while I was on the coffee run this morning," he replies without hesitation or apology.

Guilt rakes at my conscience, but I suppress the feeling. Stealing cars is one of my lesser crimes in any case. If I start feeling guilty about every single one of my sins, I won't make it through the day.

A flash of unwelcome memory flits through my head. The image of a masked man whose eyes are fixed on me just before the light goes out from behind them.

I remember how hard I pushed that knife into him. The memory makes me shudder.

"Esme?"

I flinch at Artem's voice.

His eyebrows rise at my reaction. "Something wrong?" he asks.

"No," I say quickly. "Nothing."

He keeps his eyes on me a moment longer before he pulls out of the motel and we start the drive out of the city.

We drive for about half an hour, mostly quiet. Anytime things get a little too bustling, he veers off into narrow little by-roads that seem to go on forever.

After a while, we stop in front of a secluded diner situated off the beaten track. Artem parks the car in the gravel lot and we walk inside together.

The interior of the diner is old school, neon and chrome and fluorescent everywhere. Barstools line the breakfast counter and little booths dot the outer rim of the restaurant. A few folks sit, nursing cups of coffee or stacks of pancakes. Hardly anyone looks up as we enter.

Artem and I find a booth away from the windows and sit down to the smell of bacon and eggs. Almost immediately after we've sat down, a waitress appears between us with a bright smile.

"Hey, guys," she says—Midge, according to her nametag. "What can I get for ya today?"

She looks a young fifty, with curling blonde hair that's only just starting to get grey at the roots. Her eyes slide right over me but they really pop when they land on Artem.

It's amazing—and extremely annoying—how he seems to appeal to so many different women.

"Esme?" Artem says.

"Um… I'll have the pancakes," I say, choosing spontaneously. "And a coffee, please."

"I'll have the bacon and eggs on toast," Artem tells her. "A coffee for me as well."

She scratches our orders down on her pads and then hustles away. Artem and I sink into an easy silence as we look around at the rural folks enjoying their breakfasts.

In no time at all, Midge is back with a tray balanced on her shoulder.

"Here you go, lovebirds," she says. "Breakfast is served."

She sets down our plates and our coffees and heads back to the counter. I use my fork to cut out a sliver of pancake, dredge it through syrup and butter, then pop it into my mouth.

Is it the best pancake I've ever had?

No.

But does it taste like the chef really poured all his love and effort into it?

Also no.

Still, I'm starving, so no complaints from me. I take the whole thing down in record time, hardly taking even a second to breathe between bites.

When I finally reach my limit, I look up to find that Artem is watching me with a tiny smile playing at the corners of his mouth.

"What?" I ask defensively.

"Nothing," he says, leaning back in his seat. "Just admiring."

I frown to cover the blush rising to my cheeks. "Admiring what, exactly?" I ask. "A pregnant woman scarfing down her weight in pancakes?"

Artem nods. "Something like that. It's always nice to see a beautiful woman who also appreciates food."

"I take it you haven't been around many of those women." I ask.

"Only once," he replies. "A long time ago."

Something about his tone prevents me from asking more. And before I can obsess about it too much, Midge appears between us again, her smile aimed at Artem.

"How's everything, guys?"

"Great," Artem answers without even looking at her. She hovers anyway, still keeping her attention focused on him.

She throws me a cursory smile every now and again, but it's more out of politeness than anything else.

"Well, is there anything else I can help you with today, handsome?" she continues. Her voice is irritatingly chipper.

"Nothing," I interrupt curtly with a tight smile. "Just some peace and quiet while we enjoy our breakfast."

Her eyebrows rise just a tad, but she keeps the smile on her face as she walks away. I spear another piece of pancake and pop it into my mouth, trying to ignore the fact that Artem is staring at me.

"What?" I demand, when he doesn't stop.

"Was there a reason she annoyed you?" he asks.

I narrow my eyes at him. "I'm sitting at this booth, too," I respond. "She was only talking to you."

"That's not true."

I roll my eyes. "Of course you wouldn't notice something like that. Typical."

"What's typical?"

"You get the attention all the time, so of course you don't notice it."

"I wasn't aware this was a common occurrence," he says.

"There was that slutty air hostess on the plane when we flew to Hawaii," I say before I can stop myself.

Artem's eyebrows rise. I know he knows exactly what I'm talking about.

"What made her slutty?" he ask, with barely-concealed amusement. His laughter is pissing me off, truth be told.

"The fact that she was basically offering herself up to a married man," I reply. "With his wife on the same fucking plane.

I don't know why I've allowed myself to be roped into this conversation, but I'll go ahead and blame my hormones.

"It upset you that she was hitting on me?" Artem asks.

I take a huge mouthful of pancake and pretend I can't talk for several seconds. Artem takes a sip of his coffee and leans back, waiting patiently.

When I finally swallow, he smiles. "Finished?"

I sigh. "I didn't care that she was hitting on you," I say, trying to sound convincing.

Artem laughs. "It's amazing you managed to keep your pregnancy from me for so long," he remarks. "You're a terrible liar."

"It was *rude*," I snap, jabbing my fork at him to underscore my point. "I was in the fucking plane, only a few feet away. I climbed aboard in a fucking wedding dress. I mean, she had no idea that we weren't exactly the most traditional couple. We could have been madly in love for all she knew."

"Well, she is in the hospitality industry," Artem points out. He gives me a little wink that just pisses me off more.

"That's not funny."

"Sorry," he chuckles. "It's not like I took her up on the offer."

"No. You didn't exactly push her away, though," I reply.

"Would you prefer I had?"

"Yes," I say simply.

"Alright, then," Artem says. "Next time, I'll push."

"Push hard," I tell him. "Like, off the plane, preferably."

He smiles. "Anything for you, my wife."

I turn my attention back to the remnants of my pancake to hide the shiver of sensation that those words cause in me every time.

The fuller I get, the better I feel.

"I don't have my vitamins on me anymore," I remember suddenly.

"Don't worry," he assures me. "We'll stop somewhere on the way and pick up a few things. You'll need more clothes, too."

I nod. "That would be great. Not that Cillian didn't do well picking out these clothes for me. I never got to thank him properly."

"I'm sure he's not holding a grudge about a couple items of Walmart's finest apparel."

"I'm not talking about that," I scowl. "I'm talking about the fact that he saved our lives yesterday."

"Did he? Oh, right," Artem recalls with a grin. "Don't worry. I thanked him for the both of us."

"Did you give him a hug, too?" I ask, keeping my face serious.

His mouth twitches. "Maybe."

"A kiss on the lips?" I tease.

"Watch yourself, Moreno." He shakes his head and takes another sip of his coffee.

"You and he are close, huh?" I ask. It's crazy how much of Artem's life is still a total mystery to me.

He nods. "He's the closest thing to a brother I have in this world," he tells me. "I trust him completely."

"He's clearly not Russian, though."

Artem laughs. "What gave him away?"

"The fact that he sounds like Bono doing a Lucky Charms commercial."

At that, Artem nearly spits out his coffee. It's not lost on me how much I like his laughter. How rare it is, how warm, how genuine.

"I guess I was just wondering how the two of you became friends in the first place," I continue once he's calmed down.

"I got into a fight with five fuckers who thought they could take me," Artem explains. "I would have won too, if it hadn't been for the fact that I was ever-so-slightly drunk. Anyway, Cillian stepped in and helped me out. From then on, he's always had my back. I've always had his."

"It must be nice," I say, feeling a twinge of loss. "To have a friend like that. All I ever had was Tamara."

Artem's looks at me with a careful expression, and I can tell he's wondering what to say to me.

But I don't really need him to say much. I realize that I just need the catharsis of speaking out loud.

"She was my only real female friend, you know," I continue. "I was home-schooled and Papa didn't exactly encourage me to get out and meet new people. Tamara visited a lot. She was the only one that was pre-approved and that was because she was also my cousin."

"Sounds lonely."

"It wasn't so much when I was younger," I say. "I had Cesar."

I lift my eyes to Artem's. He looks relaxed, but I can see the whites of his knuckles, the way his eyes grow still and tense as he looks at me.

"You still haven't told me... how it happened," I whisper, feeling a lump rise in my throat.

"I will tell you," Artem says seriously. "But not today."

"Why not?"

"Because it's not the right time."

"That's a cop out," I accuse.

"Perhaps."

"Artem..."

He sighs and I can feel that we've come to yet another stalemate.

"Is the story so bad?" I ask.

"It's complicated, Esme," he tells me. "There's a lot you don't know about your brother."

"You've said that before."

"Because it's true," he replies. His eyes go dark and opaque in a way that I haven't seen for a long time.

It reminds me of the time not so long ago when he was just a stranger—cold and secretive.

Which begs the question… what is he now?

"You hate him, don't you?" I say softly.

He hesitates. I know that it's only for my benefit.

"I can see it in your eyes, Artem."

He drops his gaze. I see the tense set of his jaw.

"I know you love him," Artem says at last. "I know he was a good brother to you. But that was not the man I met."

"You just saw his mask," I whisper, more to myself than to him. "You didn't see him."

"What?"

I look up at him. His head is tilted to the side with curiosity. "His mask," I explain. "I have one. You have one. Cesar had one, too. Mine was easy—good daughter. I just had to smile and curtsy and look pretty and never speak my mind. Never push back against the bars of my cage. But Cesar… His was harder to bear."

"He was the heir," Artem guesses.

I nod. "He was supposed to be like Papa. He was supposed to *be* Papa, really. Ruthless. Shrewd. Cold. But that's not Cesar. That's not how he is—how he was, I mean. You just saw the mask my father made him wear. There was a different person underneath."

He listens to me silently, taking in every word I'm saying. His eyes flit over my face as though he's searching for more clues. His jaw is still tense but the darkness lifts from his eyes a little as I speak.

"That may be true," Artem answers. "But it changes nothing. Mask or not, it didn't make his actions any less real."

Those words leave me feeling cold and I put down my fork and wrap my arms around myself.

When I look back at Artem, I can see more than just the contained anger I have come to expect when we talk about the past.

I can see pain, too.

Cesar, what did you do to him?

And suddenly, I'm scared to hear this story. My brother's memory has remained pure in my head since his death.

Yes, losing him had been painful.

But the pain was untainted.

I had mourned him freely, without complicating my grief with other unwelcome emotions.

If what Artem is implying is true, Cesar's death was not as simple as I'd always thought.

I shake my head to dislodge the creeping feelings. "Let's change the subject," I say. "I don't want to talk about this anymore."

He dips his head down in acknowledgement and we finish the rest of our breakfast in companiable silence.

Afterwards, Artem and I head to the counter to pay for our breakfast.

I watch from his side Midge steps up the cash register with a bright smile.

"Had a good breakfast, handsome?" she asks, her eyes raking up and down his tattooed arms.

"It was great," Artem answers coolly. "But I have to say, my favorite breakfasts are the ones my wife cooks for me."

Then he reaches back to where I'm standing, drapes his arm around my shoulders, and pulls me into his body, so there can be no doubt of who his wife is.

I suppress a laugh as Midge coldly passes over the change from Artem's twenty.

"Enjoy the rest of your day, hon!" I call back to Midge as we head out of the diner. Her scowl just makes my smile brighter.

Artem's arm stays around my shoulders until we reach the car.

"How'd you like my push?" he asks as he opens the passenger door for me.

"Subtle," I reply sarcastically. "But much appreciated."

He tips a fake cap at me and closes the door before circling around to the driver's side.

We drive off, leaving the diner in our wake.

56

ESME

Once we're back on the road, I fiddle with the radio, trying to find a channel with music that doesn't annoy me.

"Jesus," I complain, after I've changed the station for the fifth time. "Doesn't anyone listen to *real* music anymore?"

Artem gives me an amused glance. "You're not a fan of rap?"

I shrug. "I like some of it," I admit. "A little Tupac every now and again. But classical music is my happy place."

"Listening to you play the piano in Hawaii was one of the highlights of that trip," Artem says unexpectedly.

I glance at him, incredibly touched by his words. "Really?"

"Really," he nods. "Hands down, you're one of the best pianists I've ever heard perform."

"Uh-huh," I smile. "And how many have you heard perform?"

He gives me a grin that makes my ovaries do a little dance. "I don't need a fuck ton of experience to know when someone is good," he tells me.

My fingers twitch, a telltale sign that I've been away from my piano for too long. It feels like years since I've last played.

"You miss it, don't you?" Artem asks, as though he's just read my mind.

"How can you tell?"

"Your fingers do this weird twitching thing. I figured it had something to do with playing piano."

I look at him in surprise and he smirks at me. "Yeah, I'm observant," he says. "Did you assume my talents were limited to kicking ass and fucking?"

I snort with laughter and shake my head at him. "I'll admit, I did assume that."

"I'm not just a pretty face, you know."

I smile, but my heart can't help fluttering every time he looks at me with that tilted smile. It gives me *ideas*. The kind of ideas that would require pulling over to the side of the road and removing my Walmart t-shirt and shorts.

Unfortunately, we don't have time for that. Seeing as how there's a murderous Russian man pursuing us and all.

"So," I say to fight the rising blush in my cheeks and heat between my legs, "what kind of music do you listen to?"

"I don't listen to much, to be honest."

I can only gawk at him. "Seriously?"

He shrugs. "I'm always working," he replies. "And when I'm alone in my apartment, I like to lie in bed with silence. That's my music."

"Wow," I comment. "Very poetic. Also, boring as hell."

He smirks. "I like Viktor Tsoi. He was a Russian musician."

I wrinkle my brow. "Never heard of him. You sure you didn't just make that up to impress me?"

"He was popular in Russia," Artem tells me, chuckling. "He died young."

I stumble across a station that's playing instrumentals. It's modern day stuff from Hans Zimmer and Circadian Eyes, but it's the kind of music I like. The notes are so beautifully balanced, so harmonious together I feel the sweet melodies seep into my body.

My fingers twitch again and I notice Artem's smile.

"When we get back home, to our real home, I'll get you a piano," Artem tells me.

"Where's our real home?" I ask. Even the concept feels foreign to me now.

"The place we're running from," Artem answers immediately. "Los Angeles. That's home."

I suppress the sigh I can feel at the back of my throat and try not to think about it. My desire to stay in L.A. has waned considerably since Stanislav's funeral.

The city spells nothing but violence, chaos, entrapment.

What I really want is a quiet corner of the world. Somewhere to raise my child and play my piano.

I glance towards Artem. His profile is as impressive as the rest of him. I can see only one dark eye, the straight dip of his nose, and the thin curve of his mouth.

But I can't imagine this man in the life I'm envisioning for myself. A quiet home? Piano in the living room, a child's laughter on the front lawn?

No blood. No guns. No gangs.

It just doesn't mix. Artem and that future are like oil and water.

I turn my attention back to the road ahead, but my train of thought has led me back to what we left in Tamara's apartment.

Mischa.

His name was Mischa.

He was trying to kill Artem. He was trying to abduct you. It was self-defense.

All the justifications I've built in my head still don't stand up against the guilt, though. It's like throwing pebbles at a stone wall. They just bounce off, useless.

Did he have a wife? Did he have children? What kind of music did he like?

I take a deep breath and try throwing my pebbles again.

If you hadn't stabbed him, he would have killed Artem.

I take another breath. It doesn't help much.

He was dead. But you kept stabbing him. Why did you keep stabbing him?

"Esme."

I look at Artem with a start.

"You went somewhere dark," he says softly.

I feel tears at the corners of my eyes. "I… I'm fine."

"Do you want to talk about it?"

I open my mouth, but I shut it again just as quickly. "I think… not just yet."

"I'll be here when you change your mind."

I feel so incredibly grateful that I reach out impulsively and take the hand he has resting against the center console between us. His fingers weave into mine easily and it feels so damn good that it crowds out all the worry and guilt battling inside me.

If only all of this was so easy.

If only one simple touch could fix everything.

∼

We drive like that for another couple of hours before Artem pulls into a large mall off the interstate. The parking lot is huge but he manages to find a space close to the building.

Reluctantly, I let go of his hand and we walk towards the mall together.

As we enter, I catch a glimpse of our reflections in the reflective windows outside the building.

It amazes me how normal we look together, like an everyday couple spending their weekend in a mall. Nothing remarkable about us. You can't see my dead brother in my eyes, or the ghost of the man I killed lurking just behind my every thought.

It's just Esme and Artem.

Simple as that.

First, we head to the pharmacy on the first floor. I stock up on vitamins while Artem hovers over me looking anxious.

"First time parents?" the pharmacist asks, looking between the two of us.

"Yes," I smile.

She nods. "It's normal to worry," she says. "But try and eliminate as much stress as possible. That's the key to a healthy pregnancy."

I almost laugh, but I hold it back just in time. We leave the pharmacy a few minutes later with a bag of vitamins tucked under my arm.

"Eliminate stress, huh?" I say. "That should be easy."

Artem doesn't even crack a smile, though. It has me slowing my pace a little.

I reach out and place my hand on his forearm.

"Hey, what's wrong?"

"Nothing," he says gruffly.

He tries to keeping walking, but I stay put. He's forced to turn.

"Are you gonna start lying to me now?" I ask.

He sighs. "I guess, when it comes to the baby's health, I don't have much of a sense of humor."

I take a step forward, right into his space in that familiar way you do when you're comfortable with someone. I don't even think about it—I just do it. I'm not sure what that means for us.

"The baby's fine," I tell him. "Strong."

"How do you know that?" Artem asks.

"Call it mother's intuition," I answer carefully. "If something were wrong, I'd be able to tell."

Artem nods slowly.

I realize how badly he needed to hear those words.

Without even thinking about it, I take his hand and we continue walking.

57

ARTEM

I sit outside the changing room, waiting on Esme and clicking the heel of my boot against the floor.

I'm not the most comfortable in these surroundings, probably because I don't have much experience.

Okay, I don't have *any* experience.

But Esme insisted she needed my opinion. And apparently, I'm fucked when she looks at me with those hazel-gold eyes.

Just then, she pushes aside the grey curtain of her dressing room stall and walks out in a white dress with bow tie straps and a tight, corset-like bodice that manages to pull in her stomach and highlight her breasts all at the same time.

"Well?" she asks. "What do you think?"

She gives me a little twirl so I can admire the way the fabric clings to the curves of her hips before fanning out at her waist. It's a simple dress, but on her, it looks like a million fucking dollars.

"I think I'm *this* close to ripping that dress off you right fucking now," I growl.

That earns me an alarmed glare from a middle-aged woman passing by.

Esme suppresses a giggle and tries her best to look harsh.

"Artem! You can't say things like that out loud in public."

"No wonder I don't go out much."

She rolls her eyes at me, but I can tell she's pleased by the compliment.

Sometimes, it's easy to forget that she's only twenty-two. There are quiet moments when the silence stretches out and a haunted expression creeps onto her face. In those moments, I can tell that she's reliving experiences no other normal twenty-two-year old has to contend with.

But for now, she's just a girl trying on dresses. She looks distracted and happy.

Which is exactly the reason I swallow the intense discomfort, not to mention boredom I feel as I wait for her to tell me she's done.

She needs this.

Esme goes back into her dressing room. To my utter relief, when she emerges again, she's wearing the clothes she came in.

"Let me take that," I say, reaching for the shopping bag she's balancing on one arm.

"I can manage."

"You shouldn't be carrying heavy things," I tell her firmly, lifting the bag off her arm.

"It's hardly heavy," she says with amusement, but I ignore her.

I'm not taking any fucking chances with her or this baby.

As we head to the cash register, Esme falls into step beside me. I slow down to make sure she doesn't have to hurry to keep up.

"How are you gonna pay for all this?" she asks, with new concern.

I raise my eyebrows at her. "You think I don't have money on me?"

"You're not going to use a credit card, are you?" she asks in alarm.

"Baby, this ain't my first rodeo."

She fake-shudders. "Go back to the Russian accent. 'Cowboy' doesn't suit you."

Once I've paid for the clothes, Esme and I head back to the car. We've lingered too long, but I just didn't have the heart to ruin Esme's fun. She makes a beeline towards the black sedan, but I take her hand and pull her in the opposite direction.

"Artem?" she asks in confusion. I still feel a strange little twinge every time she says my name in that soft accent of hers. "Where are we going? The car's that way."

"I think it's time for a change," I tell her. "Something a little more spacious this time."

We walk down two rows of vehicles before I find one that meets my specifications.

It's a grey Honda that looks like it's had a few years of good use. An unassuming vehicle, the kind you see families driving around in all the time.

I glance around calmly and pull Esme towards it.

"We're stealing *another* vehicle?" she asks, with worry.

"It's a safety precaution, Esme," I tell her. "We can't afford to let our guard down."

She stands at the trunk of the car and waits anxiously until I've hotwired the engine. She needs to work on her "nothing to see here" face, but we'll have to make time for that later.

When the engine thrums to life, she gets in without a word.

There's a couple of pictures stashed into the visor over my seat. I pull them out surreptitiously and hide them before Esme can see.

If she can match faces to the car we've just stolen, it'll be another thing for her to stew guiltily over.

She has the most active conscience of anyone I've ever known. Most people who grow up the way we did have long since grown numb to causing pain to strangers.

As odd as it is, I find it refreshing. A reminder of a different kind of life. A different kind of world.

Like she's taking my hand and whispering, *It doesn't always have to be this way.*

∽

I drive out of the shopping complex quickly. Within minutes, we're back on byroads and weaving little streets just so that I can avoid all the main routes to Joshua Tree.

About forty minutes in, Esme falls asleep with her head resting against her window and one hand carelessly thrown over her stomach.

I'm not sure even she realizes just how often she touches her belly. Has she started recently or had she always done it?

I rake over my memories with her. But for the life of me, I can't remember.

Another hour on the road and it starts to get dark. I turn my headlights on and keep to the obscure little road we're on.

According to the GPS, we should be arriving in Joshua Tree in fifteen minutes.

I glance at Esme, who's started squirming a little in her seat. I can see her eyes moving furiously underneath her closed eyelids, a sure sign that she's dreaming.

When she starts to mumble and her movements become more erratic, more panicked, I pull over and park in a little patch of sand off the road.

I graze her cheek with my fingers but she jerks away from my touch, a little gasp emitting from her slightly parted lips.

"Esme," I whisper.

She groans. Her hair splays across her face as she turns. I try and brush it back, but she moves again as her breathing gets heavier and heavier.

"Esme," I say, a little louder.

She jerks forward, her eyes widening as she pulls herself from the throes of the nightmare.

As the fog clears, she blinks at me a few times, trying to bat away the disorientation.

"Artem?" she says uncertainly.

"It's okay," I assure her. "You're okay."

"I'm okay?" she repeats uncertainly.

"You were just having a nightmare," I explain. "It was a nightmare."

She shakes her head as a shiver runs over her body. "No, it wasn't."

I wait for her to elaborate, but she doesn't.

Instead, she sighs deeply and collapses against her seat as she looks out onto the road.

"Oh, wow," she says. "It's dark already."

"We're almost at Joshua Tree."

She nods absentmindedly. "Okay."

"I can find us a place to stay once we arrive."

She shakes her head. "Why don't we just camp out in the car?" she suggests.

"Here?"

I twist in my seat and look around. The model of the car allows for the back seats to be folded forward if necessary. Which would give enough space for the two of us to sleep through the night.

"We can, if you're comfortable with it," I nod.

She looks ahead, her eyes hazy with memory as she wraps her arms around her body. I pull the car back onto the road and we keep driving until we hit a patch of open desert that's dotted with twisted Joshua trees that have an austere beauty to them.

The sky is mottled with swirling greys and silvers. Only small patches of inky white clouds come through where the last of the setting sun is receding.

The desert's rugged rock formations and bristled cacti weave in and out of the landscape. Everything looks craggy, primitive. And utterly empty.

Esme sits up a little straighter, taking it all in just like I am.

I find a clear patch of desert and park. There's no coverage, nothing to block our view of the sky above.

The thick crescent moon hangs high above us. The only lantern in an otherwise dark sky.

The moment I park, Esme gets out and walks towards one of the Joshua trees a few feet away from the vehicle. She's still got her arms wrapped around her body, as though she's trying to keep herself from falling apart.

I watch her from a distance. Unsure of my place. Unsure of what she needs from me.

I decide to give her some space.

I turn to the vehicle and open up the trunk so that I can fold in the back seat. To my amazement, I find a thin air mattress under the seat, along with a pump.

I get to work blowing it up. It takes me ten minutes to get everything set up, but once I'm finished, the trunk of the car actually looks pretty cozy. I dress it up with a blanket we bought from the mall.

Only then do I allow myself to look back at Esme.

She's still standing by the same tree, but she's looking up towards the sky. Her dark hair pours around her face, flowing over her slight shoulders.

She looks like a fucking dream, a wild girl out amongst all this wilderness.

The desire to touch her, smell her, taste her drives me over there.

I whisper her name. She pirouettes slowly, like a dancer, and wraps her arms around me, burying her face in my chest. I hold her tight and kiss the top of her head.

We stand like that for several minutes, until finally Esme takes a deep, shuddering breath and pulls her head off my chest so she can look up at me.

"I don't know what to do with this feeling," she tells me desperately. "I killed a man, Artem."

Only then does it hit me just how much she's been carrying around with her this whole time.

You never forget your first kill.

I'm a fool not to have seen it earlier.

"Come," I say, pulling her towards the vehicle.

I lead her to the open trunk and we sit down on the air mattress opposite one another so that our legs meet in the middle. Her eyes trail over the stark landscape, haunted and searching.

"I'm sorry," I tell her. "I should have realized this sooner."

"I killed a man," Esme says again, looking at me. But not really at me—more like past me, through me, beyond me.

I nod. "You did what you had to do."

"Did I?" she asks. "I could have injured him without killing him. That's what I should have done."

"Esme—"

"I stabbed him until I killed him," she continues. "And even after he was dead, I kept stabbing."

"You were in shock."

"I knew what I was doing. I could have stopped."

"You were protecting me," I say, leaning forward and taking her hand. "You were protecting our baby."

Her sob escapes through her teeth and she shakes her head. "I keep seeing his eyes. The way they looked just before he died…"

"Is that what you were dreaming about?"

She nods. "You knew him?" she asks in a shuddering voice.

I get the feeling why she's asking. "A little," I acknowledge.

"Did he have a family?"

I squeeze her hand. "Will it help you to know that?" I ask.

"I don't know. Probably not," she admits. "But I want to know all the same."

She waits for my answer.

But I know that the truth will only hurt her. It will double her guilt and invite in more nightmares that she doesn't need.

I think about my child growing inside her and all the stress my world has already put on her and the pregnancy.

This baby has to be okay.

I can't do this again.

"Yes," I say. "Mischa has a wife. And two children."

She sucks in her breath, her eyes flooding with regret already.

"And you did them a favor by killing him," I finish, before she can spiral out.

"What?" she asks, her eyes going wide.

"He was a brutal man at work and at home," I lie smoothly. "His family won't miss him."

She takes that in for a moment and nods slowly. "But I still feel guilty," she says.

"That's because you're a good person," I tell her. "You have a conscience, which is a quality that precious few people have in my world."

I feel her fingers twitch beneath mine. "Doesn't that include you?"

"I have a conscience," I tell her. "I've just learned to ignore it. It's the only way to survive this life."

"Do you remember the first time you killed a man?"

I nod. "It was on my first cartel raid," I say. "We had a spy in our ranks who was playing informant to a rival cartel. We stormed their meeting, killed their men, and caught the spy who had turned against us. Stanislav had him strung up by the wrists and he put a knife in my hand."

Esme listens silently. For a moment, I think she's about to draw away from me, but she only moves closer.

"Everyone was watching. My father, my uncle, all the men," I continue. "That knife felt so fucking heavy in my hand. It might as well have been a sword."

"I tried to be confident. I tried not to feel anything. But when I looked up into his face, all my reasons for killing him seemed… inconsequential. It didn't matter that he deserved it. It didn't matter that he had betrayed us and caused the deaths of so many of our men. I saw his eyes, wide and fearful, and I hesitated."

I pause, taking a breath. It's been a very long time since I've re-lived this memory.

"He looked at me and begged me for his life. I knew better than to think I had any power to grant it to him. I stabbed him in the chest first, but he didn't die on the spot like I'd intended."

The night is cool and still. Nothing moves or makes a sound in the desert.

"He struggled and screamed and prayed, and I panicked. The more he screamed, the more I stabbed him. I didn't stop until he wasn't screaming anymore."

When I look at her, Esme has tears sparkling in her eyes. She leans in even closer and rests her cheek against my arm.

"I was fourteen," I finish.

She sucks in a sharp breath. "Fourteen," she murmurs in shock.

I nod. "The more you kill, the less you feel. It's the only way you can continue."

Esme shakes her head gently. "Killing is not something I ever want to get used to."

"Nor would I want that for you," I tell her. "But when someone tries to hurt you, you have to defend yourself. Do you hear me?"

"Yes."

"You can't feel guilty about protecting yourself," I say firmly. "Don't give them that kind of power over you. They will take advantage of it."

She nods slowly, pushing back her tears. She looks stronger somehow, as though hearing my story has helped give her closure.

"Thank you," she says. "For sharing that with me."

I lean down and kiss her forehead gently. She turns her face up as her lips seek mine out.

To my surprise, there's heat in the kiss when our lips meet. A certain understanding that's cemented itself between us in the last hour.

Not pure passion, like it's been every time before. Not just fire and lust.

Something more. Something deeper. Something more solid and real.

Her hands reach up to hold my neck. I grab her around the waist and pull her onto my lap so that she's straddling me.

The moment she's on me, my cock turns rocks hard and she grinds on it softly while my fingers twist into her hair.

I part her lips with my tongue and push inside of her, desperate for her sweetness, desperate to lose myself in her body. She whimpers and writhes against me.

I pull off her shirt and throw it to the side of the car, before I spread her out against the air mattress.

Her fingers rake over my shirt, pushing it off me. Then I pull off my pants and boxers and settle over her, my fingers twisting into the waistband of her panties. She raises her hips for me and I pull them off her slowly, my eyes lingering on her pussy.

Once she's as naked as I am, I settle over her again.

Our bodies fuse together.

Her skin feels like silk. I bend my head down to her breasts and kiss them gently while her hands trace patterns on my back.

She parts her legs for me and I can feel my cock press against her slit. She's slick with want already and I fucking love that I can do that to her. That she can do that for me.

She raises her hips just a little, but I don't enter her yet. I cup her breasts with one hand and suck the hard nipple that sticks out at me.

I do the same for the other. When both are wet and taut, I pull myself up a little and start kissing her deeply. My hand snakes down between her thighs and I push two fingers inside her, exploring her depths and priming her for my cock.

Esme shudders against my fingers. Her nails dig into my back. They urge me deeper.

"Artem," she gasps, as my fingers rub her clit and massage it slowly. "Artem, please… I want you inside me."

No man can resist those fucking words.

I pull my fingers out of her and replace them with my cock. I slide into her smoothly, but she still gasps from the pressure of being joined with me.

She's so wet that it hastens my own orgasm, but I want to draw this out. I play with her nipples as I lose myself in her moist depths.

When I feel myself on the brink of coming, I pull out and turn her on her side. Then I press my body against her and enter her from behind. Her ass works against my hips, a steady wind that tests my resistance with each stroke.

I reach over her body and start playing with her clit. She arches her head back into my chest. Her soft, downy hair brushes over my skin as she moans to climax.

Seconds later, I feel little bursts and whimpers as she explodes on my cock.

"Come with me," she groans.

I let myself go at once, releasing my own orgasm seconds after hers.

Breathing gently, she turns back to face me, with a soft expression on her face.

She says nothing. I don't, either.

It's not necessary. Our bodies are doing the talking now.

Esme falls asleep with her hand on my chest. For a long time, I just lie there and stare at her.

The chaos of the Bratva seems a far-off problem, one that I'm becoming less and less inclined to care about.

This, right here... this is what matters now.

My fingers trace the swell of her breasts and then the curve of her stomach.

It feels like, if we stay here in the desert, we might have a chance at something. A future. Happiness. Fuck, I don't know what to call it.

But something. Something real.

I have one last, hazy thought before my eyes close and I drift off into sleep: is something like that possible for a man like me?

58

ESME

PICACHO DEL DIABLO, MEXICO

"There it is!"

The porch of the lodge comes into view. Seconds later, the rest of the structure follows.

It's a slope-roofed building with weathered wood siding. The chimney is leaning over at a precarious angle.

As we drive closer, I see how neglected it is. The structure looks sturdy, but it feels like there's a layer of dust and mold that's crept into the foundations.

When Artem parks, we get out of the car and look up at the lodge together.

"Doesn't look very habitable, does it?" I say, biting my lip in dismay.

"Actually, I think it looks kinda perfect," Artem tells me.

"Yeah?"

"You were right," he nods. "This is the perfect place for us to lie low for a while. It's off the beaten path and there aren't any major hiking trails that come this way."

"There's also poor cell phone reception," I point out.

"We'll manage. The village is only a thirty-minute walk down from here, and it'll take half that time by car. We can get whatever food and supplies we need from there. And in the meantime, we can clean this place up a bit."

I purse my lips and scan the surroundings.

The lodge has been built into a natural hill that overlooks the beautiful Baja California mountain range. Woods cluster almost right up to the front door, thick and lush.

It's as picturesque as they come.

I feel a certain sense of peace overwhelm me. It feels good to get off the road and to know that we'll be staying put.

For a while, at least.

"Come on," Artem says. He takes my hand and leads me into the lodge.

He has to push the door hard, but it squeaks open eventually and we walk inside.

The space is large, with a kitchen built into one corner and a door leading to the bedroom on the opposite side. A couch has been covered over with plastic, behind which rests a table with three mismatched chairs.

I venture towards the bedroom while Artem checks out the fireplace. It's only mildly cool at the moment, but I have a feeling the temperature will drop in the night, giving us an excuse to light it up.

The bedroom is small. A bed is pushed up against one wall and it even has a mattress, but it's covered over with a thick film of dust.

Apart from that, it's practically empty.

I walk further into the room and check out the brilliant view from the window just over the bed.

Snow-capped mountain range sprawling under an azure blue sky.

Breathtaking.

I look down at the scratchings on the windowpane. Wondering if Cesar had stood there at some point, admiring the view in the same way I'm doing now.

I turn to find Artem standing in the doorway. He seems to take up the entire space, making the lodge itself look small.

I go to him without thinking about it and wrap my arms around him. It's strange how natural it feels to be in his arms now.

He kisses my head, another gesture that has become comforting and familiar to me.

"I need to scout the area," he tells me. "And secure the perimeter of the property."

I nod. "I'll try and make this place livable while you're out."

He pulls away so he can look down at me. "I don't want you doing too much," he says. "You need to rest."

I roll my eyes and walk back into the living room. "I'm perfectly capable of doing a little light spring cleaning, Artem."

He sighs. "Is there ever gonna be a time when you just listen to me without arguing?"

I glare at him. "What do you think?"

He grins. "Fair enough. I'll need to go into town to place a call to Cillian as well, but I shouldn't be more than a few hours."

"No worries. I have tons to do here to keep myself busy."

He grimaces again. "Please don't go overboard."

"Wouldn't dream of it."

He smiles and kisses me softly on the lips before heading back outside to the car. I follow along to help him unload all the supplies we'd bought on our way out of Joshua Tree.

Once the trunk is empty, Artem climbs into the driver's seat and heads back down the rocky trail that leads back to civilization. I watch him go until the car turns to the left and disappears completely from view.

At the back of the lodge, I find a small shed with brooms and mops. They could use a clean themselves, so I hold them under running water from the tap out back until they look a little more presentable.

Artem and I had bought a bunch of cleaning supplies and detergents, so I get them all out and set to work inside the cabin first.

I fold a clean duster into a triangle and wrap it around my face like an old-timey bandit. Then I dust all the surfaces, which creates something of an indoor dust cloud that took several seconds to settle.

I swept the floor twice over to get out all the dirt and debris clinging to the crevices in the wooden floorboards.

And when that's done, I go through the entire cabin with my mop.

By the time I finish, the place looks so much cleaner and brighter. My eyes dart around the space, now seeing all the possibilities to make it more personal and cozier.

I've just moved on to cleaning the stovetop when I hear the car pull up outside the cabin.

A few minutes later, Artem walks in with his arms full.

He stops short when he takes in the newly exorcised cabin and looks at me with raised eyebrows.

"So much for taking it easy, huh?"

"It looks better, doesn't it?"

"It looks amazing," he replies. "Have you rested at all since I left?"

"You've only been gone an hour," I say with a shrug.

"I've been gone for three."

It's my turn to raise my eyebrows at him. "Seriously?"

"Yes," he laughs. "How about we take a break for a bit and eat something?"

"Well... I'm almost done with the stovetop," I tell him. "But we'll need gas."

"Way ahead of you," Artem says. "I bought a gas cylinder from town."

"Why don't you get that set up, and I'll work on dinner?"

"I can help," he offers.

I smile. "Don't worry. I can manage."

He doesn't argue too much, as he goes back out to the car to get the gas cylinder. While he sorts the stove out, I look through the supplies he's brought for us.

Since we don't have a working refrigerator, they're all food items that can be stored at room temperature without going bad. Artem's also bought us a small supply of vegetables, some olive oil, and a large pot and pan.

I pull out a packet of pasta, as my meal plan for tonight takes shape. Once Artem has the stove set up, he gives me a kiss on the temple on his way out and I get to work.

I boil some pasta and use the frying pan to get a sauce going. I cut up tomatoes and mushrooms and add that to the sauce to help build flavor.

I have limited ingredients so I have to think on my feet, but I find that I'm really enjoying myself.

When the pasta's finished, I look around for plates and realize that we don't have any. I check around for Artem, realizing that I haven't seen him in a bit.

No sign outside, either.

I'm on the verge of panicking when I hear footsteps coming up from a steep slope directly in front of the cabin.

"Artem?" I call nervously.

He steps into view and gives me a broad smile.

"Where did you go?" I ask. "I thought you'd finished scouting the area."

"I did," he nods. "Which is how I found the perfect little spot for us to have our dinner tonight."

I frown, walking closer to him.

And that's when I see it: there's a narrow footpath that leads down the slope towards a flat surface that almost looks like a lookout point.

I realize that Artem's taken the porch table and both chairs down there and set up a little outdoor dining area for the two of us.

"Wow," I breathe.

"You like it?"

"It'll do," I tease. "I'll bring the frying pan down."

"The frying pan?" Artem asks, with confusion.

"Oh... well we don't have plates," I explain. "So we'll just have to eat out of the frying pan."

He laughs. "I guess there's still a lot we need to stock up on, huh?"

"We might need a fridge at some point, too," I tell him. "That is, if you want a little more variety in your meals. And if you wanna, you know, avoid salmonella."

He laughs. "You get the frying pan and I'll get the drinks?"

"Sounds good."

Ten minutes later, we're sitting at the table looking out over the most amazing mountain I've ever seen up close.

"This looks good," Artem says, gesturing to the pasta.

"Why don't you taste it first?" I say nervously.

We sit opposite each other and take the forks I've placed against the pan. His eyes are on me as he lifts a spiral of pasta into his mouth.

He chews thoughtfully for a moment and smiles.

"You can cook," he decides.

"You think?"

"My tastebuds aren't lying."

I smile. "I used to enjoy cooking when I was younger," I admit. "I'd steal into the kitchen at night and experiment. Then I'd take whatever I made back up to—"

I stop short, just before Cesar's name slips out of my mouth. I'm the one who insisted that I should be free to talk about my brother when I want to.

But for some reason, I'm hesitant to do it now.

Artem and I have been getting along so well lately and a part of me doesn't want to spoil it by bringing up Cesar.

Another part of me is terrified of hearing what else is lurking in Artem's memory where my brother is concerned.

"Back up where?"

"Uh, my room," I finish. "I'd take it back up to my room and eat it by the window."

Artem's smile comes a second too late. It's clear he knows I didn't finish my sentence the way I had initially intended.

I reach for the soda Artem bought for us and take a sip to avoid his eyes.

"It's so beautiful," I mumble, looking out at the mountain peaks.

"It really is," Artem nods. "But you are still the most beautiful thing here."

I feel a blush rush up my cheeks. But, try as I might, I can't seem to push it back.

The night sky darkens as we sit and eat. I feel more at peace than I have in a while.

After we finish eating, Artem and I walk to the edge of the slope where a large boulder forms a natural love seat facing the mountain range.

Artem sits down and tucks me under his arm so that we can enjoy the view. There's nothing but the whistling wind and the sound of crickets in the air, but all I care to hear is Artem's breathing.

He looks down at me, his dark eyes are cloudy with thought.

"I can see why your brother used to come up here," Artem says, and I freeze at the mention of Cesar.

But I don't detect any animosity in Artem's tone this time.

"It was difficult for him to adjust to life in the business," I confide. "I think this cabin was somewhere he could come and just be himself."

He nods. "Did he tell you that? That it was hard adjusting to life in the cartel?"

I glance at him, trying to decipher what that question meant. "Yes," I answer. "He was a little older than you when Papa started grooming him. He started to change."

"How did he change?" Artem asks.

I realize that we've now fallen into a fully-fledged conversation about Cesar and I feel my heartbeat pick up a little.

"Little ways," I reply. "It was a look in his eyes more than anything, like he'd seen too much of the world to be hopeful or optimistic. His smile became sad. He started talking a lot about death..."

I trail off remembering little snippets of conversations that I'd long since pushed into the recesses of my memory.

"He loved the beach," I continue. "But after Papa started his training, I started to feel like a part of him *needed* the ocean. He used to go there every chance he got. Sometimes, he'd wake up in the middle of the night and go for a run."

An old memory resurfaces. I had been a teenager and Cesar had been in the family business for years at that point.

"Cesar?"

"Little bird. What are you doing up so late?"

"What are you doing up so late?" I counter.

"I went for a run."

"It's three in the morning."

"I needed to clear my head."

"What's in your head?"

"Monsters, little Esme."

I pause, trying to see his features past the darkness. He looks like my brother and yet sometimes, I look at his face and see a stranger staring back at me.

"Does the running help get rid of the monsters?" I ask.

"No, nothing can do that," Cesar replies. "But for a little while at least, I manage to outrun them."

"You talk in riddles now. You do realize that, right?" I tell him.

He smiles. "No, I don't," he says. "You just don't understand me yet."

I frown. "I'm not a child anymore. I'm thirteen."

"Stop trying to grow up so fast," he says harshly. "I would give anything to be thirteen again."

"Because you didn't have monsters then?" I surmise.

Cesar gives me a little wink. "Exactly."

I move forward and reach for his hand. He doesn't lean in to touch me as easily as he used to. Sometimes, it feels like he wants to put distance between us, as though my presence hurts him in some way.

It might sting if I didn't know how much he loves me.

"You need to remove the mask sometimes, Cesar," I tell him. "If you wear the mask all the time, the monsters in your head will only get bigger."

He looks at me in amazement for a moment. Then he smiles softly. "Maybe you're right. Maybe you understand more than I give you credit for. Goodnight, little bird."

He leans in, kisses my forehead.

And then goes into his room before I can say goodnight in return.

59

ESME

I feel tears pooling at the corners of my eyes. Artem squeezes my hand.

"Are you okay?" he asks.

I nod. "I was just... remembering," I tell him. "Monsters."

"What?" Artem asks, his dark eyes boring into mine.

"He told me once that he had monsters in his head," I say softly. "And he tried to outrun them all the time. It was around the time Papa started sending Cesar away on missions. He was gone weeks at a time sometimes and when he returned…"

"He was different," Artem finishes. It's a statement, not a question.

"If he came home at all, he would hole up in his room and I wouldn't see him for days. Other times, he would come here first, before coming home."

Artem sighs deeply. "I've spent so long hating him," he says.

"Why?" I ask.

I feel that sense of being ready to turn a corner when you know there's something scary around the bend.

Whatever Artem says next will change everything.

He pulls away slightly so that he can look at me. His fingers inch up and he grazes them over my cheek.

"I don't want to hurt you," he says. "But I owe you the truth."

I shudder, my eyes going wide.

But I can't stop him, even though a part of me wants to.

I need to hear this.

"I want the truth," I whisper.

"I was married once... a long time ago."

I stare at him, blinking through my confusion. He was *married*?

He had never mentioned another woman before.

He had certainly never mentioned a wife.

"I don't talk about her," Artem says, as though he can see the question in my eyes. "I loved her. She was kind and strong. The type of person who saw beauty and goodness in everything, including me. Maybe that's what drew me to her in the first place. She saw something in me that I didn't see in myself. It made me want to be the person she thought I was."

His tone unsettles me. It's weighed down with fatigue as though he's speaking of distant feelings that he's been burdened with for years.

My heart trembles a little all the same.

I do feel a twinge of jealousy, but I feel more sadness than anything else.

Artem's face is stoic, nearly expressionless, but I think I know him well enough now to know that it hurts him to do this to relive this part of his past.

"But in this world, love is a liability," Artem continues. "It's a weakness that our enemies use against us. I thought Marisha was safe. We were in Moscow over the holidays. She wanted to see the town where I was born. It was meant to be a celebration of what was to come."

I don't answer. Don't move. Don't even dare to breathe.

"But my enemies found us," he tells me. "They'd been tailing us for a long time and they targeted her when she was alone in the house."

I shake my head like I can stop what's coming.

I know what he's about to tell me.

But I still can't bear to hear it.

"No..."

"He killed her in our bed," Artem rasps. "Strangled the life out of her first, and then he ripped her stomach open and left her there for me to find."

"No," I whisper again fiercely, unable to come to terms with the horrific image that's forming in my head.

I shake my head and stand abruptly, as my head starts to connect the dots, the little crumb trail he has been laying for me this whole time.

"Artem... why... what does this have to do with my... my..."

A sob swallows the rest of my words as I stumble away from him. I had asked for this story.

I had known I would regret knowing, and still I had insisted. I'd brought this upon myself.

He's as calm as the mountains that stare at us in the distance, but I can see the cacophony of emotion that stirs just under the surface.

"You asked me for the truth," Artem says. "And I need you to know why I murdered your brother."

"Artem, please…"

"I wanted revenge," he continues. "I wanted revenge for my wife… and my unborn child."

I freeze in place as the last gory detail of her murder coming into focus.

He ripped her stomach open.

I close my eyes. Two cold tears escape down my cheeks.

I want to run, I want to move, but I can't. I'm rooted to the ground, my feet cemented in place, forcing me to confront the truth I want to flee from.

"None of it is fair," Artem says coldly. "Your brother took my wife and child from me, and I took your brother from you. There are no villains or heroes, Esme. Just people in impossible situations."

I open my eyes, blinking away my tears so I can see his face clearly. I see the lines of pain that put his features in high relief.

His dark beauty shines like a beacon in the moonlight.

"Artem, I'm so sorry," I say, my voice breaking like one of the waves my brother loved so much.

"You have nothing to apologize for."

"Yes, I do," I insist as more tears streak down my face. "I have to apologize because… I still love my brother. I can't stop."

He's silent for a long time.

I finally work up the courage to look up at him.

"Do you hate me for that?" I ask.

Something flashes in his eyes for a second and he grips me tighter.

"Never," he tells me. "The man you knew was different from the man I came across. The man I came across? He was wearing a mask."

My eyes go wide at that.

I feel more tears come. But these tears are grateful.

I remove my hands from around my own body and place them against Artem's chest.

"Thank you, Artem," I say softly.

He nods, and all I realize is how badly I'm craving his touch, how much of my strength flows from him now.

I think about the hell he must have gone through in the aftermath of his wife's murder.

I can recognize that pain in him now. It simmers in the rage that I now know he keeps locked away in his chest.

He has learned to control it, but with difficulty.

I was right—knowing the truth has changed everything.

I can never look at Artem the same way again.

I can never think of Cesar in the same way again.

I love him still, but my love for him is different now. It has to be.

"How did you survive it?" I ask, looking up at Artem. "The grief. Losing her."

"Not well," he admits. "But I had Cillian then. He got me through that dark time. He told me that one day I would see a light at the end of the tunnel. I called him a fucking fool at the time, but now I can see he was right."

"He was?" I ask, grabbing that one tiny string of hope dangling before me.

"Yes," Artem says with a decisive nod. "The tunnel came to an end eventually and I saw the light. I saw the light the day I met you."

60

ARTEM

A FEW DAYS LATER

She rocks back and forth on top of me. Her hair flies wildly around her head and her lips part with a moan that sends a jolt of electricity straight to my cock.

My fingertips graze against her belly that has only just started to swell.

Esme falls against my chest, her breathing erratic and filled with notes of pleasure. I wrap my arms around her and flip us over so that I'm on top.

"Harder, Artem," she gasps. "Harder."

I bury my face in the crook of her neck and ram into her with violent thrusts. When that's not enough, I hook her legs over my shoulders so I can drive deeper.

"Yes," she moans at once as I find the right spot. She squeezes around my cock and her hands scrabble to cling to something, anything—bedsheets, pillows, my flexing thighs.

When her orgasm comes, it comes hard. Her sounds go silent and it looks for a moment like she can't breathe.

But then the levee breaks and she dissolves into an endless stream of whispers and curses and pleas to never stop.

It pulls me closer and closer to the edge, too, until I can't hold back anymore.

"Esme, I'm going to…"

She flips around frantically, takes my cock in two hands, and brings her lips right to my tip.

The suction of her wet mouth around me pulls the seed out in fiery ropes. She swallows me greedily, desperately.

It's the hottest thing I've ever seen in my life.

When I'm fully spent, Esme wipes away the tiny dot next to her mouth and settles into the sheets beside me.

"Jesus, woman," I tell her. "You're gonna kill me."

"I don't know what you mean," she says innocently.

"This is the second morning you've woken me up with your mouth around my cock."

"Are you complaining?" she asks, in a teasing tone. "Because that sounds an awful lot like a complaint, sir."

"I'm not and it isn't," I reply in a hurry. "I'm just saying, I'm liable to have a fucking heart attack the way you ride me."

She chuckles. "You're a big boy," she says, patting my chest. "You can take it."

Esme tries to get out of bed, but I grab her and pull her to me. She squirms in my arms, yelping and giggling.

"Where do you think you're going?" I growl in her ear.

"Brush my teeth…" she says, continuing to wiggle. "I've got some man's taste all up in there."

"Fuck that," I growl. "I want to lie here with you for a bit. You like that taste anyways."

"If we stay in bed, we'll end up having sex again," Esme sighs, as though it's a problem she doesn't know how to solve.

"Says who?"

She smiles. "Says me."

I flex my arm. "It's this mountain man physique of mine that's revving your engine, isn't it?"

Esme shoves me away. "Gross. Never. It's the baby. The damn baby's making me so horny."

I grin with satisfaction. I have noticed her increasing demands in the last few days, and I am all for it. My body craves hers, and I've spent the last few days exploring every last inch of it.

We haven't spoken about Marisha and the baby since the night I revealed that sordid part of my past.

But it hangs there between us in the long silences, waiting for the right moment to sneak out and say its peace.

"Oh, sure," I nod. "Blame the innocent little baby."

"I'm not—"

"You need to take responsibility for the fact that you just can't keep your hands off me," I say, cutting her off.

She narrows her eyes, but I can see the smile she's trying to hide.

"Well," she says, running her fingers over the tattoos on my chest, "now that you mention it, I've always had a thing for dark-haired Russian men."

"Is that right?"

"Mm-hmm," she nods. "With killer abs and a giant dick."

"Happy to be of service."

"You did knock me up," she points out. "It's the least you can do."

"I can do so much more than that if you let me, darling."

"Is that a threat or a promise?"

"It's whatever you want it to be, *kiska*."

"Oo, I love it when you talk dirty Russian to me." She snuggles into the crook of my arm and drops a fluttering kiss on my neck. "But don't do it now or we'll just start this whole thing all over again. Anyway, what's the plan today?"

"I've got to check in with Cillian," I tell her. "It's been a few days since our last call and I need to stay updated. I haven't been this disconnected from the Bratva since… well, since ever."

Her expression takes on that careful, weary quality that I don't like seeing. I take her hand and thread her fingers through mine.

"What is it?"

"Nothing," she mumbles.

"Don't lie."

She sighs. "Is it really so bad?" she asks. "To be disconnected from it all?"

"No," I reply carefully. "But I am the don, Esme, no matter what my uncle may be saying. I'm responsible for all the men that follow me. I need to know what's happening."

She drops her gaze. I know it's because she doesn't want me to see what's in her eyes. "Would it really be so awful if we were to just… stay up here?"

"Really?" I press. "You want to live in this cabin until we're old and grey?"

"Why not?" she counters, her chin jutting out a little. "It's peaceful and quiet and we don't have to worry about anyone trying to kill us."

"I'll kill every single man who even thinks of hurting you," I tell her firmly.

She nods. "I know that. I just wish you didn't need to."

Before I can say anything else, she disentangles herself from my arms and gets off the bed and onto her feet.

I watch as she walks naked to the chair that we usually throw our clothes on. She grabs my t-shirt and slips it over her head. It swallows her blossoming body, leaving only her legs on full display.

"What do you want for breakfast?"

"What do *you* want for breakfast?" I toss back at her.

"At this point," Esme muses, rubbing her belly, "it's really about what this little guy wants for breakfast. And I think he's craving bacon and cheese and croissants with garlic butter."

I chuckle. "Oh, just that? You don't want crepes and a seafood tower, too, princess?"

"Well, if you're offering…"

I toss a pillow at her. She shrieks and scrambles out of the room, laughing.

I get up with a yawn and follow her into the kitchen.

The place looks a lot different now than the state we found it in. It's clean, for one thing, but we also have cabinets stocked with different food products, and a small mini-fridge in the corner to store our meats, along with a few locally-grown fruits and vegetables.

Esme opens the fridge and pulls out the milk and our last carton of eggs.

"Omelet?" she asks.

"I'd do devious things to you for one of those."

She wrinkles her nose in mock disgust. "You'd do devious things to me for no reason at all."

"Touché."

Esme gets to work on breakfast, humming as she cooks. I go out to the car to check our supplies.

We should be good for another week or so up here. I wonder if there's a possibility we might stay longer. I know Esme loves the peace and quiet of the mountains.

But it's also more than that.

She's desperate to avoid the chaos that awaits us the moment we leave this cabin.

My memories unfold suddenly as I step into the crisp mountain air. I remember a conversation I'd had with Marisha what feels like a lifetime ago now.

"Where were you?" Marisha asks, her eyes bloodshot from lack of sleep.

"I was working, babe."

She flinches back from my touch, a hand falling to her growing belly. "I waited for you."

"Marisha," I sigh, "you know I have to work."

"Work," she spits. "You say that like you have a real job."

I frown. "What's gotten into you?"

She's never this combative. The woman is unflappable. It was one of the reasons I'd been so attracted to her in the first place.

"What's gotten into me?" she repeats. "Are you serious?"

"Marisha—"

"I'm terrified, Artem!" she says. "I'm terrified to bring a baby into this world. It's not safe."

"I'll keep him safe," I assure her. "I'll keep you both safe."

"One of these days, Artem, you're going to wake up and realize you're mortal, same as everyone else. You can't stop death, and you certainly can't reverse it. I don't want to lose my child to this life."

"Maybe you should have thought about that before you married me then," I snap back at her.

She flinches away from the bite in my voice.

I regret my tone immediately.

She deserves more than a short-tempered husband who disregards her fears.

"I'm sorry," I say, reaching for her hand and pulling her to me. "I'm sorry. I didn't mean that."

She sighs. "I'm so scared for my baby, Artem."

"*Our* baby, Marisha," I correct her. "And I told you, I will protect you both."

"You promise?" she asks, looking up at me with those gorgeous blue eyes.

"I promise."

I meant that. I really did.

61

ARTEM

I force myself out of the memory and close the trunk of the car. I look up through the front door of the cabin to see Esme moving around near the kitchen.

Am I repeating the same mistake here? Hadn't I just promised Esme the same thing I promised Marisha?

Why would this time be different?

I walk into the cabin just as Esme sets our plates down on the table. I join her, but I've completely lost my appetite.

"We need more milk," she says as she drains her glass. "And eggs. And bread. And, um… everything else."

I raise an eyebrow.

"Hey, I'm pregnant," she reminds me again.

"I know, I know," I say, lifting my hands up in surrender. "And it's my fault."

"Right." Esme nods, satisfied. "So you need to keep me fed and happy."

"Aye-aye, captain," I say, giving her a mock salute. "Do you wanna join me today?"

She thinks about it for a second. "I think I'd rather just stay in the cabin," she decides. "But if you happen to pass by a book store—"

"I'll see what they have."

"Thanks," she says, with a contented smile. Then her eyes glance down to my plate. "You're not eating," she points out.

I pick up my fork cut out a piece of my omelet, but that doesn't seem to appease her.

"What's on your mind?" she asks.

"What makes you think there's something on my mind?"

"That look on your face."

I smile. "I didn't realize I was easy to read."

"You're not," she replies. "But we've spent a lot of time together lately and I've starting picking up on some of your tells."

"Hmm... that's dangerous."

She laughs. "You're worried?"

"A little."

"About the Bratva?"

I hesitate. I've never been open with my feelings. It was something that used to drive Marisha crazy. She'd ask me what was on my mind all the time, and every time I would reply with the same set of answers.

Nothing.

I'm fine.

Nothing's wrong.

It's just Bratva business.

I look up at Esme, at her beautiful, empathetic hazel eyes, and I decide to be better than I was then.

"Yes," I admit. "I am worried about the Bratva. But I'm also worried about you and the baby."

Her eyes go soft. She gets up from her seat and walks around the table to me. She sits on my lap and puts her hands around my shoulders.

"I'm stronger than I look," she reminds me.

I smile, remembering that she had said something similar once upon a time, when we'd still been strangers.

"I know."

"And our baby is strong, too," she tells me. "How can he be anything else, with a father like you?"

I detect a note of pride in her voice. It makes me feel like I'm eight fucking feet tall.

I tell myself that I need to be deserving of that pride. I need to make sure she's safe.

I will not repeat past mistakes.

I will not lose another wife.

I will not lose another child.

"You keep referring to the baby as he a 'he'," I point out. "Mother's intuition again?"

She tilts her head as if she's just now noticing that tendency. "No, it just comes out that way, I guess. I honestly have no idea what we're having." Then she gives me a sneaky side glance. "Do you have a preference?"

"My preference is for healthy," I say truthfully. "Beyond that, I don't care."

She cups my face with both hands and stares at me for a long moment. I can see the optimism shining bright inside her.

The optimism that I lost a lifetime ago, if I ever had it in the first place.

"But I do hope the baby gets your eyes," I add.

"Yeah?"

"They're the most beautiful eyes I've ever seen."

"That's a big statement."

"Go big or go home, isn't that what they say?"

She laughs and kisses me softly on the cheek.

My hand settles over her burgeoning belly. I marvel at the changes her body has gone through in such a short span of time. She has a bump now, still small, only in the developmental stages, but it's undeniable.

She has a glow, too. Though I suspect that has something to do with the mountain air and the absence of stress.

"Now stop worrying and eat," she scolds, giving me another kiss before moving back to her seat.

We eat our breakfast together. When we're done, I wash the dishes while Esme spreads herself out on the sofa.

It's stained and torn in places, but it serves its purpose and even I have to admit, it's comfortable as hell.

She picks up one of the books she bought earlier this week when we went down into town together. She's been through three books in as many days and her appetite for them only seems to grow.

I slip my jacket on and kiss Esme on the forehead on my way out.

When I glance back at her, her eyes are fixed on me, a small smile playing across her face.

"What are you looking at?" I ask, wagging my eyebrows at her.

"Oh, nothing," she replies. "Just… enjoying my view. Go ahead and leave so I can get a look at my favorite part."

Laughing, I head down to the car. It's amazing how my mood lifts every time I'm near the cabin, and how quickly it deteriorates the moment I leave Esme behind.

It's like the second I lose sight of the lodge, my mind shifts back to its old ways. To tactics and alliances and violence. So much violence.

I maneuver the car down the winding track that leads to the town.

As I drive, my mind ticks off the names of all the men who have pledged their loyalty to me. They have all risked their lives and the safety of their families in order to do so.

I vow never to forget that. I owe them a debt of gratitude. I plan to repay it the moment I take back control of the Bratva.

My hands clench around the steering wheel as my mind settles on my uncle. The betrayal was all the worse because of our blood ties to one another.

But I'm starting to realize, that blood counts for nothing.

Cillian is more family to me than Budimir ever was.

I comb through every single past memory I have of Budimir, and when I do, I see each encounter and each conversation with new eyes.

I remember how he used to whisper in my ear before every meeting with Stanislav, giving me advice that directly contradicted with my father's views.

He used to set me up.

And, fucking fool that I was, I played right into his hands.

I've always considered myself closer to my uncle than my father. Now, I see that I was being played from the beginning by a man too cunning and too greedy to settle for second fiddle.

Your time is coming, old man.

I will look down at your mangled body soon and smile.

62

ARTEM

The town near Devil's Peak is a small one. There's a few different restaurants, one bar, and an essential goods store.

Driving further will take me to a stretch of hilly land where the farmers live. They're the ones who supply the local stores with fresh produce every day.

But they also supply certain parties with items when someone needed something a little more… delicate.

Like I need today.

So I keep driving through the town and into the foothills beyond. I have to drive five miles before I find a sign pointing to "Granja Hueco de Cedro."

Cedar Tree Hollow Farm.

I park right outside the main farm house just as a tall, burly-looking man steps out of the rustic structure. He's wearing mud-stained blue jeans, scuffed cowboy boots, and a grey shirt that probably used to be white in its heyday.

"Hola," he greets cautiously.

"Are you Guillermo?" I ask.

He nods and spits in the red dirt.

"I was told you had a range of exclusive products for special buyers."

"Are you a special buyer?" he asks. His tone is guarded, neutral. A tough man if ever there was one. Life out here cannot be easy.

"I think I might be."

He nods and spits again. Then, without another word, he turns and leads me through his farm to a small shed about thirty yards from the main barn.

He unlocks the door and ushers me inside.

The moment we're in, he closes the door, enshrouding us in partial darkness. The only light coming through is from the single square window on the other side of the shed.

I'm on guard. Out of habit, if nothing else.

The man thumps around and over to a long, narrow shelf space mounted on the wall, separated by a series of locked compartments.

"Cuál quieres?" Guillermo asks, clicking his teeth as though there is something stuck between them.

Esme and I have been practicing Spanish whenever I return from treks into town. I've gotten better, although she still says I sound Russian when I try to get my accent right.

"Something to shoot bears," I lie. "And plenty of ammunition."

"Bears?"

I nod. "Bears." I don't offer anything more than that.

He gives me a curious sideways glance. Then he shrugs and pops open the first compartment. Inside are a pair of Colt 1911 pistols. They look old and worn.

"I have only this now. Next month, I get more."

"I won't be here next month," I tell him. "I need a rifle now."

He nods. Spits. Shuffles over to the next box and opens that one.

Inside is a scratched-up rifle that looks like it hasn't been fired since Texas was its own country.

I grimace, but what choice do I have?

I look up at Guillermo, who hasn't taken his eyes off my face. I don't like the way he's looking at me, either.

"You've got ammunition?"

"Sí," he says. He taps a wooden crate with the toe of his boot. The bullets inside rattle and clink.

I'm used to bigger, more powerful guns, but these will have to work. I might even be able to teach Esme how to use it.

But the moment the thought crosses my mind, I reject it. Esme won't want to learn. Not after what happened with Mischa. She still wakes up in the night sometimes, sweating and muttering, "No, no, no."

"Okay," I agree. "I'll take it. I was told you had burner phones, too?"

He nods. Not a man of many words, this Guillermo. But there is a cunning kind of intelligence behind his eyes.

We haggle over the price for a few minutes, mostly with grunts and nods. His price is higher than I would normally pay, but since I don't have a lot of options, I settle with him quickly, grab my new gun and ammo along with the cell phone, and head back towards my car.

Guillermo falls into step beside me. "You just passing through?" he asks.

"That's right."

"Heard you come down to the village every other day," he tells me. His English is suddenly much more fluid than it was when I first arrived. "Where exactly are you staying?"

"In a motel a few miles from town," I lie smoothly.

"Ah," Guillermo replies, his eyes growing more and more curious.

I pick up the pace and get to my car before he can ask any more questions. He stands at the mouth of the driveway, hands crossed over his pudgy belly, watching me the whole way I go.

∼

On my way back, I stop in town and pick up fresh groceries, including a few bars of chocolate for Esme.

Then I go next door to the used bookstore that Esme stops by every time she comes down here with me.

I look through the shelves and pick out a crime thriller. The woman behind the counter squints at me through her round glasses.

"Back again," she comments.

I nod, unwilling to engage in more needless conversation.

"Cómo esta Esme?"

I flinch, not happy about the fact that this stranger knows my wife's name.

"She's fine," I mutter. Guillermo's intrusive questions have left me in a foul mood.

The woman's eyes go wide when she sees my dark expression. She keeps her mouth shut after that.

She rings up my purchase and hands it over to me without a word. Once I'm inside, I pick up the new burner phones and dial in Cillian's number.

He picks up almost immediately.

"Hello?"

"Cillian," I say.

I hear an audible sigh of relief. "You good, brother?"

"How are *you*?" I ask, ignoring his question. I can hear the stress in his tone.

Cillian has stayed close to L.A. so that he can keep an eye on Budimir and his dealings. Apparently, there has been a lot of movement lately, though little information has been leaked.

It isn't the most encouraging start. I'm hoping Cillian will have something new for me this time.

"I'm fine," Cillian says dismissively. "I did manage to get some new intel."

"Spit."

"Budimir's causing waves," Cillian says. "He's broken the treaty with the Diegos."

I hiss. "They've been our fucking allies for two decades."

"Is it any surprise that loyalty means fuck-all to Budimir?"

I grit my teeth together, my hands itching to wrap themselves around Budimir's thick, veined neck.

"That's not all, either," Cillian continues. "He's reached out to some… other people."

"Fuck," I growl. I have a bad feeling about what is coming next.

"He's trying to get into some bad shit," Cillian tells me. "Moving prostitutes. Slaves. Human trafficking, that kind of thing. The shit Stanislav swore we'd never do."

A dull ache throbs in the pit of my stomach.

"He's been gunning for that for years now," I say. "I should have fucking seen this coming."

"You couldn't have known."

"But I should have," I argue. "That's the point. I have to stop him."

"Artem—"

"This has gone too fucking far," I say, my blood feels like it's going to boil over. "He needs to be stopped now, not eventually."

"And we will stop him," Cillian assures me. "But now's not the right time. We don't have the resources and we need more information."

"The more we wait, the harder it'll be to derail his plans."

"I wouldn't count on it," Cillian says. "You are the rightful don. There's power in your name."

"Power is where the men decide it is," I remind him. "And many of them chose Budimir."

"Artem, I know you want to act," Cillian says, in his measured tone. "But Budimir is desperate to get his hands on you. That means something. It means he's scared of you. Which is why it's more imperative than ever for you to stay out of his clutches."

"I don't plan on getting caught," I snarl.

"You are not invincible, brother," Cillian rebuts quietly.

His words shiver through me, stirring up a strong sense of déjà vu. I see Marisha's blue eyes looking up at me pleadingly.

One of these days, Artem, you're going to wake up and realize you're mortal, same as everyone else.

"I have to protect Esme," I say, trying to push back my rage. "I have to protect my child. Sitting back and waiting for him to come is just asking for the fight to be brought to my doorstep."

"Then lie low a little while longer," Cillian fires back. "We need to wait 'til the time's right."

"Fuck," I growl, unable to find a counter argument.

"I'll keep you posted. Stay safe, brother. Look after your family."

"I will," I reply. "Look after yourself."

The line goes dead.

I stare out at the quiet town even more pissed off than before.

I don't belong here. I should be with Cillian, making moves, tracking Budimir's plans. *Fighting.* Not cowering like a fucking bitch.

But even as I think it, the thought of leaving Esme turns my stomach.

Esme needs me more.

I turn on my engine and drive.

Back to the cabin.

Back to my wife.

63

ESME

I'm supposed to be dusting out the sofa cushions on the porch, but I've pretty much abandoned that job completely. Instead, my eyes are firmly fixed on Artem.

He's standing shirtless near one of the larger trees just before the slope that leads to the viewing point. His body glistens with beads of sweat that cover his entire body and highlight the toned perfection of his chest, the hard ridges of his abs.

I leave the cushions on the porch and move closer. Waves of desire flash through my body and concentrate right between my legs.

It's not like I'm starving for his affection. We have sex at least twice a day. Some days, we never leave the bedroom.

And even when I think I've had enough, it only takes an hour's respite to get me wet for him again.

Artem jumps off the ground and grabs a sturdy tree branch above him. Each pull-up flexes his arms. His face is screwed up in fierce concentration.

When he drops back to the earth, he starts doing a round of push-ups. The lines of his tattoos twist and bulge with the motion.

He's so focused on his work out that he doesn't even notice me watching. Not until I walk down the porch steps and lean against the railing.

"Hey, you," he says, a smile touching the corners of his mouth. He doesn't stop moving.

"Hey, yourself," I reply. "Looking good"

He smirks. "How long have you been standing there?"

"Umm... awhile," I admit.

He laughs. "If I knew you were watching, I would have put on a show for you."

"Oh, don't worry, you did anyway," I reply. "I'm one satisfied customer. Well, partially satisfied customer."

Artem's eyebrows go up. Then he counts twenty-five and jumps down, his landing causing a small dust cloud to rise around his feet.

"Just partially satisfied?" he asks.

I touch a thoughtful finger to my lips. "I can think of another form of exercise that you could be doing," I say, feeling a blush snake up my cheeks. "One that involves me."

"Is that so?" he asks, as I walk towards him, swinging my hips a little extra just for effect.

I'm wearing a long, blue midi dress with thin spaghetti straps. It's relatively modest as far as these things go.

But Artem's eyes gloss over my body in a way that makes me feel utterly and completely naked.

"That is, if you're not too tired," I finish. I stop a few inches from him, just out of his reach.

"I'm all sweaty," he points out.

"I don't mind."

The moment the words leave my mouth, his eyes darken with lust.

He lunges towards me, grabs me, and pulls me into his body. I squeal as I slap against his hard chest.

Artem wasn't kidding—he's soaked with sweat. But when the smell of his musky sweat fills my nostrils, I swear it makes me even wetter.

His mouth closes down over mine. I shudder at the release of his breath mingling with mine.

It's easy to close my eyes and lose myself in this kiss. It makes my head spin and my knees weak. Before Artem, I had always assumed that was a phenomenon that occurred only in books and movies.

Now, I live it every day.

My hands scour over his chest and his rock-hard abs. All I want to do is lick every drop of sweat right off his body.

Something is deeply wrong with me.

His hands are rough as they run down my body and pull up my dress. I shiver against the cold mountain air—at least, until he squeezes my ass hard and I gasp into his mouth as heat flushes through me.

I love it when he's rough with me. A primal instinct gets triggered every time he grabs me. Like he's claiming me for the first time all over again.

I expect him to hoist me into his arms and carry me into the cabin. But he doesn't.

Instead, he pulls me further away from the cabin—right to the smooth stump of a tree that he'd chopped for wood to fuel the fireplace.

I feel the bark brush against the backs of my bare thighs before Artem pushes me backwards. I yelp in surprise, but then my ass lands on the stump with an *oof*.

Artem is on me in an instant. He pushes my legs apart, his fingers twisting in my hair as he pulls my head back.

I moan against him, right into his open-mouthed kiss. I'm trembling with want as I bite down on his lower lip.

The bite is a little harder than I intended. In fact, I feel the warm trickle of blood. Artem rears back in surprise.

But his dark eyes are equal parts surprised and turned on.

"So you like it rough, huh, mountain woman?" he asks teasingly.

"Is that what you'd call rough?" I fire back with a wild grin. "I've told you before: I'm stronger than you think."

Some deep, carnal passion ignites in his eyes.

Before I can correctly name it, he yanks me hard by one arm off the tree stump. Then he spins me around so that my back is to him and immediately shoves me right back over onto my elbows.

His hands scrabble against the hem of my dress. He flips it up, yanks down my panties, and then delivers one hard spank—real fucking hard, actually—to each cheek.

The burn sizzles even as he rubs the pain away.

And between my thighs is a puddle of need.

"Is this what you want?" Artem growls.

Fuck, when his voice gets that deep and rough around the edges...

"More," I gasp, even though I'm not sure how much more I can take. "I want *more* than that."

I hear a growl, low in his throat. Pure animal. Pure lust. Pure man.

I get that much wetter.

There's a tiny lull. The rustling of fabric—Artem pushing his shorts down, maybe? But when I try to look back, I feel instead his fingers seize the roots of my hair and press my face down roughly against the smooth top of the tree stump.

I moan. "I want to see you," I whimper in a frail, desperate voice.

He doesn't bother replying. Just spanks me again, harder than the first time.

I scream and try to wriggle away, but there's nowhere to go. He has me pinned here, blinded, ass in the air. Vulnerable as it gets.

His cock teases against my opening. Just the very tip—pushing and retreating, pushing and retreating.

It's fucking maddening.

"Artem!" I plead. He's killing me slowly like this. I need more of him. All of him.

Or I might just fucking explode.

"Say my name again, baby," he orders through gritted teeth.

I don't hesitate for even a second. Just a string of whimpers: "Artem, Artem, Artem…"

"Beg me to fuck you."

"Fuck me, baby," I implore. "Please, I want you inside me… Please just fuck me…"

And then he finally gives me what I'm begging for.

My husband rams himself inside me with a pressure that takes my breath away. I scream out, my voice carrying across the trees and through the mountains.

Wind laps around us, but all I'm truly aware of is how perfectly we fit together and how whole I feel when Artem is inside me.

Our lovemaking is always different. Sometimes it's slow and tender. Other times, it's fast, desperate, clinging, rough.

But this is somehow more.

Artem grips me so hard that it feels as though he's going to leave the imprints of his fingers on my hips. His hips slam against my ass, each thrust more vigorous, more violent than the last.

All I can do is grip the sides of the rough-edged bark and let each thrust drive the breath out of me.

"Fuck," Artem groans. "Fuck… I'm gonna come."

"A minute longer, baby," I gasp. "I'm almost there."

I feel his muscles tighten as he keeps fucking me, harder and harder, until I feel the wave rise.

"Yes," I gasp. "Oh, yes…"

Then the orgasm hits me, full-bore raging through my body, and for a moment, it feels like I'm being swallowed by the warmest, most luxurious ocean.

It's the best feeling in the world.

When it finally subsides, I'm glowing.

My cheek is raw from rubbing against the tree stump and my thighs are trembling from the effort of staying upright.

But I don't mind. I couldn't care less about those things.

"Fuck," Artem breathes as he pulls out of me.

I can feel his cum drip down my legs, but I don't mind the feeling. I like being his. I like that my body can make him feel the way he makes me feel.

I sigh deeply as my dress falls back down around my waist and I turn to face Artem. I run my fingers along his quivering length, realizing that there's a new sheen of sweat coating his amazing body.

"How was that for a work-out?" I ask, with a smile.

"You fucking blow my mind," he sighs.

I wrap my arms around him. "Have a shower with me."

He takes my hand in his and we walk back into the cabin, into the bathroom. I usually boil some water before I get into the tub, but I've also gotten used to cool showers. It's just quicker and more convenient. And it makes me feel stronger in the mornings, as though my blood flows a little quicker because of it.

Artem fills the tub and I start removing my clothes. He comes up behind me once I'm naked, his hands trailing over my back until they find my breasts.

In the span of a few days, I've actually *felt* them get bigger. They definitely look a whole lot bigger than when we first drove up this mountain.

"Love these beauties," Artem says, as he ducks down and slips one of my nipples into his mouth.

I sigh and kind of lean into him. He laps at my breasts until I'm whimpering all over again. Then he lifts me up and places me gently down into the tub.

When I'm settled, he sits on the edge of the tub and swings his legs over. Water spills out of the tub onto the floor and I laugh at the sight of Artem's huge, muscular body confined to the miniscule space of the tub.

It's definitely a tight fit.

"What are you laughing at?" he demands.

"Nothing," I shrug. "You look comfy."

He grabs ahold of me and pulls me onto his lap so that I'm straddling him.

"*Now* I'm comfy," he says with a triumphant grin.

I graze my hands along his shoulders, tracing the path of his many tattoos. "I just finished the book you got me," I tell him.

"Jesus, already? Well, I guess we can pick up more books when we head into town tomorrow."

"You're not interested in going today?" I venture.

"I kinda just wanna chill at the cabin today. Maybe do some repairs."

"Hmm, well I was thinking I might head into town on my own then," I say.

He frowns, but I'm expecting that reaction. "I won't be long, babe," I assure him. "We need some groceries, too."

"Esme—"

"It's just a trip into town," I tell him. "No biggie."

"I don't like it." I make a grumpy face, and he smiles. "I'm serious, Esme. I don't like sending you off on your own unprotected."

"Please, no one knows we're here," she says. "I'm just a pregnant lady out here with my husband. Totally innocent."

"Speaking of," Artem adds, his eyes growing weary, "I would prefer you didn't engage with every single person you come into contact with down there."

I frown. "What do you mean?"

"The woman in the book store knew your name," he explains.

I roll my eyes. "Oh, Daria! Of course she does," I nod. "I told her my name."

"That's my point. She knows too much."

I laugh. "She knows my name and the fact that I'm pregnant," I say. "Not exactly the most specific of information. And before you yell at me for that, I didn't volunteer that stuff to her. She guessed."

"Still—"

"She's had three children herself, so we got to talking," I interrupt him. "It was an innocent conversation."

"We still have to be careful."

"You are paranoid," I accuse him, pressing my finger to his nose.

"Possibly," he agrees. "But in this case, I'm justified."

"Artem, please?" I ask. "I'm a big girl. I can take care of myself for a couple of hours."

I see the conflict in his eyes. He desperately wants to make sure I'm protected, but he also wants to give in to me.

I have to admit, I kind of like the power I have over him.

Not that he doesn't have a fuck load of power over me in return.

"Please?"

He sighs. "You minx."

I laugh. "Is that a yes?"

"Fine," he says huffily. "But if you're not back in two hours, I'm coming after you."

"I like the sound of that," I say happily, playfully splashing a little water into his face.

64

ESME

After we get out of the tub, Artem slips on a pair of shorts and heads into the kitchen while I get dressed.

When he's around the cabin, he walks around shirtless most of the time.

That works for me just fine.

We've settled into a routine that is comforting and familiar in its domesticity. We wake up and have sex, then we make breakfast together and eat outside if it isn't too cold for me.

Afterwards, we go for a morning walk, following some of the more obscure trails along the mountain. I pack lunch if we think we'll be gone for more than a few hours.

Either way, when we get back, I'm always tired. Artem and I usually sit on the porch and talk before dinner.

Other evenings, we spend hours in bed, alternating between power naps and sex.

Artem has his workouts, while I had my books. We both do light housework, mend things that need fixing, and generally keep the cabin as livable as we can.

In fact, by the end of our first week there, it has more or less transformed into a rustic little mountain hideout, complete with all the necessary amenities, barring a few things like continuous hot water.

Every other day, Artem goes down into town for groceries. More often than not, I accompany him. On the odd days where I'd rather stay back, I kiss him goodbye and sit by the fireplace while I compose music in my head.

I've fallen into a state of marital bliss I never expected to find.

It's more fulfilling than I could have ever imagined.

After I'm dressed, I head into the kitchen to find Artem kneeling, as he works on a repair for the table. One of the legs is a little uneven, and he's putting it back in balance.

"Okay," I say. "I'm ready for my maiden voyage."

Artem gets to his feet. I can see the reluctance in his eyes.

"You sure you want to go alone?" he asks.

"I'm sure," I nod. "I'll be fine, Artem. Don't worry."

"That's probably not gonna happen," he sighs. "But I'll do my best."

I go to him and kiss him soft and slow on his lips. He grabs me by the waist and pulls me to him hard, deepening our kiss

By the time he releases me, I'm breathless.

"If that's how you kiss me every time I go into town by myself, I should go more often," I tease.

He growls. "Two hours tops, okay?"

I smile. "Got it," I confirm, before placing a final kiss on his cheek.

He releases me with a frustrated sigh and walks me out to the car. Keys in hand, I give him a little wink and set off on my little trip into town.

I know the route like the back of my hand, since Artem and I have taken this path tons of times in the last week alone. The drive down is slow, peaceful, meditative.

The town is quiet when I drive in. I go to the bookstore first and find Daria stacking books in the back when I walk in.

"Hola, Daria," I greet, giving her my brightest smile. After months surrounded mostly by Russian men, it's weirdly refreshing to speak my native language again.

Normally, she's a bright spot in these little errand runs. But today, Daria's smile is not as enthusiastic.

I sigh internally. Apparently, my scary Russian husband made quite an impression. Which means I have to do damage control.

"Hola, Esme," Daria murmurs, sliding the last book into the compact shelves. "Cómo estás?"

"Bien, bien. The belly's finally starting to come in."

"I can see that." She steps back behind her counter like she wants to keep something solid between us. "Did you like the book your husband bought for you the last time?"

"I did. It was very exciting."

"Your husband could have been the protagonist in that book," Daria comments wryly. "He certainly looks the part."

I have to suppress a smile. The crime thriller novel that Artem had picked for me last time featured a burly, growly, overprotective antihero named Malcolm Wolf, an ex-cop who starts working with a notable crime family in order to bury secrets from his past.

Daria has no idea how on the nose she really is.

"He's a little rough around the edges," I admit. "But he's a teddy bear at heart."

Not exactly true, but Daria doesn't know that.

She gives me a tight-lipped smile. "Well, as long as he's good to you."

"He's wonderful to me."

At that, Daria's smile softens to something more standard for her.

"How's that sweet little angel doing?" she asks gently, gesturing to the small belly under my white sweater.

"Good." I nod, patting my stomach affectionately. "I haven't had a doctor's appointment in a while, though. It's the first thing on my to-do list when we get back home."

I feel a strange tug at my chest when I say those last words.

Home. Where is our home? Do we even have one?

I've started to think of the cabin as our home, but I know in my heart that that's not realistic. Not in the long run.

And even if it did make for a comfortable, long-term residence, Artem would never be content to sit up in the mountains for long.

He needs something to do. Something *real.*

I'm all for that. His happiness is my happiness, after all.

I just don't want that "something" to involve a return to the world we were both born into.

The world we were lucky to escape with our lives intact.

"Well, we do have a midwife in town, if you're interested," Daria tells me.

"Really?" I ask, perking up immediately. "You do?"

"Although," Daria adds a little uncertainly, "I'll be honest, she's kind of a kook."

"A kook?"

Daria smiles. "I think the scientific term is, nutty."

"Nutty is okay, as long as she knows her stuff."

"She does," Daria promises. "It is only her bedside manner that is a little unnerving."

"I don't mind that," I say. "It'd be nice to talk to her all the same."

"Okay then," she says. "I'll write down her address for you. It's not far from here, about a ten-minute drive or so."

Five minutes later and two books richer, I get back into the car and make my way to an uphill road. It's barren and desolate, hardly anything growing at all, not even weeds.

That's not the most promising sign for a woman whose job is theoretically nurturing life.

But I promise myself not to pass judgment too early.

At the peak of the hill is a lone cottage. Almost a shack, really. The front door is painted a violent red color.

I park, uneasy already, and trudge up to it.

I raise my fist to knock, but before I can, the door is yanked open inwards.

I step back with a start as I come face to face with a tall woman with the longest silver hair I've ever seen.

She could be anything between thirty and eighty, and she's dressed in a long, flowing kaftan embroidered with elephants and birds. A dozen different, multi-colored beaded necklaces and chains hang from around her neck and massive hoop earrings adorn her ears, along with several other piercings.

She certainly looks the part.

"Hello," she greets warmly. "I sensed you were coming today."

I raise my eyebrows. "You did?"

"Of course. Please come in. I'm Aracelia."

"I'm Esme," I say with a hesitant smile.

I follow her into the house. It's pared back more than I expected, considering her eccentric fashion sense. I'd even go so far as to call it "cute."

"So, I came because I heard you were a midwife?" I say nervously. I'm wondering if maybe I'd gotten the wrong house.

"I have delivered my share of babies," she nods. "And I do practice midwifery. As well as many other natural arts."

I frown. "Like, um..."

"I tell fortunes," Aracelia says, turning to me dramatically. "I can read people's auras, perform seances when necessary and communicate with loved ones who have passed."

I raise my eyebrows. She's deadly serious. Daria was right—"nutty" is putting it lightly.

But I can't help but be intrigued. My desire to speak to her about my baby has all but disappeared.

No sense in wasting the trip out here, though, right?

"Can you read my future?" I ask.

"Claro," she confirms. "For only eight hundred pesos, I'll give you a full reading."

I should keep my money in my pocket. Go back home, laugh about this crazy idea with Artem. He'll tell me I was a fool for ever coming here, and I'd agree.

But I have an itch to do the exact opposite.

And for some reason, that's the impulse I give into.

"Okay then," I whisper.

She sweeps an arm to point me into the sitting room.

"Come this way."

I follow her to an ornate table with a chair placed on either side. I half-expect to see a crystal ball, but there's nothing in the center of the table except a small arrangement of flowers that smell fresh and fragrant. I can still see the morning dew clinging to some of the petals.

"Take a seat, please," Aracelia directs me.

I expect her to join me at the table, but she turns around and goes back into the house. While she's gone, I look around and admire her well-kept garden through the windowpanes.

I notice a pair of eyes on me, and I frown. But when I look, I see it's just a massive tabby cat staring at me from between two flowering bushes.

"Hey there, little guy," I whisper.

The cat yawns at me, bored already, and pads away out of sight.

A moment later, Aracelia appears with a pretty little pink teacup. Steam rises from the surface.

She sits down and sets it in front of me.

"It's a special mix, made of entirely natural ingredients," she tells me. "You must drink every last drop."

I raise my eyebrows. "It won't affect the baby, will it?"

She laughs. "Esmita, it's only tea," she says. "I need you to drink it so I can read the patterns in your tea leaves."

"Oh," I stammer. "Right." My cheeks color a little as I accept the tea and take a sip.

It's sweet, with a few slightly bitter notes, but it tastes comforting and I finish the cup in a few minutes. Aracelia watches me the whole time. Unmoving, unblinking.

She reminds me an awful lot of the tabby cat.

When I hand the mug back to Aracelia, she snatches it out of my hands and brings it right up to her eyes. She turns it this way and that, frowning and muttering to herself every few seconds.

"Hmm, interesting, very interesting."

To be honest, the overall effect is a little cheesy. Like she learned how to be a psychic from watching bad infomercials.

But that itch that made me say yes to her offer in the first place hasn't gone away. If anything, it's intensified.

I lean in, trying to figure out what she's seeing, but the cup is tilted up towards her.

I have to stifle a shriek when she slams the china cup back down and turns her huge gaze on me.

"You've had a strange life," Aracelia announces.

It's a pretty general deduction to make. I refuse to be so easily impressed.

I shrug. "Some might say that."

"You've felt trapped in your past life," Aracelia continues, unperturbed by my less-than-enthusiastic reaction. "You've dreamed of escape."

That's a little less general, but still in the same ballpark.

But I pay a little more attention as she went back to studying my tea leaves.

"You've suffered great losses in your life," Aracelia intones. She hasn't broken eye contact since she set the teacup down. "A sibling. A parent —no, both parents."

She's right about that.

Mama to cancer, just after I was born.

Papa to his own greed.

Cesar to the man I married.

Maybe she's not so nutty after all.

"Violence has plagued your past," the woman continues. "And according to these leaves, it will continue to plague your future."

Those words make me stop short. I stare at Aracelia, wondering if maybe I'd misheard her.

Actually, it's more like I'm *hoping* I misheard her.

"What did you say?"

"Your leaves are chaotic," Aracelia repeats. "I sense that the path you've chosen is not an easy one. There will be many challenges ahead for you."

"What kind of challenges?" I ask.

I'm leaning in, mouth hanging open in desperation, despite the fact that I told myself at the start of this reading that it didn't mean a thing.

"It's hard to say," Aracelia replies. "But I can see you coming to a crossroads soon."

"A crossroads?"

"You will have to make a hard decision at some point in the near future. It will not be easy, but trust your instincts and you might yet find happiness."

My heart is beating fast, but I try and tamp down the panic.

This is ridiculous. This woman is just a low-rent psychic. None of this is specific and she's just guessing. She doesn't have a clue what she's talking about.

I start to rise from my seat. "Um, gracias," I say. "I appreciate the reading, but I should be going home now."

She pounces forward and seizes my forearm in her two hands. "Your husband is promising you things he cannot give you."

I freeze for the briefest of moments with something like horror surging in the pit of my stomach.

Then I rip my hand away from her.

"Right," I say. "That's enough. My hus… um, I just have to get home now."

Aracelia says something else to me, but I don't hear it or bother to make her repeat herself. I just want to get out of her house and back to my own.

She stays perfectly still, perfectly upright in her seat. She doesn't blink. Just follows me with those huge eyes as I stumble to the front door and out of the house.

I drive a little too fast back through the town. In my haste, I almost forget that I need to pick up some groceries.

I turn back around and head to the grocery store. As I move along the isles, picking up milk and carrots, I feel the panic ebb slightly.

Surrounded by the normalcy of a town that now feels familiar to me, clarity sets in. I start to feel silly.

She hadn't told me anything very specific. It was all glossy generalizations that could have fit into anyone's life. I'm giving it too much power over me.

Instantly, I feel myself relax. I finish the rest of my shopping, then I get back into the car and drive back up the winding slopes towards the cabin.

Home is safe.

Home is okay.

Home is where Artem is.

⁓

Artem is sitting out on the porch when I drive up.

I can tell by his expression that he was starting to get anxious. The relief is evident on his face when I slam the door shut and stride right into his arms.

"Hey, handsome," I say. "Missed me?"

"Of course," he nods. "How could I not? Successful trip?"

"I got everything we need for the next two days," I tell him. "And… well I had a little adventure too."

His eyebrows go up. I can tell he's bracing himself to hear something he figures he probably won't like.

But when I tell him about Aracelia and her amazingly bizarre fashion sense, Artem bursts out laughing. His laughter is just the tonic I need to wipe out the lingering remnants of worry.

"I can't believe you went to a psychic."

I shrug. "I thought it'd be a laugh."

"And was it?" he asks.

I pause. "It was. Mostly in hindsight."

He laughs again and kisses the top of my head. "Well, did she tell you anything note-worthy?"

I'm about to let her warning slip, but at the last moment I hold it in. I wish I knew why.

"Nope," I reply. "Nothing at all."

"They're all hacks and con artists," he says dismissively.

"Yeah," I agree, pulling the words around myself and blanketing myself with the comfort of them.

Aracelia was nothing but a hack.

65

ARTEM

A FEW DAYS LATER

With my gun slung over my right shoulder, I maneuver over a rocky outcrop that juts over a deep ravine.

I've ventured a little further today than I usually do on my hunting expeditions, but I enjoy exploring new parts of the mountain that's come to feel like home.

In the depths of the ravine, a snow-fed river flows quickly. The same river sweeps not too far from the cabin, so following it is an easy way to get back home.

The shriek of an eagle draws my attention overhead. The bird idles around on the thermal drafts, flapping lazily.

I wish I had a camera. Esme would have loved to see him.

That thought is so normal, so mundane, that it actually shocks me into stillness for a second.

Because it *is* normal. All this is normal.

Hunting in the mountains.

Coming home to a wife to tell her about an eagle in the sky, a deer in the bushes, a goat on a distant cliff.

The problem is—that isn't my life.

It can't be.

I'm living someone else's reality. Like I'm borrowing it or stealing it for a little while.

But it doesn't fit me. It never will.

This world is not where Artem Kovalyov belongs.

I hear movement a few feet away. I go still, trying to catch a glimpse of the deer that I've been chasing for about a mile now.

I'd seen it flash through the underbrush about twenty minutes ago. Nothing since, but the animal's scent still clings to the air.

I leave the steep path I'm on and move a little higher, to more stable ground.

The path I find is broader, but it winds towards the cliff's edge. The river in the ravine thunders from below.

Up here, the scent of dried bark and crunchy leaves weaves into that pungent deer smell.

But there's something else, too. An unfamiliar scent on the edge of my perception.

Something that doesn't belong here.

More precisely—some*one*.

I stand up a little straighter, on full alert as my eyes comb the surrounding area. The trees are thick in these parts, but whoever it is that's tailing me is clumsy and obviously inexperienced in the art of stealth stalking.

Definitely not an animal—the mountain creatures are far smarter and more subtle. I creep further along the rocky trail. I take care to step only on hardened stone so I don't leave any tracks.

The mysterious strangers weren't as careful. I see their boot prints in the soil. Only one set of tracks so far.

I have a bad feeling I will soon find more.

Two steps later, my worst fears are confirmed.

A muddle of tracks in the dirt. Half a dozen men, maybe more. They clustered here and then spread out.

I curse silently.

Have Budimir's men found us?

And if so, how the fuck did they manage to do it?

I think of Esme, sitting at alone in the cabin. I'd left her sitting contentedly by the fireplace, a tell-tale sign she was composing music in her head. She's unprotected in there. No way can she fend off a group of attackers, armed or otherwise.

She needs me. I have to go back. I hope to fucking God I'm not too late already.

I turn around, ready to make my way back to the cabin as fast as I can.

Just as a group of men emerge from the forest.

They step out from behind the trees. Within seconds, I'm surrounded. Guns swivel up to aim at my chest.

I keep my expression mildly surprised as I take them in. There's only four of them—not as many as I'd been expecting.

Their faces are unfamiliar to me, and their clothes suggest that they're locals.

Definitely not Budimir's men.

The realization makes me more confident.

Despite that, however, I'm aware that these aren't just run-of-the-mill villagers. My best guess pegs them as muscle for one of the local cartels. I can see the hardness in their wolf-like expressions.

But small-time cartel men, I can handle. So the fact that there's four of them doesn't worry me in the slightest.

Still, I play it cool just to be safe, looking around at them with a slightly puzzled expression on my face.

I don't even attempt to act afraid.

Fear was never something I could fake.

"Oye, I don't want trouble," I say, even as I keep my hand firmly on my rifle. "I'm just out here deer hunting. I don't want to get in the middle of something here."

One of the men takes a step forward, marking him as the leader of this group. He's the skinniest man present, so I assume the other guys, all bigger and beefier, are his muscle.

He has narrow eyes that are too close together and a sharp, hooked nose that make him look like a cartoon villain.

The man to my left is the tallest of them all, probably an inch or two shorter than I am, and he's got a jagged scar on his face that cuts across his nose.

The guy on my right has long, white blonde hair that he's tied back in a feminine ponytail.

The fourth and final one, I note with a glance behind me, has yellowed, rotting teeth set in tobacco-stained gums. He keeps his mouth open the whole time, as though he's proud of it.

"Deer hunting, eh?" the leader says, clicking his tongue derisively.

"That's right. But no luck today. I was just heading back into town now."

"Now, there's no reason to run off," he coos. "We just want to have a little chat with you."

"About what?" I say, unable to keep the boredom from my voice.

This little shit thinks he has me scared. I can see it in the arrogant posture, the way his gun hand dangles at his side.

He's nothing to me. Out here in this rural parts, the men think they're tough. They don't know the meaning of the word.

They don't know what I've done. What I'm capable of doing if they cross me.

Motherfucker's playing with a big dog now.

"You just passing through town?"

"Yup," I say carefully. "Just passing through. Needed a little vacation and I thought I'd get in some fresh mountain air."

The leader looks around at his men as though weighing my words against their reactions. It's a lot of play-acting, in my opinion. They're trying to seem more impressive than they actually are.

"Sounds like a load of mierda to me," the leader says. *Bullshit.*

I shrug. "Then I don't know what to tell you."

The smile drops from his face and he narrows his eyes at me. "How about you tell me what you're really doing here?"

"I just did."

"Is that right?"

I suppress a sigh, getting impatient as fuck with this roundabout line of questioning. "I just told you it is."

"Then answer me this," the leader continues. "Why would some passing tourist go up to Guillermo's farm and purchase firearms if he was just here to—what was it you said?—take in some mountain air?"

Fucking Guillermo. I knew that fat bastard was shady as hell. He sold me out to local muscle for a cheap little payday.

"Need a gun to kill deer," I say. But it's a lame excuse and we both know it.

The tension in the air ratchets up another notch.

He spits on the ground between us. "There's something fishy about you."

"Me?" I say innocently. "I'm just your average guy who likes to hunt. That's all."

"Not many 'average guys' come up against four armed men and appear so cool about it," he points out.

Before I can stop the words from escaping, I snap, "I wouldn't be so cool if there was anything to be scared of here."

That's probably stupid of me, but this motherfucker is pissing me off.

The moment the words leave my mouth, I feel the atmosphere around me change for the worse.

All four men kind of straighten up, as though I made some kind of threat against them. Which I suppose is not wrong.

Maybe they're not all as stupid as they look.

"Oh, yeah?" the leader says, raising his gun for the first time and waggling it towards me. "This doesn't scare you?"

"In case you haven't noticed, I've got one of those too," I say. "Not that size matters, but mine's bigger."

"You're outnumbered, pendejo," he hisses.

He's standing there, practically begging me to be scared of him. The fact that I'm not playing into his hands is pissing him off.

I enjoy it more than I should.

I growl, "Not the way I see it."

The leader's eyes widen a little. I can see his confidence start to waver.

It's always a confronting moment when you're faced with someone who refuses to be rattled.

I've been there before, a long time ago, when I was an inexperienced pup trying to learn the ropes. Half of it is power and skill. The other half is all mind games.

Right now, I have the upper hand in both.

"You think you can take us all on?" he asks.

My fists twitch, an old habit that resurfaces the moment my old world catches up to me.

Break first. Ask questions later.

Then my thoughts turn to Esme.

I need to think of her. Everything I do from now will have a direct effect on her.

This is the first time in my life I've weighed my actions against future consequences.

"I don't want to," I reply, sidestepping his question. "I just want to be able to finish my hike, hunt some deer, and go home."

"Go home," the leader snarls. "You don't have a home here. This is our fucking territory."

"Then allow me to get off it," I say carefully. "And no one has to get hurt."

"The only one in danger of getting hurt right now is you."

"You willing to bet on it?" I ask.

Another flash of uncertainty flits across his eyes. It disappears almost instantly, but I've already caught it.

Do the smart thing, asshole. Walk away intact.

Then I see his jaw set in a determined square that I don't like one bit.

And I know he's chosen violence instead.

"I don't know who you are," the leader begins, taking me by surprise. I was sure he had cornered me here *because* he knew who I was. "But I have eyes in this town. And they whisper important bits of information to me about everything that happens here."

Why have I caught their attention?

"The word around town is there's a beautiful young woman with big hazel eyes," he says. "According to my sources, she looks a lot like Esme Moreno."

That makes my blood run cold.

Esme. They've caught her scent.

Fuck.

I have to play it cool. Esme's safety and my sanity depends on it.

For a moment, tangible fear grips my heart. I wonder if another group of men have been dispatched to the cabin.

If that's the case, I need to get to her as fast as possible.

But as desperate as I am to get to her, if I show my hand now, then I'll just be proving that they were right about who she is.

"Asma Mirena?" I ask, purposefully butchering her name. "Who the fuck is that?"

"You're telling me you don't know."

"I wouldn't be asking if I did," I growl with irritation. "Who is she? What's she have to do with me?"

The leader exchanges a glance with his men. "She's a bargaining chip," he replies. I almost lunge at him right then and there. "And a very important one at that."

"Is that right?" I say, trying to sound unconcerned. "Well, good luck finding her then."

"Her father was a notorious crime lord. Controlled quite a few cartels down this route," the leader continues. "Except that he was killed, along with his entire household. According to my sources, the only body not recovered from the massacre was Esme Moreno's."

Fuck, fuck, fuck.

It's becoming increasingly clear that my only way out of this is to kill them all. They know too much.

And the fact that Esme is on their radar at all does not sit well with me.

"And you think I know where this woman is?" I ask, playing my part up until it's clear I can't do that any longer.

My fingers twitch towards my rifle, preparing myself for the moment that is quickly approaching.

"Oh, I know you do," the leader snaps, clicking his tongue again. "Somehow you've managed to get your hands on her. Which means either she hired you to protect her, or you're the cabrón that took her in the first place."

I smile. "I'm not a fucking hired hand," I reply in a menacing voice that doesn't match my facial expression at all. My smile clearly makes him uncomfortable, because I see his eyes flash to his men. "You wanna know who I am?"

He says nothing.

"I'm Artem Kovalyov, don of the Kovalyov Bratva," I finish. My voice echoes from the mountains enclosing us. Harsh, unyielding.

The voice of a man capable of dealing out death to his enemies.

Silence follows my revelation, as I sense the stench of fear rise from all four men that surround me.

It's a more flattering reaction than I expected.

They know the name.

They know what it means.

"And the reason I don't mind sharing my identity with you," I say calmly, "is because I know none of you will tell a soul."

I allow three seconds of silence to let my words sink in.

And then I start to move.

66

ARTEM

I move fast and I move low, so that if someone fires, they'll hit the air above my head.

I slam my body into the leader first, hitting him hard around the stomach. We fall back into the dirt.

The moment he's on the ground, I somersault over him, grab his gun in the process, turn it on his men, and shoot twice.

One bullet hits Scarface in the arm. Blood spurts from a struck artery and he screams in agony as he collapses.

But the other bullet narrowly misses Blondie.

I duck behind one of the larger trees, pocket the leader's pistol, and pull my rifle out to play.

These fuckers may know my name, my legend, my reputation.

But I'm about to show them why it's all deserved.

I can hear them scrambling frantically from behind the tree, but I don't want to give them too long to re-group. So I jump out and sprint, still staying low. I fire as I move to the next cover.

One shot strikes Scarface again. He twitches and goes completely still.

The man with yellow teeth has his eyes on me. He shoots three times, but his bullets bury themselves in the trunk of the tree that's giving me cover.

I fire a few return shots blindly, but none of them find the target.

Growling, I creep backwards into the darkness of the clustered trees to reload.

"Pendejo!" the leader yells, as he finally manages to get to his feet. "Fucking Russian. Where'd he go?"

"We should have brought Antonio and Javiero," Yellow Teeth growls.

"And Guillermo," Blondie adds.

That comment sticks with me. If there are four here today, the other three they mentioned brings the total to seven who might know something about Esme and me.

Killing these bastards won't finish the job.

"You fuckers are the ones who told me that the four of us were more than enough," the leader hisses furiously.

"That was when we thought we were dealing with a fucking amateur!"

Taking advantage of their distraction, I dart out from behind the tree and fire again. This time, I'm aiming carefully.

My bullet hits the leader in the leg. He howls in pain, while his two stooges run for cover.

Scarface is still on the ground. He hasn't moved since he went down.

I move to another tree, careful to keep moving so that none of them have a straight shot to me. I need to preserve ammo if I can, seeing as how Guillermo probably won't sell me more bullets after I kill his friends.

That means I need to get closer.

I glance out from around the tree. The leader and Scarface are still on the ground, though the former is trying his best to get to his feet.

"You fuckers, come back!" he howls into the forest.

Come back? Goddammit.

If they ran, they'll alert someone. Higher-ups, maybe. And that just means more people will come looking for us.

I need to end this shit.

Now.

The leader isn't going anywhere anytime soon, judging by the waterfall of blood flowing down his leg. I'll come back for him. First, I have to stop the runners.

I take off after them. It takes me only a few short bounds to see them scampering down the mountain trail.

I drop to one knee, raise my gun, and take aim. They're moving fast, following the zig-zag of the trail. A few seconds more and they'll disappear around one of the huge boulders that dot the mountainside.

Steady...

There.

I pull the trigger. The gun recoils harshly into my shoulder.

And down the mountain, Blondie drops like a rock.

Yellow Teeth keeps moving. Doesn't even glance back. So much for being a good comrade.

I take a deep breath and fire again. This bullet narrowly misses him. Instead, a rock over his head explodes into fragments.

But it's so close that he assumes he's been hit. He loses his footing, trips to the ground, and his firearm tumbles through the air.

We both watch as it hits the ground once, twice—and then clatters over the edge of the ravine.

I keep my rifle on him as I advance down the trail. When I'm close enough, he raises his arms above his head in surrender.

I shake my head in disgust.

"That's not a gesture I recognize," I tell him as I point the gun at his head.

"Por favor," he begs. "Razor is the one who wanted to check you out."

"I don't care," I grit. "You messed with the wrong fucking Don."

Then I shoot him between the eyes.

One more left.

But just as I'm turning to head back and finish off the wounded leader, I see a large form lunge at me out of the corner of my eye.

It's Blondie.

The bullet I had fired earlier had only passed cleanly through his shoulder. He's bleeding profusely, but he still has full function of his other arm.

He manages to land a punch, but it's badly aimed and it only succeeds in pissing me off.

I avoid the next reckless punch by ducking down low. My fist darts out and hits him square in the stomach. He grunts and stumbles back, dazed.

I immediately go on the offensive. Seizing a rock in my grip, I take one step forward and smash it into his face.

Blondie's eyes roll back in his head.

Before he can recover, I cock back and bring the rock down again.

I hear the crunch of his nose breaking beneath the stone in my hand. His legs give way. He lands on his knees in front of me.

His eyes are cloudy with pain, but I can still see the fear there.

I grab his head. His muscles tense, but he's too hurt to do much more than scrabble at me uselessly with his remaining good hand.

He whispers, "Dios, no…"

"You picked the wrong man to mess with," I say.

Then I twist hard and hear the snap of his neck. He crumples to the dirt, lifeless.

I look between the two bodies at my feet.

I can't just leave them here.

But first, I have one more loose end to tie up.

So I pick up their guns and head back to the mountain edge that slopes into the ravine. When I return, Scarface is the only one left in the clearing. He's still breathing somehow, so I put a bullet in his skull.

Then I follow the trail of blood that the leader has left in his wake.

It takes me ten minutes to find him limping through the hilly forest in an attempt to escape me.

By this point, I'm really fucking irritated.

He doesn't see me until I fire a warning shot at the tree he's leaning against. At which point he jumps and then falls to the ground just like his sniveling, cowardly companions.

I walk over to him. He's trying to crawl away from me, one bloody, dirt-stained inch at a time.

"Please," he says. "Please…"

I shake my head at him. "This is the big leagues, my friend," I say harshly. "Did you really think you'd get to walk away from this with your life?"

"I… I didn't know who you were."

"Stupidity isn't an excuse."

"I have a family," he says.

I don't know if he's lying or not, but honestly, it doesn't matter either way. It won't change the outcome.

"I have a family, too," I nod, pointing the gun at his face. "This is for them."

I shoot once.

When the sound of the gunshot has faded away, I check his pulse to make sure he's dead.

Then I hoist him over my shoulder and walk back to the spot where Scarface's body is lying in the mud.

First, I heave the leader off my shoulder and into the ravine below. His body splashes into the ravine. The water swallows him whole.

I dispose of Scarface the same way, before I go back to where the remaining two bodies are lying. There's already a couple of carrion birds sniffing around, but they fly off the moment I appear.

I carry Blondie back to the ravine first and then I go back for Yellow Teeth.

Once all their bodies have been devoured by the river, I clean off their guns, retrieve my hunting rifle, and take a moment to look down at my clothes.

I'm covered in splatters of blood and there are several stains clinging to my t-shirt.

Feeling a murky sense of despair weigh down on my chest, I head back to the cabin. It takes me several more minutes before I realize why I'm feeling so strange.

The peace and serenity of our mountain hideaway has been shattered completely.

The violence of my world has reached me at last.

It forces me to confront the truth I've been avoiding since we've been up here:

There is no way to run from this.

67

ARTEM

When I finally get back to the cabin, the sun is going down. I see no signs that anyone has been sniffing around.

I head to the small shed around the back of the cabin and stash the extra guns out of sight before walking back around to the front.

As I pass by, I catch a glimpse of Esme through the side window. She's in the kitchen making dinner, and she's humming under her breath.

I can't see her bump, but I know by the slope of her arm that she's caressing it with her free hand.

Then she twirls away from the stove with the ladle in her hand, before raising it to her lips and using it as a microphone.

After the evening I've had, the sight of her puts a smile on my face. All I can do is stand and stare at her, relishing the feel of being close to her.

She will be shattered when she learns what has just happened.

And I know it's going to destroy her peace of mind.

I don't want her hurt. In any way.

I decide right then to lie.

As though she senses my presence, she looks up and catches sight of me outside the cabin. A huge smile spreads across her face, bathing her in brightness that only enhances her natural beauty.

And then her smile fades into a frown.

Her eyes squint at me as though she's trying to figure something out.

She darts away from the window and appears at the front door, before running down the stairs towards me. She stops short when she sees the state that I'm in and I see the devastation and panic in her eyes.

"Oh, my God," she breathes. "Oh, my God… Artem…"

"It's not what you think," I say hurriedly, before I can think things through.

She freezes. "What?"

I can't tell her the truth.

I can't bear to destroy the happiness that's radiated from her ever since we arrived in these mountains.

I say the first excuse that pops into my head. "It was a deer."

"A deer?" she repeats incredulously.

I nod and force a smile onto my face. "It's the craziest story, but… this is just deer blood," I say. "I'm fine."

She stares at me for a long moment.

For a second, I think she's going to call my bluff. Demand to know what really happened.

But then she smiles with relief and exhales sharply.

"Oh, my God," she says again. "For a second there, I thought... well, I thought we'd been found out."

I watch how her hands fall protectively over her stomach.

I reach for her, stopping just short of actually touching her.

"I should wash up first," I say, wiggling my bloodstained fingers.

She nods with raised eyebrows. "Oh definitely," she says. "We might even have to strip you naked to make sure we get you clean from head to toe."

And then she frowns, a little line forms on her forehead as she turns to me.

"Wait. Where's the deer?"

"What?"

"You said that you're covered in deer blood," Esme says. "Where's the deer?"

"Oh... He got away," I reply, making my tone as convincing as possible. "A stag, in fact. The big fucker was impossible. Got away from me three times before I finally managed to shoot him. Got *this* close to him too, but before I could finish the job, he bolted again and knocked me over in the process. Right here." I tap the bruise on my forehead where Blondie had clipped me.

"Really?" Esme says, looking dubious.

"I'll explain it better when I've cleaned up."

She smiles and nods. "My husband loses a fight to a deer. Can't wait to hear more of *that*."

Despite how filthy I am, she reaches up on her tiptoes and kisses the tip of my nose. Then she gives me a little wink and leads me into the house.

I follow her calmly, but my heart is hammering on the inside. Darkness settles over the mountains.

I've been playing a part the whole time we've been up here.

And now my time is up.

68

ESME

I wake up with Artem's arm thrown across my hip from behind, fingertips just grazing my swollen abdomen.

The length of him pressed up against my back, the warmth of his body cocooning me—it's the kind of security I had always wished for growing up.

Safe. Strong. Protective.

I turn slowly so that I don't disturb him and place my face right next to his. He's still in the throes of sleep and he looks so damn peaceful that I can't help but stare at him.

It's rare to see him look this way. I'm usually the one sleeping long after Artem has risen.

But on the rare occasion when I wake up to find him still sleeping, I love looking at his face, at the beautiful sharp angles and the lack of conscious intensity that makes him look so much younger. So much calmer.

Almost... at peace.

I remove his hand from around me as gently as I can and slink down along the bed, pushing the sheets away a little.

I finally convinced Artem to start sleeping naked, much to my delight. So it's easy to see that Artem's cock is at half-mast. I know it'll take only the slightest touch from me to get it standing at full attention.

He almost always wakes up with morning wood. I never hesitate to take full advantage.

Today is no exception.

I wrap my hand around the base of his shaft and rub gently until his cock hardens instantly in my grip. He stirs, but before he can open his eyes, I slip his cock into my mouth and start sucking devotedly.

He growls with pleasure and turns over a little, taking me with him. I grip his cock a little harder as I take him in a little deeper down my throat.

"Fuck," he mutters.

I want to see his eyes go wild, his jaw go slack. But I'm too turned on and too invested to stop what I'm doing to look at him.

It's a miracle that that's the case. I've only ever been with two other men in my life. Oral sex wasn't exactly fun and games. More of a chore than pleasure.

But with Artem, it's something different entirely.

Not only do I love when he eats me out, his tongue laving through my folds until I'm quivering with pleasure, but I *love* sucking him off. I love what my tongue around his cock does to him.

Once he's hard and dripping, I release his dick and wipe my mouth as I meet his gaze for the first time this morning. He looks at me with lust-glazed eyes and reaches down to pull me towards him.

I slide up and straddle his hips so that his cock stands between my thighs, nudging against my pussy. I move slowly, rubbing my wetness against his moist cock.

"You fucking tease," he accuses with a harsh laugh.

I grin and bite my lip. "Who, me?" I'm so turned on right now that I'm actually surprised by how calm I can act.

But I know I won't last another minute without feeling him inside me. Staying this close but no closer is the purest form of torture I know.

So I hold his cock in place and slowly settle down, one beautiful, agonizing inch at a time.

When I finally run out of cock and our hips are flush together, I let out a cry that reverberates around the room.

"Oh, fuck," I gasp, feeling him so deep inside me that it already feels like I'm moments away from orgasm.

I don't move at all for a few seconds. I just sit there on him, his cock buried inside me, and I wait for my pussy walls to stop clenching so hard around him.

When I can finally catch my breath again, I place my hands on his hard chest and bend down a little so that I can press my face in his neck. I breathe his musk in like a drug.

Then I start moving slowly, taking my time, riding him gently and building momentum as we go.

He lies back and lets me, watches me.

It took a long time for him to relinquish control. To let me do this—control the movement, the pace, the rhythm.

I'll always love giving all that up to him. Letting him own me completely—mind, body, and soul.

But this is good, too, when the time is right.

And right now, the time is *so* fucking right.

I know he feels the same. Artem's expression thick with lust.

But there's also another emotion there. One that I can't quite put my finger on.

I'm too fucking distracted to worry about what else on his mind, though, so I just keep riding him until my legs burn with fatigue.

When my movements start to slow, he pushes himself up into a sitting position and sucks one of my nipples into his mouth. They're so sensitive now that the feel of Artem's tongue engulfing them makes me moan and shudder with a little more urgency.

Then he holds my hips in place and starts ramming into me hard from below. I choke back a cry, my eyes going wide with shock at the strange and deliberate urgency with which he fucks me.

His eyes are intense as he rams into me from below, forcing me to bounce on his cock. I grab ahold of his shoulders and cling on tight as he stabs through me, sending what feels like electric shocks straight to my heart.

His jaw clench fiercely—almost angrily—and his hands grow tighter around my hips.

I know he's seconds away from coming.

The sight of him coming undone pushes me off the edge first. The orgasm gushes through me with violent force. It's as angry and fierce as he is.

Sure enough, he comes right after me. I stay on top of him as he rides out his own shockwaves.

When he stills, I swing one leg off him and fall to his side, nestling myself in the crook of his arm so that my head rests comfortably against his shoulder.

Artem's eyes fix on the ceiling above.

This has been happening for a few days now, I realize suddenly—as if I'm just now connecting the dots.

He falls into deep silences that make me feel like I'm alone in the cabin.

His smiles come a little less easily. And when they do come, there's a sad tilt to the set of his mouth, a muted tone to the glint in his eye.

I've been trying hard to place why this sudden change has come over him, but I've only managed to come to one conclusion: this peaceful life in the mountains is starting to wear on him.

Especially knowing that he has responsibilities elsewhere.

I know he's here for me, to protect me.

But I'm not naïve enough to believe that that's enough for him in the long run. He's not the type of man to run from his duties, and the Bratva has been his entire life.

I turn to my side and caress the side of his face, forcing him to meet my gaze.

"Hey."

He smiles. Again, I see it, the sad tilt to his lips, the worried ebb and flow of his eyes.

"What's on your mind?" I ask.

"Nothing."

He says it gently, like he has the last few days every time I've asked what he's thinking about.

But this time, I'm not willing to let it go.

"Artem," I insist, "I may not have known you for very long, but I am still your wife. I want you to be able to tell me if there's something getting you down."

He looks at me for a long moment, his eyes intentionally expressionless.

"You were thinking about the Bratva." I fill in, taking an educated guess.

He sighs. The etch of worry still clings to his features stubbornly. "Yes, I suppose I was."

I push myself up on one elbow so that I'm looking down at him. "Can I ask you a question?"

His eyes go careful instantly.

I hate that. I don't like feeling like he's keeping things from me.

He nods, but I'm not convinced.

"And you'll promise to answer me honestly?"

He nods slowly, but his eyes are still careful. Still guarded.

I decide to press on anyway. "Do you miss it?"

"Miss... it?"

"The life," I say simply, before I elaborate. "Being in the thick of it, going on missions, commanding men... Being the don."

He considers my question for a long time. "I still don't really feel like Don," he replies. "I was don for a split-second before my uncle staged his coup."

"But the rest of it?" I press.

He lets loose a long exhale. "It's all I know," he answers eventually. "I don't know any other life than the one I was born to."

I nod. I can understand that. I've even prepared myself for the answer.

But it still makes me quiver a little.

It still makes my heart sink with disappointment just a bit.

Then I feel his eyes on me, boring down. I don't meet his gaze. If I do, he'll see the disappointment. The hurt.

Maybe he'll see it either way.

"That makes you sad?" he surmises correctly. I hate that he can read me so well, on top of everything else. He's a total enigma, a black box, whereas I'm an open book, heart on my sleeve at all times.

I take a deep breath and start to stammer through what I really want to say.

"I... I just... do you think you can be happy... if you were to leave the Bratva behind?"

I know I'm showing my hand, but I can't help myself. My emotions are running high, the baby inside me is growing, and with each passing day I keep thinking about the life I want to give this child.

"I don't know, Esme," Artem says. "I never thought I'd ever want to give it up. I never thought I'd have to."

"So you don't want to give it up?" My voice quivers no matter how hard I try to contain it.

"I didn't..." he says. "...Until I met you."

I freeze for a moment, studying his face for signs that he might just be saying what he thinks I want to hear.

"Really?" I dare to ask.

"The last couple of weeks up here," he says, "they've been better than I could ever have imagined. I never thought I'd enjoy peace and quiet so much."

I smile, feeling hope rekindle in my chest.

"Artem," I say, throwing caution to the wind. "Why don't we just stay? Stay up here and leave it all behind."

He raises his eyebrows. "You mean give up my claim as Don?"

"Yes!" I exclaim. "Why fight for something that's just going to bring down a war on our heads? If you leave the Bratva behind, we can disappear. Yes, your uncle might continue to search for us, but after a few years, he'll forget. And you and me… we can be happy. Our baby can be happy."

I'm searching his eyes as I talk, looking for that fire, that spark that I know can lead us into the future I'm desperate for.

I keep telling myself that it's coming. Any second, I'll see it.

Agreement. Acceptance. Hope.

Something.

"I want our baby to be safe, Artem," I tell him, my hand falling over his chest. "I want our baby to grow up happy and secure. I want him or her to have a normal life. I don't want this child to suffer like I did, or to live up to some kind of expectation of what he should be like you did. Like Cesar did."

He breathes, slowly and evenly. Doesn't look away from me. But says nothing.

"My brother changed everything about who he was to fit into the role my father pushed him into. And it broke him. He wore his pain well, but I could see past the veneer. Past the mask."

Artem watches me silently. I can't tell what he's thinking. I wait patiently, but then I start to get nervous. He's driving me insane.

Say something, I beg silently. *Say anything.*

"Artem?"

He closes his eyes for a moment, but even when he opens them again, I can't read what's behind them.

"I'm not saying that I haven't thought about it," he admits.

"Yeah?"

Against my better instinct, hope blossoms in my chest.

He nods. "Esme... it's a beautiful idea, but reality is oftentimes extremely different."

"I know it's not going to be easy, Artem," I agree quickly. "It's probably going to take years of adjustment. But I think we can do it. We'll be together. That's the whole point—it's gonna be you and me. And our baby. We can do it *together*."

"What would I even do, Esme?" he asks. "I'm not cut out for a quiet life. I was trained to fight, to kill, to strategize and plan. I was trained to lead."

"And you'll continue to lead," I tell him, even though I have no idea what that will look like in the normal world. "It'll just be in a different way. You'll lead our family."

The doubt in his face is obvious. I'm running through images in my head.

Artem as a teacher.

As a doctor.

As a construction worker.

Each one is as laughable as the next.

That blossom of hope in my chest starts to wilt. The honest truth is that I can't see him in any of those roles.

I can't picture him doing anything other than leading the Bratva.

But I refuse to let that completely derail the future I've envisioned for our family.

"It's hard now, I know," I tell him. I'm trying so hard to keep the edge of desperation out of my voice. "But that's just because we've never entertained the possibility of a normal life before now. You yourself said that you didn't think you'd enjoy the peace and quiet of the mountains as much as you have. Right?"

"Right." I nod. "But that's also because I know this stint up here is temporary."

"Artem," I say, putting my hand against his cheek, "I don't want to have to worry about my child every second of every day. I want more for this baby than my childhood. More than yours."

"I have responsibilities, Esme," he says. "I can't just disappear. I have men that follow me. Cillian has given up everything for me. I can't abandon all of them."

"I'm not asking you to," I say quickly. "But give them new marching orders. Tell them to… to…"

"To what, Esme?" he asks. "They're not exactly the kind of men who can find a job in construction and be happy with that."

I feel tears prick at the corners of my eyes, but I push them back and sit up, pulling the sheets around my chest.

"Esme," Artem murmurs, his hand on my back.

"I'm fine," I say, but I can't stop my voice from shaking just a little.

I get out of bed as fast as I can and head to the bathroom where I attempt to pull myself together.

It was foolish of me to think that Artem would be as happy as I am to give up the old life, but the disappointment still chokes me with tears.

I cry silently in the bathroom for a few minutes. For a future that slipped through my fingers before I ever had a chance to seize it.

Then I splash cold water on my face and get dressed.

When I come back outside, Artem is waiting for me in the kitchen.

I give him a small smile and move to the cabinets. "What would you like for breakfast?" I ask, trying to gloss over our earlier conversation.

He comes up from behind me and wraps his arms around my waist. I feel his lips against the back of my head and I sigh and lean back into him.

"I'm sorry," he says quietly.

"Don't be," I say, shaking my head. "It was probably naïve of me to think that—"

"It's possible, Esme," he says, cutting me off.

"What?" I ask, going still.

"I can't make any promises," he says softly, in my ear. "And if we do it, it might take some time…"

I turn in his arms so I can see his face. "I know."

"But it's a possibility that I'm willing to think about," he finishes.

I can't stop the joy from showing on my face.

I see the smile in his eyes as he looks down at me. "Just you and me, right?" he asks.

"Just you and me," I agree. "And our baby. Our little family." I pull his hands from around my waist and place them on my belly. "This is what we'd be doing it for."

I see the conflict rage in his eyes for a moment, but it settles when he looks down at my stomach.

"Our baby," he echoes softly. He's talking to himself more than me.

Eventually, he sighs, kisses me on the head, and turns away to make coffee.

"Are you coming into town with me today?" he asks.

I had wanted to, but I can sense that he needs some alone time to process everything we've just discussed. I realize I need the same, so I shake my head.

"I think I'll just stay home and read today," I say.

He doesn't argue. Instead, he nods and kisses my forehead distractedly before moving towards the door.

When he's gone, I try to read, but I can't focus enough to get through a single page. I need something to clear my head.

Nature would be good. Wind on my cheek, mountains on the horizon—that kind of thing.

I shrug into my coat and head down the slope towards the narrower mountain trails that Artem frequently uses when he's out hunting deer.

It's a beautiful day. I spot a bald eagle circling high overhead. I end up following his flight path for several minutes, but I make sure to stick to the trail so that I'll be able to find my way back home when I want to.

Once the trail tapers off and slopes downwards towards the ravine, I stop walking and find a smooth boulder to rest on for a little while.

I pull out the bottle of water I've brought with me and take a long swig.

This place is truly beautiful. The kind of paradise I always dreamed of but never thought I'd find.

"Isn't that right?" I whisper to my belly.

I started doing this about two nights ago when I first felt a fluttering at the corner of my swollen stomach.

It was so slight that at first, I thought I was imagining things. But when it happened the second time, I knew for sure it was him. My child, moving around inside me, reminding me that in a few months we'd be meeting face to face for the first time.

Above me, I catch sight of the eagle again. He's circling around and it seems like he's only inches below the clouds.

"Maybe after you're born, I'll bring you right here and we can watch the eagles together," I say, rubbing my hands back and forth along my stomach. "And when you're older, I'll explain how your father and I planned our future together. How this was the place where we realized that our love for you, for each other, trumped everything else."

I felt another flutter, stronger this time. Tears spring to my eyes.

It's almost like he's answering back.

More flutters continue, like morse code coming from the inside of my belly.

I press my palm down against the rippling. "I'm here, little bird," I murmur automatically.

The fluttering eases and disappears.

"Little bird," I say again, testing the words out loud. I look out into the oncoming wind. "Cesar used to call me that."

It's been weeks now since I learned the truth about Cesar and his connection to Artem.

And it's been almost as long since I've thought about him in any real sense.

In all honesty, I've pushed him to the furthest recesses of my mind until I feel strong enough to process his part in Artem's tragedy.

I hate knowing what Cesar did.

I hate that he'd even been capable of doing something so horrific to an innocent woman.

It burns like hellfire to realize how much he kept from me.

He didn't want his sins to taint you, whispers some unseen voice in my heart. *He didn't want you to think less of him.*

I sigh deeply. There was so much I didn't understand back then.

Things are clearer now, and yet I'm still confused. Maybe more confused than ever.

The eagle lets out a high piping sound that catches my attention. He swoops lower. When he does, I notice that there are a few more birds flying in the huge expanse before me, squawking obnoxiously.

Ugly birds. Buzzards, I think.

It's not exactly the peace and quiet I'm looking for, so I get up and start the walk back to the cabin.

As I follow the trail back home, I notice the screeches get louder and more exuberant. The birds are flying low down the ravine, their wings leaving small ripples in the river.

Is something going on down there?

Gripping one of the trees close to the edge of the trail, I inch closer until I can look right down to the bottom.

On top of a pile of boulders, I see motion.

At first, all I make out is a mess of wings and snapping beaks.

Then I see a carcass amongst streaks of blood, and it makes sense. Some poor animal has died down there.

The birds are just fighting over lunch.

Could it possibly be Artem's stag, the one that got away?

I grip the tree a little tighter and lean in a little further so I can get a better look. I want to be able to tell Artem that I saw his stag.

But then something on the carcass gets caught on the breeze and wafted up past me.

It's a piece of a torn t-shirt.

Something thuds uncomfortably in my chest.

Stags don't wear clothes.

The ridiculous thought slips into my consciousness. I freeze, as a painful streak of realization hits me full in the face.

That's not a stag the birds are feasting on.

It's a human being.

I force myself to glance down one more time.

This time, I see the rotting flesh of what is unmistakably a human arm.

My stomach twists with nausea. I swallow back the bile as my mind races, trying to remember if I'd heard any gossip of a hiker or hikers who'd gone missing on this side of the mountains.

No, I'm pretty sure there haven't been any incidents since Artem and I moved up into the cabin.

And then I feel another painful pinch in my heart as a memory from three nights ago resurfaces.

"Tell me again how this stag managed to get away from you." I laugh. "Little deer outwits a big bad Bratva boss?"

Artem groans. "It's honestly not worth telling," he demurs. "It's actually a really embarrassing story. One I don't mind forgetting."

"I just don't understand how he got his blood all over you."

"Stranger things have happened."

I stumble back from the mountain edge as my eyes dart around, searching for the security that I felt only moments ago.

His story had been strange from the get-go. It hadn't really made sense to me, so why had I believed him so easily?

Because you love him.

Because you wanted to cling to an idealistic dream rather than face harsh realities.

"Oh, God," I breathe.

But my words are drowned out by the birds' shrieks. I don't even hear myself.

I force myself to breathe through the pain in my chest. I need to get my head back together before I return to the cabin.

I try to think through things logically. It is definitely possible that Artem had nothing to do with the dead body down the ravine. That's probably likely, as a matter of fact.

But in the same moment I consider that possibility, I dismiss it.

There are just too many clues.

Too many coincidences.

And now that the blindfold has been stripped from my eyes, I can't go back to denial.

Who was that man?

Why had Artem killed him?

Were there others?

And if there were, had Artem killed them all?

I take deep, gulping breaths until I stop feeling so off balance. But the squawk of the birds now feel like someone is trying to drill holes through my brain.

I need to get away from the sound, so I keep walking, trying to put as much distance between myself and the dead man as I possibly can.

When the sound of bird cries has faded with distance, I allow myself to slump to a seat on a mossy rock. I support my head with my hands and try once more to calm myself.

We've been found. That's the only explanation for what I just saw down the ravine.

We've been found and Artem did what he had to do. Defended himself. Protected us.

The fact that he had murdered someone isn't what's upsetting me.

The fact that he lied to me about it—that's what's breaking my heart.

When I look back up, I feel tears drying on my cheeks. I didn't even realize I was crying.

I look across to the mountains in the distance, but nothing feels the same. The serenity that accompanied me on my walk through the trail has now abandoned me completely.

That's why he didn't tell you.

He was just trying to protect you.

He didn't want the stress to hurt you or the baby.

The explanation makes sense to me. It *feels* true. Or at least, like it could be true.

But I can't help second guessing myself.

Is this just more denial dressed up a different way?

Am I making excuses for a man I don't really know at all?

Yes, I love him.

But I've learned the hard way: love and trust are two very different things.

69

ARTEM

I get home late that night. I waited until sundown to even go into town. Sitting in the car on the outskirts, watching farmers drive their wares in and out of the little village.

Once dark fell, I ventured in, did what I needed to do with my hood up and my head down, and got out.

After the confrontation with the cartel men, I've been on high alert. The fewer people who see me, the better.

Driving home after dark means I have to take the road back up the mountain slowly, too. I kill the headlights and drive carefully, flicking them on to get my bearings before extinguishing them again.

Just in case anyone is watching. Looking for signs of life, a trail that leads them right to our doorstep.

I park the car in front of the lodge and kill the engine. Mountain silence takes over, cold and austere.

I've grown used to the silence since we get here. It helps me think.

There's a lot to fucking think about.

I set the groceries down on the kitchen table and creep into the back bedroom. All the lights are out. I listen at the doorway until I'm sure that I can make out Esme's soft, even breathing.

She's asleep. Odd—she always waits up until I'm home.

But something shifted since I killed the men and threw them in the ravine. Something subtle, but I notice it and she does, too.

We're both pretending that the future we want is possible.

I don't know.

I don't fucking know anything anymore.

Because if I'm not a don, what am I?

A husband. A father. A friend.

I wonder if that's enough.

I hate myself for even asking the question.

"Artem?" comes her meek voice. "Is that you?"

I sigh and slip inside the bedroom. I undress in the dark and crawl into bed with her. Her cold hand finds mine, squeezes.

"I'm here," I tell her.

She whimpers, still half-asleep, and nods.

I lay there propped up on my elbow to stare at her. My eyes adjust to the darkness. I can make out the soft slope of her cheeks, the curve of her lips.

"You're beautiful," I whisper. I didn't realize I said it out loud until I heard my own voice.

"I bet you say that to all the girls," she murmurs back.

I know she's teasing, so I don't know why I sense a hint of disappointment in her tone.

You're reading too much into things.

Those fuckers burst the protective bubble you've created here.

You're just feeling a little off-kilter.

"There's only you," I tell her honestly.

I can sense her smile even though I can't see much of her face. Her hands fall to her stomach and she sighs deeply. My heart throbs with emotion.

Had it ever been like this with Marisha?

I honestly don't remember.

Out of nowhere, my stomach rumbles. Loud enough for Esme to crack an eye open warily.

"Sorry," I chuckle.

"Hungry?" she asks. "You missed dinner."

"A little," I agree. "Hungry for you."

I grab her and roll her on her back to look up at me. She giggles sleepily. The smile breaks through the sad lines of her forehead.

"Sorry," she says. "I'm not on the menu tonight."

"Don't care," I retort. "I'm not accustomed to following rules anyway. I take what I want."

Her brow furrows just a little bit, but her expression recovers almost immediately. "Artem…"

"You talking to me?"

My hands slide down between her bare thighs, while my eyes dip down to the tops of her breasts. It feels like they've gotten bigger in the last two days alone.

She opens her mouth as if to say something and then snaps it shut again.

"What?"

"Nothing," she replies. "It's not important."

"What you want *is* important," I tell her.

"Yeah?"

"Definitely," I nod. "I just want you to be happy, Esme."

I like this. Can't see much in the darkness. Can only hear, and touch, and whisper. It feels like we can be more honest now than we can when the sun is illuminating things.

She traces her fingers over the underside of my wrist where it's trapped between her legs.

"Even if it's directly opposed to what you want?" she asks, as though she's embarrassed to be asking the question at all.

"Esme, I know you never wanted this," I say. "I forced this on you. This life. This marriage. I—"

She grabs my hands and pulls them to her chest, cutting off the rest of my sentence.

"It was the best thing I was forced into, though," she says, taking me by surprise. "I know I'm probably setting feminism back a few decades by admitting that, but it's my truth."

I smile. This kind of intimacy isn't second nature to me.

I pull her back to me. "I want you to know that I have been thinking a lot about our plan," I tell her. "I know what you want. I'm trying to see if that's possible."

"Have you spoken to Cillian about it?" she asks.

"No, I haven't," I admit. "It's something I need to discuss face to face."

I had called him yesterday and we'd had another chat. I'd tried several times to bring up the fact that I was thinking of abandoning my claim to the Bratva and just handing it over to Budimir.

But I just couldn't bring myself to say the words out loud.

Every time I tried, my throat constricted in protest.

I want to make this decision for myself and no one else. But still, that toxic thought at the back of my head keeps ticking incessantly.

Stanislav will be rolling in his grave knowing what you're thinking..

My father is dead, I tell myself a dozen times over.

But it doesn't matter. The shame of relinquishing my right to the Bratva settles over me like a weight I can't shake.

So why am I giving Esme hope?

Because you want to believe in it as much as she does.

Sometimes I forget what sweet nectar denial is.

"Are you hungry?" Esme asks, cutting through my thoughts.

Grateful for the distraction, I focus my attention on her. Even after all this time, her hazel eyes are still arresting as ever. They draw me in every single fucking time.

"I thought we already established that I'm fucking starving," I say, grabbing her ass and squeezing hard.

She laughs and tries to get away from me, but I pin her down between my arms as I roll on top of her.

"Artem!" she screams.

I ignore her and nuzzle my way down her neck, between her bare breasts, to where her hips dip low.

"What do you think you're doing, mister?" she demands, breathless with laughter.

"Taking what I want."

It takes me only one quick pull to get her panties off. She sleeps in just that these days.

By then, I can see the lust igniting in her face. Her legs part willingly for me and I settle between them, running my tongue around her pussy lips first.

At first touch, she gasps and shudders before settling into the bed pillows with a sigh.

I tease her walls before plunging my tongue between them. Her hands find my hair and cling on her for dear life.

My cock strains in my boxers, but I ignore it for now and find her clit with my tongue. I lap at it and almost instantly, her juices flow.

Then I hoist myself up and settle over her without putting any weight on her belly. I slip two fingers inside her and explore her depths as her eyes close and she arches her neck backwards.

I finger-fuck her to a quick orgasm that explodes through her body, leaving a constellation of goosebumps in its wake.

I smile with satisfaction as I see her facial muscles relax with satisfaction while it ebbs down. She reaches for me, pulling my face down to hers so she can kiss me.

But just before our lips touch, she gasps. Her eyes widen suddenly.

"What's wrong?" I say, getting off her immediately, ready to panic.

She shakes her head. To my surprise, a slow smile spreads across her face.

"Nothing," she murmurs. "Absolutely nothing."

"I don't understand. What just happened?"

"I'll show you," she says. She reaches for my hand.

Then she takes it and presses my palm to the right side of her belly. I'm so concerned that for a moment I don't even register the tiny fluttering kick that pushes against my hand through Esme's stomach.

When it happens again, I freeze.

"Wait," I say, my eyes going wide. "Was that...?"

"A kick," Esme finishes. "Did you feel it?"

I lean in a little closer and press my palm down gently, waiting and hoping to feel another one.

And just then, I do.

It's a more pronounced kick than the last one. Almost like the little creature in there wants to say hello.

"Fuck," I breathe.

Esme staring at me with unshed tears in her eyes. She looks more fucking beautiful than I've ever seen her.

"Holy fuck," I say again.

She laughs. "It's amazing, isn't it?" she asks.

I can only nod, speechless.

Esme smiles wider and places her hand over mine.

"That's our baby in there," she says softly.

I just look at her, feeling another little kick under my palm.

It makes me feel... small and infinite in the same moment. For a second, all my worries and concerns fade and my life is put in perspective.

Nothing else matters except Esme.

Nothing else matters but the child she's carrying.

Maybe my purpose in life is the two of them.

For the first time since the Bratva takeover, I see myself walking away from it all.

I see myself relinquishing control over to Budimir, whether he deserves it or not.

I see myself living somewhere quiet and peaceful, where our children can grow up safe and normal, untouched by the violence and loss that has plagued both of us our entire lives.

I lean into the image, truly tasting it for the first time and not turning away in shame.

"Esme," I whisper, just because I want to.

She smiles. "He's saying hi to his papa."

Papa.

"It feels impossible," I say. "I know there's a baby inside of you, but it just became real."

Esme laughs, obviously amused by how amazed I am. "You've never felt a baby kick before?" she asks.

The moment the words are out of her mouth, the smile slides off her face.

"Oh, Artem, I'm sorry," she says quickly.

I grab her hand and pull her to me.

"Don't be sorry," I console, settling her into the crook of my arm so that I can keep my hand on her belly and still see her face. "It's okay."

"I didn't think. It was so stupid. I shouldn't have—"

"I think I can talk about it now," I reply. "I haven't been able to say that before."

She nods, waiting patiently for me to say whatever it is I want to.

"I never felt the baby kick with Marisha," I tell her. "I suppose it was too early. Or else, she just didn't tell me. Now that I think about it, maybe she didn't tell me."

Esme frowns. "Why wouldn't she tell you?"

I sigh, remembering the days leading up to her death. We hadn't exactly been the happiest couple, but I'd been trying.

At least, as much as I was capable of trying at that point.

"She was upset with me," I answer slowly. "She was…"

I trail off. Old fights resurface and plunge me into a past that doesn't feel like it belongs to me anymore.

"She was worried about the Bratva life for her baby?" Esme offers.

I shift uncomfortably, my hand stilling over her stomach.

Of course Esme would assume that was why Marisha had been upset with me. She was assuming that Marisha had felt the same way she did right now.

"No," I say. "Marisha knew who I was. She accepted that the Bratva was my life."

Esme's eyes dim a little with that. A flicker of hurt passes across her face.

I hadn't meant it to sound like an accusation, but I realize now that that's exactly how it sounded.

I squeeze her hand hard in mine.

"She was a different woman, Esme," I say.

"She was braver than I am, then."

I shake my head. "No," I say firmly. "She was strong. But her strength was different than yours."

Esme smiles slightly, but it doesn't quite reach her eyes. I squeeze her hand once more, reminding her to stay with me.

"She was upset about the hours I worked, the pace I was going at. She wanted me to make her a priority."

"Oh," Esme breathes. "And you weren't?"

"I was young," I admit. "I was consumed with proving myself. I wanted to be…"

"You wanted to be the next don," Esme finishes for me.

I nod slowly. "Yes, that's exactly what I wanted to be."

Her expression falls slack for a moment, as though she's weighing everything I've just said against her hopes.

"Esme," I say, pulling her face towards mine. "I never imagined I would walk away from the Bratva… until just now."

Her eyes spark a little. She wants to believe me so badly. But she's scared to hope.

I can understand that.

"Don't say that unless you mean it," she whispers.

"I do mean it. I mean it with every fiber of my being."

She leans in and kisses me hard, her lips pushing against mine with a force that parts them. I run my tongue down her bottom lip.

She trembles, her hands scratching at my shoulders desperately, hungrily.

I want to give myself to her.

I want to take everything she's giving to me.

I want Esme Moreno to know that I love her. That I am here for her. That she and our baby are the only things left in this world that matter to me.

And then I hear something outside.

A sharp sound that sounds like a boot on gravel.

I pull back at once, my mind alert and my body instantly tense.

"What's wrong?" Esme asks in alarm. She must not've heard the noise.

"Someone's here," I whisper as I rise from the sofa and glance out the open window of the cabin.

I can see the silhouette of our car, but nothing else.

"Artem…?"

"Wait here," I say, as I hurry to the table in one corner of the room and grab the stolen pistol from the inside drawer. "Don't move. Lock the door until I'm back."

Esme's eyes go wide as she watches me walk towards the door.

"Artem!" she begs, her voice barely above a whisper. "Please be careful."

I nod and slip outside.

I see now what I couldn't see before: a car parked right next to mine, blocking us in.

I creep over to the rear passenger's side, trying to peer in without being noticed. The windows are tinted dark. I can't tell if it's occupied.

I keep the gun raised, unwilling to take a chance just in case whoever has decided to pay us a visit is hostile.

More noise. Heavy footsteps on the other side of the car.

I duck low and race around the back on bare, silent feet. Someone is getting out of the driver's seat.

I creep up. Press a gun to the back of the bastard's head. It's too dark to make out much in the way of identifying features.

"Don't move, motherfucker," I snarl.

Then the clouds overhead part and the moon lights everything up with a soft white glow.

I see blond hair.

And when the man pivots slowly in place, hands raised in surrender, I see familiar blue eyes. A familiar cocky smile.

"Really?" the man says. "I come all the way up here and this is the welcome I get?"

"Cillian?" I say, in shock.

His smile widens. "Forgotten what I look like already?"

"Fuck," I breathe. I'm more thrilled than I can say. "Fuck!"

70

ESME

My heart thunders in my chest as I wait in the empty bedroom.

My immediate instinct is to run after Artem. To grab him, pull him to me, and away from danger.

I don't know what to do. His rifle is propped up at the door. Artem had explained how it worked, but I didn't want to practice. Not if I didn't have to.

I hear motion outside. And then men's voices.

"Fuck!" Artem's voice carries through the night towards me.

I gasp.

Before I know what I'm doing, I run out the door and onto the porch steps. I'm ready for the worst. Ready for anything.

Except, apparently, what's actually waiting for me.

Artem has his arms around a man who's almost as tall as he is. For one crazy second, I think they're wrestling.

Then they release one another, and I see the smiles on both their faces.

The blonde man turns and I realize who it is.

"Cillian!" I exclaim.

"Hello, Esme," he says, raising his hand and giving me a wave. "I didn't want to tell you I was coming in case my phone was being tapped. I didn't want any of Budimir's stooges on my tail. Sorry to crash your mountain hideaway. Cool spot, though."

I laugh out loud in pure joy. Artem looks like he feels the same way I do. He's beaming from ear to ear.

"Come on in! Are you hungry?"

"I could eat a literal cow."

Laughing again, I hurry inside to pull out some cold cuts and bread. It's late, but suddenly I'm just as hungry as the two men are.

They follow me into the cabin. I can hear them catch up as I get out plates and set the table for our midnight dinner.

I'm distracted, so I keep making stupid mistakes and spilling things and making messes that I then have to clean up, but neither Artem nor Cillian seems to notice.

I try and catch snippets of their conversation, but their voices are low. I'm not sure if that's intentional or not.

"... how bad is it..."

"...trafficking women and young girls... across the borders... spies everywhere..."

"... yes, they have... a couple of million... dead..."

Whatever I hear doesn't make me feel any better. I tune them out.

Once the table is ready, I move forward and sit beside Artem on the couch. The conversation tapers off instantly.

But Cillian covers it well as he turns to me with a friendly smile that instantly puts me at ease.

"Esme, you're absolutely glowing," he says, before his smile turns mischievous. "Of course, that could just be the afterglow of sex."

I smack him on the shoulder, but when I reach up and touch my face, I realize my lips are swollen from Artem's kisses.

"Excuse me for a moment," I say, then I stand and retreat to the bedroom to change into something better than one of Artem's ragged t-shirts and splash some cold water on my face.

I come back out a few minutes later feeling more composed. But I stop at the edge of the hallway and listen when I hear Cillian saying my name.

"… you look so fucking happy. I don't think I've ever seen you like this. Am I right in guessing this has everything to do with Esme?"

I hold my breath for Artem's answer.

"I feel like I'm under her fucking spell, Cillian," Artem replies. "This girl… It was meant to be a political marriage, but it's turned into a real one."

"Yeah, I can see that," Cillian agrees. "The two of you look like a fucking picture-perfect couple."

"There's no such thing," Artem says carefully. My heart quivers nervously at that.

Unwilling to eavesdrop any longer—especially after what happened last time I did that—I step out towards them.

"How about dinner, boys?" I ask, trying to sound as casual as possible.

They nod and join me at the table.

I really do like Cillian. This is the first time I've spent any real time with him and I find him to be light-hearted, funny and sincere. I can see why Artem and he are so close.

He also loves making fun of his best friend, which gets a laugh out of me every time.

But I also pick up on other things. Things they are not discussing in front of me.

In fact, there's a lot they leave unsaid. A history that doesn't include me. Cillian was a part of his life when Marisha was.

It's not quite jealousy that I feel, but it's something close.

Still, it's easy to ignore all that as we eat and laugh. The dinner conversation is light, and Cillian tells me a few stories about Artem over the years.

He's careful to stay away from anything directly connected to the Bratva, but I can feel the history of their lives in the cartel on the fringes of every story he tells.

Once we've finished eating, Artem stands. "I'm going to go check my perimeter again, make sure it's secure."

"Paranoid much?" Cillian teases.

"Can never be too careful," Artem shoots back. "Are you coming with me?"

I expect Cillian to tag along, but he doesn't. "Actually, I've had a long journey. I'll leave the grunt work to you."

Artem smiles and nods before grabbing his rifle and heading out. "I won't be more than an hour or so," he says. "You two play nice."

Once he's gone, I turn to Cillian, who's watching me unabashedly. I shift in my seat self-consciously, but he doesn't lower his gaze.

"How are you?" he asks.

It's a more intimate question that I'd been expecting. The way he holds my gaze just makes it more so.

"I'm good," I reply immediately, without giving my answer any real thought.

"You wanna try that again?" he asks with a roguish grin.

I sigh. "It's been bliss up here," I admit. "We've been living in a little bubble and... and..."

"I just broke your bubble," he guesses.

"No," I say, shaking my head. "The bubble broke before you got here."

He cocks his head to the side curiously.

I instantly regret letting that slip. I realize that that's Cillian's superpower. He makes you feel comfortable, he makes you feel like you're friends—and then you find yourself opening up about things that you really should be keeping to yourself.

"How so?"

I shake my head. "No, I... that's not what I mean... I..."

"Esme," Cillian says gently.

I stop my awkward stammering.

I avoid his eyes and play with the hem of my dress. "It's nothing," I try again.

"Is that why you won't look me in the eye?"

I raise my gaze to his and stare directly at him in defiance. "I know you and Artem are close," I say. "But you're not my friend."

"I'd like to be," he says instantly.

"I... you would?" I say, genuinely surprised by that.

"Of course," Cillian says. I don't hear a lick of insincerity in his tone. "You're Artem's wife, and Artem's as good as a brother to me. So yes, I would like us to be friends."

"You don't honestly expect me to believe that you'd keep my secrets from Artem, do you?"

He raises his eyebrows. "I guess I wasn't aware you had secrets from Artem."

Damn it.

I smile and shake my head at him. "You're good."

"I don't know what you're talking about," he says innocently.

I roll my eyes at him. "Is that why you stayed behind?" I ask. "So you could lull me into a false sense of security and trick me into giving you information?"

Cillian laughs. I can't help admiring the way his blonde curls catch the light. He looks like he should be on the cover of some all-American magazine. Ironic really, considering he's pure Irish.

"Come on now, you've got me all wrong," he argues. "I'm just trying to get to know you a little better and you're accusing me of ulterior motives."

"Well, you're asking me a lot of unnecessary questions," I point out.

He smiles, apparently unaffected by how uncomfortable I obviously am right now. "Nuh-uh," he says. "You let something slip and I simply wanted clarification."

I open my mouth and then snap it shut again, realizing that he's right. He's absolutely right—I'm the one being cagey and weird.

I exhale and try to shake off the tightening in my chest that I've been feeling for the past few days now.

"Okay," I concede. "You're right."

He smiles in satisfaction. "Listen, all I'm saying is, *if* there is something on your mind, you can talk to me. That's all. No ulterior motives. And in this case, I won't play the double agent."

"In this case?" I ask, with raised eyebrows.

He chuckles. "Well, sometimes in this line of work, double agenting is necessary."

"Double agenting?"

"It's a real word," he says confidently.

I can't help but laugh. For a trained killer, he's a little goofy.

"So, Cillian, I have to admit… Artem doesn't talk about you much."

"Ouch. My ego."

"That's not what I mean!" I protest. "I know how close the two of you are, and I know how much Artem loves and respects you, which is why it's surprising that he doesn't talk about you more."

"Ah," Cillian muses. "Well, Artem doesn't really like to talk about the past much. Anyone's past."

"Apparently."

"But in my case, I think it's simply because he feels he doesn't have the right," Cillian explains. "Especially because my past is mired in drama, heartache and betrayal."

"All three, huh?"

"Triple whammy," Cillian agrees. He casts a glance around. "Do you by any chance have alcohol in this little love shack?"

I smile apologetically. "Sorry, but it's a dry love shack for now."

"Seriously?" Cillian says, looking at me in shock. "There's no alcohol at all?"

"Sorry."

"What did Artem do, finish the entire supply before I got here?"

"He hasn't really drank at all since we've been up here. Actually, he hasn't really drank since we left Los Angeles."

Cillian's brow furrows for a short moment before a smile falls back onto his face.

"Wow," he breathes, impressed.

"What's that look?"

Cillian shrugs. "Just amazed, really," he says. "There was a time not long ago when Artem couldn't go a day without some liquid courage. I guess that's thanks to you."

I feel my cheeks blush with color again. "I don't know about that…"

"I do," Cillian asserts confidently. Then he takes a deep breath. "I had hoped for a little liquid courage of my own to tell you this story. But I guess I'll have to do it stone-cold sober."

I raise my eyebrows. "You're going to tell me about your past?" I ask.

"Yup."

"The one that's full of drama, heartache and betrayal?" I clarify.

"It would seem so."

"Wow," I say. "Not that I'm not flattered, and interested. But why?"

"Because, if I expect you to trust me, I have to trust you," he says.

I smile, feeling more and more at ease with Cillian with each passing minute.

Then, after taking another deep breath, Cillian launches into the story of his life in Ireland and growing up in a small-time mafia family.

He tells me about Saoirse, about the boy that hit on her, and everything that followed.

And I listen silently, allowing him to tell his story at his own pace.

When he's finished, he runs his fingers through his overgrown blonde hair and glances out the window at the mountains in the distance.

"So that's it," he says, turning his attention back to me. "That's my little tragedy, the one that led me to the Bratva in the first place."

"Cillian," I whisper, emotion clogging up my throat. "I... I'm sorry."

"It was a long time ago, Esme."

"Doesn't mean it hurts any less."

He smiles. I can see the hurt in his eyes for a moment.

"Your father didn't even try to negotiate on your behalf?" I ask.

"My father was—*is*—an ambitious man," Cillian replies. "The politician whose son I injured, he was powerful. My father had to choose between political advancement or his screw-up son. I guess it was an easy decision for him."

"And Saoirse?" I ask, feeling guilty for even asking.

"She moved on with her life," Cillian tells me. "And I moved on, too. As best I could."

"Oh, my God," I breathe. "Cillian... you still have feelings for her."

He smiles sadly. "Maybe," he acknowledges. "But it's probably because I haven't met the right girl yet. Artem's lucky that way."

I look at him with a start. "What?"

"Oh, come on, Esme," Cillian says. "I haven't seen Artem this happy in a long fucking time. And trust me, I've seen him at his happiest. At least, I thought so, before now."

"I don't know what to say to that," I admit.

"You don't have to say a thing," he says with a shrug. "I'm just pointing out a few personal observations."

I fall silent, letting that sink in for a moment. I can feel my fear rise to my throat.

I want to be able to talk to someone, and I realize I have no one to talk to. My family is dead. My cousin betrayed me. I have no real friends.

But Cillian is sitting here in front of me, and there's a part of me that trusts him.

There's also a part of me that desperately craves reassurance.

And he knows Artem better than anyone else.

"I'm happy, too," I start. "Artem means a lot to me. Our family means a lot to me. But... sometimes I don't know whether I can trust Artem or not."

I force the words out. Once I say them, it feels as though I'm holding my breath.

Immediately, I start second guessing myself.

Should I have shared that with Cillian?

Should I be talking to Artem instead?

"What makes you think you can't?" Cillian asks.

"I came across something a few days ago," I admit. "I saw a... a body. Down in the ravine."

"It could have been a hiker who'd fallen off the trail—"

"It wasn't," I say immediately. "We would know. There are announcements made when hikers suffer accidents, let alone die. And there were no search parties, either. This wasn't a hiker, Cillian."

"Did you tell Artem about it?" Cillian asks, worry tainting his brow.

"No," I admit. "But only because I'm fairly sure that Artem already knows."

He puts the pieces together quickly. "You think Artem was the one who killed him."

"Who else?" I ask, desperate for him to tell me that I'm insane for even suggesting such a thing.

But of course, he wouldn't say that to me. Artem has killed before, in front of me.

He wasn't about to stop simply because I'd come into his life.

"A few days before I came across the body, Artem came home covered in blood," I explain, my voice shaky. "He told me that it was deer blood. A stag that got away. There was no body to bring home to show me."

"Esme..."

"Why wouldn't he tell me?" I demand. "Why would he lie?"

"If he did lie, it was probably to protect you," Cillian says immediately.

I had been expecting that response, but it still disappoints me for reasons I cannot fully understand.

"We promised to always be honest with each other."

Cillian gives me a look that clearly tells me how idealistic a notion that is. "Honesty is important in any relationship," he agrees. "But it's not always realistic."

I sigh. "Apparently not."

"I'm just saying, you should talk to Artem," Cillian says. "Ask him straight out."

"And what if he lies to me again?"

"And what if he tells you the truth?" he counters. "What if he has already told you the truth?"

I roll my eyes. "Come on! A stag that got away? But not before covering him in blood first? What did he do, wrestle with the damn thing?"

Cillian leans forward and puts his hand on mine. The gesture is unexpected but surprisingly, it doesn't feel totally foreign.

"Esme, I know you're going through a lot right now," he says. "But Artem is, too. He's just not so good with baring his soul, ya know? You've got to drag shit out of him. The way he used to cope with his anger and pain was to drink. And he's obviously not doing that anymore. Which tells me one very important thing."

"Which is what?" I ask.

"You are important to him," Cillian concludes. "Maybe the most important thing."

"I doubt I trump the Bratva," I say bitterly.

"Oh, I wouldn't be surprised if you did."

I stare at Cillian's face, at his too-blue eyes and I marvel at the fact that hardened men who have lived their lives in a constant state of power play can still exhibit so much empathy and kindness.

Something about that realization makes me want to ask a question that I probably shouldn't be asking at all.

"Do you think I can trust him?"

Cillian smiles. "I trust Artem," he says. "I trust him with my life. And I think you should, too. Especially because he loves you way more than he loves me. Though I'll never cop to that in front of him."

I smile just as we hear the sound of heavy footsteps on gravel.

I look up at the doorway and try to straighten out my expression into something neutral.

A second later, Artem walks through the door with his rifle hanging over one arm.

"Everything's quiet out there," he says. "We're good."

"Did you do a thorough job?" Cillian asks sternly.

"Fuck you," Artem replies.

Cillian looks to me and gives me a wink. "See?" he whispers. "Dude loves the fuck out of me. Don't get jealous."

I suppress my laughter. "I'll try not to be," I say as I stand. "I'll get you some linen so you can make up the couch. It's not the prettiest one out there, but it's really comfy."

"Don't worry, I'm not fussy," Cillian replies.

Artem scoffs.

Cillian flips him off and the two trade barbs while I get the linen for Cillian.

Having him here has already improved Artem's mood. I actually do feel a twinge of jealousy at that.

I feel immediately ashamed of myself and tamp it down under a smile.

"Goodnight, boys," I say before heading into the bedroom.

I know they'll want some time to talk in private.

But I'm lying in bed for only half an hour before Artem joins me in bed. He assumes I'm sleeping at first, so he pulls me against his body and kisses my neck softly.

"I'm awake," I say gently.

"Did we keep you up?" he asks.

"No, I couldn't hear you from in here," I tell him. "Not that I was trying to."

He chuckles and kisses me again. "You two had a nice chat while I was out?"

I try and figure out if there's subtext to his question, but if there is, I can't seem to pick it out.

"We did," I nod. "It was nice getting to know Cillian. He's an easy guy to like."

"That I can't argue with," Artem nods. "He was always the charmer."

"What does that make you?" I ask.

"The don," he replies without hesitation.

I turn into him and catch the whites of his eyes in the darkness. They're laser-focused and determined in a way that scares me a little.

I can feel it between us—all the things we're not saying out loud. I wonder if he feels the same.

I think about straight out asking Artem about the dead man I'd seen in the ravine, like Cillian had suggested.

But I can't quite form the question because I'm so terrified of the answer.

So when Artem leans in and kisses me hard, I let him. I reach down and cup his erection, pulling him closer to me and pretending as though I have nothing more to say.

Because I can feel it coming, even though I'm not quite ready to admit it.

I can feel our bubble shattering. Can sense the outside world at our doorstep, and I know choices need to be made soon.

I just don't want to make them tonight.

So for now, for just these next handful of moments, I sink into Artem and lose myself in him.

For tonight, I pretend everything is going to be just fine.

71

ARTEM

We make love in the midnight moonlight filtering through the window. Soft and slow and quiet, so we don't disturb Cillian on the couch.

Esme gives a desperate little cry as she comes.

When it's my turn, I bury my mouth against her throat and erupt into her.

I would give anything for this woman. For the child growing inside of her.

They mean everything to me.

Once our breathing calms, Esme turns into me and takes a deep breath.

"That was amazing," she says, tracing my tattoos the way she does every night before we fall asleep.

"At your service, ma'am."

She giggles a little, her laugh softened with drowsiness. "I like Cillian," she tells me.

"Yeah?" I reply. "Apparently, the feeling is mutual."

"What did he tell you?" she asks. For a moment, she looks a little nervous.

"Nothing I didn't already know."

She smiles, but I can sense the stress underneath it. I've been sensing it for the last couple of days now.

Not for the first time, I wonder if there's something she's not telling me.

Just like there's something I'm not telling her.

"What were you and Cillian talking about out there before you came to bed?" Esme asks.

"This and that," I reply vaguely. "Mostly just... business."

"Okay."

Esme falls silent. I turn back into the conversation Cillian and I had just before I left him sprawled out on the sofa with his legs hanging off the end.

"She's special, Artem."

"I know," I nod. "You guys had a good talk?"

"I think trust is difficult for her," Cillian answers carefully. "But I think I made some headway. Pretty sure she likes me."

"Cocky motherfucker."

"Can't really blame her," he continues, with a shit-eating grin. "I am charming as fuck."

"Maybe it's time for you to hit the road, Jack."

Cillian gives a self-suffering sigh. "You're just lucky she saw you first," he says confidently. "That's the only reason she's with you right now, instead of me."

"That's the only reason?"

"And obviously my cock is way bigger than yours."

I laugh. "You know you're the only one who can get away with saying that shit to me, right?"

Cillian gives me a little wink and his smile falls back into seriousness. "She really is great, Artem," he says. "I think the two of you could be really happy together."

Cillian catches the uncertainty in my eyes. He's the only person I don't hide it from.

"What's wrong?" Cillian asks.

"Esme wants me to walk away," I say.

"Walk away?" Cillian repeats.

"From the Bratva."

"Ah."

"You don't seem surprised."

Cillian shrugs. "I suspected."

"What do you think?" I ask, because he seems unwilling to volunteer his opinion.

"If you're asking me what you should do, you're asking the wrong man," he tells me, turning away.

"Because you'll tell me to keep fighting?"

"No," Cillian says. "Because I don't know what it's like to have a family to fight for."

"Cillian..."

"Listen, Artem," Cillian cuts me off. "This is your decision. And I'll support you no matter what. Even if what you decide is to give up your claim to the Bratva."

Hearing it from his lips feels strange. Like we're talking about someone else's life.

"My father will be rolling in his grave right now," I mutter.

"Stanislav is dead," Cillian retorts, though his tone is respectful. "He doesn't give a shit what happens in this world anymore. Don't let a ghost determine what's right for you."

I smile. "Fuck, you're a lot wiser than you look."

"At last," Cillian replies. "Some fucking recognition."

"It's good to see you again, brother.".

"Missed me, huh?"

I roll my eyes. "Don't fucking ruin it."

Cillian laughs. "Go on. Get to bed. Your woman is waiting for you."

"We have a lot to discuss."

"Tomorrow," Cillian replies. "There'll be time enough for that tomorrow."

I nod and head for the bedroom, but I pause just before opening the door. "Cillian?"

"You want a goodnight kiss?"

Laughter bubbles to my lips, but I manage to keep my expression straight.

"If I do decide to leave the Bratva... what will you do?" I ask.

The question has been weighing on my mind for over a week now. I don't miss the crestfallen expression on Cillian's face, before he covers it up with a blithe smile.

"Tomorrow," he says. "We'll talk tomorrow."

"Artem?"

I blink and my eyes focus on Esme. She's looking up at me with those gorgeous eyes. They look like molten gold under the moonlight.

"Where'd you go?" she asks gently.

"Sorry, I was just thinking about… everything."

"You wanna talk about it?" she asks.

"Not tonight," I say, mimicking Cillian's sentiment.

She opens her mouth to say something but then she snaps it closed at the last moment and nods.

"Okay," she whispers, but I can see her eyes are swimming with thoughts of her own, thoughts that she's still keeping close to heart.

I press my lips against her forehead. She curls up in the bedsheets.

It takes several more minutes for her breathing to relax. When it does, I check to make sure she's really sleeping before I disentangle myself from her and stand.

My mind is so wide awake, so alert, that I know I won't be able to sleep for several hours.

In my old life, when I got into this mood, I'd head to a club with Cillian and we'd spend the night getting drunk and fucked up.

That is not what I crave anymore.

I realize with a start that it's been several weeks since I've last touched alcohol. And perhaps that's why I've been feeling things in such a raw, unadulterated way.

Clarity is something I need now, but it isn't necessarily the most comfortable feeling to be faced with.

I'm standing by the window, contemplating a midnight run, when my ears catch a sharp sound.

I still, my eyes turning alert as I scan the darkened horizon.

The sound didn't sound natural at all. In fact, it sounded suspiciously like a signal off one of the perimeter traps I'd set earlier this evening.

Which meant a very large animal had ventured closer to the cabin that it had ever done before, or else...

We have some unwelcome visitors.

I snap the window shut and draw the blinds down.

I'm making my way to the door when Esme sits up suddenly.

"Artem?" she says, her voice panicked already. "What's wrong?"

"Nothing," I reply, but I don't sound convincing. "I just... I heard something and I need to go check it out."

She frowns. "Why do you look so... tense?"

"I think one of my perimeter traps got tripped," I admit.

"Someone else is here?" she asks.

"That's what I'm going to find out."

"Artem..."

I move to the side of the bed and grab her hand.

"Don't worry," I tell her, trying to infuse my voice with confidence. "It's probably nothing. I bet it's just that stag that got the better of me, remember? Back for revenge."

I expect her to laugh. Instead, she frowns, a different kind of frown than I've ever seen from her before.

"Take Cillian with you," she begs.

"I don't need to," I say calmly. "I'll be back soon. Stay in bed."

"But—"

"Esme!" I bark.

She quiets at once. Her lip trembles.

"Stay in bed," I order.

"I'll be back soon."

I close the door on her. When I turn around, Cillian shoots off the sofa, obviously still wide awake.

"What's wrong?" he asks, taking in my tense stance.

"Something tripped one of my perimeter traps," I tell him. "I need to go check it out."

"Let's go then."

"No," I tell him firmly. "I want you to stay here with Esme."

He doesn't like that one bit. "Artem, you might need back-up."

"It could be nothing."

"And what if it's not?"

"Then I'll handle it." I loop the rifle over my shoulder and tuck the Glock in the back of my jeans. "I have two more guns in that drawer over there. Ammo is under the kitchen cabinet. Keep Esme safe."

I head out of the cabin, with adrenaline pumping through my veins.

Darkness is my only real cover as I move deeper into the woods where my traps lurk.

None of them will succeed in stopping an attack of any kind. They're merely meant to alert me to the presence of intruders.

I'm a few steps shy of the nearest trap when I hear a voice in the shadows.

"Fuck."

I freeze at the muttered curse. My hand grips my gun. I slink backwards to find coverage behind the trees.

I don't know who's here, what they want, how many there are.

Until I have more information, I need to play this carefully.

Common sense tells me that the safest bet is to get back to the cabin, grab Cillian and Esme, and make a run for it.

But I've done enough running in this lifetime. I hated it then and I hate it now. It's not in my nature.

My first instincts are to stand my ground and fight.

To protect my family by putting myself in between them and danger.

And to beat danger into the fucking ether.

More muffled sounds emerge in the distance. I prick up my ears and pay attention.

By the sound of it, I'm guessing that I have at least four men to deal with. Possibly more coming from the east. It's hard to say exactly because of the wind causing a low whistle through the trees.

I see movement off in the distance. I pause, darting behind a thin willow that leaves me exposed on the other side.

I raise my gun. Keep my eyes peeled. As they adjust more to the darkness, I start to see silhouettes moving through the trees now.

They're coming towards me without caution. That tells me that they still don't know I'm here.

At this point, the element of surprise is all I have.

I stay still and lie in wait.

A tall figure steps into view. I can't make out individual features but I see enough to know that I don't recognize him.

I think about Razor and his band of misfits near the ravine the other day.

It is possible he had more men at his command than I had initially suspected. Which suggests they are here now to exact their revenge.

The thought makes me slightly more confident. If these men fight like Razor and his idiots, then I have nothing to fear.

Still, I'm not about to celebrate until their bodies are lying at my feet.

Stanislav's old words ring in my head.

Even a dead snake's venom can still kill you.

The tall man stops only inches away from me. When he turns to look at his comrades, he shows me the back of his neck.

I strike instantly.

I grab him by the throat and smash his head into the same tree I'm hiding behind. I smell the release of fresh blood at once.

I don't wait to find out if a single strike was sufficient. I ram his face against the tree a second time.

When I pull him away, his eyes are wide and glazed with shock.

His lips move. Before he makes a noise that gives away my position, I twist his neck hard. A dull snap rings out.

And his eyes go cold and lifeless.

I drag his body to a dark corner and cover it with some loose branches. Hopefully, his friends won't come across it before they come across me.

Then I continue pushing forward. Two other figures only lurk a few feet away.

I move stealthily, taking care to time my footsteps so the crunch of leaves meld with sounds of the forest creatures.

"Where's Suka?"

I stop moving and listen.

"Went that way. Come on…"

"I told the fucker to stay with us."

The second voice is closest to me. I pull out the sleek switchblade I bought in town and move as fast and as quietly as I can.

He sees me right as my blade finds his throat.

His eyes bulge in terror.

And one smooth, seamless cut robs him off his life.

He falls to the forest floor with a thud. I dart back behind another tree.

"What the fuck was that noise? Where are you?"

The new man is about to turn the corner. When he does, I know he's going to see the body and he's going to alert the rest of them.

I try to time it, but he's faster than I expected. He sees me coming before I can reach him.

I'm halfway across the distance when he unleashes his gun.

It fires just as I tackle him to the ground.

By some miracle, it misses. The bullet buries itself in the dirt. I don't wait to see if he fires again.

Instead, I snatch the gun right out of his dumbstruck hand and turn it on him. No explanations, no introductions, no apologies.

I just fire it into his face.

The gunshot makes me wince. But I've just announced my presence to the whole damn mountain range, so the guns might as well come out to play.

I hear more coming. I curse viciously under my breath.

By my count, I would guess at three more men, at least, and that's a modest estimate.

And they're coming fast. Too fast to hide.

I hear raised voices a quarter-second before they emerge into the clearing.

I dive for cover and start firing with abandon. I hit one man in the shoulder and one in the chest.

The latter falls to the ground instantly and I know I've made a kill shot.

The others take firing positions or fan out. I duck behind a rock outcropping and curse again under my breath as I replenish my ammo.

The adrenaline is still coursing hot through me, but now there's worry and a twinge of fear.

All I can think of is Esme.

Stay with her, Cillian. Don't fucking leave her side.

We're still close enough to the cabin, that both Cillian and Esme will have heard the gunshots.

I'm hoping that Cillian is in the process of getting Esme out of these fucking mountains as soon as possible.

But I can't be sure and it's driving me fucking crazy.

Focus, Artem. Think about this later.

For now, you need to concentrate.

New determination gives my muscles fresh strength as I peer around from the boulders.

I can see four men, all large and all armed. They are dressed differently than Razor and his men were, but I don't dwell on it.

Instead, I dart between trees just long enough to get another round of bullets in the air, forcing the attackers to scatter for cover.

Fuck.

There's too many of them.

It's starting to dawn on me that if this becomes a fight to the death, I might not make it out of these woods alive.

I may be more skilled than all of them, but guns don't care about skill. They'll kill you no matter how good you are.

One bullet is all it would take. One bullet, to make my wife a widow, to leave my child fatherless before he is even born.

Fuck that.

This is not the day I die.

I burst out from behind the tree, a gun in each hand as I fire like a madman with nothing to lose.

The moonlight glitters above me, illuminating the blood seeping out from the dead bodies that litter the leaf-covered floors.

One man crumples to the ground.

Another.

Another.

Then my gun clicks—empty.

And in the silence that follows, I hear at least a half a dozen guns cock at the same fucking moment.

I freeze even before I hear the command.

"Stop or we will kill you!"

I'm surrounded now from all sides. Six men in front of me, and at least that same number behind.

If I start firing now, I might take down a few more, three, maybe four if my aim is precise.

But it would still end the same way—with a dozen bullets in my twitching body.

"Stand down."

"Who the fuck are you?" I growl.

I can't tell who's in charge and I don't recognize the voice barking at me to stay still.

But something tells me that these are not the men I thought they were.

Footsteps approach. The men in front of me part like the Red Sea.

I frown as a figure walks through the darkness towards me. When he crosses into the lone moonbeam piercing the trees overhead, my blood runs cold.

He throws back his hood and pulls down his face mask.

I keep my eyes locked on his.

I don't want him to see my fear.

I don't want him to see my fury.

I don't want him to glimpse how much I wish I'd told Esme the truth.

Because if I die here—and that's looking more and more likely with each passing second—the last thing I'll have said to her was a lie.

The man's face is lined with age, but his eyes glow with the hunger and ambition of a man fifty years younger.

Budimir smiles at me.

"Hello, nephew."

TO BE CONTINUED

Artem and Esme's story will finish in Book 2 of the Kovaylov Bratva duet, GILDED TEARS.

CLICK HERE TO GET IT NOW!

MAILING LIST

Sign up to my mailing list!
New subscribers receive a FREE steamy bad boy romance novel.

Click the link below to join.
https://sendfox.com/nicolefox

ALSO BY NICOLE FOX

Kovalyov Bratva Duet

Gilded Cage (Book 1)

Gilded Tears (Book 2)

Princes of Ravenlake Academy (Bully Romance)

Can be read as standalones!

Cruel Prep

Cruel Academy

Cruel Elite

Bratva Crime Syndicate

Can be read in any order!

Lies He Told Me

Scars He Gave Me

Sins He Taught Me

Belluci Mafia Trilogy

Corrupted Angel (Book 1)

Corrupted Queen (Book 2)

Corrupted Empire (Book 3)

De Maggio Mafia Duet

Devil in a Suit (Book 1)

Devil at the Altar (Book 2)

Kornilov Bratva Duet

Married to the Don (Book 1)

Til Death Do Us Part (Book 2)

Heirs to the Bratva Empire

Can be read in any order!

Kostya

Maksim

Andrei

Tsezar Bratva

Nightfall (Book 1)

Daybreak (Book 2)

Russian Crime Brotherhood

Can be read in any order!

Owned by the Mob Boss

Unprotected with the Mob Boss

Knocked Up by the Mob Boss

Sold to the Mob Boss

Stolen by the Mob Boss

Trapped with the Mob Boss

Volkov Bratva

Broken Vows (Book 1)

Broken Hope (Book 2)

Broken Sins *(standalone)*

Other Standalones

Vin: A Mafia Romance

Box Sets

Bratva Mob Bosses (Russian Crime Brotherhood Books 1-6)

Tsezar Bratva (Tsezar Bratva Duet Books 1-2)

Heirs to the Bratva Empire

The Mafia Dons Collection

The Don's Corruption

Printed in Great Britain
by Amazon

23445512R00344